# Praise for *The Murmur of Bees*

"Segovia's nostalgic novel, inspired by family anecdotes, offers seductive prose . . . It resembles García Márquez's fiction but with its own northeastern Mexico tenor. [*The Murmur of Bees*] . . . is a very interesting read, it is one of the books of the year with unforgettably well-crafted passages."

—Hojeando, *El Norte*

"*The Murmur of Bees* is a story of love, brotherhood, and the inner struggle to heal the pain left by the Mexican Revolution."

—*Milenio Diario*

"*The Murmur of Bees* by Sofía Segovia is one of those magical novels where reality meets the enigmatic; some call it magical realism, others letting the imagination speak. I subscribe to the latter."

—Todo Literatura

"An absolutely wonderful read . . . where we can perceive a strong and precise language, full of poetry."

—Eduardo Antonio Parra, author

"*The Murmur of Bees* . . . transports the reader to prerevolutionary Mexico. A brilliant novel, very well constructed and undoubtedly one of the most outstanding of 2015."

—*Top Cultural*

"In *The Murmur of Bees*, Sofía Segovia has achieved an entertaining and profound family saga where the fiction and reality of her country resonate."

—*El Nuevo Herald*

"[*The Murmur of Bees*] . . . is a story that invites the reader to make the most of their senses, a 'sensual and sensory' story that 'smells like the honey of bees and the orange blossoms of the Morales Cortés's orange trees.'"

—*Vanguardia España*

"Sofía Segovia is the new voice of Mexican narrative. In the pages of *The Murmur of Bees*, the reader breathes a Marquezian air and finds a magical realism that is very much Sofía's own, one that does not resemble anything previously known."

—Wendolín Perla, editor

"Oranges, bees, and a very special child combine to perfection in this novel by Sofía Segovia."

—*Página 2*

# THE
# MURMUR
## OF
# BEES

# THE
# MURMUR
# OF
# BEES

## SOFÍA SEGOVIA

*Translated by Simon Bruni*

**amazon** crossing

Previously published as *El murmullo de las abejas* by Penguin Random House Grupo Editorial in 2015 in Mexico. Translated from Spanish by Simon Bruni. First published in English by AmazonCrossing in 2019.

Published by AmazonCrossing, Seattle

www.apub.com

Amazon, the Amazon logo, and AmazonCrossing are trademarks of Amazon.com, Inc., or its affiliates.

ISBN-13: 9781542040495 (hardcover)
ISBN-10: 1542040493 (hardcover)
ISBN-13: 9781542040501 (paperback)
ISBN-10: 1542040507 (paperback)

Cover design by David Drummond

Printed in the United States of America

First edition

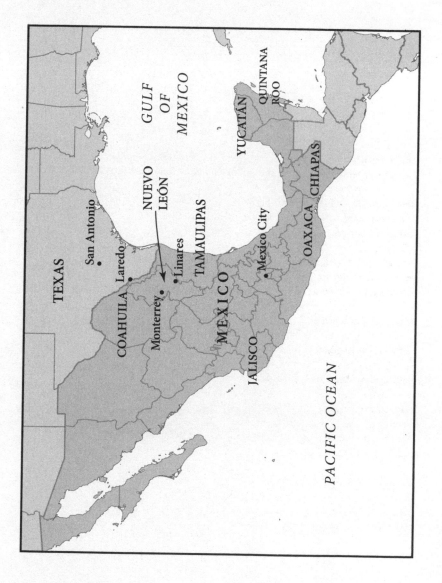

# 1

## *Blue Boy, White Boy*

That early morning in October, the baby's wails mingled with the cool wind that blew through the trees, with the birdsong, and with the night's insects saying their farewell. The sounds floated out from the thick vegetation but faded a short distance from their source, as if halted by some magic spell while they went in search of human ears.

For years, people remarked how Don Teodosio, on his way to work on a nearby hacienda, must have passed right by the poor abandoned baby without hearing a peep, and how, in search of a love potion, Lupita, the Morales family's washerwoman, crossed the bridge that would take her to La Petaca without noticing anything strange. *And had I heard him*—she said that evening to anyone who wanted to listen—*I would have at least picked him up, because as horrible as he may be, I don't know who could have abandoned a newborn baby just like that, left him there to die all alone.*

That was the mystery. Who from the area had shown signs of an ill-advised pregnancy recently? To whom did this unfortunate baby belong? News of such indiscretions spread faster than measles in that town, so if someone had known, everyone would have.

Yet, in this case, nobody knew anything.

There were all kinds of theories, but what captured the collective imagination was the theory that the baby belonged to one of the witches of La Petaca, who, as everyone knew, freely gave their favors of the flesh. A witch who, having produced such a deformed and strange-looking boy—a punishment of the Almighty or of the devil, who knows?—had gone and thrown it under the bridge, to leave it to God's mercy.

No one knew how many hours that baby spent abandoned under the bridge, naked and hungry. Nobody could explain how he survived the elements without bleeding to death from the umbilical cord left unknotted, or without being devoured by the rats, birds of prey, bears, or pumas that were plentiful in those hills.

And they all wondered how old Nana Reja had found him, covered in a living blanket of bees.

Reja had chosen to spend the rest of her days in one place, outside one of the sheds they used for storage on the Hacienda Amistad. It was a simple, windowless structure, identical to several others still in service, built behind the main house to hide it from social visitors. The only thing that distinguished this shed from the others was its overhanging roof, which enabled the old woman to remain outside whether it was winter or summer. The overhang was nothing more than a lucky coincidence. Reja hadn't chosen the place for protection from the elements, but for the view and for the wind, which blew down to her from the hills. Just for her.

The old woman had chosen this as her resting place so long ago that no one living remembered when she had occupied the spot or how her rocking chair had appeared there.

Now, almost everyone believed she never got up from that chair, and they supposed it was because, at her age—and how old she was nobody could say—her bones no longer held her up and her muscles no longer responded. For when the sun came up, they saw her sitting there already, gently rocking, more from the wind than from any movement

2

of her feet. Then, at night, nobody noticed her disappear, because by that time they were all busy going to sleep.

All those years on the rocking chair caused the townspeople to forget her story and her humanity: she had become part of the scenery, put roots down into the earth she rocked upon. Her flesh had become wood and her skin a hard, dark, furrowed bark.

Passing by, no one said hello to her, just as nobody would greet an old, dying tree. Some children observed her from a distance when they made the short trip from town in search of the legend; only rarely did any of them have the guts to go closer to check that it really was a living woman and not one carved from wood. They soon realized there was life under the bark when, without even needing to open her eyes, she dealt the daring adventurer a good blow with her stick.

Reja did not abide being the object of anyone's curiosity; she preferred to pretend she was made of timber. She preferred to be ignored. At her age, she reckoned, with the things her eyes had seen, her ears had heard, her mouth spoken, her skin felt, and her heart suffered, she had been through enough to make anyone weary. She couldn't explain why she was still alive or what she was waiting for before she departed, since she was no longer of any use to anybody and her body had dried up, so she preferred not to see or be seen, not to hear, not to speak, and not to feel.

Certain people Reja did tolerate, such as the other nana, Pola, who like Reja had seen her best days long ago. She also tolerated the boy Francisco because once, when she had still allowed herself to feel, she had loved him intensely. But she could not stand his wife, Beatriz, or their daughters. The wife because Reja had no desire to allow someone new into her life, and the children because they seemed insufferable.

There was nothing they needed from her and nothing she wanted to offer them, for old age had relieved her of her servant's duties. She'd had no part in the running of the house for years, and that was how she had started to become part of her rocking chair. So much so that it was now hard to see where the wood ended and the person began.

Before dawn, she would walk from her bedroom to the shed, where her moving seat awaited her under the overhanging roof, then close her eyes so she wouldn't see and her ears so she wouldn't hear. Pola brought her breakfast, lunch, and dinner, which she barely touched because her body no longer needed much food. She got up from her chair much later, only when, through her closed eyelids, the fireflies reminded her it was night, and when the wooden rocking chair, which grew tired of the constant proximity long before she did, pressed and pinched her hip.

Sometimes she opened her eyes on her way back to bed, though she didn't need to open them to see. Then she lay on top of the covers— she didn't feel the cold, because her skin did not let even that through anymore. But she did not sleep. The need for sleep was something her body had given up. Whether it was because it had slept as much as a being must sleep over a lifetime or because it refused for fear of falling into eternal slumber, she did not know. She hadn't thought about that for a long time. After a few hours on the softness of the bed, she would begin to feel the pressing and pinching that reminded her it was time to go visit her loyal friend, the rocking chair.

Nana Reja didn't know exactly how many years she had lived. She didn't know how she'd been born or what her full name was, if anyone had ever bothered to give her one. Although she supposed she must have had a childhood, she couldn't remember it or her parents—if she ever had any—and if someone had told her that she had sprouted from the earth like a pecan tree, she would have believed it. Nor did she remember the face of the man who gave her the child when she was a young woman, though she did recall seeing his back as he walked off, leaving her in a hut made from wood and mud, abandoned to her fate in a strange world.

Be that as it may, she would never forget the powerful movements in her belly, the twinges in her breasts, and the sweet yellowish liquid that emerged from them even before the only child she would have was born. She wasn't sure she remembered that boy's face, perhaps because her imagination played tricks on her, muddling the features of all the babies—white and dark—she suckled in her youth.

She clearly remembered the day when she arrived in Linares for the first time, half-starved and freezing to death, and she could still feel her baby in her arms, pressed tightly against her chest to protect him from the icy January air. She had never been down from the sierra, so it was natural that she had never seen so many houses in one place, or walked down a street, or crossed a square; nor had she ever sat on a public bench, and that was what she did when weakness made her knees give way.

She knew she had to ask for help, but she didn't know how, even if it wasn't for herself. She would ask for help for the baby she held in her arms, because for two days he hadn't cried or wanted to feed.

That was the only reason she had walked down to the town she sometimes contemplated from afar, from her hut on the sierra.

She had never felt such cold, of that she was certain. And perhaps the inhabitants of the place felt it, too, for she saw no one walking outside, braving the freezing air like she was. All the houses seemed unapproachable. The windows and doors had bars, and behind them, closed shutters. So she stayed sitting on that bench in the square, wavering, growing colder and more afraid for her baby.

She was unsure how long she remained like that, and perhaps she would never have moved—would have become one of the square's statues—had the town's doctor, who was a good man, not come walking through the square just then and been shocked to come across such a desperate woman.

Dr. Doria had left his house in spite of the cold because Sra. Morales was about to die. Two days earlier, the woman had given birth to her first child, with a midwife tending to her. Now the husband had called on the doctor in the early hours, alarmed by his wife's fever. Doria had to coax her to tell him where she felt the discomfort: in her breasts. The infection manifested as a sharp pain when the baby fed.

Mastitis.

"Why didn't you tell me sooner, Señora?"

"I was embarrassed, Doctor."

Now the infection was more advanced. The baby was crying nonstop because it hadn't fed for more than twelve hours—the mother couldn't bear to breastfeed it. He had never seen or heard of a woman dying from mastitis, and yet it was clear that Sra. Morales was dying. The ashen skin and that sickly shine in her eyes told the doctor that the new mother would soon give up the ghost. Dismayed, he took Sr. Morales out into the hall.

"You must allow me to examine your wife."

"No, Doctor. Give her some medicine, nothing else."

"What medicine? The señora is dying, Sr. Morales, and you have to let me establish what from."

"It must be the milk."

"It must be something else."

The doctor did his utmost to convince him: he promised to touch and not look, or to look but not touch. In the end, the husband agreed and persuaded the dying woman to allow the doctor to palpate her breasts, and worse still, to examine her lower stomach and groin. There was little need to touch anything: the intense pain in her pelvis and the purulent lochia emerging from the ailing body betokened death.

The cause of maternal death and a way to prevent it would one day be discovered, but for Sra. Morales, that day would come too late.

There was nothing to be done but to keep the patient as comfortable as possible until God said enough.

To save the baby, the physician sent the Morales's servant boy to find a dairy goat. Meanwhile, Dr. Doria tried to feed him with an improvised bottle filled with a solution of water and sugar. When the goat milk arrived, the newborn did not tolerate it. He was certain to die a slow and terrible death.

Doria was still worrying as he made his way home. He had said goodbye to the husband and father after declaring there was nothing more he could do.

"Be strong, Sr. Morales. God knows why He does things."

"Thank you, Doctor."

As he walked through the square, he caught sight of the woman of black ice, which struck Dr. Doria as a small miracle, for he was exhausted, and with the cold, he was walking with his head down. She was sitting right in front of the bronze plaque announcing that the Morales family had donated the bench to the town. Compassion cut through his fatigue, and he approached the woman to ask her what she was doing there and whether she needed help.

The man spoke too quickly for Reja to know what he was saying, but she understood the look in those eyes and trusted him enough to follow him to his home. Once inside the warm house, Reja plucked up the courage to peek at the baby's face. It was blue and lifeless. She was unable to suppress a groan. The man, as the town's doctor, did what he could to revive him. If she had been able to speak in spite of how numb she was from the cold, Reja would have said, *What's the use?* But she could only groan and groan some more, besieged by the image of her blue son.

She didn't recall the doctor undressing her, nor stop to think that it was the first time a man had done so without climbing on top of her. Like a ragdoll, she allowed herself to be touched and examined; she reacted only when the physician brushed against her enormous, warm breasts, tight and painful from the milk that had built up. Then she let herself be dressed in thicker, cleaner clothes without even asking to whom they belonged.

When the doctor guided her back out onto the street, she reflected that at least she would feel less cold when she was returned to the same bench. She was surprised when they passed the square and continued down a road that led them to the door of the most impressive house on the street.

Inside, the property was dark. As dark as she felt. Reja had never seen people as white as the woman who received her, though there was a shadow over her face: a sadness. They sat Reja in the kitchen, where she kept her head down. She didn't want to see faces or eyes. She wanted to be alone, back in her hut made of wood and mud, even if she died of cold, alone with her sadness. Better that than endure the sadness of others.

She heard a newborn crying, first in her new-mother's nipples and then with her ears. That was how her body had reacted every time her child cried with hunger, even when he was out of earshot. But her baby was blue now, wasn't he? Or had the doctor saved him?

The throb in her breasts grew stronger. She needed relief. She needed her baby.

"I miss my boy," she said softly. Nobody in the kitchen with her seemed to hear, so she ventured to repeat it more loudly: "I miss my boy."

"What is she saying?"

"That she misses her boy."

"What's that about her missing something?"

"She wants her son."

The doctor arrived with a bundle in his arms and passed it to her. "He's very weak. He might not be able to nurse properly."

"Is it my little one?"

"No, but he needs you just the same."

They needed each other.

She opened her blouse and offered him her breast, and the child stopped crying. In the relief she felt as, little by little, her breasts emptied, Reja observed the baby: it wasn't her boy. She knew it at once—the noises he made when he cried, suckled, or sighed were different. He also smelled different. For Reja, the effect was the same: she wanted to lower her face to inhale deeply in the hollow of the neck, though she thought they might not allow it, because among other things, the clearest indication that she was holding someone else's baby was its color. While hers had gone from a dark brown to a deep blue, this one was gradually turning from bright red to white.

They all observed her in silence. The only sound in the kitchen was the baby sucking and swallowing.

Alberto Morales had fallen asleep, watching over his dying wife. After several days of his spouse's moans and the newborn's incessant cries, he had gotten used to the idea that, while they made noise, they were still alive. Now, he was woken by the deafening silence: neither was his wife moaning nor the baby crying. Anguished and not daring to touch his wife, he ran in search of his son.

In the kitchen, he found the servants and Dr. Doria standing around what he supposed was his child's body. Noticing his presence, they all stepped aside to let him through.

He looked at his baby suckling the darkest breast he'd ever seen.

"We found a wet nurse for your son."

"She's very black."

"But the milk's white, as it should be."

"Yes. Will the boy be all right?"

"The boy will be all right. He was just hungry. Look at him now."

"Doctor, my wife was quiet when I woke."

That had been the end of Sra. Morales.

Reja stayed away from the process of mourning: the wake, the burial, and the wailing. For her it was as if the señora had never existed, and sometimes, when the boy let her, when she allowed herself to listen to the silent call of the hills, she could almost believe that this baby that hadn't come from her body had sprouted from the earth. Like her, with no memory of anything other than the sierras.

Something stronger than maternal instinct took hold of her, and for the next few years, the only thing in Reja's world was the baby. She imagined she kept him alive for the earth, his helpless mother, so it never occurred to her to stop offering him her breast after his first tooth, or even a full set of teeth. She would simply say, *Don't bite, boy.* Her milk was nourishment, comfort, lullaby. If the boy cried: to the breast; if the boy was angry, noisy, feeling down, sad, bad-tempered, snotty, or sleepless: to the breast.

The boy Guillermo Morales enjoyed six years at Nana Reja's breast. Nobody could get the idea out of their head that the poor child had almost starved to death, so no one dared refuse him anything. But one day the Benítez aunts arrived to visit the poor widower, and shocked to see a boy almost of school age latched onto the servant's black breast, they insisted to Sr. Morales that the kid should be weaned.

"It's not as if he's about to starve to death, man," one of them said.

"It's scandalous, Alberto," said the other. "Obscene."

At the end of their visit, as a favor to the bewildered father, the pair of spinsters took Guillermo off to Monterrey for a time, realizing there was no other way the boy would listen to reason or get to sleep, since he had never done so away from the breast of his nana Reja.

They left Reja with empty arms, and so full of milk that she left a trail wherever she went.

"What're we going to do, Reja?" the other servants asked her, tired of cleaning up behind her.

She didn't know what to say. All she knew was that she missed her boy.

"Ay, Reja. If you're going to be like this, best it doesn't go to waste."

And so they brought her malnourished or orphaned babies to feed and glass bottles to fill, because the more she nursed, the more milk she had to give. Then the widower Morales married his second wife, María, the younger sister of his late spouse, and together they gave Reja twenty-two more little ones to feed.

In the following years, Reja would never be seen without a child at her breast, though she remembered Guillermo Morales with particular fondness: the first child she wet-nursed, the one who saved her from being utterly alone, who gave her a purpose that would keep her fulfilled for years.

Of course, Guillermo himself returned a short time later, but not to the old house in the square. Tired of living in the bustling center of Linares, his father had made the extravagant decision to abandon the family mansion and live on Hacienda La Amistad, which was located just outside the built-up area of town. There he grew into a man and started his own family. When he inherited the estate following the death of his father—victim of nothing other than old age—he also inherited his nana Reja, who wet-nursed his children, too, when they arrived.

A strange situation: a father who'd fed from the same breast as his children. And yet, when he'd suggested finding another wet nurse and giving Reja a rest, his wife had firmly refused: What better milk than their nana's? There was none. Guillermo gave in, though he avoided thinking much about the situation and tried to pretend he had no memory of his prolonged turn at the breast.

It was at La Amistad that Reja grew old, as did Guillermo, his nana seeing him die of an infection. And like his father before him, when he bequeathed the estate to Francisco, the only son who'd survived epidemics of dysentery and yellow fever, he also bequeathed old Nana Reja, along with her rocking chair.

But she had not nursed the children of Francisco and Beatriz. Time had dried Reja, who no longer remembered how many local children had lived thanks to her abundance. She didn't even remember the last white drop that had emerged when she squeezed her breasts or how they had once tingled even before she heard the cry of a hungry baby.

That morning in October 1910, the inhabitants of the hacienda woke as they did every day of the year, ready to begin their routine.

Pola opened her eyes without turning to look at her roommate's bed. After decades sharing a room with her, she knew that Nana Reja came and went unnoticed. The sounds of the hacienda were starting up: the laborers arrived with their tools to head to the sugarcane fields, and the house servants prepared to begin the day. She washed and dressed. She had to go to the kitchen to have coffee before leaving for town to buy freshly baked bread from the baker's shop in the square. After finishing her milky coffee, she collected the money that Sra. Beatriz always left in a tin can.

It promised to be a sunny day, but she needed her shawl because, at that hour and that time of year, the cold night air persisted. She took the shortest path in the direction of town, as she did every day.

"Off to town, Doña Pola?" Martín, the gardener, asked her, as he did every day.

"Yes, Martín. I won't be long."

Pola liked this routine. She enjoyed going to fetch the bread every day. It meant she could find out the latest goings-on in Linares, and see from afar the boy, now a grandpa, whom she'd liked so much when she was young. She walked to the rhythm of the constant creaking of Reja's rocking chair. She liked walking down the road flanked by giant trees that led from the estate to the center of town.

Back when she still spoke, Nana Reja had told her how the widower Alberto Morales had planted them when they were little more than branches.

On her return, she would take Reja her breakfast, as she always did.

Nana Pola stopped all of a sudden, trying to remember. What about Reja? As she did every day, Pola had passed by the black rocking chair. Many years ago, she had given up trying to converse with the old woman, but it comforted her to think that, like these old trees, Reja remained, and that perhaps she would remain forever.

And today? *Did I see her when I went past?* She turned around.

"What did you forget, Doña Pola?"

"Have you seen Reja, Martín?"

"Course I did, on her rocking chair."

"You sure?"

"Where else could she be?" said Martín, following Nana Pola at her brisk pace.

They found the chair still rocking, but Reja wasn't in it. Alarmed, they returned to the bedroom the nanas shared.

They did not find her there either.

"Martín, run and ask the workers if they've seen Nana Reja. Look for her on the way. I'll let Sra. Beatriz know."

Beatriz's routine did not involve rising early. She would wake with the certainty that everything was underway: the bread and coffee already set on the table, the gardens being watered, and the clean clothes being ironed. She liked to start her days listening to her husband doing his ablutions, dreaming and from a distance, and then wake herself, still wrapped in the sheets, by saying a Rosary in peace.

But that day, in the Morales Cortés house, there were no ablutions, no Rosary, and no peace.

# 2

*Echoes of Honey*

I was born within that pile of masonry stone, plaster, and paint a long time ago. It doesn't matter how long; all that matters is that the first thing I made contact with outside of my mama's belly was the clean sheets of her bed, because I was lucky enough to be born on a Tuesday night and not a Monday. Since time immemorial, the women of her family had changed the sheets on Tuesdays, like decent people did. That Tuesday, the sheets smelled of lavender and of the sun. Can I remember it? No, but I imagine it. In all the years I spent living with my mama, I never saw her change her routine, her habits, the way she did things as God intended: on Tuesdays, the beds were made with linen that had been washed the day before with bleach, then dried in the sun, and finally ironed.

Every Tuesday of her life, with just one, painful exception that was still to come.

It could've happened the day I was born, but it didn't. Mine was a Tuesday like any other, so I know what those sheets smelled like that night, and I know how they felt on the skin.

Although I don't remember it, on the day I was born the house already smelled how it would smell forevermore. Its porous stones had absorbed the good aromas of three generations of hardworking men and three of women who were sticklers for cleanliness with their oils and soaps; the walls were impregnated with the family recipes and the clothes boiling in white soap. The scents of my grandmother's pecan sweets; of her preserves and jams; of the thyme and epazote that grew in pots in the garden; and more recently of the oranges, blossoms, and honey—they always floated in the air.

As part of its essence, the house also preserved the laughter and games of its children, the scolding and slamming of doors, past and present. The loose tile my grandfather and his twenty-two siblings trod with their bare feet and my father trod in his childhood was the same one I trod as a boy. That tile was a betrayer of mischief, for with its inevitable clunk, the mother of the time would be alerted to whatever plan her offspring had hatched. The house beams creaked for no apparent reason, the doors squeaked, the shutters banged rhythmically against the wall even when there was no wind. Outside, the bees buzzed and the cicadas surrounded us with their mad, incessant song every summer evening, just before nightfall, while I was immersed in my final adventures of the day. As the sun went down, one began to sing and the rest followed, until they all decided at once to fall silent, frightened by the impending darkness, I suspect.

It was a living house, the one that saw me born. If it sometimes gave off the scent of orange blossom in winter or some unattributable giggles were heard in the middle of the night, nobody was scared: they were part of the house's personality, of its essence. *There are no ghosts in this house,* my father would say to me. *What you hear are the echoes it has kept to remind us of all those who've been here.* I understood. I imagined my grandfather's twenty-two siblings and the noise they must have made, and it seemed logical that, years later, remnants of their laughter could still be heard reverberating here or there.

And in much the same way, I suppose my years in that house left some echoes of me there—*Shush, boy, you're like a cicada,* Mother would say to me—and the house left its own echoes in me. I carry them inside me still. I'm certain I carry my mama and papa in my cells, but also the lavender, the orange blossoms, my mother's sheets, my grandmother's calculated footsteps, the toasted pecans, the clunk of the treacherous tile, the sugar caramelizing, the *cajeta*, the mad cicadas, the smells of old wood, and the polished clay floors. I'm also made of oranges—green, sweet, or rotten; of orange-blossom honey and royal jelly. I'm made of everything that touched my senses during that time and entered the part of my brain where I keep my memories.

If I could get there of my own accord to see the house and feel it again, I would.

But I'm old. The children I have left—and now, even my grandchildren—make my decisions for me. It has been years since they allowed me to drive a car or write a check. They speak to me as if I didn't hear them or couldn't understand them. The thing is, I'll admit: I hear, but I don't listen. It must be that I don't want to. Granted, my eyes don't work as well as they did, my hands shake, my legs tire, and my patience runs out when my grandchildren and great-grandchildren visit me, but while I'm old, I'm not incompetent. I know the times I live in and the outrageous price of things; I don't like it, but I'm not unaware of it.

I know exactly how much this journey will cost me.

I may be old, but I don't talk to myself or see things that aren't there. Not yet. I know a memory from reality, even if I grow more attached to my memories than to reality with each day. In the privacy of my mind I go over who said what, who married whom, what happened before, and what happened after. I relive the sweet sensation of being hidden among the high branches of a pecan tree, reaching out, plucking a pecan, and opening it with the best nutcracker I've ever had: my own teeth. I hear, I smell, and I feel things that are as much a part of me today as they were yesterday, and which spring up inside me. Someone can tear open an orange nearby, and the aroma transports me to my mama's kitchen or my papa's orchard. The mass-produced bottles of

16

cajeta remind me of the tireless hands of my grandmother, who would spend hours stirring milk and sugar over the fire so it would caramelize without burning.

The sounds of the cicadas and bees, now rarely heard in the city, force me to travel to my childhood, though I can no longer run. I still search with my nose for a trace of lavender, and find it, even when it's not real. When I close my eyes at night, I hear the clunk of the floor tile, the creak of beams, and the shutters banging, even though, in my townhouse, there are no loose tiles or beams or shutters. I feel like I'm at home, the one I left as a child. The one I left too soon. I feel like it's with me, and I like it.

# 3

## *The Empty Rocking Chair*

Beatriz Cortés de Morales would remember that morning in October 1910 for the rest of her life.

They had knocked on her door insistently, and thinking they had come to tell her one of the sugarcane fields was on fire, she left the warmth of her bed to open up. It was Pola, crying: they couldn't find Nana Reja anywhere. Wasn't she in her bed? No. She wasn't in her rocking chair? No. Where else could the little old lady be?

Dead, lying out there in the bushes, probably.

Beatriz had known Nana Reja her whole life because, having been neighbors for generations, the Morales and Cortés families often visited one another's homes. Though she'd always known her future husband, she fell in love with him when she was sixteen, when Francisco Morales returned from his civil engineering studies at the University of Notre Dame and asked her to dance with him to a romantic song during the Holy Saturday festivities.

Since her father-in-law died and Francisco inherited his properties, Beatriz had shared responsibility for everything, including the now-missing old woman.

The Morales family mobilized the hacienda workers: some to ask around the town, others to look among the bushes.

"Could a bear have taken her?"

"We would've found paw prints."

"Where could she have gone, if she hasn't moved from her spot in thirty years?"

There was no answer to that question. Alive or dead, they needed to find her. While Francisco coordinated the search on horseback, Beatriz went to sit in the nana's vacant chair, which creaked as it felt her weight. She thought it the right place to wait for news, but soon asked Lupita, the washerwoman, to bring a different chair. As much as Beatriz tried, she couldn't manage to control the rocking chair, to which her body's contours were alien.

She sat for endless hours on her own chair beside Nana Reja's, which rocked by itself, perhaps helped by the wind that blew down from the mountain or maybe purely out of habit. Mati, the cook, brought her some breakfast, but Beatriz had no appetite. All she could do was look into the distance. Try to make out any far-off movements. Some interruption in the monotony of the crops or in the improvised and intact beauty of the hills.

How lovely, the view of the mountains and sugarcane fields from there. She had never admired it from that viewpoint, and now she understood the initial charm the place had held for Nana Reja. But why look eternally out toward those endless, unchanging hills? Why look always toward that dirt road winding through them? And why look constantly in that direction, if her eyes weren't even open? What was she waiting for?

While she awaited news, Beatriz, a practical-minded woman, concluded they were unlikely to find the nana alive. Her pragmatism therefore also permitted her to make concrete plans for dear Nana Reja's wake: they would wrap her in a sheet of white linen and bury her in a coffin of fine timber that Beatriz had already sent for. Father Pedro would conduct the mass, and the whole town would be invited to attend the funeral of the most long-lived woman in the region.

Of course, without a body, there would be no wake. Could there be a Requiem Mass without the deceased?

As for the rocking chair, she couldn't decide on the best thing to do. They could burn it, or turn it to sawdust and spread it around the garden, or put it in the coffin with the dead woman. Or they could leave it where it was as a reminder of the body that occupied it for so long.

It would have been sacrilege to let it go from being an extension of Nana Reja herself to serving a practical use again for someone else. That much was certain.

She studied the old chair, because she had never before seen it vacant. It had never been repaired or maintained, but it held together. It creaked a little when it rocked, yet seemed immune to the weather and the elements, like its owner. There was a symbiosis between the chair and its owner, and she imagined that, while one lived, so would the other.

Beatriz realized with alarm that someone was running toward her on the road through the sugarcane plantations.

"What is it, Martín? Have you found her?"

"Yes, Señora. Sr. Francisco sent me to fetch the cart."

Beatriz watched him hurry off in search of the wagon. They had found the body, she thought, and despite her practical woman's mind, she felt a heavy sorrow. Nana Reja was incalculably old, and it was to be expected that she would die soon, but Beatriz would have liked for her to depart in a different way: in peace, in her bed or rocking in the wind on her chair. Not like this, attacked by a wild animal, perhaps, alone and no doubt scared, exposed to the elements on that road that disappeared into the hills.

Too long a life for it to end like that.

She shook off her sorrow: there was much to do before they arrived with the body.

When the men returned with the loaded cart, it was clear that the plans and preparations had been for nothing: defying all predictions, the nana was alive.

# 4

*In the Shade of the Anacahuita*

Francisco would later describe how some laborers found her, a league and a half from the house. They came to him, upset, because when they finally located the old woman, she refused to answer them or move from where she was. So Francisco sent for the cart and then went himself to the place where Reja was, sitting on a rock with her eyes closed, rocking in the shade of an anacahuita. She held two wrapped bundles: one in her apron, the other in her shawl. Francisco approached softly so as not to alarm her.

"Nana Reja, it's Francisco," he said, heartened when she opened her eyes. "What're you doing so far from the house, Nana?" He asked without expecting any answer from the old woman, who had fallen mute years ago.

"I came to find him," she said quietly, her voice croaky from old age and disuse.

"Whom?"

"The baby that was crying."

"Nana, there're no babies here," he responded. "Not anymore."

In reply, Reja held the bundles out to Francisco.

"What are they?" Francisco took the bundle wrapped in the apron, then quickly dropped it, startled. It was a beehive. "Nana, why were you holding this? Have they stung you?"

As the hive hit the ground, the bees still living inside came out in a rage, in search of the culprit. Some laborers ran to get away from the danger, pursued by the insects, but in unison the bees stopped their aggressive foray and returned, as if called home. The shawl-wrapped bundle that Nana Reja still held moved, and Francisco and some workers who had resisted the temptation to run from the enraged bees were left dumbstruck, especially when the old lady hugged the package to herself again, continuing to rock it as if it were a child.

"Nana. What else do you have there?"

Then the bundle burst into wails and frenetic movements.

"He's hungry, boy," said Nana Reja as she carried on with her constant swaying.

"May I see?"

As he unrolled the shawl, Francisco and his men at last saw what the nana had in her arms: a baby.

Their horror made them step back. Some of them crossed themselves.

# 5

## *Ribbons and Lice*

I was never allowed childish illusions about the source of babies. I always knew that the story about the stork was just that: pure make-believe for inquisitive children. My mama never pretended with me like most ladies of her time did. If I threw a tantrum, she would tell me how many hours she had spent in labor with me; if I disobeyed her, she bemoaned the pain of giving birth. After some of my pranks, had it been possible, she would have made me pay dearly for every contraction.

My mama was a good woman. It's true. She just couldn't explain where I came from. I don't mean the physical aspect of it: she was very intelligent, and though she lived in an age of modesty, she knew that the consequence of marital intimacy was children. The problem was that she had assumed her fertile period was over: my two sisters were already married and had made her a grandmother. My arrival late in her life came as a surprise.

With this in mind, it is easy to understand my mother's shock when she realized she was expecting a baby at the unlikely age of thirty-eight. I can imagine how hard it was to confess her condition to my elder sisters. Worse still to her friends at the Linares Social Club. And I understand her desperation when, after having two señoritas with their ribbons and lace, she gave birth to a little boy complete with mud, head lice, and dark-skinned toads.

And so, my mama had me after she had started playing grandmother. She loved me and I loved her very much, but we had our problems. I remember how, unable to cover me in flounces and bows, she insisted on dressing me up like a little Spanish lord, in outfits she made herself. But I was anything but lordly. And I was not at all Spanish, either, though she insisted on clothing me in little embroidered suits copied from the latest magazines from Madrid.

To her dismay, I was always covered in food or dirt, or in dog, cow, or horse crap. My knees were always grazed, and my blond hair was stiff and dark with mud. The snot that hung from my nostrils never bothered me. The handkerchief embroidered with my name, which my mama stuffed into my pocket every day, I used for everything except wiping my nose. I don't remember this, but they say I preferred eating beetles to the chicken or beef liver the nanas made for me—on my mother's orders—so that my cheeks would color pink.

Now that I'm a father, grandfather, and great-grandfather, I admit I wasn't an easy child to deal with. Much less manipulate.

My mama complained all her life that, after I finally learned to speak, my favorite words were *no, I do it*, and *not fair*; that no sooner could I walk than I started to run; that once I mastered traveling at speed, I climbed every tree that appeared in front of me. She did not know what to do with me. She felt too old and thought she had already done her job as a mother with her two grown-up daughters, who were almost perfect.

She had a girl who was the apple of her eye, she would say: for my elder sister Carmen, it has to be said, was beautiful. When she was little, my mama curled her blond hair and took pleasure in people calling her an angel, a darling, a beauty. Later, Carmen broke half the hearts in town, first when she left for Monterrey as a student and then when she married. Married and living elsewhere, she never mentioned it, but I know my sister was embarrassed that the legend of her beauty was kept alive on the town's streets. For years, my mama kept the countless letters of eternal love and slushy verses from all the unrequited admirers Carmen had, before and after she married. Anyone would think they had been written to my mama from the way she treasured that pile of papers like trophies and showed them off at any opportunity.

She would also say that she had a girl who was the apple of her ears, because my other sister, though pretty, was distinguished more by her voice. My mama would make Consuelo sing to anyone who came to visit, and her melodious voice always received praise.

"She has the voice of an angel!" they all said.

I've never heard angels sing, but I suppose it was true: my sister possessed an angel's voice. What few people knew was that behind that voice she hid a demonic temper. Not even at the worst of times did she lose her melodious tone, of course, and her every sentence was pure poetry. She could say, *Don't come near me, you flea-ridden brat, you're disgusting,* and still sound like an angel to Mama's ears. *I'm telling him fairy tales,* she always replied when mama asked what she was saying to me.

I didn't much care what she said, for she was a stranger who did not really belong in my world. For years she was like one of the witches from those fairy tales; I knew she was using her voice to enchant everyone, to make them believe she was good and sweet as an angel, especially my mama.

I was one of the few who was immune to her charms. My mama couldn't understand why I didn't fall head over heels for my sister whenever she visited. She could not comprehend why I preferred to spend the day far away, or why, when I was sent on a visit to Monterrey, I would choose to stay at my elder sister Carmen's house. *Your sister's such a good girl, so nice, so sweet,* my mama would say to me, attempting to soften or improve our relationship.

There were two angels in the family, and there was the boy, which was me. When my mama talked about me, she would say, as if apologizing, *This is the boy*. Or, *He's the runt*. She never said that, in me, she had the son of her dreams. She would never have had the audacity, or perhaps it never occurred to her. *Ay, Dios!* she would say all the time. I can't remember ever bumping into my mama in the halls of my house, in the courtyard, dining room, or kitchen, without her letting out a loud sigh. *Ay, Dios,* she would say, blowing out a little, *just look at that hair, that snot, those clothes, look at how dirty he is, how untidy, how suntanned, I'm too old for this, ay, Dios!* Before long, her sighs shortened. Gradually it became just the *Ay, Dios!*, then just *Ay!*, and then not even that: a snort.

I was always noisy, my voice shrill. My body was a refuge for every tick, flea, or louse that needed a home and sustenance, so there was little point in my mama letting my blond curls grow. Out of necessity, I was always close cropped. Like an orphan boy.

*Ay, Dios!* Sigh.

If I had been entirely in the care of my mama, I might have ended up wearing more bows than my sisters. Circumstances saved me from this fate, because my papa, who was a grandfather before I was born and had resigned himself to working the land only to bequeath it to his sons-in-law, would not allow anyone to turn the son who had arrived so late in his life into a wimp. And while he had never interfered in his daughters' upbringing, from the moment he learned a male had been born to him, he began confronting my mama about mine. He was well aware there was no place for the fragile in our land and in our time, with war surrounding us and sometimes coming to visit.

Those confrontations with my papa must have troubled her. She adored him, which was strange for a wife of almost forty, so she took a step back from my hands-on upbringing to keep the peace. My papa, meanwhile, had neither the time nor the inclination to be responsible for me, first because he did not know what to do with a baby or a little boy, and later because he spent his time going here and there, supervising and defending the cattle ranches in Tamaulipas and the orchards in Nuevo León.

Nonetheless, I had many arms just for me. My Nana Pola would leave me with the cook, Mati, who would hand me over to Lupita, the washerwoman, who would drop me off with Martín, the gardener, who after a while would leave me in the good company and care of Simonopio. He didn't pass me on to anybody until night fell and someone came out of the house asking where the boy was.

# 6

*Wings That Covered Him*

Simonopio's arrival was an event that marked us irreversibly. A family watershed. Later, it became the difference between life and death, though we would not understand this until we looked back on it from far in the future.

My papa would berate himself for the rest of his life for how he reacted when he first saw Simonopio.

I suppose that, as well traveled, well learned, and well enlightened as he felt, he had not completely thrown off the superstition that existed in a town not far from a community of witches. And perhaps the situation that day had weakened his conviction: first the empty rocking chair, the missing nana, the certainty of her death, the search among the surrounding bushes that extended ever farther from the house; then the discovery, the talking nana, the warlike swarm from the apron-swaddled hive; and finally a newborn baby with a disfigured face, wrapped in the nana's shawl and a living blanket of bees.

As far as first impressions go—and first impressions are always important—Simonopio, as the nana insisted he be baptized in spite of my parents' and the priest's objections, had not made the best. The campesinos asked their master to leave the monstrosity there, under the anacahuita, by the side of the road.

"It's God's will, Señor, for this boy is the devil," Anselmo Espiricueta insisted.

By then my papa had recovered from his initial reaction. Drawing on all the strength conferred upon him by knowing himself to be a man of the world, a man well traveled, well learned, and well enlightened, he had shaken off superstition in order to focus on the mystery.

"That's absurd. We don't believe in those things here, Espiricueta," he said, before continuing his gentle questioning of the nana.

From the few words the little old lady uttered, Francisco understood where she had found the baby and in what circumstances. How and why the old woman had walked up the mountain to the bridge, under which she found the baby, nobody would ever comprehend. *I heard him* was all she would say; *I heard him.* Whether superstitious or enlightened, everyone knew it was impossible to hear the faint wail of a child abandoned under a bridge several leagues away.

That was the great mystery, and it grew even greater and was granted eternal life when Don Teodosio and young Lupita said they had not seen the boy when they passed the same place shortly before. How was it possible that the old woman had heard him? There was no imaginable answer. No believable answer.

"I can't even hear my wife talking next to me at lunch," said Leocadio, a peon on the hacienda, to anyone who'd listen.

But there was a fact nobody could deny: the wooden, immobile old woman had left her little world to go to the rescue of this unfortunate child, and had seen fit to carry him off, beehive, winged friends, and all. When my papa was about to shake off the bees that completely covered the newborn's body, Reja stopped him.

"Leave them, boy," she said, wrapping the baby up again.

"But, Nana, they'll sting him."

"They would have done that already."

29

Annoyed, he ordered his men to put Nana Reja on the cart, but she clung fast to her bundle, fearing they would snatch it from her and follow through on their threat to leave the baby to its fate once again.

"He's mine."

"He is yours, Nana," my papa assured her, "and he's coming with us."

"And the beehive too."

Reluctant but taking great care, my papa covered it with the apron again before lifting it onto the cart. And only then did they begin the journey home, to the empty rocking chair.

# 7

## *White Drop, Holy Drop*

Francisco Morales felt little of the certainty with which he had answered his nana. *He's coming with us,* he had said. Yes, but why? What were they going to do with a child that had entered the world already marked? Abandoning the boy did not cross his mind, but he could hear what the peons were saying under their breath, especially Anselmo Espiricueta, the newest employee, who'd refused to ride on the cart with the newborn. Had the devil kissed it? Made a pact with it? Was it the devil himself or a divine punishment? Ignorant superstitions. And yet, Francisco could not see how a baby with a hole for a mouth could survive a single day, and he did not know what he could say to subdue the ignorant prejudices of the people that would surround him for however long he lived.

Near the town, he had ordered Espiricueta to turn off. On the one hand, because someone had to ask Dr. Cantú to come to the house to examine the old nana and the unfortunate baby, and on the other, to get him away from the child and his already nervous entourage. He did not need the southerner with his apocalyptic prophecies to put more ideas into their heads.

"And don't start with that gossip about the kiss of the devil, eh? Let's not go around telling tales of sorcery. The nana found a baby that needs help, and that's all. Understood, Anselmo?"

"Yes, Boss," Anselmo Espiricueta replied as he ran off.

When he reached the town and saw Juan, the knife grinder, Anselmo did not resist the temptation to explain to him, in confidence, that he had some shocking news—the nana, the bees, a witch's baby—before continuing his spiel with all manner of terrible predictions.

"Evil will befall us, you'll see."

And so it happened, as things tend to happen, that before Anselmo had even found the physician, all Linares knew about Simonopio's misfortune and the possible blight on the Morales family and all its descendants.

Dr. Cantú, being the serious and professional man that he was, had responded immediately to the Moraleses' call without stopping to answer the questions of the foolish and the superstitious. He was surprised to find himself riding to the hacienda behind a cart carrying a casket. It was a shame: he had thought there had not been any deaths in this business with the old woman and the baby.

When he reached the house, he found the nana where she always was: settled into her rocking chair, surrounded by the family and its most trusted domestic staff. The fact that the nana had moved at all was reason enough to be surprised. He struggled to believe that someone of such advanced age had suddenly rushed off on an adventure up a steep road, let alone that she had returned from it having come to no apparent harm. And with a living baby in her arms?

If Francisco Morales was saying so, all he could do was believe it.

"Who died?"

"No one," Francisco replied.

"Then who is the coffin for?"

When they turned around, Martín and Leocadio were there bearing the heavy box, waiting for instructions. The doctor was intrigued; Francisco, confused; and Beatriz, alarmed: the coffin! She had completely forgotten the preparations she had made when the nana was missing, when she had sent Leocadio to the town to fetch a casket. Now Francisco was looking at her in surprise.

"Er . . . it's in case of an emergency."

Beatriz went over to tell Martín to cover the coffin in thick canvas and store it in the shed, out of everyone's sight. When she returned, Dr. Cantú was asking to examine the child.

They did not allow him to approach the bundle the old woman was holding without putting on a pair of thick leather gloves, the property of some day laborer, *because the bees are everywhere, Doctor.* As he opened the shawl wrapping, he saw what they were saying: hundreds of bees wandered the baby's body. He wondered how to shoo the insects without alarming them, but Reja took care of it. Cantú did not know whether, helped by her hardened skin, the woman felt she was immune to bee stings, or whether she just knew they would not dare sting her.

Whatever the reason, with great calm, she proceeded to brush them off without angering them.

The baby remained alert and tranquil. The doctor was surprised to see him watch the last bees that flew around him and then into the hive that someone had hung from one corner of the overhang with some wire. He noticed that the unknotted umbilical cord was beginning to bleed, so he tied it with some suture thread.

"This baby was left to die, Morales. They didn't even try to leave it to fate: he could have bled to death. As a matter of fact, he should have bled to death."

And yet he had not bled to death, even with the umbilical cord like a running hose. And against all logic, he had not a single bee sting. He had neither been devoured nor killed by exposure to the elements. This combination of factors added to the mystery that would forever surround Simonopio.

"The boy is surprisingly healthy."

"But, Doctor, the mouth?" asked Beatriz, concerned.

The lower jaw was perfectly formed, but the upper one was open from the corners of the lips to the nose. He had no lip, upper front gum, or palate.

"He was kissed by the devil," someone in the crowd said. Espiricueta.

"It's no devil's kiss," the doctor replied firmly. "It's a malformation. It happens sometimes, like when a baby is born without fingers or with too many fingers. It's sad, but natural. I have never had to tend to a case, though I've seen it in books."

"Can it be fixed?"

"I've read there is a procedure, but it's dangerous and painful. I wouldn't advise it. Best leave it in the hands of God."

The boy would be this way for as long as he lived.

"Children like this do not live for long: they die of hunger because they cannot feed, and if by some miracle they can, the liquid drowns them, since it enters the respiratory tract. I'm sorry. I very much doubt he will survive more than three days."

Before ordering a dairy goat brought or sending for a wet nurse, Francisco requested the presence of Father Pedro, for if this boy was going to die, he needed to be baptized as God intended. The goat arrived before the priest, and the nana requested that a cup be filled with a little warm milk and a little of the honey beginning to seep from the beehive. She soaked a corner of her shawl in the mixture, and squeezing the material drop by drop for over an hour, she fed the baby until he slept.

By the time the priest arrived in a great rush, loaded down with oils and holy water to anoint and baptize the ill-fated child, he found him awake again and with his mouth open, awaiting each sweet, white drop that fell onto his tongue and rolled down it. They had already washed him and dressed him in fine diapers and the white robe the Morales girls had worn in their baptism, which Beatriz had retrieved from a chest. Given the rush, for they expected the boy would die at any moment, the ceremony began without interrupting the feeding. And so, from a drop of white to a holy drop, with the nana on one side and Francisco and Beatriz on the other, Simonopio's body and soul were saved.

# 8

## *War's Harvest*

That day he had lost the entire maize crop. It hadn't been the most abundant, but he had kept it going in spite of the plague of insects. To save it, he had taken care of it as if it were his own daughter. He felt almost as if he had caressed every cob.

But they had snatched it from him. They arrived to take it once the infestation had passed, once it had been irrigated enough, once it had ripened, once it was tender and juicy and his workers had harvested it under the burning April sun, which sometimes, like this year, could be worse than in July. They arrived to take it when every last corncob was in the wooden crates and about to travel to markets near and far.

*It's for the army,* they told him before turning away.

Francisco Morales had no choice but to watch the full crates disappear by the cartload and, in silence, say goodbye to a season's work.

*But it's for the army,* he said with sarcasm to console himself as he poured a whiskey. They had left him not one ear of corn for his dinner. Not a single peso for new seeds. *For the army,* yes, but for which of the many?

In that war, the armies were just one army, he decided, but one that endlessly shed its parts, like the hourglass-shaped wooden doll a Russian classmate had once shown him at university.

*It's a* matryoshka. *Open it,* the Russian had said to him.

He noticed that the matryoshka had a subtle incision around its middle. He pulled and it opened. To his surprise, inside he saw another identical doll. Then another and then another and another, ever smaller, until he counted ten.

That was how the army—the armies—of the Revolution seemed to him: from one emerged another and another and another, each of them identical, each with the same conviction that it was the nation's official army and that, therefore, it had the right to violate whomever it pleased. To kill whomever it pleased. To denounce whomever it pleased as a traitor to the fatherland. And each time they passed through his land, it seemed to Francisco that, like the Russian doll, they grew smaller, if not in number then in their credibility and sense of justice. In their humanity.

That harvest was the least of what the war had taken from them. They had lost Beatriz's father when one of those armies intercepted him on his way to Monterrey and accused him of treachery for offering dinner to General Felipe Ángeles—his childhood friend and the new, but brief, governor of nearby Coahuila—an enemy of the deposed president Carranza.

The war had taken their peace, their tranquility, their certainty, and their family, for *bandoleros* would come to Linares to kill and rob. They took any women they came across. Beautiful or ugly, young or old, rich or poor, they made no distinction.

Francisco had thought it astounding that such a thing could happen in the modern day. Then he learned that, in war, even modernity evaporated.

His daughters were beginning to leave childhood behind—they were young, pretty, and rich. Fearing they might one day be sought out, Francisco and his wife sent them to board with the nuns. They were safe in Monterrey, but their parents grieved their absence.

They also lost their men if they did not manage to hide when one of the armies passed through: no questions asked, without explanation, they were conscripted to fight. Francisco lost two of his peons this way, which was not easy to forget, because he had known them both since they were children.

Him—men like him—the levy overlooked. Renown and wealth still counted for something in 1917. The war did not require his flesh for another shield, but it still stalked him, winked at him, and threatened more than* his maize, for the maize they took that day would not last long. It would never sate a voracious appetite that demanded everything.

The war's armies now wanted land like his. Land and freedom, they insisted. They all fought for the same thing, and he—men like him—had nowhere to take cover from the crossfire. The only possible outcome with the land reform—which all sides claimed to defend as their own—was to lose land. The only option was to hand it over to someone who wanted it but who had never sweated for it, who would never understand it. To offer it meekly the day they came and knocked on his door, in the same way he had let his crop go that day: in silence. It was that or die.

That was why he had not dared to object when they came for his maize. Not even his renown would shield him from a bullet between the eyes. A crop of maize was not worth dying for. He loved the land that his ancestors had passed down to him, but there was something that he valued even more: his life and the lives of his family.

Until now, all he had managed was to redistribute his lands in his own way: to place some of them in the names of trusted friends. These measures were insufficient. There was no legal way to register the remaining lands in Beatriz's or the girls' names, so large tracts remained vulnerable to expropriation. That was why he was now sitting in his office, drinking the single glass of whiskey he allowed himself each day earlier than usual.

."Francisco?"

Beatriz wouldn't appreciate him getting drunk *because I've lost* or *because I'm going to lose everything and there's no way out.* Because how did one defend oneself against legal theft?

". . . so Anselmo wants to use soap on them."

He would drink his whiskey. One. As he always did. He would enjoy it, even if he knew it would not give him any answers. Then he would stand up and go walk through the sugarcane fields. He would force himself to take each step. He would caress every stalk, if necessary: it was the only trick he had left to avoid going into the red.

". . . Simonopio."

"What?"

"I think you mean 'pardon me?' Your mama brought you up better than that. What are you thinking about, anyway?"

Tired of all the responsibility and uncertainty, so defeated that he could barely deal with what already existed, let alone proceed with plans for the future—such as expanding the plantations, hiring more campesinos, building more barns for equipment and crops, extending the workers' lodgings, and buying the coveted tractor—he, too, wondered what he was thinking. Why he was wasting so much time sitting there. Why he did not feel up to anything that afternoon beyond his whiskey.

Even if all the crops came through, even if they were sold at the best price, in their entirety, without being stolen by the rustlers or the government for its armies, it might all still be of little use. He might end up working his fields so that someone else could harvest them, so that someone else could occupy his property. Why invest time, money, and effort in these inherited lands if he did not know to whom they would belong in a month or a year?

Would it not be better to buy properties in Monterrey? To enjoy what was left of his daughters' youth? The war had stolen time from him, on top of everything else. He wished he had more time for his wife, for his daughters; more time for the boy who had arrived in their lives.

That day, he realized to his surprise, there was time. That day, the war, by taking his maize in a 100 percent tax, had taken away his planned work. However, it had left him time. It had left him with a rare day when his hands were empty, with no maize to protect, no goods to deliver. He would stop grumbling, then. That day, he would not waste any more time on the war or the reform. Or on the lost maize.

The whiskey could wait until the usual hour. The sugarcane could wait for his visit. He would use this time for something else.

"Francisco, I'm speaking to you!"

"Pardon me, pardon me," he said as he left the glass of whiskey half-drunk on the table and went to hold his wife and smile at her, as he did only when they were alone.

"Ay, Francisco . . ."

"At your service, ma'am?"

"No! Stop fooling around. I came to tell you that Anselmo wants to use soap on the bees to kill them. He says they're messengers of the devil, or some nonsense. He won't shut up. I don't even know what he's saying anymore."

"Tell him no."

"I have! Do you think that man listens to me? No. You go. I left poor Nana Reja sitting on the rocking chair, waving her stick. She's furious. She even opened her eyes!"

"And Simonopio?"

"Simonopio's never there when Anselmo arrives. I don't know where that boy hides himself."

Neither the years nor the stern lectures had persuaded Anselmo Espiricueta to give up his superstitions, thought Francisco, frustrated. He looked at his whiskey. He looked at his wife, sorry to abandon the game they had started playing. The war and the land left him with little time for Simonopio, but today Francisco would give him some. He would defend the boy's bees for him, because they were his, because they had arrived with him, because although Simonopio had always had hands to take care of him and godparents to watch over him, Francisco—on his monotonous rides from ranch to ranch—was plagued by the thought that the bees were the boy's primary guardians. Killing them would be like killing a piece of Simonopio. It would be like orphaning him.

Besides, though the bees had gradually covered the roof of Reja's shed and no one dared go in there to store things, they never hurt anybody. Most people had become accustomed to their presence around the boy. They seemed interested only in Simonopio, and he appeared interested only in them. His life would be hard enough with the bees by his side. What would become of him without them?

They had arrived with the boy. There must be a reason for it. Francisco would ensure they were left in peace.

"Let's go."

That day was Simonopio's; it was his bees'. Some other day, Francisco would also find a way to defend his land.

# 9

## *The Bee Boy*

At Nana Reja's feet, Simonopio learned to focus his eyes by watching the hive. Even as a baby he learned to distinguish them individually, watching them leave the honeycomb early and awaiting their punctual return in the afternoon. He lived his life by the bees' schedule and soon learned to crawl away from the mat to follow his tireless companions around the garden.

The day would come when he would follow them beyond the boundaries of the garden and beyond the hills that he could see.

Reja, who had resumed her wooden motionlessness, kept silent but constant watch over him. She no longer fed him herself, but since the beginning, she had made it clear that the bee boy was to be fed goat's milk and honey, first with a cloth, then with a spoon, and later with a cup. In the early days, she did not allow anyone near the child for fear that somebody with bad intentions might harm him or somebody with good intentions might drown him by feeding him like an ordinary baby. The only people with permission to go near the child were Beatriz, Nana Pola, and Lupita.

Reja would never have let Beatriz feed him. Beatriz was always in such a rush to be somewhere else: if she wasn't supervising the house or her daughters, she was at her club's social events. Reja also knew that, if she allowed it, Beatriz would turn Simonopio into an indoor boy, a child of books. That was not Simonopio: Simonopio was for the outdoors, for the wild. He was for reading life, not books. When Beatriz wanted to see and hold the boy, she had to go to Reja's rocking chair to do so.

Pola was old and patient, and in Lupita, though she was young, Reja saw a goodness that enabled her to look beyond the cavity in Simonopio's face. Both would feed the child until the last spoonful, unhurriedly. Nana Pola and Lupita would never kill Simonopio, not with bad intentions or good.

And while no one else felt welcome when they approached, once Simonopio became mobile like any other normal boy, he would approach them, always with his version of a smile. Those closest to the Morales house stopped being frightened by the boy's deformed face, and in time they began to feel familiarity and affection, even forgetting the defect that marked him. They heard him coming near and welcomed his presence, for with his pleasant personality, he was the best company while they did their daily work.

As the years passed, it became clear that, though he had survived and grown proficient at eating, Simonopio would never master communication. The consonants made with the tip of the tongue, which are most of them, escaped back into the cave that was his mouth. And while he could pronounce any sounds that emanated from the back of the mouth, like *ka*, *ga*, and *ha*, as well as all the vowels, most people with whom he spoke lost their patience too soon. The little noises and mumbles baby Simonopio tried to produce to imitate them made them feel most uncomfortable; the words he tried to pronounce without success, even more so. Unable to understand him, some thought he not only had a facial defect but was also soft in the head—and that, consequently, he could not understand them either. *Poor Simonopio,* some well-intentioned people began to call him. *Poor Simonopio is distracted and stupefied by the bees; he laughs by himself, he can't talk, he pretends to sing, he doesn't understand anything.*

How wrong they were.

Simonopio would have loved to sing the song that Lupita was intent on teaching him to pronounce, even if *Peter Piper picked a peck of pickled peppers. A peck of pickled peppers Peter Piper picked* was beyond his capabilities. He would have liked to talk to people about the songs they sang of vain women, abandoned women, railway women, soldier women. He would have liked to discuss his bees and ask everyone why they didn't hear them, given that they spoke to the others, too, as they did to him. Had he been able, he would have talked about the song the bees sang into his willing ear about flowers on the mountain, faraway encounters, and friends that had not made it on the long journey home; about the sun that would beat down hard one day but be covered in storm clouds the next. Then he would have liked to ask Lupita: *Why do you hang out the clothes you washed, when it's about to rain and you'll have to rush to take them in? Why are they irrigating, when it's going to rain tomorrow?* He would have liked to ask his godfather why he had done nothing to prevent the crops from dying on an icy night last winter; did he not feel the cold coming? And what about the constant impossible images that crossed in front of his closed eyes—or about the events he saw before, after, and while they happened? What did other people see when they closed their eyes? Why did they close their ears, nose, and eyes when there was so much to hear, smell, and see? Was it just him and nobody else who heard and listened?

How could he discuss these things when his own mouth disobeyed the signals he sent to it, when all that came from it were nasal grunts and goose honks? He couldn't do it, so he didn't. Simonopio learned that the great effort required to say the simplest things was worth making only if someone would understand, if someone was interested.

At Nana Reja's motionless feet, which her rocking chair always pointed in the direction of the road that had brought them together, Simonopio mastered the art of silence.

# 10

## *Broken Promises*

Beatriz Cortés was sitting where she was entitled to sit as chairwoman of the organizing committee for the Linares Social Club's annual Holy Saturday dance. For months, she had been insisting they should resume the tradition she had enjoyed so much in her adolescence and childhood. In the warless past, the annual dance had been a magnet for the families of noble descent of Saltillo, Monterrey, Montemorelos, and Hualahuises, who made the trip each year without fail. Around the big event, several days of activities were also organized on the various haciendas and ranches of the local hosts. Everyone enjoyed the occasion: the older generations, now married, reuniting with friends from their youth; and the young meeting one another and, perhaps—if they were lucky—finding and winning over the love of their life.

Many ladies of Linares society had refused at first to take part in the organization of the event, but Beatriz persuaded them of the importance of returning to the customs of the past. *They won't come,* they had said. *They're all afraid they'll be robbed on the way. Nobody will come. What's the point?*

Perhaps they were right, but Beatriz had to try. How long did it take for a tradition to be lost forever? Less than the eight years it had from the same affliction she suffered from in life: great potential but few achievements, and grand promises broken.

For life had promised great things to Beatriz Cortés.

From the cradle, she had understood she belonged to a privileged and respected family that lived from its hard work on its lands. She had known her place in the family was solid, with an unusually affectionate and attentive father and a mother who, if not affectionate, was intelligent and firm. She was aware that, save a deadly attack of dysentery, she would live a long and worthwhile life. It was a given that Beatriz Cortés would meet and befriend the worthy people of Linares and the region. That she would share a classroom and, later, motherhood with the daughters of the best families. That they would always be her friends, and together they would grow old in full view of all, enjoying an old age full of grandchildren. Of course, before the grandchildren, there would be many children. And before the children, marriage to the ideal man. And before even that, a youth full of suitors who would seek to attend the parties where she would be, so they could court her.

Early in life, she knew what kind of a man she would marry: one from the area, the son of a family of noble descent. She knew it before she was of the age to put a name and a face to her chosen one. They would have many sons and daughters, and most would survive, she was certain. And by her husband's side, she would see many successes and some failures—salvageable ones, of course. There would also be frosts, droughts, and floods—the inevitable cycle.

She counted on the certainty that all the promises life had made her were, or would be, fulfilled in proportion to the work and effort invested. In life, only potential was free. The outcome, the achievement, the aim came at a high cost, which she was prepared to pay. So Beatriz Cortés was unstinting in her efforts to be a good daughter, a good friend, a good student, wife, mother, charitable lady, and Christian.

How did one woman persuade an entire foolish nation to lay down its arms, return to work, and start producing again? How did a woman pretend that the events happening around her did not affect her? What could she do to change the trajectory of a bullet? Of ten bullets? Of a thousand?

At that moment in time, she was sitting at a table, surrounded by women feigning interest in preserving the old traditions with a dance that might happen in six months' time, when none of them were sure they would live that long. They were discussing flowers, announcements, invitations, visits, and venues, when really each of them was thinking about crops that had failed or had rotted for a lack of transportation or buyers. They were thinking about the sudden, unwanted, violent visits from hostile armies, and the death notices that followed. They were thinking of the sons who were growing into men and who, should the armed conflict continue, could be dragged into the endless fighting. They were thinking of the daughters who would never meet the man that life had promised them, because at any moment he could receive a bullet to the heart, the head, or worse, the stomach. A young man whom they would have been destined to meet at some dance in five or ten years' time, but who might now be nothing more than maggot-filled nourishment for a nopal. Who might become sterile dust instead of planting life in the belly of a woman, the one who would have been his wife had the first shot not been fired one fine day, and had that not been answered with a second shot and followed by an endless volley.

Her own daughters liked that little game: *Mama, who am I going to marry?* they would ask. Beatriz understood, of course. She had played it herself with her mother and her cousins when she was a girl. Was there a more important unknown in the life of a young woman? *Whom will I marry? A handsome man, I'm sure. Hardworking, brave, from a good family.* Now Beatriz refused to play it with her adolescent daughters, daughters of this Revolution. She would not make them any promises or help them construct the fiancé they would have in their dreams, for she was not sure he would even live until the day when they might meet.

Beatriz herself felt lucky; Francisco Morales was the man life had promised her, the man she had conjured in her youthful imagination. He was everything she could wish for: handsome, from a good family, hardworking, brave, educated, and landed. Back then, there had been no war, no sign of conflict to mar or complicate their courtship. They married after visits, dances, traveling fairs, and days in the country. They were satisfied with each other, and they had the necessary resources at their disposal; life and the future seemed secure. And at first, life had kept its word: Carmen was born a year later and Consuelo two years after that.

Years of peace and hopes for the future.

At one time, before the war, with all of life's promises tangible and in front of her, Beatriz had felt lucky to be a woman of that time and lucky that her daughters were women of the new century. In that era of wonders, anything was possible: the modern railway shortened distances and moved goods and people in large quantities. Steamboats propelled travelers across the Atlantic to Europe in a few weeks. The telegraph communicated the birth or death of a family member—from a great distance and on the same day—and allowed businessmen to quickly strike a deal that would have taken months to arrange before. Electric lighting galvanized an array of nocturnal activities, and the telephone, though still not widely used, kept people in touch with far-flung friends and relatives.

And yet, far from coming together due to all these wonders, people were intent on dividing themselves. First, in Mexico, with the Revolution. Then, all over the world, with the Great War, which at last seemed close to ending. But not satisfied to fight and suffer in that war, now the Russians were waging their own at home, brother against brother, subject against king. The news had just arrived that in July, after months in captivity, the tsar, the tsarina, their four daughters, and the little prince had been surreptitiously assassinated, their bodies disposed of so that no one would ever find them.

Beatriz did not know much about Russian royalty or the reason for the conflict, but it had shaken her to learn that, with the twentieth century in full swing, a king had been murdered along with all his off-spring, including daughters of a similar age to her own. Her imagination tortured her: time and again, in her mind's eye she saw the faces of two disfigured, bullet-riddled girls. Always the same two. They had the faces of her daughters.

And so she concluded that Russia and the rest of the world were closer to home than it seemed. In her region, too, horror stories were circulating about entire families disappearing, women being kidnapped, and houses set on fire with the inhabitants inside. The war between Mexican soldiers, between enemies, was a tragedy, but the worst thing was that it also reached people of peace. People who sought only to work and live as a family, who desired simply to bring up their sons and daughters, see them grow to adulthood, and let God decide after that.

When the Revolution broke out, Beatriz had felt safe in her little world, in her simple life, shielded by the idea that if you bothered no one, no one would bother you. Seen in this way, the war seemed distant from her. Worthy of attention, but distant.

After the severe federal punishment that followed Governor Vidaurri's bid for independence in the middle of the previous century, the people of the state of Nuevo León preferred to keep safely away from this war's swings of fortune. *It's an ill wind that blows no good,* Beatriz had thought.

Now she knew she had deceived herself: somehow, she had persuaded herself that, if she did not feel it to be her own, the war would not touch her or her loved ones.

At first, she had been young and idealistic enough to support the principle of nonreelection and the right to a meaningful vote. "Effective suffrage, no reelection" had seemed an elegant sentence, deserving of a place in history. Surely it was what the country needed to renew itself and embrace the modernity of the twentieth century. Good sense would prevail, the war would soon end with the much-wanted departure of the eternal president Díaz, and peace would be restored.

In the end, the only sensible person in the whole story had been President Porfirio Díaz himself when he released his grip on power, realizing that the indefensible was not worth defending; he packed his bags and left for exile after a few months of clashes. That was the outcome for which everyone had hoped. The desired victory. Period. With that, the drama should have ended.

But no.

Very soon, the main characters in the farce they called the "Revolution" forgot their agreed-upon lines and took on lives of their own, writing their own dialogues and monologues of betrayals and shootings. The original script disappeared into oblivion. Some wanted to blast their way to land and wealth that did not belong to them; others wanted to sit in the big chair. It occurred to no one—or no one had the desire—to bring two chairs together, talk without bullets, and keep talking until peace was brought about. They made an obedient people take up arms and placed them under the command of madmen who killed indiscriminately and without the slightest care for military ethics and courtesy.

Then the war ceased to be a distant curiosity and became an insidious poison. Beatriz's self-deceit came to an end in January 1915, and the armed struggle arrived in her home and her life to stay, like an unwanted, invasive, abrasive, destructive guest.

That was when it knocked on her family's door, which her father opened with a naivety for which Beatriz still could not forgive him.

According to some of his fellow passengers, Mariano Cortés had boarded the train at the last moment, after saying a hurried, agitated goodbye to his son-in-law. He greeted the handful of other passengers in the first-class coach and took his seat. He was reading peacefully when a battalion blocked the tracks on the hill known as the Alta, taking advantage of the engine's deceleration due to the slope. Some witnesses said it had been the Villistas. Others said the Carrancistas. They all breathed more easily when they learned it was not a general attack on all the passengers: the battalion was looking specifically for Mariano Cortés in order to kill him.

Later, they would say how he had gone out into the open field, where soldiers were waiting to seize him. According to a witness who was in a good position to hear, the soldiers accused him of fraternizing with the enemy, wherefore they declared him a traitor to the fatherland and deserving of the death penalty. Immediately.

*I am not a traitor to anyone, and you are no one to judge me. But if you must kill me,* the witness to the accused's words repeated, *shoot me in the chest and not in the face, so that my wife may recognize me.*

And so, they stood him alongside the train and, in front of the rest of the passengers, fired six bullets into his chest and stomach. Mariano Cortés returned home dead, but recognizable for his wake.

In the town, her father's death was romanticized. He had been dressed in his best suit for the journey, tall and upright, with the winter sun on his brow and the cold wind ruffling the hair that he always let grow too long. Standing, alone, facing the battalion. What guts! What love he showed for his exquisite wife with his final words! But none of them had been present when the cart arrived bearing the man of flesh and bone. The lifeless father with a flaccid expression, perforated, bleeding, and covered in the bodily fluids that had escaped as he died. Where was the romance in that? Where was the dignity?

All Mariano Cortés left behind when he died was a deep void.

Now they had to keep enduring the mournful tributes and accept that they were well intentioned. Beatriz continued to do so, though the rage and hatred that filled her at times like this, when she succumbed to introspection, frightened her. If she loved her father, why could she not forgive him for dying? As a good Catholic, why had she been unable to look the bishop in the face since that moment in the middle of the Requiem, when he said that her father's death was God's plan, that He sent ordeals as a blessing to those who deserved them most and were most able to endure them? And why did she now look with suspicion and anger at the people of worth, the cream of society, with whom she was supposed to mix?

Perhaps because she knew that one of them had been her father's betrayer.

*A dinner killed him,* the locals said. And at the wake, between embraces, the mourners said, *God took him because he was a saint; There was no one as good as he was; God needed him; God needed another angel in heaven;* and *What joy for the Cortés family to have an angel to look over it now.* And to herself, Beatriz said, *The war's bullets killed him, not a dinner, not God. The betrayer that reported the dinner held in honor of General Ángeles killed him. He was killed by the man who had him pulled off the train and made him stand there and wait meekly to be filled with lead. He was killed by a small-minded, vindictive man who did not deserve to hold the office that he refused to give up. Each of those wretched gunmen killed him.* And finally, *His naivety and meekness killed him.*

War was waged by men. What could God do against their free will?

And who had gained anything from her father's senseless death? Nobody. The war had not suddenly stopped because a supposed traitor was dead.

As if the six bullets that hit their target had not been enough, the Carrancista soldiers—for the circumstances suggested it had been they—proceeded to kick the body, as though to make sure that the soul would find its way out through one of the many new holes in its shell. And they left him there to move on to something else, to continue their reign of terror, without taking a single step toward peace.

For the Cortés and the Morales Cortés families, on the other hand, life changed beyond remedy. They had become the great losers: almost four years later, Sinforosa, Beatriz's mother, was not even a shadow of her former self, overcome with grief and the fear of more reprisals. Now she lived with her only daughter, for when she lost her husband, she lost her essence, her strength, and even her ability to take care of her home and herself. Beatriz's brothers, Emilio and Carlos, had given up the promises life had made them and were performing the duties of their murdered father. Beatriz was losing in her attempts to cling to her own life's promises despite suspecting that they would never be entirely fulfilled. She was losing opportunities for family plans, put on hold because they were currently inconvenient or impossible. She was losing by hiding her pain to support her mother and her husband. She was losing because, instead of germinating more children in her belly, she germinated fear, suspicion, and doubt in her mind. And worse still: she was losing the absolute belief in herself that she had felt all her life.

The life she was living now did not resemble the life that Beatriz Cortés was supposed to have. In spite of it all, the sun rose and set each day—though even that sometimes disconcerted her. Life went on. The seasons came and went in an eternal cycle that would not stop for anything, not even for Beatriz Cortés's sorrows and truncated hopes.

In the town, almost four years after his execution, they still remarked with admiration on the dignified comportment and the final brave words of Mariano Cortés. This was no consolation to a daughter who had lost her father in a moment of violence. Beatriz repeated it to herself every day: *I am a grown woman, I am a wife, I am a mother. I don't depend on my father anymore, I have my own family, and we are well.* But it was one thing to say it with her head, and another for her heart to believe it and stop sending pain signals to her soul.

Because it was a lie that a woman left her parents' home to become one flesh with her husband: for all that she loved him—and she loved Francisco because he deserved it—such a thing had never occurred to Beatriz. In her world, a woman took her parents' home with her wherever she went: to school, on a foreign voyage, on honeymoon, to bed with her husband, to the birth of her child, to the table each day to teach her children good posture and good manners, and—she believed—she would even take them to her deathbed.

In her world, a woman never left her parents behind, even when the parents left her.

And now, in the anonymity that darkness provides even in the marital bed, Francisco had begun to talk about the possibility of giving up everything—lands, family traditions, and friendships—to start from scratch. Buy some land and start again somewhere else. In a burgeoning Monterrey.

With the intimacy and immediacy that came with sleeping shoulder to shoulder, Beatriz had said: *Francisco, go to sleep.*

She had not allowed him to continue. She did not want to listen to any more. She did not want to lose one more single thing.

"Beatriz. What's on your mind? Don't you like the flowers we chose?" Aunt Refugio Morales's voice broke through her absorption.

"Hmm? Oh! Yes . . . I like them. Carnations are always nice," she replied, though she doubted they would be able to come by flowers of any kind.

"There's time. It's only October. I think we can order them in February to make sure they're delivered on time," Mercedes Garza went on, her voice weak, labored, hoarse from so much coughing.

"And what if they don't arrive?" Aunt Refugio asked. She could always be counted on to be clear and direct.

"If they don't arrive, then they don't arrive," said Lucha Doria. "What color are we going to order?"

"Red?" asked Mercedes Garza between coughing spasms.

"No. Not red. Any other color, whichever you want," said Beatriz sharply. She preferred a color that would not resemble blood. Seeing that Mercedes's cough was not relenting, she asked, "Are you all right? You look dreadful."

"No. I woke up today feeling as if I'd been beaten. I think I'm coming down with a cold, or perhaps traveling while pregnant wore me out. Or something. I'd better go home to bed."

They all agreed it was a good idea and got up with her to leave. As she came out onto the street, Beatriz was surprised to see Simonopio waiting for her, anxious, sitting on a bench in the square. More and more often, the boy had been straying away from the house without telling anyone where he was going or what time he would return, but it was strange to see him walking in the town. Stranger still to see him stop there.

Beatriz knew that Simonopio did not like being among so many strangers that did not take kindly to him. She suspected that they remarked on, and even mocked, his peculiar physical features in front of him, quite without shame. And how had he known exactly where she was?

Simonopio came up to her and took her hand urgently, indicating that she should follow him.

"You're very hot," said Beatriz, touching his forehead. "You have a fever!"

He did not turn to look at anyone else. He only had eyes for her.

"Do you feel unwell?" Beatriz asked with alarm.

"Ay, Beatriz. What patience and what Christian charity you have," said Mercedes Garza between coughing fits, but Beatriz ignored her, as she did the other ladies who, crowding around them, were saying, *Poor boy, what a mouth, but what beautiful eyes.* When one of them went to stroke him like a pet, Simonopio did not let her. He kept pulling insistently on Beatriz's hand. She let him separate her by a few paces from the group.

"This boy's never sick," she said to them when he insisted on pulling her farther away. "*Ándale*, quick, let's go."

Beatriz turned her head to wish her old school friend a speedy recovery, but Mercedes Garza did not hear her—she had turned the corner.

# 11

## *The Spaniard Arrives in October*

Someone had to be the first to die that October of 1918. Why not Mercedes Garza?

After her meeting with the other social club ladies, she arrived home, requested a cinnamon tea, and announced that she was going to lie down for a while to rest. At lunchtime she had not gotten up to eat, but nobody was alarmed. At nightfall her husband arrived home from their ranch hungry, expecting his wife to tend to him.

"Ay, Señor, the señora felt a little unwell. She's been in the bedroom for some time now," the cook informed him.

The door was locked. Mercedes did not answer. Sergio Garza ended up going in through the courtyard window, only to find his wife lying on her side, the unfinished cinnamon tea on the bedside table. The luggage set the couple had just used on their trip to Eagle Pass, Texas, remained half-unpacked, which was strange, since Mercedes was a very particular and tidy woman. He knew she had been so excited about the fabric she had bought that she could not have let a day go by without going to see her seamstress to order some new maternity dresses. All of this was evidence enough, but Garza had to approach and touch his wife's cold flesh to be sure.

Dr. Cantú arrived half an hour later to confirm what Garza already knew.

"What did she die of, Doctor?"

"Heart failure," answered the physician with certainty and authority, though really, he would have liked to admit he did not know.

He did not like lying. At first glance, he could see she had not been poisoned, stung by an insect, or attacked by some criminal. But how could a woman who was healthy in the morning be dead by the afternoon? All he knew was that Mercedes Garza had died from cardiac arrest, for nobody dies without their heart first stopping. He was confident he had stated nothing but the pure truth.

"What do I do now?" the dazed widower asked.

For now, they had to keep vigil over the young mother and then bury her.

Shaken—because it was not every day that a woman of such standing or of such a young age died under such mysterious circumstances—the mourners at the wake wept and offered condolences to the widower, and since there was no explanation for the sudden death, they offered him words of comfort: *She was an angel who is now with her baby,* or *She was a saint and God needed her in heaven, because he always takes the best, and she was the very best.* Nobody, not even the husband himself, was able to say at what, precisely, Mercedes Garza had been the best, but as God intended, one must always speak well of the dead. All of them, even Mercedes's husband, knew that the deceased was bad-tempered, had been conceited since childhood, and mistreated her servants. In short, they all knew she was far from a saint and even less of an angel. But that day, the deceased, since she was dead, would be forgiven her every transgression.

That was the protocol.

Tomorrow would be another day. But while today lasted, *What a beautiful wake* and *What a moving funeral, how lovely she looks, how well they prepared her,* the ladies of Linares's high society said.

"And that poor child!"

It was the best-attended wake of the year. Everyone who had been acquainted with the woman or her husband felt obliged to go. Not even the knife grinder missed it, though the señora still owed him for his last visit. The mysterious circumstances surrounding Mercedes Garza's death aroused a morbid curiosity in everyone: *What did she die of? Nobody dies from a cold, do they? Who was the last person to see her alive? Who helped her when she felt unwell? Who was her closest friend? Who's to blame for not accompanying her home, for not recommending an excellent infusion? How grief stricken does the husband look? Who will take care of those poor children? How long will it be before he marries again?* They discussed all of this in whispers, faces close together, but only between Rosaries, because otherwise it would have seemed in very poor taste.

After the burial, infected by the sorrow of Mercedes Garza's inconsolable widower and poor motherless children, not a single eye nor handkerchief was left dry. That day, many moist embraces and used handkerchiefs were shared. In the end, Sergio Garza's right hand was sore from so many commiserative handshakes, and inexplicably, his legs and entire body ached too.

Could it be his heart's pain spreading everywhere?

That October of 1918, Mercedes was the first to die, but she would not be the last.

The next day, Dr. Cantú received another summons to the Garza house: Sergio Garza was unwell. The barely conscious patient had a burning fever, he was delirious, and he was struggling for air. His lungs were full of water, and his lips and feet were purple. Acute pneumonia, the doctor diagnosed, with confidence now. But Garza was young, healthy, and strong, and the doctor could not explain the ferocity of the attack, the speed with which the illness—whose progress was usually observable—had come on.

He had not yet finished tending the sick man, knowing that there was little he could do for him, when he was summoned to the home of another patient.

That day, the following one, and every day for the next three eternal months, Dr. Cantú had no rest. No consolation. No knowledge that would help him to help.

It took him a couple days to realize that the speed at which the infection—which seemed like a flu—was spreading was abnormal. That it was of a different nature to anything seen before. It took him a couple more days to send telegrams to alert Governor Nicéforo Zambrano to the alarming death rate in the Linares area.

In Monterrey they already had the same problem, so the governor's response was slow, occupied as he was awaiting instructions from the nation's capital on how to deal with this evil that had spread not just through Nuevo León but across all the states along the US border. By the time they managed to identify the plague, they did not have the energy or creativity to invent a name themselves and instead adopted the one that the entire sick world had decided to give it: Spanish flu.

In a way, Mercedes Garza had been lucky to be the first to die, for hundreds of people said goodbye to her with great pomp and ceremony. Her mournful funeral would have been etched in the collective memory for years to come had it not been for the events that followed.

By the time her widower died three days after her, nobody had the inclination, the energy, or the good health to witness his burial, let alone attend a prolonged wake. By then, at least a third of Sra. Garza's funeral-goers were lying in bed in various stages of the same illness.

When Sergio Garza was in the throes of death, Father Pedro went to administer last rites to him. Then, at the foot of the coffin, he said a few ceremonial words—the bare minimum—before the man was placed in the same grave as his wife.

The sole witness was the gravedigger, Vicente López. The priest, who was in a rush to get to midday Mass, left the cemetery without making sure the grave was filled. And Vicente López left without doing it: *What for, if their little ones are going to join them tomorrow or the next day?*

The gravedigger was no clairvoyant, just an observer. He had heard the Garza family's servants say that the children already showed clear signs of the same illness. A shame: you didn't have to be a doctor to know there was no hope for them.

Once they had delivered their master's body, the servants no longer considered themselves bound to the family. Each went their separate way to try to save their own skin. Some thought one of the witches of La Petaca had given the Garza family the evil eye, and they refused to spend another moment in that house, afraid the power of the curse would extend to them too. The only one to stay to the end, because she had nowhere to go and because her devotion was greater than her superstition, was the orphans' nana, for the children's grandparents and other relatives had neither the health nor the courage to enter that infected house.

By then Vicente López was even busier than Dr. Cantú. At first the physician had tried to visit each house, as was expected of him, and to do so with the usual respect, but the reality was too much for him.

It was too much for everyone.

Afflicted by the curse of which the superstitious spoke or the infection the good doctor described, too many were dying every day. It became necessary to establish a system for collecting the corpses: once a day, early in the morning, in the company of one of his sons, Vicente López traveled the streets of Linares in a cart in search of the dead bodies. He found them wrapped in sheets and dumped in front of the houses; it was not practical to come and go from the cemetery every time someone died. At first, the good families demanded the personal service they were accustomed to, but they very soon lost the desire and the energy to make demands. They limited themselves to leaving a message on the cadaver stating that it was such and such, a devout Catholic, may the Lord now have him in His presence; and then, please bury him in the crypt or grave of the family such and such. Within a few days of the outbreak, nobody stayed on the street to see off the bodies, send a final blessing, or cry. There were other sick people to tend to in the house.

So Vicente López collected corpses in the morning and spent the rest of the day digging the family graves of the rich or throwing the bodies of the poor in the mass grave that, with each swing of his spade, grew ever larger.

Those who died in the night or early morning arrived at the cemetery still fresh. Those who passed away later had to wait until the following day, and so they suffered the natural yet cruel transformations that death brings to a body, whether poor or rich, in full view of the family. *Because we're all equal in death,* concluded López in a moment of philosophical lucidity.

The Garza children had the good fortune to die at night. One from the natural causes of the illness. The other suffocated by a pillow held firmly over his face with great love and decisiveness. Although she would take the crime to her grave, his nana hoped with the last ounce of fervor that remained in her soul that God would not make her pay too dearly and would understand she had no longer been able to bear such enormous suffering in such a dear, tiny body.

The gravedigger found her on the street, inert and badly wrapped in her white shroud, lying between the two little boys she had so loved. He lifted one and then the other onto the cart. When it was the nana's turn, López expected to feel the cold of a soulless body, but it burned with fever.

"I can't take you like this!"

She opened her opaque eyes.

"Take me," she said.

"But, lady, you're still alive . . . Why're you lying out here?"

"So I die now and not later. Because if I don't come out to die, I'll die inside, and then who'll bring me out onto the street? There's no one left . . ."

That nana was the first person López found alive, but she was not the last. Mothers with dying children who waited with horror for the hours of darkness to pass, knowing that the cart would soon come by, would take them outside and shroud them even if there was still life in their bodies. Nothing could be done for them except try to make sure they arrived fresh at the cemetery. Some remembered to send them off with a blessing or with a little pendant pinned to the shroud.

Soon Vicente López no longer asked or checked. He understood the practicality of it and took them all, dead or alive, for he knew from experience that many of the living would be dead before the end of the journey. Some clung to life a while longer. Those he left beside the pit for the elements and the disease to finish off. He could take them near to their final resting place, but to push them in while they still lived was quite another matter. No: he would leave them to die alone, as God willed it.

Several times a day he would check on them. *Ready?* he would yell from a distance, while he labored to make the mass grave bigger or buried the day's dead. There was always at least one that answered, *No, not yet.*

And one after the other, they all succumbed. There was just one among them, always the same one, who replied that he was still there.

This one spent his time listening closely for the moment when he would be called or when his guardian angel would come for him. He waited for his soul to finally leave his body. Eventually, tired of seeing the days go by, of patiently waiting and waiting to be summoned into the presence of God, of watching the gravedigger bury body after body, he began to grow bored. He started to feel the stone that was digging into his backside. To feel hungry. Then he was overcome by a craving for some delicious *empalmes con frijoles y asado*. The bugs crawling over his body and biting his skin began to irritate him. He passed the time listening to the gravedigger's comings and goings, and he tried to keep count of the dead being rolled into the grave, though he always lost track. He arranged and rearranged the shroud his mother had wrapped him in while she gave him his final blessing and said, *Go with God, my son, we'll see each other there later.* He presumed that, when one's own mother gave one up for dead, one should also accept it; what else can one do?

He could remember the high temperature and discomfort of the first few days. And in his moments of lucidity, when the fever's grip eased, he lamented the things he had not had time to do. He lamented that he had never returned his friend's boots to him and that he had never sent that love letter to Luz, his neighbor, after stealing a kiss. But once he was lying on the street, with his mother's blessing on him and the cart about to collect his body, what did it matter?

He had arrived at the cemetery in a daze from the illness, without much memory of the journey in the cart. Three days later, with his fever lifted, lying on the edge of the pit, he felt completely alert. Alert and fed up.

Little by little, he had moved away from the edge for fear of rolling off as he slept. Of falling in by accident and being given up for dead. Or falling and breaking his neck and actually dying. Each time the gravedigger asked whether he was dead yet, he answered *No*, first in a weak voice and later more forcefully. *Not yet.* On the third day, he yelled with all the might he could muster that he was still there, and *Can I have some water?*

He had witnessed the deaths of each of the bodies on either side of him. Each had died differently: one in silence and the other making a great deal of fuss—coughing, choking, and wailing—but neither of them, he was certain, suffered one moment's boredom or hunger. If they had had the time and clarity to think of a wish, they would have wished only to end their torment as quickly as possible. He therefore reached the conclusion that, in the process of dying—well or badly—there was not much time or energy for boredom. So he decided to stop devoting his time to dying.

*Itching's a sign of healing,* his mother always said. Well, now he had his own version: *If you're bored, you're getting better.*

And truth be told, he was also itching. Fiercely. All over his body. While the dead were being eaten by the insects of the dead, he was being eaten alive by the ones that prefer warm flesh and fresh blood. Living flesh.

He stood, took off the shroud, and folded it carefully. Though his legs were shaking, he walked for the first time in many days. He plodded forward, slowed by weakness and wary of frightening the gravedigger, though López did not bat an eyelid when he saw him in a vertical position.

"No, compadre. Nothing frightens me anymore."

With some help, he climbed onto the cart, this time so the gravedigger would take him back to town and straight home—without stopping at the cantina that he had also been dreaming of since the day before—for he was eager to give his mother the good news of his recovery.

"She best find out from me and not from someone else. Can you imagine her reaction, Don Vicente?"

"Uh-huh."

There was little time to imagine it. When she opened the door and saw him, his mother—who in her sorrow had pictured her son infested with maggots in the green sheet she had wrapped around him when he was dying—managed only to let out an ear-piercing scream before collapsing, killed by shock, as the rest of the family and the neighbors who peered through their windows looked on in astonishment.

Practical as ever, and aware of the long funereal journey ahead of him, Vicente López asked the young man who had been his only return passenger, "Will you help me lift her onto the cart?"

And equally practical, as one necessarily becomes on returning almost from the gates of heaven, he answered "Yes" and "Poor Mama, her time had come." And since he had with him the green sheet that had been his shroud, he wrapped his mother in it, a little unhappy about the dirt it had accumulated in the last three days but certain his mother was beyond worrying about such things.

One by one the neighbors came out of their houses, which they had not dared to do for days, to marvel at the events and then share the news.

At the time, the doors to the cathedral were kept locked because the federal government had ordered all gathering places to remain closed: theaters, movie houses, bars, and of course, churches. For a while, poor Father Pedro had defied the order, saying that nobody had the right to close the House of the Lord, much less refuse Communion to believers, even if fewer and fewer attended. Sick but soldiering on, he had died suddenly three days ago while reciting the Credo in the first mass of the day. The handful of churchgoers had run out without even crossing themselves. His body had to wait all day and all night for the grave-digger to come by and collect it, watched over by his young assistant, Father Emigdio. The now-familiar sound of the cart approaching had freed him from his vigil. Since then, a frightened Father Emigdio had kept the doors locked. He did not dare even to look through the peep-hole when someone knocked, asking to come in and pray.

He was the only person who prayed there at that time. And that was what he was doing right when they came and knocked insistently on the cathedral doors. Surprised and alarmed by the many fists that thumped the doors with such persistence, he made an exception and opened the peephole.

"A miracle, Father! A miracle!"

"What miracle?" Overcome with emotion and longing for them to tell him the disease was gone, he flung the doors wide open.

"Lazarus has risen!"

# 12

## *Letters and Telegrams*

News of the resurrection of Lázaro de Jesús García—for that was what the fortunate return passenger had been called since the day of his baptism—spread through Linares in a matter of minutes. Some would soon accept the truth and view the news as a mere curiosity, with nothing more than anecdotal significance. But others clung to the hope brought by good tidings at a time when everything seemed like hell itself, and they would have lynched any birds of ill omen who dared refute the miracle. To this day, some still tell the story—swearing it was witnessed firsthand by a great-uncle or great-grandmother—that on one of the most terrible days in the history of Linares, a Lazarus rose from the dead by God's hand.

That day, as the news spread through the town, Lázaro was elevated to divine status. After plucking up the courage to leave the cathedral, young Father Emigdio decreed that the restoration to life of a local parishioner was a sign of the forgiveness of God, who had punished the poor community so much already, making the just pay for the sins of others, for as its very name indicated, the epidemic was the fault of the socialist, apostate Spanish who strayed ever further from the Church.

Then, overcome with emotion, he went to the home of the last living postal employee.

"Álvaro. Open up the post office for me. I must send an urgent telegram."

Despite the postman's initial refusal and his doubt as to whether anyone was at the Monterrey office to receive the telegram, the priest persuaded him with the promise of eternal salvation. Thus, he sent the first telegram of his life to the archbishop in Monterrey: URGENT stop MIRACLE HAPPENED IN LINARES stop LAZARUS RISEN stop CONFIRMED BY ME stop RESPOND URGENTLY stop.

Father Emigdio did not know whether the telegram would reach its intended recipient, but that day, by a stroke of luck—good or bad would be determined later—Governor Zambrano in Monterrey, despondent due to the public health crisis, also required the special services of a telegraphist. While sending official telegrams reporting the number of dead to date, the governor received the good news—*At last, some good news!*—and sent it immediately to its ecclesiastic addressee.

When he received the message, the archbishop of Linares, Francisco Plancarte y Navarrete, hastily called a Mass of Thanksgiving to be held the next day. *Lazarus resurrexit* would be the topic of his sermon. On his death two years later, in 1920, an inspired script for the failed sermon was found among his belongings, along with a letter written in his own hand, unfinished, drafted with the intention of formally asking Rome to send an emissary to attest to the miracle.

In Linares, on the day of the extraordinary event, the people made a pilgrimage in the hope they could see and touch the one who had risen from the dead.

Many townspeople had seen him dead and wrapped in a shroud. From the safety of their homes, they had peered out of windows and witnessed the final blessing that his now-deceased mother had offered. And they all knew with a certainty that sat firmly in the gut, as Lázaro himself had also known, that there is nothing more final than a mother's mortal blessing. Later, they had seen Vicente López lift the body on top of the others he had collected on his journey of no return. Sra. García had mourned her son in the proper way: she had lit the candle that she usually saved for Easter and closed the shutters. Lázaro had died. Many had witnessed it, but now they saw him come back from the grave: he breathed, he walked, he spoke. If all this evidence failed to convince anyone, the fact that Lázaro stank of death after three days of lying among corpses was enough to persuade even the most skeptical.

Lázaro was happy his recovery brought so much joy to his neighbors and the people who came from farther afield. He had never been the recipient of so much attention, but he did not understand that, when they called him "Lázaro" and touched him with such emotion, they were not thinking of him but of the well-loved and famous friend of the Messiah. And when they cried, *You have returned!* and he replied, *Yes, I've returned,* the others thought it was from heaven, but he meant from the cemetery.

After elbowing his way through the pilgrims, his neighbor, the father of the girl to whom Lázaro wrote the letter that he never sent, took the opportunity to hug him tightly before starting to cry. Knowing that the neighbor had at no time liked him, Lázaro would never have dared to declare his romantic interest in his daughter, but he decided to seize this moment of intimacy.

"Don Luis: before I went, I wrote a love letter for your daughter Luz."

At that, the man's crying intensified, and Lázaro turned to his brother, Miguel, in search of an explanation. Miguel García made a sign with his forefinger, running it from one side of his throat to the other.

Luz was dead.

The man who would have been his father-in-law had Lázaro had the courage to send the letter, had Luz accepted it and accepted him, had Lázaro not fallen sick, had he not kissed her and therefore infected her, and had she not died, looked him hard in the eyes.

"Did you see her there?"

"Er. Um." In all likelihood, without knowing it, he had witnessed the girl's body being heaved into the grave. "I think so."

"Did she seem happy?"

What kind of question was that? Lázaro felt an urgent need to get away from there, to flee into his home and lock the door behind him.

"Er. I don't know. There were already a lot of them; it was very crowded," he said, imploring his brother with his eyes to help him get out of there, to help him escape their morbid neighbor.

He was desperate for a bath to wash away the smell of urine and worse. He was desperate to sit or lie down: the muscles in his legs were refusing to hold him upright. He wanted to eat something, even just some cold leftovers. Then perhaps he would be able to understand what was happening to everyone. It was as if, in his three days' absence, they had all lost their minds.

The crowd insisted that they wait for Father Emigdio to return from the telegraph office to lead the official Rosary, but Miguel García said they would wait inside, that the others must understand that coming back to life was not easy, that it required a great deal of effort, so Lázaro must be allowed to rest.

The brothers went into the house, but before they closed the door, they heard Don Luis, the father-in-law that would now never be, cry out between sobs:

"If only you had brought her with you!"

# 13

*Get Up and Go*

Dr. Cantú was just several blocks away, but the news of Lázaro's return had not yet reached him.

The doctor did not believe in modern miracles. To his close friends, he insisted he believed in only the miracles that had been worthy enough to be mentioned in the Old and New Testaments. Except, one could not call oneself a true Mexican without believing in the miracle of the apparition of the Virgin on the Hill of Tepeyac, who had at any rate been considerate enough to people like him to leave evidence of her visit.

In his opinion, the Virgin of Guadalupe marked the end of the age of miracles.

He supposed that daily life, science, and his knowledge of human nature had turned him into a doubting Thomas. The things he considered miracles in recent times came not from the catechism but from the great advances of medicine. He was certain that, with modern vaccines and medications, man would soon defeat death.

For him, that would be the greatest miracle.

Nonetheless, at this time of persistent death, his faith in science and medicine had been put to the test. The supreme self-assurance he felt as a member of the global medical community had been shattered in just a few days. He was exhausted, tired in body but even more so in spirit, weary of seeing people die.

He felt ready to believe again in some divine miracle if only God would do him the favor.

Of course, as a young man, when he had decided to become a doctor, he had been aware that he would see his patients—friends and strangers—die. He considered it the only certainty that life gave everyone equally: sooner or later, everybody would die. It might be slowly or suddenly, but they would die. And so he had accepted it and he had assumed the responsibility: he would witness the deaths of children, young people, old people. He would be with them in their final moment, until the time came when they would see him die.

This disease, however, had entered their lives treacherously, without warning. Now he traveled around the town wrapped from head to foot in thick clothes, with a scarf over his mouth, protective gloves over his hands, and his head covered. He visited the endless dying and did not dare to have skin-to-skin contact with them. He visited those to whom he could not give words of reassurance or hope in their agony, and those whom, in his outfit, he could not offer the comfort of seeing a friendly face at the end of life. For whenever they saw him arrive, they knew that it was to sentence them to death.

He had begun that day with a sadness he could not shake. He was gripped by the idea that the disease would not stop until it finished off every last living person. Such was the situation in the town, in the country, and in the world: no one who was infected survived. And though he clung to life like anyone else, it terrified him to imagine that he might be the last man standing.

He had tried to convey to the inhabitants of the town how important it was to remain in quarantine, to not leave the house if anyone was sick, and needless to say, to also stay at home if one was lucky enough to have no infection in the family. Following the instructions of Dr. Lorenzo Sepúlveda of the Monterrey Hospital and of Governor

Zambrano, he had requested that, in addition to closing public places, people and goods not be allowed to enter or leave. The postal service was now at a complete standstill because its workers had been among the first to die. An occupational hazard, with so many letters passing from hand-to-hand. Sepúlveda had also sent an urgent appeal to the federal government to stop the trains so that the infection would be fenced in and contained in the northern states. But his request had fallen on deaf ears, and the disease had spread all over the country.

The miracle would have been if those arrogant fools with the fate of the country in their hands had listened in time to the voices of the experts. Now it was too late.

The reality was that all manner of instructions could be given, but people needed to eat and they needed supplies. Some considered feeding the soul as important as feeding the body, so they, too, disregarded the order to not attend Mass. Father Pedro himself had refused to accept that the illness was capable of entering the church, much less spread and grow during the sacred ceremony. But this disease did not respect holy places, rituals, or people, as the pig-headed and dead Father Pedro must now know, wherever he was.

Nor did the disease respect medical personnel. The town's already limited hospital, founded by the ladies of high society, had closed its doors after the death or desertion of its nurses and the rest of its staff. Now Linares's doctors and any surviving medical staff who dared do so roamed the town, like Cantú, visiting houses where they were not welcome.

As he crisscrossed the town between one tragic visit and another, for the first time, the doctor dared to ask for a miracle, believing only such a wonder could save Linares.

He was not expecting a reply, let alone an immediate one, when he came across a group of people walking in a hurry. They were going together to see the miracle of a Lazarus, they told him. *God's honest truth, Doctor. He expired, and now he's back from the grave with messages from the dead for the living,* they told him.

Dr. Cantú was used to the extravagances of these simple people. Often—most of the time—they turned something ordinary into something extraordinary, and elaborated on the simplest explanations so much that they ended up confusing rather than clarifying the point they were trying to make.

He had always devoted some of his consultation time to people who could not afford to pay, who proudly traded homemade cheese or a dozen eggs for an appointment and a remedy. Hardworking people who rose at dawn and had not a moment's rest until nightfall. Anyone would have thought, therefore, that when they spoke they would get straight to the point and be sparing with words, but no: much of the time he spent with them was wasted on trying to understand the convoluted descriptions of symptoms given by the patients themselves or by their mothers, who sometimes required more attention than the patients. In addition to doctor, he had to be translator, linguist, and fortune-teller.

This was the case of a mother of two, a widow since the day before, whom he had just visited:

"Ay, Doc. This flu sure has hit everyone in the house hard—there's no one fit to mend the others. We're all sick, Doc! My old man didn't have time to say a word. One second he was there, and the next he was God knows where. Even I can feel it coming on, and there won't be no shakin' it. And now this lad's got some rashes which're comin' out like rashes, but they're bumps, or who knows what they are? And he's got little bumps on his weenie as well and on his little nuts and butt cheeks, where they're worse still. Then he's got that thing in his mouth, you can't see it, but you can tell it's there just by lookin', and I don't know what it is, but it's somethin'. Poor as we are, all I can do is wash it with alcohol, but not even that stops the itchin'.

"And worse: my girl, just look at her. Her chest's rotten. She ain't far off chokin' to death. The snot built up with the cough, and she's drownin' in it. And the cough's gettin' worse. She's got what I call a dog's cough, and around here, above the lungs, you can hear all the muck in there: her little chest goes *gurr, gurr, gurr.* Sometimes I can see her breathin' ain't working . . . It must be the cough, that's what I say."

"And has she had a fever?"

"Oh, no. No fever. Just a nasty temperature that heats her up good and hot, till her little heart's thumpin'. And it never goes down. And then there's the cryin' all day, and she don't sleep well from all the hallucillusions."

Explaining to the mother that her son had touched poison ivy and then his private parts and mouth was very easy.

"The boy's healthy, in spite of the rashes. Don't put any more alcohol on him; it won't do him any good. And he must stop touching himself, even if you have to tie his hands. Send him to the pharmacy for some ointment to cover the eruption. And sew a bar of lead into his underpants. That will help."

Giving bad news had become part of his daily routine, but that did not make it any easier—next, he had to explain to this devoted mother that there was no way to save her daughter.

"All we can do is keep her comfortable. Sit her up with pillows to help her breathe more easily. Dab her with cool cloths to bring her temperature down. Keep the windows open, and don't go near her when she coughs. Wash your hands, Señora. Whenever you touch her, or touch her things, wash your hands. If you're not careful, you'll be infected and so will your son."

"Just give her a vaccine against the chokes, Doc. I'll get the necessary."

But it was not a question of the necessary, of money, or of willingness. He wanted to believe that a vaccine would someday be found to make influenza nothing more than a bad memory in humanity's long history, "But today, Señora, today," Dr. Cantú said to the distraught woman, "there is no vaccine at any price. I'm sorry."

How he would have loved to have been able to prescribe the new aspirins that the Germans had invented, but it was a sophisticated, costly medicine, made even more expensive by the Great War. They had been easy to obtain in the United States before the conflict, but now, with the recent theory that the Germans had launched a bacterial attack by means of their Bayer aspirins, they no longer sold them even across the border.

At first, the pharmacy had endeavored to procure willow bark, the source of the main component of aspirin. It was not as effective as the German tablets, but an infusion of the bark helped a little with the pain and fever. Unfortunately, the small amount the pharmacy acquired had been used up in the first days of the Spanish nightmare.

Frustrated that he could not do more, the doctor went away from that house knowing that the girl's hours were numbered. He would not be surprised if the mother soon followed, for her eyes looked glassy.

It was then, on his way to another tragic visit, that he dared ask for a miracle, and then that he found the group in the street proclaiming it. He joined them so they could take him to the place where the phenomenon had occurred. He did not know what he would find there, but he wanted to believe it would be something different from the constant tragedy of recent weeks. That would be enough.

By the time they arrived, the man they were already calling Lázaro the Resurrected of Linares had gone into his house.

"We touched him, Doctor. We saw him clear as we can see you now. We smelt him and he smelt of pure death, Doctor, rotten-like . . . and you can't fake that, right? And we knew he wasn't going to last, because Doña Chela was rushing around giving him traditional remedies and cleansing rituals. Didn't do any good. Then the poor woman howled to the heavens after she left him there, all wrapped up on the street. The gravedigger took him off to the cemetery, still fresh, all floppy, and he was a goner for three days, he was. Just like the Lazarus in the olden days, the real one. But this one's our very own: the Lazarus of Linares!

And when he got back today, the first thing that happened was his mama died, Doctor. I bet they switched 'em round in heaven, one for the other. She was a saint, Doña Chela: look how she traded her soul for her son's . . . a true saint. Later, Lázaro told good Don Luis he saw his daughter Lucita in the land of the dead, may God have her in His holy glory, and by anyone's reckoning he does, because Lázaro saw her happy 'fore he came back here. Now folks are lining up to ask him 'bout their dead, but right now they're not ready to open the door to give 'em an audience."

It was not the miracle he had imagined, and like any self-respecting skeptic, he needed to see it to believe it. He knew that when he went into Lázaro García's house he would find a logical explanation. But later on, when he found time to recount the events of that afternoon to his wife and friends, he would admit that, for a moment, hearing the people who had gathered there, his hair had stood on end.

As a doctor, he felt entitled to knock and demand they open the door to the García home to him.

He found Lázaro freshly bathed, lying in bed vomiting. In the absence of his mother, his brother, Miguel, had warmed up the *cabrito en salsa* from the day before. The mere smell of the goat meat had been enough to make him feel sick, but he knew he needed to eat. At the second mouthful, his stomach rebelled.

"How many days have you gone without food, Lázaro?"

"I don't remember, Doctor. I can remember the three days in the cemetery, but I can't remember how many days it's been since I fell ill. More than a few, I'd bet, because my clothes are all too big for me."

"Well, you can't start with something so heavy. Start with toast and chamomile tea, but slowly: small pieces and sips, bit by bit, so that your stomach gradually gets used to the food."

Miguel took the plate of cabrito away and went to make the tea and toast. There was a persistent knocking on the door, which Miguel answered on his way to the kitchen. It was Father Emigdio. Dr. Cantú nodded a greeting.

"I've just sent a telegram to the archbishop to announce the miracle of our Lazarus."

Dr. Cantú preferred not to contribute anything to that line of conversation. He wanted to hear the story from the mouth of the supposed risen one.

"What happened, Lázaro? They tell me outside that you came back."

"That's right, Doctor. The plain truth is that I was fed up, so I thought it best I come back."

"You mean you got bored?" asked Father Emigdio, somewhat indignant.

"Well, yes. Imagine: all that was happening was that I was watching more and more dead people arrive, and then more dead people again. And then I thought how happy my mama would be to see me well, and just look what happened. Now I'm here and she's there."

"You decided to come back yourself?"

"With the help of God and His angels, of course," the priest cut in.

"I kept an eye out, Father, to see if the angels would appear to show me where to go, but they didn't. So, yes, it was just me. Who else? Of course, the gravedigger helped me onto the cart and brought me here, Doctor."

"He got you out of the grave?"

"Oh, no. He never put me in there. He's a good man. He'd never have done that. Just imagine. He left me at the edge with the other ones that weren't ready yet."

"Ready?"

"Ready for the pit. All the others eventually went, but not me. I waited and waited to be called, all blessed and everything by my mama, and nothing happened. I tried to wait, but I got tired of it, so I got up and walked until I found Don Vicente. Then he put me on the cart and brought me home."

"They say that you told Don Luis, your neighbor, that you had seen his daughter . . ."

"Well, what could I say to him, with him hugging me like that? I tell you, Doc, I saw a lot of dead people, and God only knows whether I saw her. Maybe. I was embarrassed to ask Don Luis what time or what day she'd died, or what color her sheet was, but the honest truth is that, bored as I was, I took to counting them to pass the time. And he asked me whether I'd seen her, so I said yes, I think so. And then he asked me why I hadn't brought her with me. But you won't see me going in that pit—not a chance. Rummaging through those rotten, stinking bundles to find my neighbor, as much as I liked her—no, sir. And anyway, if Luz died, she should stay where she's meant to be, right? What do you think, Father? The dead shouldn't be wandering around, visiting Papa, should they?"

"You came back to visit your mother, Lázaro. Remember?"

"I did, Father, but not Luz."

"And did you see a bright light as you returned?"

"In the day I saw light; at night I couldn't see anything. That's how I know I spent three days there, Father. I would've liked to have come back sooner, but the truth is, it was a while before it occurred to me, because at first I was really sick. But then, when I got bored, I realized I'd gotten better, so I just got up and walked."

"Just like Lazarus."

"How could it be like anyone else, if that's who I am?"

"Lázaro García. Explain one thing for us," Dr. Cantú interjected, suspecting that, if they went on like this, they would go around in circles for eternity. "Did you come down with the Spanish flu?"

"Yes, Doctor. In no time I felt like I was choking to death."

"With a very high fever and aching body?"

"As much as my mama tried, may her poor soul rest in peace, it wouldn't go down. I couldn't even think anymore, and everything hurt so much I couldn't move, much less breathe. My skull and my brain hurt so much I wanted to rip my head off, and the compresses my mama made for me did nothing. By the time my mama said, 'Son, you're not going to get better, you'll have to go now because Don Vicente's coming,' all I wanted was to die."

"That was when you died?" the priest asked.

"No, Father! Like I keep saying, I got bored!"

"Okay. When was it you died, so that you could return?"

"Who said I died? I never said I died."

"But you returned!"

"Well, I went in good faith. My mama said to me, 'Go,' and I went. She wrapped me in my sheet, and I tried not to move too much. But after three days, I got tired of waiting, and I came back."

"To be clear: You fell sick?" Dr. Cantú asked.

"Yes, Doctor."

"They took you in the cart to the cemetery?"

"Yes, Doctor. The gravedigger put me on there."

"But you were alive when you went?"

"Uh-huh."

"You were alive? Your mother sent you to be buried alive?"

"Don Vicente never buried me, Father. He kept asking: 'Are you still alive?' And I always said yes. The other poor folks gradually went quiet, and then they were ready."

"Ready for the pit. Dead, you mean."

"Yes, Doctor. But not me, as much as I tried. So I came back here when I was able to get up. What is it, Father? Why are you making that face?"

The information he had just received, processed, and accepted hit Father Emigdio like a bucket of icy water. "There is no miracle! What am I going to say to the archbishop? What am I going to say to all the people waiting outside?"

"Tell them, Father," the doctor suggested, thinking it would reassure him, "that there is no resurrected one because he was never dead. But tell them that we now have the first sufferer of this influenza who has survived, and that, Father Emigdio, is the best possible miracle. Then tell them to go home, because this isn't over yet."

The visit ended when the little tea and toast Lázaro García had managed to ingest itself returned to air and light, and propelled itself with uncommon force onto the priest's cassock. There was more noise than quantity, really, but some things not even a saint can endure. Feeling disgusted, as well as snubbed, Father Emigdio turned to leave the house, thinking it would be best to face the people and get it over and done with.

Dr. Cantú's day had improved immeasurably. He was under no illusions: he knew that the miracle of Lázaro the Survivor did not mean the end of the infection and the deaths, especially after the hours the crowd had spent gathered together, talking and coexisting in close proximity.

He did not know how much longer the epidemic would last, but now he knew that at least some would manage to survive in the town, in the state, in the country, and in the world.

For Father Emigdio, on the other hand, it would be the worst day of his life. He had started it shut away, afraid, behind the cathedral walls. Now he knew he should never have opened the doors, but he had let himself be infected by the excitement of the faithful, and his day had been filled with a wonder that his own faith had prepared him to blindly accept since he was a boy.

He had never believed himself worthy enough to see one of the great miracles in person, but today he had thought he was sharing the joy that important figures from the Bible must have felt on witnessing God's greatness. He had participated in and was perhaps even an instigator of the fervor that had blossomed that day on the street where the Lazarus of Linares lived. What's more, committing the sin of pride, Father Emigdio had announced the miracle prematurely to the archbishop of Linares, a claim that he now had to retract, humiliating himself, in the second and last telegram of his life. And as he went out onto the street like a bird of ill omen and announced that everything had been a misunderstanding, because, since Lázaro had not died, he could not have been resurrected, many people forgot his sacred status as a priest and cursed him for having made a fuss over nothing and for conning them. Some accused him of being a Judas the Betrayer for trying to draw them away from the faith with the miracle of Lázaro the Resurrected. Among these was Álvaro, the postman, who was waiting for him in the crowd and from whom Father Emigdio needed another favor.

"Come along," he said to the disappointed Álvaro, "let's go write another one."

He left in a hurry—spattered in vomit, frightened of the heated atmosphere, and disappointed in himself—to write the telegraphic message: URGENT stop ERROR IN LINARES stop LAZARO NEVER DIED stop NEVER RESURRECTED stop JUST RECOVERED BY HIMSELF stop FORGIVE ME.

The reply that the governor of Nuevo León was expecting from the capital had not yet arrived, so this new telegram surprised the patient telegrapher who, between the two messages from Father Emigdio, had shaken off his depression by thinking about the Lazarus. He was in no hurry to send this latest bad news to the archbishop, thinking, in his renewed depression, that there was no rush when it came to bad tidings and that it could wait until the next day.

For his part, Father Emigdio, equally depressed, returned to the cathedral. He bolted the doors and, feeling very tired, went to bed, where he would spend the last night of his life. Because, in opening the door that day and going out to celebrate the failed miracle, infected with the fervor that surrounded him, he had also become infected with the disease. Luckily for him, his agony was as short as Mercedes Garza's had been.

That day, Lázaro the Resurrected ate, rested, and regained his strength, so it might be considered a good day. But thereafter, he would become the only man in the world—because no other case had ever been known—to be nicknamed with his own Christian name. And the nickname would catch on so quickly that very soon everyone—except his brother—would forget what Lázaro of Linares's original name had been.

And his infamy would accompany him for the rest of his life: he would never find a woman who wanted to spend her life or even a night with him. His reputation as a good-for-nothing would not, by itself, have prevented him from finding a partner, for women that fall for such men have always existed, in spite of concerned parents insisting, *My child, don't marry that man: he's a good-for-nothing.* Words in the wind. But none would forget or come to terms with the enduring mental image of Lázaro: dead, half-decomposed, stinking of rotten flesh.

Though Lázaro had returned to life and soon regained his health and good looks, all of them, even Celedonia Grajeda, the ugliest girl in town, would refuse with a shudder to share their flesh with a man and to touch it against a body that had lain rotten and worm ridden in the mass grave.

Aware of his misfortune and infamy but longing to be married, Lázaro was forced to search for a bride in nearby villages. But as everybody knows, in those villages, news travels fast, and news like Lázaro's even faster. In none of them would he find a woman who would have him or even share the warmth of her body with him in a simple and fleeting dance.

# 14

*Simonopio's Sinapism*

In the years that followed his recovery and until the day of his death, I suppose, when they saw him pass by, the people of Linares—whether believers or unbelievers—continued to call him Lázaro the Resurrected of Linares in gossipy or reverential whispers, depending on where the person was on the scale of faith. The coincidence of him sharing his name with the famous figure from the New Testament helped to perpetuate the amazement of the people, many of whom, before the famous incident of his miraculous return, had never had a word to say about him except to declare that he was a good-for-nothing.

I remember Lázaro. Not from the days when he was newly back to life, because that was years before I was born, but I do remember how he was much later, when little remained of the man he might have been, when all that remained of him was pure legend.

There was nothing extraordinary about him, physically speaking. All I remember is that he was a silent man with an unhurried gait. And very tall. Even if, to a child, everyone seems tall. Did he have brown, black, or green eyes? I couldn't tell you now. Was his nose snub or aquiline? Again, I couldn't say. I watched him pass by with some admiration because, from a young age, I was very fond of listening to stories and reading tales of adventure, and one of the most exciting and wonderful was the Gospel's recounting of the death and return of Lazarus.

Or it was to me, at least.

Truth is, I could think of no greater adventure than a journey to and from that place that Lázaro must have reached when he gave up life. I, who at that age had traveled no farther afield than the family orchards and Monterrey, imagined that such a man must return with much to tell. I wanted to know everything: *Did you cross the river? Did you see Charon? Did you fight the souls in purgatory?* Or *What is God's face like?* But my mama, letting out a sigh, would tell me, *Don't even think about it,* and *Don't be so silly.*

The day would come, years later, when I would ask Mama to call him, to invite him to visit me—prevented as I was from going out to find him, with or without permission. By then I had forgotten about the adventures and wanted only to ask him what one has to do to return from there.

In one of the few lies she would tell me in her life, my mama assured me that she had tried to find him, but that Lázaro had left Linares for a while.

"When he comes back, we'll find him, won't we?"

Years later, my mama would tell me this detailed anecdote about our Lazarus in a half-joking, half-sad tone. Perhaps it was the same tone in which Dr. Cantú had told it to her. It could not have been easy for her to battle with my childish obsession with the matter. But also, I think that when she told the story of Lázaro again, she could not help but remember the story of all the people who suddenly disappeared from her life forever in those final months of 1918—or afterward—in what must have seemed to her like a blink of the eye.

She might say, *When we were girls, Mercedes and I would hide in a hollow in the trunk of a pecan tree so that her sister Luisa wouldn't find us,* but she refused to talk about the last time she saw her friend alive, much less about being unable to attend her funeral or about how that entire family disappeared from this earth in less than three days. She spoke about Aunt Refugio, about how clever and prudent she was, but she never mentioned that, on the one day her prudence had let her down, she had invited her inseparable friends Remedios, Amparo, and Concepción to spend the period of forced confinement with her and play a canasta tournament meant to last as long as the quarantine.

All of them spinsters and of an advanced age, they accepted the invitation, pleased for the company and to continue the rivalry they had begun years before, when it became clear to them all that they would never be married and they discovered the card game. Since then, they had earned reputations as ferocious competitors, and it would not be the first time that they spent entire consecutive days without going outside, their minds on the private canasta tournaments they organized at one of their houses.

The Spanish flu meant little to them except another opportunity to do what they liked most. And without silly interruptions, to boot.

By then, they knew about the infection and the death of the Garza family, who, as everybody knew, had traveled to Eagle Pass, Texas. *Who knows what kind of people and filth they must have come across in that town of cows and cowboys?* they said between games. Perhaps this was why it did not occur to Aunt Refugio that, fine and trusted ladies of decorum that they were, her friends might arrive laden not only with suitcases but also with the same invisible and undesirable passenger the Garzas had brought back from Texas. And much less did she imagine that, whether with an ace, a joker, or a three, they would cheerfully pass it on with each card that exchanged hands.

The four friends were found two days later, each of them sitting in her seat, motionless, holding her cards.

They would have sooner died than end a game before it was finished.

The man who found them would say to whoever wanted to listen that, while the notebook showed Refugio and Remedios were way ahead on points, in their last game of canasta, all of them had lost.

The three most acute months of the Spanish influenza crisis left the survivors of Linares and of the whole world with scars that would never heal and voids that would never be filled.

It is now known that there was nothing Spanish about that influenza. Spain, since it was not involved in the Great War, was simply the first to report the infection to the world. Hence the name. Experts have tried to determine since then whether it began in Boston or in the military barracks of Kansas or Texas; it was exported from there to warring Europe in spring 1918 and to northern Mexico that fall. Some say twenty million or even fifty million perished, and just in Mexico, three hundred thousand—perhaps up to five hundred thousand—died from the virulent disease. It is a well-known fact that the yellow fever epidemic a few years before and the new so-called Spanish pandemic killed more Mexicans than all the bullets fired during the Revolution.

Still, in January 1919, in Linares, these details were of little interest, because absences were not measured in numbers or statistics: they were measured in grief.

When the townspeople gradually tried to resume life—the daily routine, the rhythm that had been laid down over generations—the postmen, the butcher, the grinder, and their entire families were gone. The milkman and several of the garbage collectors no longer traveled the streets. The gravedigger, Vicente López, and two of his sons were gone. The young daughter of the owner of a grocery and tobacco store had to take over the business, without knowing where to start, when her father and three sisters died. Many farmhands and some owners of ranches and haciendas had disappeared. Several ladies from the social club would never worry about the flowers or music at future events again, and many founding members who had signed the club's memorandum of association would never lay eyes on the social hall they had longed to see built. The position of parish priest at the cathedral was vacant, as was the job of headmistress of the girls' primary school. The best carpenter had not finished training his son and apprentice. On the desks of the girls' and boys' schools, the absentees had left unopened books and notepads with blank pages. There were lessons that had ended abruptly and would never be learned, and friendships that would never be forged. The town was full of friendless friends. There were also many young widowers who had to learn to live without their wives, and many widows whose lives and upbringings had not prepared them to be breadwinners. By the same token, there were a great many childless parents and parentless children.

Perhaps it was from that pain and those absences that the saying I remember from my childhood in Linares emerged: "The unhealthy year of 1918, when the Spanish flu was the worst ever seen."

I guess that, for those who stayed in the town and witnessed each death, slowly growing accustomed to the horror of seeing the cartful of bodies go past every day, to seeing loved ones or acquaintances walking one day and riding as lifeless passengers on the cart of death the next, the blow was gradual, and resignation came ever more easily.

My parents did not stay to watch anyone die. They did not wait for their people or for themselves to drop, infected, one after the other. Simonopio saved them.

"He saved us with a fever he invented," my mama would say on the few occasions she said anything on the subject.

He had never fallen ill. He had never even had a simple cold. But the day Simonopio went to find my mama after her meeting with the ladies from the club, his fever gradually rose until it made him convulse and lose consciousness. Dr. Cantú could not see any cause for such a rise in temperature: that morning, the boy had jumped out of bed with all his usual energy. There was no swelling in his respiratory tract, the lungs sounded clear, and his kidneys and liver felt normal. He was neither vomiting nor suffering from diarrhea. His joints were not swollen either. The doctor doubted it was polio, because my mama had noticed nothing strange in his walk, but there were countless other possible causes: a latent eruptive fever, appendicitis, or meningitis, for example.

He could open up the boy's right side to examine him, he told my parents, but if it was peritonitis, nothing could be done for him anyway. He would be cutting the body open purely to see what the child would end up dying from. If it was meningitis, the prognosis would be even less encouraging.

The doctor's advice was to wait, observe, keep him hydrated, and do everything possible to lower his temperature with cloths soaked in cold water from the waterwheel, or rags soaked in alcohol. They could give him the Bayer aspirins the physician knew my parents had bought on a trip to the United States when the pills were still sold there. They would help with the fever, pain, and swelling if, by grinding and dissolving them in water, my parents were able to persuade Simonopio to swallow them.

"You must prevent any more convulsions, but be aware that the fever is a sign of another ailment that might be killing him."

When he arrived home that night, an urgent message awaited Dr. Cantú. That was when he found Mercedes Garza dead.

The first to learn of her death and arrive to hold a wake were her parents, brothers, and sisters. At two o'clock in the morning, by which time the body had been washed, dressed, and prepared for an open coffin in the parlor, the rest of the family members, friends, and acquaintances began to arrive, all ready to accompany the widower on his night's vigil. At dawn, some left to rest, eat breakfast, and prepare to come back later, while others arrived to continue the wake.

In this coming and going of people sharing the widower's pain, of prayer chains and gossip before the mass and burial, my parents were not present.

They, too, had been awake all night and must have prayed, but I assume it would have been for the boy who had come to them from the sierra. No sooner had his temperature gone down a little and they relaxed their vigil than it suddenly went up again, making him convulse in a way that frightened them all. When they learned of Mercedes's death, with great sorrow they dedicated some prayers to her as well, but they never considered leaving the boy, their godson, the son of nobody and of everybody, who had brought so much joy with him.

They worried about Simonopio but also about Nana Reja, who would not move from his side. They had sent for her rocking chair so she would be more comfortable, but they were concerned that the pain of seeing her beloved little one die would cause her irreparable damage. They tried to explain and prepare her for what was certain to happen, but if anyone remained calm, it was her. Serene but active for the first time in years, she gave herself to the task of keeping Simonopio hydrated. As she had done when the boy was just a bundle in her arms, she squeezed a constant drip of milk into his mouth, with added honey from the bees that accompanied him all his life.

At that time caring for the sick was mostly women's work, but my papa, worried as he was, did not want to go far from Simonopio's room. Running the hacienda took him away some, for work did not stop even when a death was near, but as soon as he had given his instructions, he returned. With the compassion for which she was known, my mama gave him jobs to keep him calm and make him feel he was doing something to help. If more goat milk or cold water was needed, she would ask him, and he would send for it. When it was time for another dose of aspirin, my father would grind the tablets, taking care not to waste a single precious gram.

The day after Mercedes's burial, when they heard that there was a strange, devastating, deadly epidemic in Linares and Monterrey, for a moment they thought Simonopio must have caught it, as many who had attended the wake and funeral had.

"But where?"

"The day he came to wait for me when I had my meeting. Perhaps Mercedes passed it on to him."

"No, remember he already had a fever. And he would've infected us by now."

My papa gave strict instructions that no workers from the hacienda or their families must go to Linares for any reason.

"And if they go, they'd best not return."

He gave instructions to Anselmo Espiricueta to stand guard at the entrance to the hacienda with harsh but necessary orders, under the circumstances: *Anyone who wants to leave can leave, but we won't let them or anybody else back in. Not even Dr. Cantú.*

If needed, Espiricueta had permission to fire his rifle.

Simonopio's fever remained a mystery, but while it was clear it was not the same illness attacking and killing so many in Linares, my papa wanted to prepare for every possibility. He remembered a cure that, according to his maternal grandmother, was infallible against any affliction of the lungs, from a cough to pneumonia. He sent for a piece of canvas, which he smothered on one side with a thick layer of mustard, and he applied it to Simonopio's chest.

"What're you doing, Francisco?"

"A sinapism for Simonopio."

He remembered Grandma's sinapisms. They were very unpleasant, but every time one was administered to him against any congestion, he was cured. Sometimes, just knowing they would put one on him cured him. He hoped that the heat the mustard produced in contact with the skin would draw out any malignancy from Simonopio's chest.

"Leave it on until I return."

My papa had been planning to go fetch my sisters by train from Monterrey when the news reached him that Governor Zambrano and the public health authorities had ordered a quarantine across the northern part of the country and the closure of public places, including the schools. The railway service had also now been suspended.

"I'll go in the car before they close the roads on us. No one must leave the hacienda," he reiterated.

In those days, there was no road like this one—wide, paved, and free of potholes. With the poor state of the rural lanes between the two towns, it would take him many more hours to arrive by car than it took by train. But there was no train, and nothing would deter him: he was intent on bringing Carmen and Consuelo back from Monterrey.

Later, he would tell my mama that, driving through the streets of Linares that morning with the car windows firmly shut, it was as if he were passing through a ghost town, as if life had ended. The streets were devoid of living people, but there were shrouded bodies dumped in front of houses, some of them dear friends. He saw that the stray dogs, normally wary after a long education of kicks and beatings, were now beginning to lose their usual caution: they were sniffing around the bundles, attracted by the smell of death. It would not be long before they made up their minds to dig into the feast that the Spanish flu had left for them.

So he stopped, the only time he would dare do so in the entire journey. Afterward, he would admit that, before plucking up the courage to open the door, he had taken a deep breath and held in the air, for two reasons: fear that the infection was alive in the Linares air in search of new victims, and fear that the streets would smell of dead townspeople. He did not want to live the rest of his life with that memory.

With his lungs full of the clean air from his car, holding his breath, he climbed out with the .22-caliber rifle he always kept under the seat and fired three well-aimed shots. The five surviving dogs fled, frightened by the bangs or because they did not wish to share the fate of their partners in crime. He allowed them to scamper away, struggling because the air stored in his lungs was running out but satisfied he had scared them off for the time being. They would be back, he knew. The sickly sweet smell of decomposing flesh would embolden them.

As he returned to the car, he saw Vicente López—the only living inhabitant of the town he came across—turn the corner and approach with the cart already half-full. They waved at each other. The gravedigger collected the bodies my papa had protected from being devoured and then lifted the dead dogs onto the cart as well. Only then did my papa continue his journey, speeding away and hoping the dogs would not end up in the same grave as the humans.

The road to Monterrey, already long and difficult at the best of times, had never seemed so punishing to him, worried as he was for poor Simonopio and for the well-being of my sisters. He knew they might have already been infected in the communal living space of the boarding school, but he didn't care. If anyone in his family had to die or if they all had to die, they would do so together.

When he arrived at the Sagrado Corazón, only a few pupils remained. He didn't let my sisters pack or say goodbye to anybody. Though they were still dressed in their uniforms, he made them get in the car, and they set off.

It is easy to imagine that Carmen sat calmly in the car, content with the arbitrary decision, while Consuelo made my poor papa's head spin all the way home with her grumbling and fussing. About what? I don't know. About anything. She always found a reason to be unhappy and would make it known to whoever would listen. Imprisoned in the car, my papa would have had no escape. But that wasn't what happened. Well, Consuelo was true to character, but Carmen surprised everyone. From comments made years later—reliable accounts of the event—it is known that Consuelo arrived home in a foul temper, and Carmen, far from exhibiting her usual equanimity, was angry, punishing my papa with her silence. What's more, to my papa's surprise, she had been the one to berate him most for ordering them to come back with him like little girls.

To make matters worse, as they drove into Linares, my father informed them of his latest decision: they would not go near the dying town. Avoiding the most densely populated streets so his young daughters wouldn't have to stare death in the face, he explained to them that, when they arrived home, the whole family would pack what they needed to relocate to Hacienda La Florida for a while, in the hope that the disease would not reach them there.

"For how long, Papa?"

"As long as necessary. Until people stop dying. Or stop falling ill."

My sisters had grown accustomed to living through one catastrophe after another, but not to life stopping altogether. They could barely remember a time without war, and yet they knew that every year they would plant crops, in spite of it, and later they would harvest crops if there was anything to harvest, regardless of the threat of a famished battalion passing through. People also carried on with their plans as much as possible: despite the war—and our parents always told them there was nothing worse than a war—there were weddings, births, baptisms. There were parties and days in the country. If an army was known to be prowling the surrounding area, people would stay close to home, but they would still go out to do their shopping. The milk reached the houses without fail, and friends met in the afternoon for a snack. That was the life they knew: the one that stopped for nothing. Not even for the death of a beloved grandparent.

At their age, they were still strangers to the pain and irreversibility of death, for although they had attended the burial of their grandpa Mariano Cortés, the grown-ups had protected their feelings—the naive sensibilities of young children—from the violence of his death almost four years earlier. In their juvenile minds—for juvenile minds have evolved very little since the first adolescent existed—Grandpa had died because he was a grandpa, and old people die because it's natural for them to die, while young people live forever and are immune to everything.

Now it seemed as if an eternity had passed since Grandpa Mariano's death, just as the days they would spend without seeing their friends in Monterrey or Linares because of their father's whim would seem eternal.

Because it seemed—and they had complained at length about it to each other—that our father announced and feared many calamities that had yet to happen, such as the threat that an army of bandits passing through would steal all the pretty young women, which was why he had sent them to board at the nuns' school in Monterrey. Or the threat that men might come one day to snatch their lands from them by law or force. Time passed, and as yet, none of that had happened. Maybe the Spanish flu was just another of these catastrophizing exaggerations.

Our father was firm: they would not see their friends even to say hello. There would be no trips to the square. There would be no parties. He knew they thought they would die of boredom in their exile on the remote hacienda. But he also knew they would survive the tedium and, with a little more luck, the epidemic as well.

In an attempt to be kind and patient, as they climbed out of the car, my papa told them that they could read as much as they wished at La Florida.

"You can even read that novel you like so much, that one about heights."

His well-meaning comment was not well received by either of them: since he had not given them time to pack, he had forced them to leave behind not only *Wuthering Heights* but also their new favorite novel, *Emma*. And no, they had no desire for him to lend them any of his books—who was interested in reading *A Tale of Two Cities*?

My mama used to say that the moment Simonopio heard my papa coming into the house and irritably informing my sisters that Dickens's novel contained romance, too, and not just killing, he woke up, alert and free of fever or weakness.

And that was that: one minute he was motionless, burning up; the next it was as if the last few days of unconsciousness and convulsions had never happened.

My papa, delighted to see the boy cured thanks to the wisdom of his grandmother, instructed them to continue the treatment for a few more hours to prevent a relapse. Then he left to organize the family's relocation and speak to the workers who lived with their families on the hacienda. He could do nothing for the people who lived in the town, but he could save as many lives as possible. If they had not visited

Linares in the last two days, they were welcome to travel with the family, he told them. They would find a way to house them all on La Florida, where, with luck, all the families would be far enough away from the sickly air of Linares. The men would make the short journey each day between the two haciendas to tend to the sugarcane and other crops on both, but they would not visit the town or have contact with anybody from Linares.

When he finished his speech, Lupita was waiting for him.

"Doña Reja says Simonopio can't stand his little chest wrap any longer."

"Well, he'd better stand it."

The family moved to La Florida the next day. All the workers decided to go with them.

We now know that the epidemic lasted three months, but on the day they covered all the furniture in sheets, when they locked the windows and doors, my family did not know when they would return or if they ever would. The house had never been left unoccupied, even when the family spent a few days on another hacienda.

This would be the first time they left it abandoned.

I managed to grasp what my mama was saying when she admitted, years later, that when the last door was bolted, her heart had tightened in her chest until it squeezed tears from her eyes, hidden but painful tears.

They were leaving behind the house, and they were also leaving behind mementos such as photographs, my sisters' childhood clothes, the tea set my mama had inherited from her grandmother, the English dinner service she had bought on her only trip to Europe with her father, and her Singer sewing machine.

But her tears were not for the house or for the things. That abandonment hurt, though she knew that the house, with everything that filled it, would be there waiting for them when they decided to return. But that final bolt marked something worse: their abandonment of the town's people, of her two brothers, of all their cousins and aunts and uncles, of her fellow club members, of the family's friends. Their abandonment of all the people who gave Linares life. Who would still be there when they were finally able to return?

My mama's tears, which she quickly got under control, came to her eyes because, that day, it was as if the world were ending.

After locking up, they turned away from the house and did not turn back. My sisters were already waiting for them in the car. They had my grandmother with them, of course, and all the domestic staff and almost all the hacienda workers traveled in other vehicles with their families.

Only Anselmo Espiricueta and his family were missing from that caravan of one car, four carts, and a pickup truck.

To my papa's great displeasure, he learned from another campesino that Espiricueta had obeyed the order to stay on the hacienda to guard the entrance, but keen smoker that he was, he had sent his wife to the grocery store in the center of Linares the day before to buy tobacco and rolling papers. Knowing that Espiricueta's family, as unsociable and unfriendly as they were, always kept its distance from the rest of his workers' families, my papa felt there was little danger that any infection had spread to the rest of them. But he did not think it prudent to take the Espiricuetas to live in the close proximity that awaited at La Florida. They would stay on La Amistad. My papa wished them luck and good health, but Espiricueta did not accept his good wishes.

"You won't take us, but you take Simonopio. He's the sick one. He's the one who brought the disease."

"Still on about that? Simonopio had something different, and he's better now. You knew the danger and knew my orders: you should not have allowed your wife to leave, let alone ask her to go to town and run an errand for you. Had you followed my instructions, you would have had to shoot her rather than let her return."

"Then maybe I shoulda shot you, Señor, when you came with your daughters."

For the rest of her life, my mama rued my papa's overly patient decision not to respond to that seditious comment, taking it as nothing more than a rash outburst.

"This is only going to get worse, Anselmo. Here on the hacienda you have provisions. For you and your family's own good, forget about your tobacco, because as things are, that vice of yours is going to kill everyone."

And after this declaration, he turned around and climbed into the car that would lead the caravan of people and supplies.

Out in the open for the first time in days, Simonopio traveled in the first cart behind my family's automobile. My papa had finally given in and allowed him to take off the mustard sinapism but told him that he had to remain lying down for the whole journey. Martín drove the cart with Trinidad, one of the campesinos, accompanying him. Nana Reja sat beside Simonopio, silent and with her eyes closed as always. Pola, Lupita, and the rocking chair were also with them, of course.

My parents spent the whole journey between the adjoining haciendas discussing Simonopio's illness and sudden recovery. The discussion would continue for years, but they would never settle their doubts or get to the bottom of the mystery. My mama always took the view that it was no coincidence that the unexplained fever had struck Simonopio just as the Spanish flu gripped Linares, keeping her away from the town and preventing them from attending her friend Mercedes's deadly wake or returning to town in the early days of the epidemic. The boy's recovery also seemed suspect to her: *What a coincidence that, as soon as you returned saying we were leaving Linares, he woke without a temperature. No aftereffects, no discomfort,* she argued.

"It was a miracle," she insisted.

My grandma Sinforosa, certain that such a declaration could come only from Rome, would always say, *Ay, my girl! How? How could it be?* And my sister Consuelo would say, *Enough arguing! What does it matter?*

My papa could not think of any arguments to refute what my mama said, but he did not want to agree with her either. I suppose it would have meant getting into more discussions and questions that were hard to explain or grasp. It would have meant openly accepting that, aside from the strange circumstances of his birth and his arrival in the family and even aside from the inexplicable way that more and more bees followed him, Simonopio was not a normal boy. And so, all the way to the hacienda, my papa insisted, as he would insist for the rest of his life, that he had saved Simonopio's life with a sinapism.

# 15

## *The Abandoned Body*

The day when the plague and death arrived in Linares, Simonopio woke very early feeling perfectly calm. Nothing had alerted him to what was coming: neither his bees nor the bright sun nor the cloudless skies. It was a beautiful fall day. An ordinary October day.

Simonopio woke only with the certainty that the Morales girls would soon arrive for a long visit, and that was good.

Later, worried that the red horse could twist its leg in a pothole, he ran to fill it with earth. He was pleased when he was able to get there in time; had it injured itself, the horse would never have recovered.

Satisfied with his day's good deed, he would have liked to have gone running up into the sierra, following his bees as far as he dared go, but his affection for Lupita kept him close. He did not want her day to be ruined because she had to wash the clothes twice, so he kept watch while Lupita sang and washed, for when she finished, the basket of clothes was going to fall onto the muddy ground while she was distracted, looking at Martín.

What's more, Simonopio knew that Martín was not right for Lupita. Not because he was a bad man; it was just that, as much as she wanted it, Lupita would get nowhere with him.

To save her happiness that day, Simonopio would offer to carry the basket, knowing that she would not allow it, believing it too heavy a load for him. But Simonopio would insist in order to keep her attention, so she would not notice the presence of the man who made her mind wander. And without the distraction, there would be no stumble, and she would not have to wash all the clothes a second time as a result.

But then, with no warning, between a clean shirt and a dirty under-skirt, he saw the new thing, the bad thing that was coming, so he forgot Lupita and abandoned her to her fate as she yelled, "Where're you going, Simonopio?" from behind him, surprised by the suddenness of his departure.

He ran without stopping down a path he rarely traveled toward the town square. That was where his godmother was, in the big house where people like her gathered.

He knew that folks were looking at him as he passed, but he did not care: he had to get her out of there, he had to take her far away. So that she would live, he needed to get his godmother out of the town. The urgency he felt was great. Sometimes things were hazy at first, but with patience and time, everything would become clear. While he waited outside, he did not know whether there would be a fire, whether some army would pass through firing indiscriminately, or what. But looking around the square filled with people doing what they did every day, strolling in a leisurely, carefree way, he could not shake off the certainty that something terrible was about to happen.

When he saw the ladies come out of the building, he knew: the pretty pregnant lady carried death inside her. She was poison that would kill whatever it touched. Poison that would kill even after she was dead. That very same day.

He saw it. He saw death spread across the square, through the streets. He saw the bodies piled on top of one another on the full cart. He saw them cast outside the houses. He saw the street dogs feasting.

He saw the deaths of the Morales family, one after the other. With them, he saw the end of the potential of the child that did not yet live.

And he did not know what to do to stop it.

When Simonopio approached his godmother, he was already hot and sweaty from running all the way there, from the anxiety. Beatriz interpreted his body heat as fever and was alarmed. Then he knew that his temperature would save many lives.

That is what he did: he let himself fall ill. And now all the passengers on the caravan heading to La Florida would live. He could do nothing for the people they were leaving behind, but his godparents and the girls, Grandma, Nana Reja and Nana Pola, Mati and Martín, and all the other workers and their families were safe.

If they had allowed it, he would already have been waiting for the family at La Florida. He knew all the shortcuts through the hills. The bees had shown them to him. He knew it was important, which was why he'd paid close attention when he followed the swarm, but he did not yet know why. What he did know at that moment was that the family was traveling away from death and heading toward life.

He felt happy. Relieved. Even with his silence, he had found a way to make himself understood—on this occasion, at least. It had not been easy, and perhaps, if he had had more time, he would have thought of some other way.

For now, Simonopio just lay on the cart obediently. He enjoyed the cool morning air and the warmth of the sun on his face. He had never spent so long between four walls as he had in recent days, and when he returned to his body, his first instinct had been to run to the hills, to leap into the river, to listen to his bees.

Bodies that fell sick, like his, were not allowed such freedom. He knew that four days had passed since he had made himself fall ill and that he had caused the family anguish; now he must pay. And this was his punishment: to keep his body in an unnecessary and annoying state of rest despite how he longed to run, to see his bees swirling above him, even if he was unable to follow them into the air no matter how they insisted, and then watch them give up and fly away. On top of this, he had to suffer the searing heat on his chest where the mustard from the sinapism had burned him. Though that pain was the least of his worries.

He had seen the look of relief and satisfaction on his godfather Francisco's face when he had woken. His godfather proudly told him that he had cured him with his sinapism, and Simonopio would never refute it: one should never contradict an act of love. After hours of the treatment, Simonopio had gestured at them imploringly to take it off, because it burned. But he knew that his godfather's peace of mind depended on a few more hours of a sinapism for his godson, so he had put up with it.

The sinapism had been administered to Simonopio, yes, but he knew that it had served to cure something in his godfather. Perhaps it alleviated the anguish or pain in his heart. Yes, the mustard burned, but Simonopio understood how hard his days of sickness had been for Francisco Morales and knew how hard the coming times would be. While he was able, Simonopio would gladly do what he could for him. He hoped that the curative effect of the sinapism, which he had tolerated with so much patience and stoicism, would also heal all the wounds his beloved godfather's heart would soon, inevitably, suffer.

Because they were heading toward life, yes, but that did not mean that life would be easier.

# 16

*Dust Thou Art . . .*

If he was not supervising his cattle ranches in Tamaulipas, Francisco Morales made a daily trip to inspect the work on his various haciendas. Weeks had gone by and there was still no infection on La Florida, which gave him the satisfaction of knowing he had made the right decision.

Even so, he knew being far from home was not easy for anyone.

To avoid thinking about her two adult sons left in Linares, his mother-in-law did not leave the kitchen. She spent the time perfecting her cajeta, which she stirred and stirred, relentlessly. She switched the wooden spoon between hands, but she never allowed anyone to relieve her of her work, even though the constant circular movement wore her out to the point that, at night, the spasming muscles in her arms, shoulders, and neck needed rubbing.

Still, she stirred endlessly and would not accept help. She did it by herself, she said, because the work was hypnotic, and while her mind was under the almost narcotic influence of her labor, she forgot everything. She forgot her sons, the husband she had lost. She forgot what might have been and what might be. The work was tiring for her arms but restful for her soul.

Understanding this, Francisco made sure they were never short of goat milk or brown sugar. Which was why liters of cajeta were produced each day, shared out by Sinforosa at snack time between the workers' children, who, thanks to this generosity, gradually grew plump.

Meanwhile, Carmen and Consuelo went through various states of mind. Sometimes they were happy, sometimes sad. Sometimes they cried without any provocation whatsoever. At other times they screamed with fury at some offense, real or imagined, but then returned to being complicit in a secret that made them double up with laughter. Worst of all was when they went through all these states in a single day; Francisco would rather smell the charred hair and flesh of the cows he branded than try to decipher each change of tone or look in the eyes of his daughters.

During that time, he moved cautiously through the house, trying not to be caught and become embroiled. His admiration grew for Beatriz, who seemed both unsurprised and unfazed by the adolescents' outbursts. To keep them busy, she would give them tasks: to teach the youngest children to read, and to educate the older ones in arithmetic. When they had done that, she asked them to give everybody music lessons. As expected, Carmen was the more patient and persevering in her lessons. Consuelo would disappear when Carmen was distracted; she did not have, nor would she ever have, any patience for other people's children.

Francisco tried to understand them. It was not just boredom that was making them this way: they were not used to such basic living conditions. With no electricity, they had to give up their activities at an early hour. They were in the habit of ending the day reading under an electric light, not an oil lamp. And, accustomed to having an icebox at home, they would normally have their drinks with ice, even in winter. But here there was no cooler and no electricity, for they were costly luxuries the family had installed at their house on La Amistad over time, electrifying the social rooms and then moving on to the private areas. The kitchen had been the most recent project, though Francisco hoped to continue very soon with the servants' quarters and the campesinos' houses. But that was an expensive project. For the time being, he had no plans to invest in electrifying the hacienda on La Florida, as his daughters were now requesting each time he refused their requests to return to the modern luxury of Linares.

Beatriz remained impassive at all times, but Francisco knew it was a mask she put on each morning when the sun came up. Every night he heard her tossing and turning in bed. He was aware of her getting up to go check on the girls in their bedrooms. She also checked the locks on the doors, made sure no candles or oil lamps were lit, and confirmed that the woodstove had gone out completely.

In the mornings, Beatriz pretended she was perfectly rested. She joined Francisco for breakfast. She woke Carmen and Consuelo so that they would perform their duties. She organized the day in the house, the routine cleaning and the deep cleaning. In the kitchen she made sure that nothing was wasted, that not a crumb went astray. From time to time she would go out to see Nana Reja. While they did not complain, neither the nana nor her rocking chair could get used to their new location or their new view: the former barely ate, and the latter hardly rocked. Beatriz did not know who was suffering most, and she worried.

But she kept going. She kept going because she had to. She would finish one thing and move on to the next, until everything was done, until she had no option but to continue her embroidery by the light of an oil lamp. She kept her body busy so that her mind did not have the energy to wander, to think about anything else, to explode.

Francisco was grateful for the brave front she put up, because it gave him the strength to also put on a mask each morning, to say goodbye with a smile, and to leave her in charge of whatever happened on La Florida while he went about his various tasks in the surrounding area and farther afield in Tamaulipas. Much like his mother-in-law stirring her cajeta, he had his ranches and plantations to exhaust his body but give respite to his mind.

Beatriz had nothing to bring her comfort. She kept busy all day but without anything really bringing her peace. She knew that her workers also missed their homes, which were simple but their own. They all had a roof over their heads at La Florida, but little privacy. Just one family of servants normally lived on the hacienda there, in an old building of twelve large, independent rooms—originally built to house more campesinos than had inhabited it in recent years. With the sudden invasion, it had been filled, a family in each room.

While they slogged away or followed a yoke of oxen during the day, on La Florida or on La Amistad, the men told themselves everything was back to normal. Lost in hard work, they forgot that their families were living in exile as far away as possible from the town. Then, when they returned before nightfall, they were surprised by their wives' ill humor and did not understand it.

It was the wives that felt the real pressure, for they had no privacy or time away from one another through the day. They had to share a kitchen and washhouse. They had to live with the mayhem of so many children together in one place with nothing to do. They had to take turns cooking for everyone, cutting back on the provisions not grown on their land and, thus, hard to replenish, such as salt, pepper, white flour, rice, beans, and potatoes, all things they had bought from the Chang brothers before the ban.

Francisco had seen to it that they procured everything in large quantities, but since nobody knew how long their exile would last, they had to be sparing. He was not worried they would go hungry. On his ranches they had plenty of meat and milk from the cattle and goats. All trade had ceased since the onset of the epidemic, so the idea of slaughtering however many animals were needed to feed his people did not trouble him. The plantations meant they had homemade brown sugar, and there would be no shortage of onions, squash, and carrots grown on their vegetable plots. If needed, he would also buy food from his campesinos. They had plenty of their own maize and lime to make cornmeal in the mill, where they also ground the sugarcane.

Beatriz had recently brought it to his attention that the workers were holding back some of the sugarcane extract in order to ferment it and make aguardiente in a still they'd rigged up from some old copper pans.

"The women are complaining, Francisco. Especially about the unmarried men who have no family responsibilities. They keep everybody awake, they say, particularly Trinidad, who's a heavy drinker, but not a good one."

Worse, they could not go to the bathroom in the middle of the night for fear of unwanted advances from some drunken seducer, single or married.

Francisco was not a teetotaler: he enjoyed a beer once in a while. Carta Blanca from the Monterrey Brewery was his favorite, and ever since the ice factory had been set up in Linares, he had liked it ice cold. He also enjoyed his daily glass of the whiskey that he brought back from his trips to Texas. But the alcohol content in the aguardiente that his workers distilled scorched the throat and made the stomach burn. With a few swigs of this liquid, any man would lose his good sense, so combining the potent liquor with the close quarters in which they lived was an invitation to disaster.

Therefore, he confiscated the ingenious distilling contraption, though he knew it would affect his men's morale. Believing that the remedy for any demoralization was work, he kept them busy with tasks on the haciendas. It was what they were accustomed to, part of their daily life. The hours they spent tending to the plantations, with no help from their wives, wore them out. They would return to La Florida with no desire to do anything except eat and go to bed early, without making trouble, aware that more work awaited them the next day.

The only one that dispensed with his routine duties was Anselmo Espiricueta. Francisco allowed him to stay at home because, a week after the caravan's departure, his wife had fallen ill and died the same day, and it had not stopped there: four of his children were now dead or dying. Only the father, the eldest son, and the youngest daughter remained in good health.

Francisco did not know how one disease could attack some and have mercy on others, but he did know that this particular tragedy could have been avoided.

The fact that the woman fell sick a week after the warning he had given his worker told him that Espiricueta had ignored him and sent his pregnant wife into town again—for more tobacco, no doubt.

Francisco Morales had never been one of those people who go through life saying, *See, I told you so.* In fact, he hated comments like that—what did they achieve? They were just wasted words, when there was no longer any way to repair the damage. However, he had never been so tempted to grab somebody by the shoulders and yell, *I told you not to go to town, I told you your smoking would kill them!* Somehow, he found the strength to keep his mouth shut, for Francisco could not imagine the anguish and the magnitude of the grief that such a loss could cause in any man, not least one whose responsibility for his family's infection must be weighing heavily on his conscience.

All Francisco could do for them in the circumstances was to leave packages of ready-made food near their house. The first time, he also left Bayer aspirins, but the next day he found them moist on the ground, wasted. He was sad to see something so precious and so expensive squandered. He did not offer them again: he could not afford to leave his own family without medicine, in case they needed it.

Beatriz was the one who had the idea to send the family food when they heard of the woman's illness. She also suggested they summon the doctor, but Espiricueta categorically refused to receive him. And now he was paying the price for his decisions.

What began as an act of kindness on Francisco's part to help a man, to help a desperate family, eventually became a nuisance. Perhaps it was

Espiricueta's lack of commitment to his work, his lack of effort, or simply the weight of his expression, which held something his employer could not decipher. That look in his eyes, a look that all the good treatment— a home, food, schooling, good company—had not lightened. It might have been that Francisco suspected Espiricueta beat his wife, that he had noticed the usually friendly Simonopio avoided him, or that Beatriz found the man repulsive.

Now, with the family decimated, Francisco struggled to admit even to himself that he had been mulling the idea of getting rid of Anselmo Espiricueta for some time. Each time he had considered it, sympathy had gotten the better of his determination. If he had dismissed the father, the wife and children would have been left homeless, without work or earnings. Hopeless, again. He also knew that, if he fired Espiricueta, nobody else in the region would give him work.

And with good reason.

He could not let him go. Much less now. He did not believe in kicking people when they were down, and it was not possible to fall lower than Espiricueta. Francisco could not turn back the clock or return his wife or children to him. All he could give him was continued employment and, with it, some peace.

He felt a presence beside him.

"Simonopio, what're you doing here?"

That day, Francisco had left La Florida with no company other than his campesinos, whom he transported in the pickup truck. There was much to do every day. The social life of Linares might have halted, but the land stopped for neither death nor mourning. Each day the cows and goats waited for someone to milk them and the plantations had to be irrigated or harvested.

He could have sent the campesinos on foot; the distance between La Florida and La Amistad was short. But Francisco believed in investing the body's energy in the day's tasks and not the journey, and while the route was not steep, it lacked shade and was very hot, even in fall. If the debilitating hours of sun were impossible to avoid, then they might as well be spent working. He took care of the transportation. Obtaining gasoline was neither easy nor cheap, but he preferred to spend money on fuel than to waste man power.

Now, suddenly, right beside him, the newly recovered boy had appeared, having found his own way there. He was not out of breath, nor did he seem hot from the effort. Francisco knew Simonopio liked to stray from the house, but he'd had no idea the boy was brave enough to venture such a distance. He felt the urge to tell him, *Don't stray so far, you'll get lost in the mountains, Simonopio; the bears might eat you, boy,* but he contained himself. Francisco did not like wasting energy or words, and at that moment he was certain Simonopio had no need for his. Clearly, he had arrived where he had wanted to arrive, without anybody's help. In this moment of insight, Francisco understood that the danger of being eaten alive had ceased to exist for Simonopio in the first few hours of his life, and that, should he decide to walk to the Antipodes, the boy would never lose his way.

And not only that: in that moment, Francisco accepted that, with Simonopio, there were no coincidences. If he was there, it was for some compelling reason.

"Were you looking for me?"

Simonopio gestured for Francisco to follow him to the abandoned family house. Francisco had not been back in the house since he and his family had locked the door. And he had not felt the faintest urge to return by himself. Reluctant but curious and certain that Simonopio must have a good reason to lead him there, he entered.

Francisco had expected that the oppressive emptiness and silence of the house would be heartbreaking, so he had decided not to set foot in it until he returned with Beatriz and his daughters by his side. He was surprised to find, as he walked in, that his heart neither tightened nor stopped beating. Not even the oppressiveness he had so feared materialized. The awareness that he was back did not make him shudder.

He looked around. Four weeks of neglect, and everything was already covered in a thick layer of dust.

It occurred to him that houses die when they are no longer fed with the energy of their owners. He wondered whether the ancients had experienced the same thing: the Mayans, the Romans, the Egyptians. He wondered whether, when they abandoned their homes, when they left their villages after some catastrophe, never to return, they had caused the death, deterioration, and then ruin of houses, villages, and temples.

Much like what was happening now in Linares: *The plague's here, let's go.* Then, a few years or a generation later, nobody would remember the original settlement, which, under sustained neglect, bit by bit, dust mote by dust mote, would return to its mistress, the earth. For dust thou art, and unto dust shalt thou return: as certain for living cells as it was for any heap of bricks, whether Roman, Mayan, or Linarense.

In this particular case, the heap of bricks being suffocated by dust was the one that formed the protective shell around the hopes and dreams of generations of the Morales family.

And he would not let it die.

"Give me a hand, Simonopio."

Not even as a boy had Francisco's responsibilities included cleaning, washing, or dusting. But at that moment, he felt compelled to do it, even if he had no idea where to begin or where the women of the house kept the cleaning equipment.

The house reeked of neglect, a smell his nose recognized despite never scenting it before. Maybe this was the smell given off by dying bricks, like the sickly sweet aroma that emanated from dead flesh during decomposition, he thought. He looked around the whole house, confirming that the dust indeed covered everything: floors, banisters, curtains, valances, doors, windows. Sheets protected the furniture, but they were also covered in an extremely fine powder that managed to find its way through cracks imperceptible to the human eye, covering memories and remnants of entire civilizations.

Simonopio knew where the soaps, oils, cloths, and feather dusters were, as well as how each thing was used. He handed Francisco a duster.

Francisco would be the first man in the Morales family to devote his time to these tasks that, until now, had belonged solely to the women. And these tasks, to his surprise, would bring him peace, comfort, and a challenge once a week when, in the company of Simonopio—always present on the day set aside for this almost military campaign—Francisco fought against a bitter, invincible, indefatigable enemy. It did not matter how much care and effort he and his army of one soldier devoted to the task of banishing their adversary from their kingdom: it immediately began its slow, silent return, intent on smothering Francisco Morales's hopes for the future.

# 17

## *The Singer and Its Rat-A-Tat, Rat-A-Tat*

The truth is that Simonopio did not take my papa to the house to see the dreadful state it was in. He had nothing against doing the cleaning, I suppose, and much less against helping his godfather in that or any other task. What he wanted was to drop a heavy hint that my papa should take my mama's beloved—but burdensome—Singer sewing machine.

Later, my papa would admit the grand gesture he made to keep my mama sane during that forced exile had been Simonopio's idea, though it had taken him a while to understand what the boy was trying to tell him. On the first visit to the house, he attacked the enormous machine with the feather duster after Simonopio pointed at it emphatically. On the second visit, Simonopio had to take out trimmings, thread, and buttons, and then carry everything in boxes to the pickup truck to make himself understood: they had to load up the heavy machine and transport it to La Florida.

It was one of the first sewing machines for domestic use, but it was not like the light, practical ones we have now—though I admit I have not seen one for many years. At that time, the mechanical machines of heavy iron were mounted on a piece of solid wood furniture. Once its place in the home was chosen, the great hulking thing would never be moved again. To say it weighed a ton would be an exaggeration. I've never established its precise weight, but it was more than any normal person—or four—would want to lift, I can assure you.

I suppose my papa had learned to trust in his godson's instincts, and worried as he was about my mama's state of mind, he decided to make the effort to take it to her. He thought perhaps she would use the time to teach Carmen and Consuelo to sew, as she had always wanted to do, or spend it sewing the season's garments. Not everyone had such a machine, and my mama treasured hers. My papa thought the surprise would make her happy.

I don't know whether you have to be as old as me to have learned that women can never be fully understood. Their minds are a labyrinth that men are only permitted to glimpse from the outside when they want us to, when they invite us.

Until then, the labyrinth remains a mystery.

My papa found his wife making candles with the beeswax Simonopio gave her from time to time. He led her to the truck, where Simonopio and the rest of the workers who'd helped lift the contraption onto the vehicle had gathered, all waiting to see her face beam with surprise, excitement, and gratitude.

Contrary to their hopes, when she saw the cargo, my mama turned around without saying a word and strode off. Crying.

Years later, she told me that she never knew where all the tears that sprung forth that day had come from. She would always refer to it as "the day I cried for no reason."

She had cried over her father's death, of course, but that was a discreet, dignified crying filled with pride, with no outbursts or drama, though not without bitterness. Knowing my mama, she would have made use of her embroidered handkerchief, careful as she always was not to show her natural—but uncomfortable and shameful—secretions. It had been elegant and justified crying.

But there's crying and there's *crying*.

The person who burst into tears when she saw the mass of wood and metal that was her sewing machine could not have been her. From the instant she laid eyes on it, she did not recognize herself. At that moment—she would say—she was thrown into a trance, and only a tiny part of her brain remained intact, asking her, *Who are you? Do you not care about the spectacle you're making of yourself?*

My mama left the group of several men and one boy speechless, stunned, not knowing what to do or say. Together they had made an enormous effort to transport the machine from its usual place to the truck without its parts falling off or the pedal tipping. Then some of them walked back while others steadied the machine on the bumpy ride in the cattle track. They knew, of course, that they still had to haul it down and position it in its new place, but they were willing. What none of them wanted was to return it to its original location.

"What shall we do, Boss?"

"Go rest. We'll see about it tomorrow. You, too, Simonopio. Don't worry, go have a bite to eat."

My papa didn't go to find my mama straightaway. He listened to some survival instinct and waited to be called for dinner before he went to see if his wife was calmer. He found her in the bedroom, sitting on the armchair that she mostly used for sewing by hand or for her embroidery. It was dark, but she had done nothing to light the room. My papa lit the nearest oil lamp.

There they remained, not caring that dinner was going cold.

Dr. Cantú wrote them a brief note once in a while and left it at the entrance to La Amistad for my papa to find on his visits. So far, my papa had received three: the first two very short and far from encouraging, and the third one a little longer but very odd. In his hurry, the doctor had not explained himself very well when he wrote about the over-crowding at the cemetery, a failed rising from the dead, and a survivor.

Since the communication was one-way, he had no means to request more information from the doctor, to ask questions, or to receive spe-cific answers. Cantú was already doing enough by sending his notes. My papa must have resigned himself to it, guessing the doctor would not have the time, between patients and deaths, to write long accounts, to make full lists of those who had perished, or to remember whether he had already mentioned the death of such and such. Indeed, in each letter he repeated the names of some of those who'd succumbed. The information therefore served to tell them only whether civilization still existed, and not the details and fate of all their friends and relatives.

Despite his frustration with the patchy information, riddled with gaps and ambiguities, my papa was grateful for Mario Cantú's distraction. He was grateful for not knowing. He felt some relief concluding, for want of information confirming otherwise, that his brothers-in-law still lived, because it was clear that the circumstances could change a great deal from letter to letter.

My mama did not know, either, whether it was better to receive this news that only tormented her or to remain oblivious to everything.

However, when my mama saw the sewing machine on the truck—the one that had given her hour upon hour of peace, the one she'd positioned in the brightest part of her sewing room, counting on the fact that it would not be moved even after her death—she let out all her well-hidden, pent-up anguish, for she believed that the end of the world had arrived. That it was real: they were the last survivors. That they would never return to the life they had known. That they were isolated forever. That they would never order flowers for the spring dance. That the fabric she had ordered for the girls' ball gowns would never arrive. That her daughters would never find husbands if there were no flowers, gowns, or boys. That if there were no fabric, there would be no use for the machine, because she had no loom and, at any rate, did not know how to use one. Then she pictured herself unpicking their old clothes in order to remake them, again and again, until the wool was threadbare from use. She saw herself with no flowers to take to the cemetery. But if the cemetery was full and everyone was dead, who would've laid her brothers to rest? Who would bury the last person standing? The risen one that Dr. Cantú had written to them about?

All these thoughts came to her at the same time, in that tiny instant of afternoon when she stood in the shadow of the pickup truck. And that was the little glimpse my mother gave my father into the labyrinth of her thoughts.

My mama believed him when he promised her the world hadn't ended, and she felt reassured. My papa then left her there, still in the darkness of her bedroom with the one oil lamp he'd lit, to tend to some extremely urgent task. A task he made up, according to my mother, so he did not have to see her like that anymore. My father might never have understood that episode, his wife's "breakdown," but his wife certainly understood him.

Calm now—comforted by her armchair and in particular by her reunion with the hope of life, new clothes, future sons-in-law, and grandchildren—the small amount of good sense that had persisted during the outburst witnessed by her husband, workers, and godson returned to occupy its rightful position in my mother's ordinarily even-tempered mind. It returned strong. It returned offended and complaining to her that it had been *some tantrum you threw. And in front of everyone. Aren't you ashamed?*

But my mama, who at her age had learned there was no pain—and now shame—that would stop her, got up from the chair, took off her apron, splashed cold water on her face, and seeing herself in the mirror, ignored the question. And then she went to find my papa.

"Come on. Let's get them to serve dinner again."

The next day, the Singer was in its new, albeit—to my mama's relief—temporary, place in the room my sisters had taken over for their romantic reading.

But there was no fabric suitable for sewing. My poor papa was a country man, and as such, he knew nothing of sewing or fabric. And he had not brought any. At the end of the next day, my papa arrived with another offering for my mama.

*He brought me everything they could find in my sewing room,* my mama would say. *The trunks full of calico, the summer and winter fabrics. He brought all the thread. And also feathers, beads, sequins. He even brought the trunks of yellowing old curtains that I was going to send to the convent! We had to store everything in one of the bedrooms because it didn't all fit in the sewing room.*

Nonetheless, not with all the materials in the world could my mama have made hardworking seamstresses out of my sisters. Before their exile, sewing had never held their attention. My mama had thought that when the modern machine arrived, it would arouse their interest, but she soon concluded her daughters would stretch only to darning socks and sewing on buttons, nothing else. Now that she had them captive, as my papa would say, she made another attempt, albeit a failed one. This time, the problem did not stem from my sisters. My mama realized that, while she was an excellent seamstress, she was a dreadful teacher. She lacked the necessary patience. Seeing another person sitting in front of her Singer sewing machine—whether it was one of her daughters or another student my papa found for her—would put her in a very bad mood. She would start by telling them that the pace of their pedaling was wrong. Then she would try to show them how to baste or change the needle, but seeing the novice's clumsiness, she would say, *Move over, let me do it.* That's how she would end up doing the whole thing, telling them, *Oh, what lovely work you've done!*

My mama always admitted that the sewing machine saved, if not her life, her sanity. And she was grateful more to Simonopio than to my father for it. Though they never discussed it openly, both of them understood that their godson had suggested the sewing because he knew it brought her peace.

How right he was: while my grandma found peace with her constant stirring of heated milk in the kitchen, switching hands each time she finished a Mystery of the Rosary, my mama needed the soothing rat-a-tat, rat-a-tat, rat-a-tat of her machine. Rat-a-tat, rat-a-tat, rat-a-tat, for hours. When she sat a student down to sew, the change of rhythm drove her crazy. It was her machine, and it had to go rat-a-tat, rat-a-tat, rat-a-tat. Not rat-a . . . tat, rat-a . . . tat.

I never saw the machine in its temporary home at La Florida, but sometimes I imagine that the rhythm of my life is based on the rat-a-tat, rat-a-tat, rat-a-tat that would always accompany me years later, from my first days in the womb and until adulthood, ensuring my mama's clearheadedness.

My heart, your automobile, time—it all moves forward and ages at that rhythm. Rat-a-tat, rat-a-tat, rat-a-tat.

With the rat-a-tat, rat-a-tat, rat-a-tat of her machine in those days of exile, my mama made ball gowns for my sisters and practical clothing for her fellow refugees. In addition to two skirts with matching blouses, she sewed a Sunday dress for Margarita Espiricueta, the only surviving girl in that unfortunate family. With the remnants, she decided to also make her a ragdoll, which was so beautiful and so coveted that soon she had to make a dozen more for all the workers' young daughters.

And since she had plenty of time and anguish to spare, she kept sewing, guessing her friends' daughters' sizes, hoping that the Spanish organdy blouses she accumulated would fit. That they wouldn't seem out of fashion or too childish. She made skirts and blouses of all sizes in more practical fabrics for the girls of the charity school, for when they went back to class.

Later she would admit that, had their exile continued, she would have carried on making clothes until the fabric ran out. That she would have sewed even if the combination of materials and thread was not right or in good taste. If absolutely necessary, she would have unpicked old clothes and even new ones in order to reinvent each garment, so that she didn't have time to think or give in to sorrow.

Immersed in this creative endeavor, my mama did not contemplate—she refused to contemplate—that some of the people she'd worked so hard sewing for would never need new clothes again.

# 18

## *Land Will Always Be Somebody Else's*

From the position he had chosen at the top of a hill, Anselmo Espiricueta observed the caravan of cars and carts in the distance. They had warned him in advance that the boss and his family would arrive home that day, but since they had not specified a time, he made a special effort not to be there to welcome them.

He spied on them while sitting against a tree, for his clothes were insufficient to protect him from the icy morning wind. But there he stayed, bearing it, waiting, bitter, wishing he could be at home covered in blankets. Where he came from, people wrapped up a little more in the rainy season, but other than the arrival of a hurricane or two, there were no climactic surprises, and so he did not need much clothing in order to cope with life. In the North, one had to wear thin clothes, short sleeves, long sleeves, garments of cotton and of wool, thicker clothes, and clothes that were thicker still, and then one had to know which ones to wear depending on the day, which could start warm and turn ice cold by lunchtime.

It was not his first winter there—he had arrived in the North eight years ago. But he still did not understand the cold. Where did it come from? Who sent it and why? And when it went away, where did it go? Where was it kept? And also, how did the cold manage to get inside him, into his flesh and bones? However much he wrapped up, the cold always found a way to seep in, and sometimes it seemed that, while it began outside—near the trees on the hills, perhaps—it ended up occupying his entire body until it made him tremble. As if it were trying to shake apart his skeleton, to dismember him, to scatter his parts around that land that held him prisoner.

He had arrived there without knowing it even existed, in search of an elusive North. Of course, here they called the region "the North," but now he was certain there would always be a more northern North. This was not the North he longed for. It was not the one he had left his old life behind for. It was not one that was any good to him, when it offered nothing but a life full of work, scorching heat, dry air, rare clouds, ice, and now also disease and death.

They had been passing through, intending to move on, when something squeezed his wife's belly hard and made her expel the daughter she had inside prematurely. They had seen some disused land and settled on a little piece of it that Anselmo claimed as his own, with his family as witnesses. With sticks and branches, he and his eldest children had built the Espiricuetas' first dwelling. They had had nothing more than they were searching for: land and freedom.

"We're gonna build a brick house soon, you'll see."

And they would have their own tobacco field and their own animals, he promised himself. For the first time, on that little piece of land, Anselmo Espiricueta felt he was the master of his own time, of his free will, and of his destiny. Until then, he had lived a life of brutal punishment and poorly paid and thankless work. The revolutionary air he had breathed in the South had seduced him, and he had understood he would have to go in search of land and freedom himself to have any hope of finding it. He had heard that anyone could get rich in the North and that there was still much unclaimed land. And he wanted it.

He would no longer live at the mercy of others. After making this wish, Espiricueta did not have the patience to wait.

The risk that his employer would snare them on their escape from the South was great. The chances of climbing onto the train and going unnoticed were slim. But he preferred to take the risk, to die and see his wife and children die, rather than spend another day as a serf, waiting meekly for the beating that would finally kill him.

There, in the distant North, which at first—for a few weeks—he had believed was the North for which he had yearned, he had felt like lord, owner, and master. His children would never see him humiliated or knocked down by a foreman again. They would not have to stand aside for anyone, to let anybody through, to try to go unnoticed. They would not have to be less, to have less, or to count their beans every day.

In that North, there would be no more hunger, no more poverty.

However, it was one thing to want it, to think it, to consider it; seeing it through was quite another. A few days after settling there, they had no beans left to count or share out: they were all hungrier than ever, and crueler still, their thirst was no less acute, perhaps worse. Their bodies had never felt such heat, and however much they searched, neither Anselmo nor his sons could find water.

People who take for granted that water always falls from the generous sky to wet the earth do not develop the skills needed to find it deep underground. If it does not rain today, then it will tomorrow, they thought; but the days passed, and the rain they longed for never arrived. The vegetation around them was foreign, strange, and they soon realized they would obtain no food or even a single drop of moisture from it.

With traps and spears, they managed to kill rabbits and opossums, but they did not provide enough nourishment for the whole Espiricueta family, and they were no replacement for water.

Hunger and thirst, the new masters of their existence, subjugated him and his offspring faster than any whip.

Anselmo Espiricueta heard the cart approaching on the same day his wife told him her breasts no longer produced milk. *Better we crush the kid than let it starve, Anselmo.* But he was proud of one thing that set him apart from most: all his children had been born alive, and all had survived. They had not lost any to the runs, to fevers, to anything. Nor would they lose any to hunger, he promised himself. So, when he heard the horses' hooves and the wheels of a heavy cart grow nearer, he ordered his eldest sons and daughters to position themselves, threateningly, on each side of the track of fine, dry, airborne yellow dirt that now covered the members of his family.

Now, years later, he would not know exactly how to explain why he went out to meet the cart. He wanted something. He wanted to save his family. He wanted to block the path through his property, to rob the people on the cart of something, even if just their feeling of safety. If their efforts were interpreted by the group they intended to accost as a plea for help, it was only because of the arrogance of the driver, the leader of the group.

Francisco Morales glanced at the pathetic troop that blocked his path and did not think for one moment that his life was in danger. It never occurred to him that he was looking at desperate souls who would have killed him for a drink of water. So bedraggled were they—covered in dry and desiccating dirt, their cheekbones protruding, their dark skin turned deathly pale, their lips parted and covered in a thick layer of white foam, and their eyes bulging—that to him, they looked like nothing more than hopeless beggars. He thought them so poor, so insignificant, that when he saw the shack they had built, he never suspected an invasion or an attempt to appropriate his land.

It soon became clear to Anselmo, despite the thirst and hunger also thickening his mental processes, that this enormous, pale-skinned, fair-haired man was the real lord and master of every stick and every stone the Espiricueta family had used in those days when he had thought he had his land and freedom. Conveniently, he quickly forgot his initial attempt at aggression and felt that servile part of his soul, that backbone of the spirit so accustomed to bowing down, do so again—defeated by the presence of a great lord prepared to help them, by the humiliation of being stripped of everything in an instant, yes, but also overcome by the ambition to survive above all else.

Were they lost? *Yes, lost,* he replied, swigging water. Did they stop because of the baby? *Yes, cause of the little one,* he said, looking at his children, now restoring the moisture to their dried-out cells. Can you work the land? *I know a little.* Are you from the South? *The south of the South.* Do you have anywhere to stay? He could feel his moist tongue's gratitude, but looking at the humble shack they had built themselves when they still had strength in their bodies, he answered, *No.* Do you need work? *Yes, Boss, I need work.*

*Yes, Boss. Yes, Boss.*

Since then, they had remained in this North sometimes of fire and sometimes of ice, prisoners of their will to live and the unexpected and cruel kindness of these people who offered only false hope, taking from them the land that had begun to feel like their own, preventing them from continuing their journey farther north with their *Not a good idea* and their *Why go there when you don't even speak the language?*

The greatest cruelty was the offer of land and a home, which rekindled Anselmo's hopes of independence.

Spanish was not Anselmo's mother tongue, and his previous experience did not include speaking to the landowner, only with foremen, who switched between the first language they shared with Anselmo and Spanish at their convenience. The fast, relentless words of this northern landowner entered one ear, reached his mind like a whirlwind inside his head, and then escaped out of the other ear as quickly as they had arrived. He managed to retain only the words that invaded his heart.

Would he like to have his own plot, his own house? *Yes, Boss.*

Morales had him taken to the two-room house.

He understood the apologetic words that the men who took him there spoke on the way. *It's a very basic house, and it's been empty for a long time. And it's far away, but it's better than nothing.*

While the other workers' houses had been built more recently to form a little community, with a plot of land for each one, the one allocated to Espiricueta was separate from the hacienda's cluster of buildings. Espiricueta did not care: when he saw it, he thought it a much better and bigger house than any he could have imagined.

He understood that wild animals had made their nests there, since it was cool and dark, but it would be easy to flush them out and make it habitable again. Since neither of the two windows had shutters, he would find a tree and make some himself at the next opportunity. As for the isolation, Espiricueta had no interest in having neighbors snooping on them or criticizing his wife or children. They had lived crammed together with other families in the South, and this house gave them the chance to do as they pleased. The house was also built directly on the field he was offered—his house, his field—where he would work shoulder to shoulder with his sons.

He understood that the boss was a fair man who paid well, as the men told him when they instructed him to turn up early the next day to work. That with his first wages, he would buy his first seeds to sow the allocated family plot, and that they, or someone, would lend him the tools needed to fix the house and prepare the field.

The problem arose when Espiricueta realized that Morales was making a promise in which the land would belong to him, but it did not, and that the house would also be his, but it was not. He would have to work double time—work the boss's land and his own—to pay rent with each harvest so that eventually, if he saved, he could buy the plot and leave it to his children when he died.

Anselmo Espiricueta did not have the patience for all that saving and waiting. Why wait until he was so old he could no longer straighten his back before he owned his own plot? Why must he live life bowing to a master, any master? He did not care whether it was a southern or a northern master. He had left the South, risking his own neck and his children's, in order to escape poverty. In his eagerness to start a new life, he had not hesitated to leave behind the language of his childhood, the moist earth of his birthplace. Why would he want to wait patiently in this land of biting cold and searing heat?

At first, Señora Beatriz had seen to it that they received supplies for several weeks and used clothes for the whole family. They had accepted it: the only clothing they possessed was what they had been wearing when, in total darkness, they left the tobacco estate where they had been predestined to spend their lives. They were also sent soap and a lotion for lice, fleas, and ticks, which they had been forced to accept. *They don't want dirty, foul-smelling folks near them,* thought Anselmo. *Is that why they gave us a house so far from the others?*

Then came the worst insult: the offer to pay for the Espiricueta children's schooling. To send his daughters to the charity school for girls, his sons to the one for boys. *They're good schools,* the señora assured him. The Morales girls went to the same school, though they called it "college," because they went to the side for elegant señoritas of high society, the side for those who could afford to pay. Then she spoke to them about the opportunity to better themselves by learning their letters and numbers, but Señor Morales was not present, so Anselmo set aside his reverence and put an end to the monologue.

"No, Señora. My children won't be doing that. What for? What good will it do them? We need the boys for the sowing and harvesting. And what could they teach my daughters there that would be of any use? To be better maidservants? Best they stay here, where they can be useful."

Señora Beatriz had rushed away, disturbed.

The years that passed had not made Anselmo Espiricueta forget his ambition for land and freedom. The idea was beginning to be bandied around in the area, but the workers on the hacienda and in the town did not seem to understand it: *Why would they want to give us land for free, land we haven't bought?*

They believed that life smiled on them by giving them good work and the chance to better themselves by planting their own plot. By educating their children. Anselmo thought that all the consideration, all the kindness, and the lack of beatings had ended up taming them, had made them conform. But he had learned from every lash of the whip and every blow he had received in his life, and the good treatment did not fool him: it was just a crueler form of control.

As he cut the sugarcane every day—a task that required only strength and rhythm—planted it, or loaded it onto the cart, he promised himself, as he had done from the beginning, that this would be the last day he would work for someone else. That he would leave this place, with or without his family, in search of the land he knew awaited him. He did not know where it was, but he would have to search for it, find it, and defend it better than they had defended the little tract of land they had taken as theirs between La Amistad and La Florida. He would plant tobacco, which was what he knew best.

However, his treacherous belly, full and grateful, subdued his willpower, so it proved very difficult to turn around and leave the place, with or without children.

Years later, there he still was, waiting with ambition and without patience, in the freezing place that had stolen his time, wealth, strength, and family: his wife and most of his children had met their end in that icy inferno with the plague that had come upon them.

Now he had lost almost everything, and if he had disapproved of Simonopio before, now he was convinced that all his terrible predictions on the day of the boy's birth were coming true. War had arrived a few days after the boy, and since then, the misery had continued: the disease and death of so many, and in particular his family, were caused by the evil that Simonopio had brought. And he had warned the boss: *That boy was sent by the devil, and he's gonna bring us nothing but disaster, you'll see.*

And had that arrogant lump listened to him? No, of course he hadn't. What did Anselmo Espiricueta know if he couldn't even read and write? *All I know's what life's taught me. What I learned in the firelight at midnight, listening to the old shamans.*

As he got to his feet, his back stiff and sore from holding it in the same bent position, resting against the tree for so long without taking his eyes from the road the caravan of healthy people had driven down, Anselmo Espiricueta promised himself he would never forget that they had taken the cursed child with them.

"And left us to die like mangy dogs."

# 19

## *The Return to Life, Another Life*

The three months of exile had marked Beatriz Cortés de Morales. They had changed her. Sometimes she felt as if she had spent what should have been the best years of her life as a silent spectator in a drama in which the lead role was her double: sharing the same name and identical features, but with an adversarial temperament.

Who was this woman who could not get through to her own daughters? This woman who had sent them to be brought up by nuns and then spent her days feeling upset because she had lost them, because they were growing up outside her supervision—and who, now that she had them all the time, found it impossible to strike up a conversation with them beyond the most basic social courtesies between mere acquaintances?

When she walked into the sewing room, which she shared with her daughters when they read, she often found them whispering between themselves, as was natural for young girls to do. When they saw her come in, they would immediately fall silent. They never confided in her like they had when they were little, and it was not unusual for them, when they noticed her presence, to rush out, giggling and pulling vexed faces.

Beatriz no longer recognized her daughters and did not know how to repair their relationship. She had no idea how to strike up even a simple conversation with them. Her daughters did not want to be with her. They did not want to speak to her. What she had hoped would be an opportunity—albeit a forced one—to spend time together had become an exercise in tolerance. They did not want to sew, though that did not surprise her: they had never liked it. They did not want to help teach the children of the families sharing their refuge, whether the subject was music, reading, or games. In the evenings after dinner, when the busy day was over, they would refuse to sing or read for the family. All they wanted was to be with each other, though by no means in absolute peace: such close coexistence wore them down and made them explode at one another or at everyone else.

Whenever Beatriz found something to say to restore harmony, Carmen and Consuelo would look at her with surprise in their eyes, as if to ask, *What are you talking about?* Whatever had happened an hour or two ago was now history, and they had no intention of revisiting or remembering it. They changed subjects, moods, interests, and conversations at a giddy speed. A speed that Beatriz had neither the mind nor the energy to match. A speed, it seemed to her, that made her age.

It was not just her daughters she blamed for her distress.

Her concern for the people who had remained to face death in Linares had stopped her sleeping, and since she never managed to fall into deep sleep, the house itself put her on guard several times each night. La Florida creaked like any old house, but its creaks were not like the creaks that lulled her to sleep at La Amistad. The same could be said of the house's smells, its dimensions, its hallways, its colors.

In the day, it did not matter so much. But each night, exhausted, she was overcome with a burning desire to run away and keep running until she was back lying in the bed where her married life had begun.

Instead of running out, terrorizing any wild animals that roamed those sierras by night, Beatriz wandered in silence through the halls of La Florida. It was not the time for sewing, as much as she would have liked to, so instead she inspected doors and windows that she had locked herself earlier on. She checked the oil lamps several times, in complete darkness, to be certain none of them remained lit, especially in her daughters' bedroom. While she was there, she would tuck them in, even when it was not cold; stroke their brows; brush the hair from their faces. Then she would sit at the end of their beds to gaze at them while they slept.

In the day, it was if she did not recognize them, but in the solitude of night, she was reunited with her little girls. That was when she had understood them well, when they breathed the same air as she did with no complaints, no running off. In the darkness, interrupted only by the moonlight, they seemed to shrink under their sheets, to take up less space in the bed, to return to a shape and size that she recognized. Sometimes she lay down with one of them. Sometimes she dozed a little, enveloped in their breath. She recognized her daughters in their open mouths as they slept or in their little sighs and snores. At night, as they dreamed, they did not run off, and nothing got between them: they were hers again.

Dawn caught her with scissors in hand. She did not want to wake the house pedaling her Singer, but nothing prevented her from starting a new project, starting a new pattern, cutting some fabric. She would light one of the oil lamps she had invested a good part of her nocturnal efforts ensuring was not lit, and she would start her day. She received her husband with a smile, as she always had. Then she accompanied him to breakfast and said goodbye at the door, wishing him a good day and sending a few secret blessings with him. What she requested and promised before God for the good of her family, she did in the privacy of her mind, because if Francisco had known how much protection she requested for him in particular, he would have realized his wife was not the pillar of strength she pretended to be.

Simonopio knew. He was always there when they opened the door in the morning. He stared at her while she said goodbye to her husband. Then he approached her with an offering: some beeswax or a small jar of honey. Beatriz grew accustomed to the taste of the honey sweetening her coffee. It became such a part of her ritual that, with the simple act of pouring a fine trickle into her cup, she found some peace, renewed spirits, and the energy to continue with the strange routine of that place. To deal with her unrecognizable daughters, with the slights and spats between the servant women, or with another servant alarmed by a rash on the stomach of one of her children. Simonopio observed her, and Beatriz had the feeling that the boy knew things she would not even admit to herself. It was he who had found the antidote to the implosion she had felt coming. It was he who had suggested bringing her the Singer. Beatriz knew he had sensed that her sewing machine would make her happy or at least soothe her desperation; that it would keep her sane.

Sometimes she wanted to say to him, *Tell me what you see with those eyes, Simonopio. Tell me how far they see, when they probe me. How deep into my body, into my soul.* For some reason, because the eyes were Simonopio's, the scrutiny did not unsettle her. It seemed natural to her that she had no privacy with Simonopio. There was never any judgement or disapproval in his eyes. Simonopio was who he was, he was how he was, and all one had to do was accept him, just as she knew he accepted her.

As the weeks passed, the weather changed. It turned cold, and with the fall in temperature, Simonopio's gifts to her became rarer. She did not know much about bees, but she supposed that they took shelter in winter and needed their honey. In response to the silent apology Simonopio offered her every day for the shortage, Beatriz reassured him that it did not matter: she had been storing the surplus in jars and had enough honey for two or three months. *And who knows, by then your bees might have some more for you, Simonopio.*

Although the weather had changed and Simonopio's features were left bare, the lifelong companions that normally perched on him absent for the winter, he would wander off, as he did every day, to explore the mountain paths. During one wakeful night, Beatriz concluded that the bees were more than just a coincidence or a curiosity for Simonopio. They accompanied him; they guided him; they watched over him. It troubled her when he went out alone, without his guardian angels. She sensed that without them, he was vulnerable, but there was no way to stop him. He did not know how to stay put. If he was given a task to keep him near the house, he would do it willingly, but when Beatriz looked at him, she could see the longing in his eyes. She made sure that he ate well and wrapped up warm. That he took some food with him in his knapsack. All she could do for him was to let him go and, each time he left to wander off into the wooded wilds, to send more secret blessings with him.

From blessing to blessing, the days, the nights, the months passed. Three months.

If leaving Linares had been hard, returning proved, unexpectedly, to be harder still. The very thing she had been looking forward to for almost ninety days—doubting sometimes that it would ever be possible—had robbed her of the desire to sew from the moment Francisco told her that the number of infected and dead were in sharp decline. That they would wait a week or two longer before deciding, though he anticipated they would return to La Amistad and Linares very soon.

The time had come to return to the reality of Linares, to count the dead, to mourn them. To hand over her daughters again for strangers to educate them, to pass out all the clothes she had gathered in a corner of her sewing room to the living who remained.

Two days before leaving, she found Carmen alone, crying. Consuelo had chosen that day to tire of her sister's company and had locked herself in their bedroom to invent new ways to do her hair.

Alarmed to see the calmer and more even-tempered of her daughters crying, Beatriz sat with her and tried to string together and understand her single-word utterances: her friend Mariqueta Domínguez's cousin, the handsome one. A debutantes' ball at Monterrey Social Club at the beginning of September. Her dance card full. Two waltzes and a lemonade with Antonio Domínguez. Love letters from him to her and from her to him, though they had seen each other only that one time.

She listened stoically to the news from the lips of a sobbing Carmen. She did not interrupt her to say that she was very young and that not so long ago she had been playing with dolls, though it was what came to mind with each of her daughter's words. She had the urge to tell her, *See what happens when you read so many romantic novels?* But she resisted, of course.

Beatriz and Francisco knew the boy's family through mutual friends. Though she lived in Monterrey, María Enriqueta was boarding at the Sagrado Corazón. And while Beatriz did not understand the practice of living separately from one's children when it was unnecessary, she had been glad the girls had forged this friendship at school. Mariqueta returned home every weekend and often invited Carmen and Consuelo to visit her, to have lunch with the family or attend some special event, such as Antonio's sister's debut at the Monterrey Social Club.

"And you hadn't met Antonio Domínguez until then?"

He had just graduated with a degree in engineering from MIT and had not visited Monterrey in two years. He was a good boy, handsome, hardworking, from a good family, and he had asked Carmen to marry him.

With this announcement, the air left Beatriz's body. Carmen did not give her time to recover it.

"And now he's dead!"

"How do you know?"

"I don't know it, but I can feel it. I haven't received a letter from him for three months!"

"Nobody's sending or receiving letters. The postal service has been suspended. You know that, Carmen."

"I know. But they stayed in Monterrey. They had nowhere to go like we did. What if he fell sick? What if he died? What if he's forgotten me?"

"Look, Carmen, I can't guarantee he's well. But what I can guarantee you is that, if he is healthy, he hasn't forgotten you." In fact, Beatriz had no grounds to make such a guarantee, but she went on. "I also promise you that, as soon as we're able, we'll send a message to Mariqueta so that she knows you are all right. Everything else, we'll wait and see."

Carmen was reassured after the talk with her mother, but Beatriz had to rush off and lock herself in her own bedroom to regain her breath and study herself in the mirror, as if she would find answers there.

At last she understood the changes in mood, her daughters' whispering, their secrecy, their complicity, though she would have been grateful if—after bearing the separation from her sweetheart in silence for three months—Carmen had kept her secret for a few more days. At least until they had returned to Linares.

The mirror gave her no answers. Nor did it offer any hope or promises.

She had had to vow to Carmen that she would say nothing to Francisco. Beatriz had agreed both reluctantly and gladly. She did not like keeping secrets, especially from Francisco, but at the same time, what was the sense in worrying him so soon? And what if the Romeo of Monterrey had, in fact, died of flu? It was not that the future mother-in-law wanted the candidate for son-in-law to be dead—far from it—but it was possible that all of Carmen's plans would evaporate in an instant.

Her husband was already weighed down with enough worry. On their return to Linares, she would of course find the best way and the best moment to give him the news. In the meantime, she would spare him this new source of anxiety.

For the time being, Beatriz was a new, albeit reluctant, accomplice to her daughter's love life. When they sat at the table, between mouthfuls, Carmen would give her complicit looks and little smiles, to which she was expected to respond in some similar way. The problem was that Beatriz did not understand them; sometimes she wanted to answer, *I'm very sorry, I don't speak that language.*

Not anymore.

She wanted to say to her: *I think I remember speaking it, learning it, but at some stage, I don't know when, I forgot it. Whether it was from neglect or because it's a language to which only young people have access, I don't know.*

She said nothing, afraid to break the fragile connection.

As a young woman, Beatriz had always reflected on how it would feel to grow old. She observed her mother—old fashioned, elderly, diminished, prudish—and wondered if a person woke up one day saying, *This is the moment my old age begins. Starting today, my brain will stop tolerating new ideas, my taste in clothing will stop evolving, my hairstyle will remain the same forevermore, I will read and reread the novels that brought me pleasure in my youth with nostalgia, and I will let the next generation—whom I no longer understand because I only speak "Old"— make my decisions for me, because I have nothing to teach them anymore. I'll be company for everyone, but little more than that for anyone.*

She was too young to be old, but when a mother has a daughter whose mind is set on marriage, she cannot help but conclude that the years are running away from her. *At thirty-three, I'm beginning my old age.* That would be another tough piece of news to share with her husband: *Francisco, as of today, we're officially old.*

No. It would not be easy to give him this news.

With her new burden, the last two days had felt like an eternity. There was much to deal with as soon as they set foot on La Amistad. Now it was as if the three months of isolation, while not exactly pleasant, had at least given them the illusion that they could continue living a life in which their worries were not minor but were ultimately intangible.

They were returning, yes, even if, on the way to the hacienda, Beatriz could not stop thinking that they were not going back to the life they knew before October, that everything had changed, that they would have to explore their new life as if it were a new world, a new frontier. And now the intangible problems they had merely worried about would become palpable: they would become real. Now she felt an urge to tell the caravan of refugees to return to their exile, if that would mean they could prolong the illusion of the existence of the life that they knew before the Spanish flu and her young daughter's childish romances.

She did not dare do it, of course, for the old Beatriz would never shrink from a problem or a responsibility. Then she thought that this would be one of her new challenges: to find the old Beatriz again, to rescue her from the miasma that enveloped her. As for adopting new hairstyles and fashions, she would wait and see: it would depend—she supposed—on the hairstyles and fashions. And as for nostalgia for the novels of her youth, that was a luxury she could allow herself once in a while. However, not even in her old age would she become anybody's shadow or be left drifting, at the mercy of other people's decisions. She would never allow herself to grind to a halt. And under no circumstances would she ever allow a grandchild of hers to call her anything other than Grandma Beatriz. No Gran, Granny, or Grandmom. She would make that very clear from the beginning.

What was more, bit by bit, if possible, she would reunite the two parts into which her consciousness had been split: the old one and the new one. She would be one again and would leave behind the stand-in that she had discovered in recent months.

The question, then, was: Which of the two—new or old—would win the battle to define Beatriz Cortés thereafter? The new Beatriz felt a special admiration for the old one—her character had had certain redeeming qualities—but she also hoped she would not reemerge with such force that she would cancel out the wisdom the new had gained.

When she arrived, the first thing the new Beatriz did for the old one was to walk into the house at La Amistad without shedding a single tear. Immediately, seeing its state of neglect, she ordered her mother, daughters, and servants to clean: *Take off the sheets, don't shake them inside the house, move furniture, fetch dusters. Don't even think about complaining, Consuelo. Wash the dishes and pans, change the bed linens; it's all filthy, and the dust will suffocate us.*

Surprised when Francisco joined her on her rounds and at his repeated comments on how clean the house was, with so little dust, Beatriz told him that there was indeed remarkably little dust on the furniture and floors, but *have you seen under the armchairs and beds? And on the dishes and utensils!* It was as if all the dust had gathered there; mountains were forming.

She did not understand when Francisco went away looking upset. She supposed it must be because she had never spoken to him about dust or dirt before. Her mother had warned her before she married: never speak to your husband about everyday housekeeping, because he won't be interested. Beatriz had heeded the advice and doubted that Francisco even knew where they kept the mops, brooms, and dusters.

Once the cleaning gang had been set to work, she opened the chest containing the collection of clothes she had sewn.

She hoped the blouse and skirt were the right size, though if they were not, she could easily make some adjustments. She put everything in a bag along with the doll she had made from the remnants of the fabric.

She had been surprised not to find Anselmo Espiricueta waiting for the procession's return. She would have to visit him to offer her condolences. It was cold, and it was a long way to the Espiricuetas' home, but the ground seemed dry, so she wrapped up warmly and decided to go there on foot. After a few steps, she noticed Simonopio walking beside her.

"You know I'm going to see the Espiricuetas, don't you? Don't come if you don't want to."

Simonopio kept walking, and Beatriz, while surprised, was grateful for his company. She did not want to face the widower alone.

From a distance, it was clear that Jacinta Espiricueta's absence was taking its toll, even if she had never been very strict. The house looked sadder and more neglected than ever. They had never done much to improve its appearance: the shutters on the windows were more like fixed boards, with wide cracks that did little to protect from the light or drafts. But now there were also pots and pans and garbage everywhere, and weeds grew unfettered where the house met the earth. They seemed to sprout from the foundations.

Beatriz had felt very sorry for Señora Jacinta ever since she met her: famished, suspicious, overrun with children, devoid of hope. Beatriz had thought that by giving her husband work and the family a home, she would lift her burden a little. But she soon learned that the assurance of work, their own land, and good treatment would not soften Espiricueta's wife.

Though it went against her firm commitment to Christian charity and she struggled to admit it to herself, Beatriz was uncomfortable with the Espiricueta family living on La Amistad. The husband's manners, the wife's despicable attitude, and the furtive eyes of both disturbed her. And while Beatriz did not in all honesty seek praise or gratefulness, she admitted that she could not help but notice the complete lack of gratitude from both Espiricuetas for the opportunity that they had been given for a new life, new friendships, and new skills.

Francisco looked at her with surprise whenever he offered to send Espiricueta to do some special task in the house and Beatriz turned down the offer. *I'll wait until Gabino or Trinidad are free. There's no hurry,* she would reply. She did not want to feel the weight of those resentful eyes on her. She did not want him near her daughters or Simonopio. She did not want that man inside her house or touching her things.

She had been nervous leaving him at La Amistad unsupervised when everyone had gone into exile, even if the circumstances were exceptional and justified. By day, she knew there was no way of entering the house without a key, but during her interminable sleepless nights, she imagined Espiricueta exploring the house with his eyes, with his hands, with the bare soles of his feet. She imagined him opening their drawers or sleeping in their marital bed at his leisure.

On several occasions, she had considered asking Francisco to get rid of him, but she would never have dared. She did not want to request a man's removal just because she did not like him. And now she was going to the home of these poor wretches because she knew that—after what the family had suffered, after its loss—now it was impossible to even contemplate throwing them out onto the street.

Simonopio decided to stay out of sight of the house and sat down to wait on a stone behind a bush. Beatriz was not surprised. Whenever Anselmo Espiricueta was close, Simonopio would disappear. It was as if the boy remembered what the man had said about him the day they had found him abandoned, or as if he sensed the ill will that the campesino still harbored toward him, as if he knew about his superstitions. It was as if he did not trust him.

"I won't be long."

In the half-light of the winter afternoon, the house seemed like nothing more than a black-and-white photograph: no bright colors interrupted its gray monotony. As she approached its silence and darkness, she thought she would find it empty, as if the surviving members of the Espiricueta family had responded from a distance to her secret wishes and left for good of their own accord—northward, perhaps, as they had always wanted—without anybody asking them to do so. Without saying goodbye to anyone. Without telling anyone.

If this were so, the mystery of the Espiricueta family's disappearance would live on forever in their community on La Amistad and in all Linares. It would become good material for a legend: what remained of an entire family disappears by the hand of the father who, driven mad by the death of so many of his children, wound up killing the few that survived, perhaps burying them alive, determined in his madness to fill all the graves he had already dug. Then, witnesses—the sweetheart of a cousin's friend, a friend's sister, the teacher's grandmother—would swear that the man, a vile murderer, a possessed or, at the very least, tormented soul, would roam the area forevermore, endlessly searching for his family members. He would wander the region blaming any living person he encountered for his irreversible loss, destined never to remember—or never to want to remember—that it was he who was to blame for his own misery.

And like many other legends, this one would travel through time and space, transcending generations and geographical boundaries. The tale of bloody sightings and loud wails would be retold with ever-increasing eccentricity, until the collective consciousness forgot the origin of the story and the name of its protagonist, and they all believed it belonged to them: from Chiapas to Guanajuato to Texas.

She felt a shiver run from her feet to her head. She knew she did not have a fertile imagination and that the idea that had wormed its way into her mind was almost identical to the legend of La Llorona—the Weeping Woman—that had frightened her so as a child. The thought of the woman who had lost her children and was destined to wander aimlessly, endlessly crying out for them, still scared her. She did not deny it. The idea that she might know the protagonist, the origin, of a possible legend firsthand—even if that idea came from convoluted reasoning spawned only by her imagination in that moment—made her come out in goose bumps.

She knocked on the door without wanting it to be answered.

# 20

## The Story That Was Told, Is Told, and Will Be Told, Perhaps

Simonopio knew almost all the paths: short ones, long ones, wide ones, narrow ones. He knew the paths of animals and the paths of men. Some had even been made by him when he came and went in pursuit of his bees, which rarely kept to the man-made tracks. But he did not know all of them, and some he had not traveled to the end or even to the point where the bees called it a day and decided to begin the journey home.

For him, until now, only one path had been forbidden. He never understood why, but he had blindly obeyed; so until that day, he had never followed the track that would take him straight to Anselmo Espiricueta's house.

He could feel in the air around him that his swarm grew agitated every time the man with the irreconcilable grudges approached him. It was their way of warning him to flee when they felt Espiricueta close, to avoid crossing paths with him on the tracks where they might meet. Even so, sometimes Simonopio would stop at a crossroads of two paths near Espiricueta's house, aware that the path on the left would take him straight there, and he felt drawn to the forbidden, to the unknown. But since it was a section of the hills that even the bees avoided, he had always obeyed them: *Not there, there's nothing good there,* they often reminded him.

He knew the hostility that the man had felt toward him since they met the first time: Simonopio, a newborn baby, and Espiricueta, a newcomer. How could he not know it, when he thought he could remember it? Or perhaps it was that—much like the old bees told the young bees about each success and failure of the past, to repeat the victories and to avoid the mistakes—his bees had told him so that he would never forget that first encounter. Or perhaps it was the looks Espiricueta gave Simonopio at every opportunity: intense, heavy, dark, ominous.

Between Espiricueta and him there was a story that not even the wind knew yet. It was a story still unfolding that had begun on the day Simonopio was born, but it was also a story that had not yet happened: suspended in stasis, on hold thanks to his bees, but not dead or brought to an end.

It was a story that was waiting patiently. Waiting to exist.

This he knew with certainty. He had always known it, just as he knew the likely stories of others; all he had to do was search the corners of his mind to see them—his own stories or those of other people. Some stories—whether his own or not—he saw very clearly from start to finish. In certain stories, he could make out how they came to be before they had begun, though he did not have a clear picture of the outcome. Other stories materialized from nowhere, with no warning: they just happened.

Some future events—seen in full or in part—were so desirable that he waited for them impatiently. Others made his hairs stand on end when he thought about them, and preferably would never come to pass.

Francisco Morales had taken to telling him stories while they secretly cleaned the house. Simonopio always listened intently, for it was what he knew how to do best in a one-sided conversation, as any conversation in which he participated ended up being, silent as he was. He also listened because he was aware of his godfather's need to express himself, even if it was merely through stories that he himself had been told as a boy. But his main reason for being such a committed listener was that nothing fascinated Simonopio more than the stories told by other people, whether through songs or tales.

*This is a legend,* Francisco would say to him. *And this one's a fable.*

When it came to legends and fables, Simonopio also liked the ones told by Soledad Betancourt, the storyteller at the Villaseca Fair. She told her stories orally, from memory. He listened to her every year without fail in the marquees that went up on the outskirts of Linares. It was not that the woman arrived each time with a complete repertoire of new stories. He wondered at how she often told the same tales, but with little twists that she added masterfully to renew them, to make them fresh, more dramatic, or more terrifying. His godfather, clasping a feather duster, had told him some very similar stories—which, under his control, in his voice, charted their own new course.

Simonopio knew there were stories that one could read in books, with black words on white pages. He was not interested in those, because once printed they were indelible, unchanging. Each reader had to follow the order of words indicated in those pages exactly, until they each arrived inexorably at the same outcome.

Comparing the two storytellers, Simonopio had learned that, just as the words of a story told verbally had the freedom to change, its characters, the challenges they faced, and the ending were also free to change.

His favorite story was the fable Francisco told him about a lion and a coyote in the land of light. Simonopio wanted to be the brave lion, like his godfather suggested to him.

"In a fable, the animals possess human traits, their virtues and flaws. If you know the fable, you can choose to be the gazelle or the mouse, but I think you must be the lion, Simonopio. Just remember to watch out for the coyote."

Happy that his godfather had compared him to such a majestic character, Simonopio thought constantly about how to be the lion of the tale, how to live up to his godfather's praise. And it delighted him that his was a story that had never been written down.

Being in possession of that story meant Simonopio could make endless changes, could add or remove characters as he saw fit and give them the traits of the people around him. And he was the lion. Though his mind sent him on thousands of different fictitious adventures, he was the lion. The coyote was always the same, as well, and as much as Simonopio tried, not even in his most skillfully constructed narratives did he manage to remove that character from his story. He suspected that, for as long as there was a lion, there would always be a coyote.

While that fable was just one tale, an invention, the stories Simonopio stored in his mind—the ones only he knew or saw—spoke to him of reality.

The stories of Villaseca and those of his godfather had taught him that he who has a story in his mind, he who does not put it in writing, enjoys the freedom to reshape it at will, and Simonopio thought he had the power to do the same with the stories of real life that he saw in the privacy of his mind. They were not written, either, so he felt it was his duty to be a good, albeit silent, narrator. To twist them, like Soledad did at Villaseca. If, by filling a hole, he could erase an unhappy ending for a horse, then he did it. If allowing himself to fall ill for a few days changed the fate of many of his characters and saved their lives, he would not hesitate. He could not stop those future stories; he could not choose which ones to tell or know them all in full and in time to make plans and changes, like Soledad and Francisco Morales did. But there was always some adjustment he could make, as minor as it might be.

About his own story, which he knew would come—the latent story about him and his coyote—he still did not know what to do.

Simonopio was not a boy who allowed fear to control him. Every day on his walks, he came across bears and pumas in the wild and looked them in the eyes to say, *I am the lion, you go your way, and I'll go mine.*

But never until that day had he walked down the forbidden path, and Simonopio knew that an accidental encounter with a wild beast was preferable to a collision with the man who had made this track, pressing down the earth with the weight of his footsteps, his envy, and his grief.

He had to admit that, in a way, he was glad to have the perfect excuse to invade Espiricueta's territory as his godmother's escort, with his bees not there to forbid him. Finally, he could sate the curiosity he had always felt: What was there, or what was missing from there, that made the bees avoid the place?

What he discovered with each step he took toward the epicenter of that living piece of land was the same thing he perceived in its tenant's eyes: that there was only disquiet and unhappiness there. That the land breathed but would struggle to allow any crop to live. That the air blew and brought oxygen, but it also poisoned something deep within the cells. That life there was heavy, dangerous, dark, ominous.

His curiosity sated, he decided that, like his bees, from that day onward he would never set foot on a single grain of earth that Espiricueta occupied.

It had not been easy to take the turn that he had never dared or been allowed to take before. It was the pressure in his chest. It was his body's instinctive rejection when it breathed that air, and the instruction the bees had given him all his life. It was, of course, because of the risk that he knew he would run.

In spite of the fear, which almost paralyzed him and which he had to hide so as not to alarm the woman under his protection, Simonopio remained steadfast in the task of accompanying and watching over his godmother, observing her closely all the way: Was she short of breath, like he was? Was the palpable weight of the atmosphere affecting her? Was she turning pale? Was her pace slowing as they drew closer to the house? *If so,* thought Simonopio, *we'll stop and go back.* But no. Beatriz

Cortés had a mission to complete, and nothing distracted her from the obligation that she had imposed on herself. So, despite his unease, Simonopio walked on with the firm intention of avoiding the coyote's lair, of remaining hidden.

He promised himself that he would not detonate the future that day.

He longed, at that moment, for the company of his bees, for in their absence he felt blind, restricted to what his body's eyes could see and the limited information he obtained with his immediate senses from the physical world around him. He was aware that this was the normal state for any person, but for him it equated to extreme myopia and deafness, because without his bees, he could not see or hear beyond the hills. Without them, he could not see behind him or observe the world from above when he chose to do so. In their absence, Simonopio could not smell the exquisite aroma of the pollen, just as the bees did.

Without the bees swarming around him, coming and going, the information he received from the world was linear; while with them, from the moment he had begun to feel sensation, he had grown accustomed to perceiving the world as it was: a sphere.

As much as he wanted to, he could not summon them now. They did not necessarily sleep when winter arrived; rather, the bees hid away in their honeycomb for as long as possible, sharing the heat of their bodies, particularly during a severe winter like the one they were enduring that year. They remained in their beehive, which grew in size and prosperity under the shed roof they had been invading and covering, hexagon by hexagon, with their wax structure. And there they remained for months, living off the fruit of their tireless work the rest of the year.

Simonopio visited them often. He laid his hands on the firm structure of the living honeycomb, vibrant with their buzzing. Without coming out, they welcomed him, they consoled him in his solitude, and they asked him: *Do you need us?*

Just the knowledge that they would come if he called for them, ready for anything, calmed Simonopio. They would go wherever they were needed without hesitation, even to this undesirable place, if Simonopio called for them—but at great cost: with the low temperatures, most would die. That day, in that place, he was afraid, but that was not enough to make him call on his bees to sacrifice themselves. The day to summon them had not yet arrived.

Sitting on a rock behind a bush, waiting for his godmother to finish her duty, watching over her from a distance, Simonopio was not ashamed to admit that what terrified him most was the knowledge that, one day, he would face Espiricueta. He did not know where, how, or when it would be, and that caused him great anguish. That day, the man did not appear to be at home, Simonopio concluded with relief when the youngest daughter timidly answered the door.

It would come, but today would not be the day of the lion and the coyote.

He had no choice but to wait for time to make his story real. What he did know was that the day would arrive, that it could not be put off, and that his loss would be enormous and irreparable. Without knowing the story in advance, he was certain it would change everyone's lives.

If, by avoiding Espiricueta, by evading him, he managed to prolong the wait, to grow strong until he lost his fear, to learn what he needed to know in order to change the words and elements of this inevitable narrative; if he bought himself enough time to grow physically, mentally, and spiritually; and if over this time he gradually became the powerful lion he imagined, then he would continue to avoid it for as long as necessary. Because Simonopio was certain that the tale the bees, the wind, and the trees would one day tell about him and Espiricueta would be a story of the kind one hoped would never happen.

"What're you doing here, devil?"

Surprised by the violence in the voice, Simonopio turned around to see Espiricueta charging toward him, ready to deal him a blow with the stick he carried in his hand.

# 21

## *Gaps That Were Left*

Sometimes when we do not have someone in front of us—in plain sight, in constant contact—while we know it does not mean that they no longer exist, it's as if it were impossible that they should carry on without us, that they could continue to exist without our physical influence. Perhaps this stems from the depths of our early childhood, when we are reluctant to lose sight of our mother for fear of her disappearing.

I don't know if it's happened to you, but it has to me. It still does. Right now, as we travel away from my family, from my home, when it's almost time for lunch and I know that the food is being prepared, I struggle to accept that, even though I'm not there, the broth or stew is still bubbling away, the same smells that are always there when I'm present are still wafting around the house, and the food will still taste the same in my absence.

This phenomenon does not occur, of course, when one goes out to buy some milk from the store on the corner. It occurs, to me at least, when one goes away, when there is a goodbye involved—or an interval, you might call it.

When I was away studying and returned for the holidays, it seemed very strange to me that my mother had had the initiative in my absence to change the upholstery on an armchair or donate the books from my childhood to younger eyes and minds. Then, when my own children studied elsewhere, I called them often so that they would not forget my continued presence in the day-to-day world: the daily routine where we feel hungry and eat, where our teeth rot and we have fillings, where we come down with diarrhea—not too often, hopefully—and treat it with an infusion of estafiata, grown in a corner of the garden. Where the light bulbs blow and we change them; where our electricity bill is double the usual amount, and seething, we just pay it; where sometimes we fight, but most of the time we're happy; where we have dinner with old friends or even make new ones.

All of this in spite of your absence.

Of course, I know it's not like this, that they won't forget me and I won't them, but it's the first time I've tried to explain the concept to someone. I hope I've managed it. And no. I'm no more senile now than I was an hour ago, when we got into the car. I'm not senile, but at my age, I think I now have the right to say whatever I want. And this is what I want to say: my memories, my impressions come with me. I don't know about yours, but my reality goes with me wherever I go and leaves behind its capacity to reinvent itself, to develop.

I imagine that, in much the same way, my parents thought they would return to a town frozen in time, fossilized. A Brigadoon. But no. Life—and death—continued without them.

It was not until they arrived back in Linares that my papa admitted to my mama the anguish he had felt when he drove through the town on the day he went to collect my sisters in Monterrey. During the three months of isolation, he had kept it to himself to avoid worrying her. But on their return, when the context was different, he allowed himself to confess that the experience had horrified him and kept him awake for several nights, for whenever he closed his eyes, he saw the empty streets again and the dogs hungry for human flesh, and he heard the sound of the horses and the funeral cart on the paved road. Even after receiving a few sporadic letters from Dr. Cantú and learning that life in Linares went on, albeit in a strained atmosphere, my papa struggled to imagine or remember the streets full of living people, like they had been before.

After thinking about it for many years, I've reached the conclusion that, with his last glance at his ancestral town after the arrival of the flu, my papa experienced the phenomenon I have been trying to describe: you leave a place or say goodbye to someone, and thereafter, you feel the existence you have left behind is frozen by your absence. On that last drive through Linares, my papa had been left thinking it was the end of the world. The end of his world, at least. All the usual sounds, smells, and sights had been wiped out, and I'm certain that he had the impression—a primeval instinct, perhaps—that all the bodies strewn on the roadside were people who had suddenly dropped dead as they went about their daily business, with no warning.

His first impression when they returned once and for all was, perhaps, of a gray Linares. In that January of 1919, Linares was icy and overcast, and the people walking in the streets wore black mourning clothes. The circumstances might have prevented them from saying goodbye to their loved ones at the grave, but as my grandmother used to say, decent people knew how to mourn properly: by wearing black for a full year.

My parents discovered a kind of mourning that they struggled to understand. People had lost husbands, wives, parents, children, or friends, and they wore black, but they went about their daily business as if nothing had happened. They were happy to be alive, I suppose. I would have been, too, frankly. In the new reality that the influenza brought about, it is easy to believe that people who were honest with themselves could admit such a thing—that they could think *My sister died* and *What a shame, but how nice that I didn't*—even if saying so in front of others would have been in poor taste.

I do not wish to make light of the pain they must have felt at the loss of loved ones. Anyone who has been bereaved knows that the survivor's recovery is a torturous road.

We must consider the time. Imagine so many around you suddenly falling. Falling like flies, as if the air had suddenly been filled with poisonous gas. I imagine that, at the end of such an onslaught, only the flies that kept their distance, that went unnoticed, that were lucky, would survive. But once the harmful substance had dissipated, what would the survivors do? Get back to their lives.

Life waits for no one.

If you're a fly, you keep flying and being a nuisance. If you lived in Linares at that time, you could never stop going out to the fields or ranches to tend to your crops or animals. You might close the store for a few days because of the initial shock, but you would open it again because, even if your relatives were sick or dead, your needs and the needs of others—those who sold to you and those who bought from you—persisted. If you lived at that time, you could not avoid having to go out to buy food, and not a day could pass without washing diapers or underpants, even if you sent your mother to the cemetery two hours earlier. In the midst of this crisis, you had tooth decay, infected toenails, and stomach upsets—slight or severe—that you put up with for a while before having to seek help from a doctor, if you could find one. Others went out to sell goat milk, or whistles, yo-yos, and spinning tops in the square, in the hope that there were still children alive to buy them.

Knowing that the pandemic was over, the new gravedigger must have been only too glad to respond when he was called to bury a Christian, because he knew that they would be sending him someone quite dead, someone who had perhaps suffered a welcome and understandable heart attack. An ordinary death. If a mother or a father had lost a child, they had others to feed, so they had to go back to work, and that was that. With no fuss or extra patience from anybody, not even themselves.

The initial compassion and attention Mercedes Garza and her family received when she fell ill and died were not experienced by anyone else in those three months. There were no women to bring food to fellow mothers when they lost their husbands, nor anyone to dry the newly orphaned children's tears. By the time the Spanish flu had completed its cycle, there was nobody in Linares who had not lost someone, so there was no one to ease the sorrow of others with their condolences.

By the time my parents arrived, ready to offer their sympathies to all and sundry, nobody wanted to hear them. They had already changed the subject. They had turned the page in that story. They had survived it.

There was nobody with whom to discuss the absence of the usual postman; the storekeeper that knew them; or Father Pedro, who had baptized my sisters and Simonopio, because all they said was *Yes, the other one was better* or *This priest's a better speaker*. Those who stayed in Linares saw one, ten, or twenty such figures die. They were sorry, of course, but the urgent need to fill the gaps left by their deaths forced everyone to be practical and to say, for instance, *Don Atenógenes, the butcher, has died; may God have him in His holy glory, and may He send us another butcher soon. Amen.*

Their need for meat, groceries, worship, and sharpened knives was greater than their pain and sorrow. Such is life.

My parents, who had not expected to come up against all of this, struggled to understand it and to be practical themselves. For example: it was hard to offer sympathy and commiseration to a mother, a friend younger than my own mama, who had buried a daughter less than three months prior and was two months pregnant now. My mama, who—while I don't wish to boast—was a paragon of refinement and good taste, did not know what the correct protocol was in such circumstances.

They also faced the sudden loss of dear friends.

Though they had received news of the death of this or that person in Dr. Cantú's brief notes, they had departed and taken their reality with them. They understood what the deaths meant rationally, but while they were in isolation at La Florida, their lives did not change one bit. Going back and suddenly being faced with the absence of friends, relatives, and acquaintances meant experiencing all the pain at once.

Those who had remained had suffered drip by drip, but my parents were caught in a downpour.

Isolated from everything, they had almost managed to believe that the war had also disappeared in their absence. But no. Not even the influenza, as deadly as it proved to be, was enough to stop the violence. And while a great many inhabitants of Linares had died in those three months, the deaths made no dent in the local population, for more and more families arrived every day from the rural areas, in search of refuge from the plundering, the kidnappings of women, and the levy.

Thus, when my parents returned to their previous life, they found it full of gaps that absent friends and acquaintances had left, but also lumps made by the new and unfamiliar faces that appeared in front of them from nowhere, as if by magic.

My grandmother was also suddenly confronted with the fact that her two sons, whom she had been so distraught to leave behind when she went to La Florida, had not only survived but were carrying on with life as if nothing had happened and nobody had missed them. She had known, from the occasional messages she received, that they were still alive, which she attributed to all the prayers she had said for them while she prepared her cajeta.

During her absence, and in spite of the public health crisis, they'd taken good care of their land, but they'd also had the energy to fall in love and to woo the objects of their affection. Emilio was engaged. Carlos was now married and about to make Sinforosa a grandmother for the third time—the first grandchild with the family surname—but those events had not necessarily occurred in the proper order.

Had my grandmother stayed in Linares—and had she still been the woman of days gone by, before life executed her character by firing squad—she would have immediately given Carlos, her youngest son, a dressing down for being so loose and lustful. She would have told him in no uncertain terms to behave like a man of integrity and marry the girl. Then she would have sent them away, to live out of sight for a while, far from the gossips of Linares high society, so that nobody would question the dubious news of a premature grandchild.

Under these new circumstances, Grandma Sinforosa gave an enormous sigh of relief at the fact that Carlos had done the right thing without being told to do so: she learned that María de la Luza Garza's father had not even had to demand that Carlos honor his obligations to his daughter. As a decent man, as a gentleman, he had gone to the family's home, asked for her hand in marriage, and sent for the priest, who married them there and then in a discreet ceremony with only Emilio accompanying him.

The hasty marriage had caused something of a scandal. The well-intentioned said it was in very poor taste to have married in the absence of the groom's mother and amid all the loss of life: they had to remain in mourning for a year, as was only proper, and all social events were supposed to be put on hold. Not least something as joyful and auspicious as a marriage. The not-so-well-intentioned remarked on the audacity of the new couple: *In the family way with so many people dying,* and *When did they find the time?*

My grandmother noticed all her friends doing mental arithmetic as they asked about her new grandchild's arrival, but she did not care. She was grateful she was no longer the woman who would have tried to hide an untimely pregnancy, sending her son away before her grandchild was born. Families had to stay close, because as she had learned, one never knows what might happen. The spark had gone out of her some time ago, and this new grandchild made her realize that it did not matter what tragedies befell them: life went on.

On the first day after their return, when my mama left for her tour of sympathy at the Espiricueta household, my papa took the opportunity to go into town, thinking he would find it in a similar state to when he drove through on the way to collect my sisters.

He was amazed to find that the streets were busy.

The mayor, Carlos Tamez, was outside the post office, where there was a constant flow of people coming and going. They greeted each other hurriedly, both anxious to continue on their way. As the mayor walked past, my father asked him whether the postal service was now operating.

"Partially," he replied.

There was staff, but since they were just beginning to reorganize themselves, one had to go through to collect one's letters and telegrams oneself.

"You're going to need a wagon," said the mayor before heading off.

It was an ominous and cryptic message that my papa did not understand until he walked into the post office, found what awaited him there, and then returned home for what would perhaps be one of the worst experiences of his life.

By nightfall he was calm again, thanks to the efforts and reassurance of my mama, who in dealing with my papa's unusual and sudden fit of rage had forgotten her own, equally unusual fury—less sudden in her case because it had been growing slowly since her visit to the Espiricuetas.

She would bemoan this for the rest of her life: *Why did I let it happen? Why did I not tell him when there was a chance to fix it?*

Because the perfect course of action can only be seen in hindsight, which is why we fill life with so many *should haves*. In that moment, with the blindness that comes from living in the present, my papa's temper was fiercer than my mama's.

# 22

*Letters That Arrived*

When he walked into the little post office, Francisco Morales was surprised at the activity and the new faces. The former postmen were not there, though the new supervisor seemed familiar; later, he would learn it was the former boss of the garbage collectors. For the growing town, it had made sense to appoint a postmaster who knew its streets and neighborhoods, replacing the one who, after twenty years of service, had succumbed to the flu—perhaps from an infected letter or from the deadly sneeze that took Doña Graciela by surprise at the post office, giving her no time to take out her embroidered handkerchief.

After him, his subordinates had also met their deaths, one of them, Álvaro, for being the hero or the idiot—depending on who told the story—for coming out of hiding to heed Father Emigdio's call and write two deadly telegrams.

Now everyone was new to the business of handling and sorting the letters in a practical way. They knew the streets, but first they had to read the handwriting—whether fine or crude—of the sender. With the rush of missives that arrived or that had to be sent when the service was resumed, they felt as if they were drowning under a sea of paper. They did not know where to begin: all of a sudden, they had three months of good wishes, condolences, death notices, interrupted business, last-minute confessions, and everything else.

Adding to the novice postmen's confusion was the desperation of the local population to receive news from friends and relatives. In their attempt to complete their inventory of survivors, they milled around in the small space, demanding to be seen to immediately and as a matter of priority.

Francisco decided he would wait a day or two. He did not want to become entangled in the human knot that had formed there. When he turned to leave, the postmaster called out to him.

"Don Francisco! Don't go! We have your correspondence. Well, some. There might well be more letters in the pile. But we already have masses of letters for your address. Take 'em, for mercy's sake. Clear some space for us here. Hey, kid! Bring Don Francisco's!" Joaquín Bolaños said to his assistant, before turning back to Francisco. "They sent these to us from Monterrey in their very own bag, to save us the trouble."

The boy returned carrying a white calico sack. It looked like a pillowcase, but it was stuffed with rectangles of fine paper and tied up to protect its contents. The people there, who were waiting anxiously for perhaps four or five letters, stared at it in amazement: Who had so much to say? To whom? And why?

"All of these are mine?"

"Well, not exactly yours, no. But they're for *one o'* yours."

"One of my what?"

"One o' your daughters."

"I don't think so. There must be some mistake."

"Nope. We checked each one of 'em, and the writing's nice and clear. Eighty-nine letters, all of 'em for Señorita Carmen Morales Cortés. We reckon they're love letters."

Francisco took the sack before he could make out what the people were murmuring. He did not need to hear, because he could guess. *Love letters for Carmen Morales. Who are they from?* they would be thinking. And *Will she reply?*

He had parked his car near the square, ready to continue with the visits he had planned for the day, so he headed there, slung the sack into the automobile, and climbed in after it. The smell of paper and ink invaded his nose. He forgot about the remaining visits. Instead he went home, furious because his daughter's name was now making the rounds, and anxious to know who had devoted so many words to her.

Neither Carmen nor Consuelo were at home when he walked in. Nana Pola informed him that they had gone to see the Ardines twins and that Beatriz had not yet returned from her visit to Espiricueta.

Alone, he inspected the letters and confirmed they were indeed all for Carmen and all from the same sender: a certain Antonio Domínguez Garza. They had obviously been written over the course of three months, though he did not know whether the young man had taken them to the post office one by one or, knowing that they would not be sent until the public health crisis was over, had kept them in order to send them all together at a more recent date. At any rate, a fortune had been spent on postage stamps to send some letters that Francisco now wanted to burn without knowing anything more about them.

The fire was crackling. It would have been very easy to set them on fire, a few at a time, and watch them slowly burn. It would also have been easy to open them one at a time to read what this Antonio was saying to his daughter. But he did neither, as much as he felt the need. One never opens another person's letters or reads them without permission, he had to remind himself.

He would not open them out of good manners, but he did want to kick something. He would have liked to have had something solid to punt—Antonio Domínguez, for instance—but he had to make do with the pile of letters that had formed on the floor as he took them, one after the other, out of the sack.

With frenzied blows, he made the letters fly in all directions, scattering them around his study.

It was at this moment that Nana Pola arrived carrying his hot chocolate, as she did every winter evening if the master was at home. She reached the door but did not dare step through it. Accustomed to seeing him calm in any situation, Pola did not have the courage to speak. Without spilling a single drop of the chocolate she had so carefully prepared, she quickly closed the door and went back to the kitchen, hoping that Señora Beatriz would soon return, because somebody had to do something.

The sight of Francisco Morales lost in a violent dance all around the room, his face flushed, snorting from some indecipherable exertion, would be very difficult to forget or to explain.

She had to send for the señora immediately.

"Martín!"

Martín ran off down the path that led to Anselmo's house. With luck, he would bump into Señora Beatriz on her way back; if not, he would search for her farther on. Alarmed by the urgency with which Nana Pola had ordered him to fetch Señora Beatriz, Martín hoped that the señora had not continued on another path to visit someone else. He was no more than halfway when he found her, in the company of Simonopio. In the early winter half-light, from a distance, he noticed they were both walking fast, holding hands. Simonopio was keeping pace with his godmother. He seemed distressed, disturbed by something. In the minute it took to reach them, Martín tried to guess why they might be in such a state. Señora Beatriz also had a grim face and was holding Simonopio with her left hand and carrying a stick in her right. Martín could not believe that Simonopio had done anything to displease or enrage the señora, who was generally patient and even-tempered. What was happening? They had been back only a few hours, and already everything had been turned upside down. They had not even had time to enjoy their homecoming.

"Señora Beatriz! Pola says Don Francisco's having a fit!"

Beatriz did not ask any more questions. She dropped the stick and Simonopio's hand and lifted up her obstructive underskirts on each side to double her pace. She did not care if Martín caught a glimpse of her ankles. Her priority was to reach the house as quickly as possible. Pola received her there with the same announcement: Francisco was having a fit. In his study.

"Now all you can hear is silence—"

"And you left him like that? On his own?"

"I was afraid because of the puffing and snorting. I thought it best to close the door and send for you."

"Call for the doctor, Pola. Quickly. Go on."

At the closed door to the study, Beatriz hesitated. She was frightened of what might await her. Would she find him alive? And if he was alive, what did Pola think Beatriz could do for him if he had lost consciousness? She felt her eyes well up. She controlled herself and went in.

She had pictured him crumpled on the floor, but he was not—he was sitting in a reclining position in his armchair, his back to her. She approached him gingerly, slowly, until she could see him from the front. His eyes were closed, but he was frowning. He was sweaty but breathing. His face was red all over.

She had never seen a victim of a stroke before and had no idea how to help him. She did not know whether to move him so that he was lying down or to leave him where he was. Nor was she certain whether she should speak to him or shake him out of his stupor, or whether it was better if he came back to his senses of his own accord, in his own time. Should she give him water, or not? Give him ammonia to smell?

She ventured to touch his face. When he felt the contact, Francisco opened his eyes so suddenly that it made Beatriz jump.

"What?"

Wavering between shock and relief, Beatriz opted for indignation.

"I thought you were dying, that's what!"

"Of course I'm not. Who said that?" he asked without moving from where he was.

"Oh, forget it. It's clear you aren't. What's all this mess? What happened here?" In the respite that her relief at her husband being alive gave her, she noticed the envelopes scattered across the floor.

"The consensus in Linares is that they're all love letters for Carmen."

"Ah. There's an opinion on the matter in Linares?"

"What do you think? Eighty-nine letters don't go unnoticed, Beatriz."

"That many?" She began picking them up and making tidy piles while Francisco observed her without moving. They were a little battered, but none were open, and it appeared that none had been destroyed. They were all from Antonio Domínguez.

Francisco noted that Beatriz did not seem surprised.

"You already knew that Carmen had a sweetheart in Monterrey?"

"I only found out a few days ago."

She told him what she knew about their daughter's romance and about the amorous suitor's family and social pedigree.

"I was going to tell you very soon; it wasn't a secret. I was just putting it off, that's all. Until the right moment. Now we'll have to speak to her about making a serious commitment."

"Not in his dreams! She will not marry so young. Anyway, who is he? He could be a fortune hunter, a libertine, a seducer of young ladies—"

"No! He's a young man from a good family, like I said. And I don't think he would dare play games with someone like Carmen. But he's not from Linares: if they marry, they'll live in Monterrey. Just imagine. What would we do? How often would we see her? And of course, they must not marry immediately: Carmen must finish school and wait at least a year for the mourning."

"A year for each death would be better."

"I don't think so. At that rate, we'd never be grandparents. And I do want to be a grandmother, even if our grandchildren end up living far away. Just not so soon. In any case, we need time to come to terms with the idea that we could be grandparents, that we're old, don't you think? The news that I had a daughter with marital intentions hit me like a bucket of cold water, to be honest. I was only just getting used to this phase of our life, and now we're entering another, the same one my mama's in. And it has been hard: growing old isn't easy."

"First we will have to see whether we like the suitor before there can be any wedding. The grandchildren will come later. It's a long way off."

"Well, if I grow old, that means you'll be growing old, too, you should know."

"I'll never grow old, and if I don't, then I won't let you either," he said to her, pulling her onto his lap.

That was how Carmen found them when she came crashing into the room, brimming with joy.

"Is it true a lot of letters came for me?"

"Who told you?"

"They told me in town, on the way home. First Doña Eufemia told me that she saw that there were three sackfuls. Then other people. They all wanted to know who they're from."

"Doña Eufemia . . . I told you all of Linares would know about the famous letters, Beatriz. One sack. There was just one sack. And you, Carmen: I'd like you to make it clear to this Antonio that I do not like the fact that, thanks to him, you're the talk of the town. And if you are going to read the letters, afterward you will pass them all on to your mother so she can check them. His tone and his intentions had better be the right ones. And if you reply, you must also read your reply to your mother, to avoid any misunderstandings or more gossip. If that's not to your liking, we can burn them right here and forget about the whole business."

Carmen quickly agreed but took her time sorting the letters by date before opening the first one.

Nana Pola plucked up the courage to come in to announce the doctor's arrival.

"How embarrassing," Beatriz said. "I had him come for nothing! I thought you'd had a stroke. I'll tell him it was a misunderstanding, so that he can go."

"No, tell him to come in. With all the thrashing around, I injured my back. I can't move," he admitted.

Beatriz looked at him closely.

"Didn't you just promise me you'd never get old?"

# 23

*Verses That Win Hearts*

While her father recovered from his fit with the help of aspirin and hot-water poultices, Carmen read her letters out loud in the presence of her mother, who was forced to admit that, not only did they show the respect due to a young lady of good family, they also expressed a devotion that seemed sincere, passionate, and at all times well mannered. In the first few letters, Antonio made Carmen promises and asked for promises in return. He asked for her consent to write to her parents, to obtain their permission to begin the courtship. In the most recent letters, he continued to make promises, but in his anguish at the prolonged absence and silence of his sweetheart, his hope for a future together was replaced by his fear that Carmen no longer graced the world of the living with her presence.

He transcribed songs for her and clumsily translated some of the classic poems of English literature into Spanish. He was also brave enough to include some of his own imperfect but impassioned pieces. Beatriz did not know whether Carmen noticed the difference, but she liked Antonio's originals the most—if not for their quality, then for the devotion they expressed. In spite of her surprise at Carmen's new romance and her firm belief that her daughter was still too young for it, Beatriz was deeply moved by the strength of feeling that her daughter had elicited in the young man. If somebody was going to love her, a mother could hope only that her daughter would be loved well and for the rest of her life. And that was how, with his verses and declarations—and with the good intention of wanting to ask her permission—Antonio Domínguez won the heart of the woman who would become his mother-in-law. With each page, Beatriz cared less about their initial obstacles and objections. She did not know her future son-in-law, but she hoped to meet him, to learn more about him. She wanted to see the love and admiration that he felt for her daughter in his eyes. The war would end, and it would become easier to visit them in Monterrey when they married. They would find a way to ensure that the grandchildren did not miss their grandparents, inviting them to visit often.

The young man had not yet mentioned dates, just promises, and while there was no reason to fear Carmen would threaten to marry before she was sixteen, Beatriz began to think that her firm conviction that her daughter must wait until she was seventeen could soften if the young lovers decided to marry sooner.

If one thing had been beaten into Beatriz in the years of war and months of infection and death, it was that life offered no guarantees, and regardless of how many plans had been made, events outside of one's control could easily spoil them. From the first line Carmen read from Antonio Domínguez's letters, the hard shell of cynicism that had formed around Beatriz had begun to soften. Nothing would make her change her mind: she still thought that life did not make promises. For her, that was a simple fact. But she had based her decisions on this precept for a long time. And now she wanted to think that, while life did not make promises, sometimes it offered opportunities. Beatriz recognized that Carmen had a chance to live and to give life, to start afresh, with new enthusiasm and faith in the future.

She therefore concluded that it did not matter whether Carmen married at sixteen or seventeen: the important thing was to seize the opportunity and not let it go. She realized with nostalgia that they were leaving behind the childish games of "Who will I marry?" that a mother and daughter play, a question to which there was never a concrete answer, until there was. And now there was. And she wanted to say to her daughter, *Here he is; it's time; this is what life is offering you. Don't let it go.*

With each paragraph that they read, Beatriz Morales de Cortés gradually turned her back on past sorrows, hardships, and complaints, and began to look with relish at future opportunities. For everyone. For Carmen—she decided to believe—there would be more joy than suffering. And what more could a mother want for her daughter?

For the first time in a long while, she felt that the deaths, disease, and war were not the end; life went on, and at times like this, she took pleasure in it. Naturally, eighty-nine letters cannot be read with due care in one sitting. They stopped to have dinner and later again for another bite to eat. On her mother's insistence, Carmen's reply had to wait until the next day. *Who knows what silly things you might say at this time of night?*

"And the same goes for me. Time for bed."

The next day, they had Martín take Carmen's letter to the post office. With the appropriate discretion, it contained the necessary information: *I am alive; I received your letters; I don't know when I will return; my parents have given me permission to be your fiancée.* Martín left with the letter but returned with nine more, though just one was from Antonio Domínguez. The rest, to the Morales family's surprise, were also professions of love for Carmen, written by young men of Linares who, hearing about the large shipment of letters from Monterrey the day before, had seen the door open to courting her.

The replies to them were kind but emphatic: *Thank you, I am spoken for.* Even so, not all of them desisted from their attempts: years later, letters that would never receive a response continued to arrive, and Beatriz would keep them forever. Her daughter was engaged, but in a world with so little good news, why not appreciate young love—whoever it came from—which wanted only to let itself be known?

# 24

## *Life That Goes On*

My sister Carmen would not marry immediately. After much discussion, my parents decided that my sisters must return to the Sagrado Corazón, in spite of the romance. The violence and pillage of the war hadn't abated, even after three months of the influenza epidemic. The levy remained a real danger for the men, and women could also disappear in an instant and never return. I suppose all of this was worse in other states, but in Nuevo León, we were not exempt from it. My parents thought that Carmen and Consuelo were at greater risk from the possibility of bandoleros attacking Linares than they were boarding in the protection of the nuns. Carmen's suitor would have to wait.

But it wouldn't be easy for them to support my sister in their courtship. Determined that neither of their daughters would marry a man they did not know well, they had to think of a strategy to enable the sweethearts to see more of each other—with the utmost propriety, of course. It would not be enough just to allow them to leave the boarding school from time to time with their friend, the young man's cousin. Indeed, they were afraid it would be frowned upon that a young woman of good family should see her fiancé in the absence of her parents.

So, my papa, who had already devoted a great deal of thought to fast-developing Monterrey as an opportunity to leave, as a respite from the crossfire of the war—and from the stagnation and uncertainty of the countryside—announced to my mama a few days after learning of the courtship that, protest as she might, it was time to build or buy a house in Monterrey.

"And no, it's not to go live there. I know you don't want to. It's to be closer to the girls. That way Carmen can see Antonio under your supervision, because one does not marry blind. And anyway, it's a good investment."

His final point was, perhaps, mostly for his ancestors' ears.

"But the tractor you need, the peons' houses, the electrics . . ."

"We have savings, and if they're not for something like this, what are they for? I've already used some to buy land there, and look: nothing happened."

With my mama concerned about the changes that were about to happen, my papa finally informed her, without much fuss, about the properties he had purchased. When there was no explosive response on my mama's part, to avoid tempting fate—to distract her—he continued explaining the plan.

My sisters could stay in the house when my mama was in the city, and they would join the Monterrey Social Club so they could go to the dances.

My sisters liked the idea. The problem was that my mama had not returned to Monterrey since my grandfather was executed. It was not the city she objected to: it was the journey. She was worried about the dangers of traveling by train. When my papa told her he would send her in the car, though it would take longer, she was no less afraid. Train or car, it made no difference. My papa could hardly criticize her for her fears, for they were well founded. He couldn't promise her that nothing would happen, that there was no danger, just as he couldn't promise her that she would be safe if she remained in Linares.

My sisters were very beautiful, especially Carmen, and not by chance: they inherited it from my mama, who, despite having a daughter of marrying age, was very well preserved. My papa knew that the risk of her being snatched while in transit was almost as high as it was for my sisters. And in order to stay as close as possible, watching over her since the incident that made them decide to send my sisters to board in Monterrey, he had not given the Tamaulipas ranches the attention they needed. Carmen's engagement opened up the possibility of the family living in safety in a new home in Monterrey, at least while he was away on his ranches.

Though my mother swore—and would fulfill her oath—to never spend more than a week away from her home by my papa's side, they quickly bought a house on Calle Zaragoza, at the time the best location for families of means. It was of modest size but extremely modern: fully electrified, with running water in the kitchen and an indoor bathroom. At first this had seemed extravagant to Beatriz, but she grew accustomed to it almost immediately.

That was how Carmen and Antonio, despite both of them being in mourning for a year—for in Monterrey there had also been many deaths from the Spanish flu—were able to conduct a quite conventional courtship when my mama was in the city. They danced at the Monterrey Social Club; they dined at home with my mama. And when my papa came to visit, the fiancé's parents would invite them to some family event. When my sister returned to boarding school in my mama's absence, the couple wrote to each other twice a day, missing one another and impatiently planning the event that would bring their lives together in the winter of 1920.

As it turned out, they didn't marry until the winter of 1921, though everything had been ready for the wedding for a full year. What happened—and my parents would later point out the irony of initially worrying so much about the young age of their enamored daughter—was that Señora Domínguez, Antonio's mother, died of acute hepatitis in October 1920, shortly after the couple notified the

Church of their engagement in August of that year. Antonio, obliged to remain in mourning for at least a year, postponed the wedding.

"Look, Francisco. You must promise me something," my mama said to my papa during their son-in-law's year of mourning. "If I die this year, don't even think about postponing Carmen and Antonio's wedding. If we carry on like this, their whole life could pass them by with all this death. Life waits for no one, and death takes us all. Let them marry, and that's that. Something discreet, if they want. Without much celebration. Honestly, it would offend me if it weren't discreet; I would be more offended if they grew old before marrying because of my imprudence."

"Would flowers be allowed in this context?" asked my papa and, after receiving the pinch that he deserved, added, "Don't even say it; you've never been imprudent in your life. And don't even think about starting now."

# 25

## *The Coyote That's Coming*

The day that Simonopio accompanied Beatriz Morales de Cortés to offer her condolences to the Espiricueta family was the day when he took refuge again in his nana's bed.

Simonopio had slept peacefully in Reja and Pola's bedroom all his life, first in a Moses basket and then in a crib. When he was four, they urgently made him a bed.

His godmother had walked in one night, looking for Nana Pola, and saw him lying in his crib, ready to sleep curled up in a ball. She approached to stroke his brow and tuck him in, but then stopped.

"Just look at you, Simonopio! When did you grow so much?" He, of course, offered no reply. "You don't fit anymore. If you keep sleeping here, you'll grow all rolled up like a snail."

Two days later, Simonopio found a large bed with no rails in place of his crib.

He did not want to turn into a snail, and he liked the idea of stretching his legs, but he would miss the bars that kept him inside, that protected him. He knew he would be unable control his movements in order to keep away from the edge. The first night, he could not sleep. After that, he slept but would wake suddenly, startled by the feeling in his stomach of falling into a void. Simonopio was not afraid of hitting the ground; he was afraid of the void. Of falling forever.

In the following months, he developed the habit of sneaking with blanket and pillow into his nana Reja's bed, where he fell fast asleep between his protector's warm body and the wall.

Reja, who did not sleep, noticed when the boy climbed in with her, trying not to disturb her, afraid perhaps that she would stop him and send him back to his own bed. But she never did. She did not care if the bed ejected her before her customary time in the mornings, stiffer than usual and groaning a little as she moved and got up, which she had never done before. She was not used to having someone so close, whether in the day or night, but if she was not there to offer comfort to her boy, what purpose did she have in life?

Simonopio was an active child, even when he slept. Sometimes Reja thought he followed his bees in his sleep, just as he did when he was awake: he moved his legs as if running and his arms as if flying. He also preferred to be closer to his nana's tough, woody skin than to the hard, unyielding wall. As the night wore on, Simonopio gradually conquered more and more territory of the shared bed, leaving her with little space to rest—insufficiently and poorly—on the edge of the cliff. Reja was not scared of the void; she was scared of the hard floor. She was afraid that, when she hit it, her bones would shatter like glass.

Nana Pola could not help but notice so much unusual movement in their bedroom. When months went by and the situation did not improve, she spoke to Simonopio one night, as she tucked him in.

"You can't go to sleep in your nana Reja's bed anymore; she's very old and aches all over. I don't know what you're frightened of, Simonopio, but you're a big boy now. You're safe here. I bless this room every night. No witches or ghosts can come in here. No monsters can fit under your bed, either, because it's very low and they're very big, as they say. And we don't have any dolls that wake up and walk around at night, because we sent them all off to the storehouse. Now sleep tight."

This list of beings that he should fear would never have occurred to Simonopio, but if the room was blessed every night, that was enough to reassure him. He was not afraid of them. What continued to terrify him was falling and—asleep—never finding his way to the floor. Falling and falling without end and never waking up. And he did not believe any blessing would protect him from that. But Nana Pola was right: he was a big enough boy now to understand that, though he needed his nana's protection at night, she was too old to give it to him without certain consequences. He had to be brave.

He was brave and he was inventive, so finding himself denied the protection of his nana's body, he dragged a chair to the edge of his bed. It was not the complete enclosure that his crib had offered, but the high backrest served the purpose of tricking his sleepy eyes in the darkness. It took him several more weeks to achieve peaceful sleep once more, but he never bothered Nana Reja again. One day he forgot to push the chair against his bed when it was time to sleep, and gradually he forgot the fear that had prevented him from resting properly. And in time he completely forgot that he had once needed to have Nana Reja near him in order to sleep.

Nevertheless, on the day when Beatriz let go of his hand to run off ahead of Martín, the bird of ill omen, Simonopio had stopped there, alone, rooted to the spot in the middle of the path. He was not afraid for his godfather Francisco's health: he knew that something had happened to upset him and nothing more. Frozen there, Simonopio was afraid that he was falling, falling without end, that he would never find the ground. Because of his recklessness—because he had gone where he should not have gone—he was sure that he had set in motion his story with the coyote, and he did not know what to do to remedy it.

Because sitting on his rock behind the bush, while he waited patiently for his godmother to finish her visit, he had heard a noise that alerted him just in time to turn around and see the man approaching fast with a stick, ready to strike him. He managed to avoid the first blow by reacting nimbly, but he knew he would not be able to dodge it forever: he could read in Espiricueta's eyes that he would not stop until he had killed him.

Only Beatriz's scream stopped the man—just. She approached, furious, armed only with a ragdoll. Simonopio recognized it as the doll his godmother had made for the Espiricueta girl, the one with the silent eyes. She reached them with the look and sense of purpose of a bee defending its swarm. Simonopio was glad to have her by his side.

"Whatever is the matter with you? How dare you?"

Halting the blow did not mean that Espiricueta had contained his rage or put down his stick. Beatriz stood between Simonopio and his attacker.

"What I wanna know," Espiricueta snapped back, "is what this possessed wretch is doing at my house. How many times's he been here to bring us bad luck?"

"Why would you think he would do that?"

"My wife died on me. Then my children."

"And that's why I came: to offer my condolences," said Beatriz, trying to calm herself and rediscover the pity she had felt for this man who had lost so much.

"What good will they do me? Go give 'em to someone who has a use for 'em. Far as I'm concerned, this one killed my family. I don't want no condolences or pity. I want the last two kids he left alive to live. I want the ones he took given back, like that fella what came back from the grave."

"Anselmo. I understand your grief and your desperation, but how can you think that Simonopio is to blame in any way? It was a disease that attacked the entire world!"

"I told you nothin' but misery'd befall us. My field's never borne what the others have since he arrived, and then my family dies on me like no one else's does. Why only me?"

"A great many people died, Anselmo. All over the world."

"That might be, but no one died on you."

"Aunts, relatives, friends. And your family, Anselmo."

"No one."

They were not going to get anywhere like this, so Beatriz changed the subject and adjusted her tone to a more conciliatory one.

"Well, I brought you some things for your little girl. If she needs anything else, let us know. If you want, we can enroll her at school so—"

"No. All they do there is teach 'em to be servants, and she won't be nobody's servant. Know what I need? I need you to take your charity to someone who wants it. There ain't nothing we want from you. Or do you think a doll's going to bring my girl's mama back? Take your boy and tell him to never set foot on my land again, 'cause next time, I'll kill him."

The threat made Beatriz hold her breath and lose the color in her face. She let out the air little by little. Simonopio noticed that the hand that still held his wrist was trembling, but her voice was firm.

"And I warn you that if you go anywhere near him, things will go very badly for you. You'd better not so much as look at him. Is that clear? And let me tell you one thing: this land is not and never will be yours."

Beatriz did not wait for a reply. She seized Simonopio by the fore-arm and sped off with him without looking back. She gripped him in one hand, feeling him take to the air behind her like the ragdoll that she still held in her other. Her breathing had not returned to normal, and Simonopio thought that not even Espiricueta would dare challenge her when such bravery and such fury was expressed in her face. As the path widened, Beatriz remembered the doll she had devoted so much time to making, thinking of Margarita Espiricueta. Without a second thought, she cast it into the undergrowth so that it would slowly rot, like any of the scarce plants and animals that inhabited that barren land. Then she found a strong stick with which to replace it in her empty hand.

"Don't worry, Simonopio. Everything's fine. He would never dare," she repeated to him every so often to reassure him, albeit without slowing down and without letting go of the stick.

They encountered no danger on the path—just Martín with his news of Francisco Morales's supposed fit. And there Simonopio remained, frozen to the spot in the middle of the icy wilds, with no godmother or bees, his only company a discarded piece of wood that he knew would be useless should he have to defend himself in the story that, he was certain, had begun that day.

He could not regain his breath, and it was not from the effort of their trek but from fear.

No. His story would not end in a stick fight, nor would it end that day; of that much he was sure. But he still did not know when, which was why he was terrified: he felt as if he were falling endlessly, awake but with no control, unable to find his balance again on the firm ground of certainty. Then he remembered the warmth of his nana protecting him from the void, and he ran to find her.

# 26

## *This Land Is Not and Never Will Be*

yours. Never. Not. Yours. Not yours.

Anselmo's chance to thrash the little demon had been brusquely interrupted by the hag. But what could he do? Ignore the boss's wife? Kill the boy in front of her? He would have liked to, but he was not stupid. Because then what?

So he had contained himself—though he had not stopped wanting to do it—but stood his ground to defend his territory until the woman left with her demon.

Still blinded by rage, it was some time before he remembered that he was still holding his arm aloft and gripping a stick in his hand, but when he saw his daughter come out of the house, looking for her absent benefactor with a sparkle in her eyes that he had never seen before, perhaps from the excitement of putting on the new skirt and blouse the Morales woman had given her, he felt the weight of the cane again and the rough texture of the thin edge that dug into his callused hands.

His urge to strike out revived, he went for her for accepting the charity and gifts that were no doubt the result of the guilt felt by those who have everything.

He beat her to make her take off the new clothes, right there outside, before making her go back into the house and heat up the comal. When it was hot, he set her to cooking chilies. Before he could feel the sting of the hot and spicy smoke of the toasted chilies in his lungs or eyes, Anselmo Espiricueta left the house, closing the door and shutters tight; and there he left her, crying, pleading, burning inside from the chilied air, just as his parents had punished him whenever he misbehaved.

Espiricueta went out into the icy elements, convinced that with his punishment he would banish any inclination to be poor and lowly from his daughter's soul.

He saw the skirt and blouse lying where they had fallen and picked them up. He headed into the hills along the path that the meddling hag had taken. When he reached the point where it widened, satisfied that he was far enough from the house, he threw them in the undergrowth so that they would slowly rot, like any of the scarce plants and animals that inhabited that barren land.

"My land."

His land.

# 27

## The Roof That Breathes

Simonopio spent every remaining night of that icy winter taking refuge in his nana Reja's warm bed.

When he heard her arrive at night to lie down, he would climb into the bed after her, using—without knowing it—the same tactic he had perfected at the age of four: carrying a pillow and blanket and moving with as much stealth as possible, for fear of being turned away. It took him a long time to fall asleep, both due to the narrowness of the bed and to the thoughts that insisted on going around and around in his head, trying to find a way out of the predicament he had gotten himself into. In the end he slept, because his child's body demanded it and his mind gave in.

Nana Reja remained silent, as ever, saying nothing and asking nothing: not *What's the matter?* nor *Why are you so frightened?* nor even *There's nothing to be afraid of.* Simonopio suspected that she knew, that she sensed something monumental was happening to him, and that was why she never dared tell him to stop being afraid or that there was nothing to fear. She lay awake, motionless, as Simonopio knew she always did at night in her bed, even without the Simonopio-shaped lump that visited her without asking permission. When he opened his eyes with the first light of the morning, the bed was cold. His nana was no longer there: she had gone back to her eternal place, sitting on her rocking chair under the shelter of the shed's overhanging roof.

Simonopio had heard his godmother Beatriz say that, especially when it was cold, Nana Reja should no longer be allowed to spend her time keeping guard out in the elements. That an elderly woman her age could die from exposure. But there was no persuading the little old lady made of wood. She did not care about the changes in weather or the elements. All that seemed to matter to her was not leaving her post as a deaf, mute, and blind lookout. When Beatriz asked Martín or Nana Pola to lift her up and carry her to the warm kitchen, Nana Reja reacted with a forcefulness that could hardly be misinterpreted: she shook her stick vigorously, managing to strike Martín—who was not quick enough to escape—on his legs. As for Pola, Reja would not dare hit her for any reason, but nothing stopped her from waving her stick in a wide arc when she sensed Pola was close.

Nothing and nobody would convince her to change the routine she had followed for decades.

Not even Simonopio, who also worried about her.

He was eight: he was not a baby anymore. He knew that he disturbed her at night, but the experience on Espiricueta's land had shaken him, and for the time being, he needed to feel protected, at least while he was in the unconscious state of deep sleep.

He spent the days rebuilding his courage. Since the cold refused to go away, his bees came out very little, and when they did, they remained close to the large structure with which they had colonized the shed roof. They came out to exercise their wings and—perhaps—their instinct a little, but not all of them did so. Or at least, not all at the same time.

Simonopio did not want to go anywhere without them. Not for now. He had wandered near the house for days, surprising everyone with his constant presence, because with his continuous expeditions into the wilds, his appearances had been increasingly rare.

Before everyone in the household began to quiz him about his well-being, when he knew he would not even be able to offer a response, it occurred to him that he could help his nana so they stopped bothering her with all their worrying and, of course, so she would not be cold. Simonopio suspected she did not feel the cold on her hardened skin, but perhaps in her ancient insides she did, without realizing it. He knew it was not time for Nana Reja to die, but he also knew certain situations could easily change because of a stubborn refusal to protect oneself.

Since it was imperative that Nana Reja not be cold in the day, so that she lived for as long as she was meant to, Simonopio lit a fire for her, which eased everyone's concern for the little old lady and for him. Keeping a fire going—while making sure the smoke did not reach his bees in their hive—was a nonstop task: Simonopio fed the fire with wood all day, every day, until the weather turned. The bees came out of their cozy enclosure without difficulty, and he felt strong enough to stray from the house again.

Because, since the night when he returned to his nana's bed or the first day he spent sitting at her feet, watching over her and keeping her warm, Simonopio had known that he could allow himself only a short break. That soon he would need to go out into the world again to prepare himself, before the world—the violent one—came looking for him. But in those days, when they all praised him for being so attentive and protective of Nana Reja's well-being, without imagining that he was also looking out for his own, he could not shake off the desire for the cold to last a little longer. For the truce to continue for just another short while. At the same time, he was aware that desire did not come into such matters: the cold would disappear when it had to disappear, and when it did, his period of artificial serenity would end, and he would have to face up to the consequences of his grave error.

When he thought of this, sitting to one side of a motionless Nana Reja, he was besieged by fear, like the cloud of smoke from the fires he lit himself. Because the end of winter was the time limit he had given to his fear and paralysis. To his sleeping all warm and safe beside his nana. To the task that anyone could do of endlessly adding log after log to the fire. Simonopio decided that, before the final bee came out to enjoy the freedom of spring, before they all left together on their epic journey, he would take his pillow and fold up his blanket. He would leave behind his nana's warmth and protection. He would also leave behind Nana Pola's nocturnal blessings against monsters, animals, dolls, and everything else. He would transport his bed with or without help. He would clean Nana Reja's shed, which nobody used as a storehouse anymore because of the bees, and move in there to sleep, to wake up, to grow, to become strong.

At first, Francisco and Beatriz Morales were against Simonopio sleeping in such isolation and rustic conditions. They also argued—with good reason—that the shed had been built as a storage space. That it was not meant to be anybody's sleeping quarters, much less the bedroom of a dear child they would have taken to sleep in the main house on the day of his arrival had Nana Reja only allowed them to, without caring if Consuelo had a tantrum because of the strange and ugly baby.

Every time Simonopio moved his bed and placed it in front of the shed, Beatriz or Francisco sent someone to return it to the house.

"No, Simonopio. You can't sleep there. If you don't want to sleep with the nanas anymore, come to the house with us."

They continued to explain to him how the bees had gradually taken possession of the rafters of Nana Reja's shed—because they had not dealt with the problem in time, they admitted—and that now it was too late: for years, nobody had been brave enough to store tools or anything else in the storehouse.

"How're you going to sleep there, Simonopio?"

As they asked him the question, in spite of the boy's expected silence, the answer—clear, logical—came to them by itself. And if they had not been persuaded by the fact that there was no one better for that space than Simonopio, who was rarely seen without his bees, they would have witnessed Nana Reja—who nobody ever saw move, speak, or show any interest—attempting to remove her beloved boy's bed from their shared bedroom herself.

They laid down some rules, of course. First, that before moving there, Simonopio must clean the shed. And second, that he allow them to build an adjoining bathroom and make a window to improve the ventilation and natural light in the space. For the time being.

Simonopio gladly agreed: he did not want to put his bed where the nocturnal dolls that Nana Pola had sent to some unspecified storeroom might have been left and forgotten. He would do the clearing out.

The window would be made whenever it was made, but he wanted to move in right away. Before he could lose his determination, he went straight to the shed to try to open the door. Rusted and swollen from neglect and years of disuse, the door would not budge. Simonopio could not manage it alone and had to persuade Martín to pluck up the courage to help him.

"All right, Simonopio; if I'm with you, I suppose they won't attack me."

His bees had never attacked anyone, with or without him, but he had no means to explain that to Martín. And, given what was coming in the future, he thought with some regret that it was convenient for people to have that misperception: *Don't go near Simonopio's shed, or you'll get stung to death by a bee or a thousand.*

He had spent much of his life sitting in the shade of the protruding roof, keeping Nana Reja company, learning the lessons of life that the wind and the bees taught him. But that day, having repaired the door, Simonopio went inside the shed for the first time.

It was true that it needed a window, not just because of the darkness but also to get rid of the stuffy smell that had built up over the years. The floor was firm, covered in the dust that even the swollen door had been unable to keep out, and in two corners, a buildup of honey that the bees had allowed to escape had crystallized over the years.

None of it bothered him. He would leave the door open all day and let the fresh aroma of wild herbs clean the stagnant air imbued with the smell of men returning from work, oil for the plow, spilled kerosene, broken plant pots, rotten rope, old sacks both empty and filled with earth, scaffold boards, and rusty pieces of metal. To the rhythm of the rocking chair's creak outside, where Nana Reja looked out, as ever, to the road and the hills, he dragged everything from the shed.

He left the stalactites and stalagmites of soft, crystalized amber honey intact in their corners. They belonged there.

On the last shelf was something that, at first glance in the half-light of the shed, Simonopio thought was a piece of canvas. On closer inspection, he noticed the canvas covered something: an enormous box. He could not move it by himself.

When he finally persuaded Martín to help again, Simonopio was surprised at the man's alarm when he saw the box, and at first, he did not understand why he was so afraid. It seemed a very fine box to him, though he had not opened it. Then he hesitated. What if it was where Nana Pola had stored the nocturnal dolls? It was not nighttime, but it was quite dark inside the shed. He was afraid the conditions were conducive to the dolls coming to life, to them coming out to scare him.

Simonopio ran out behind Martín, frightened by the product of his imagination.

After regaining his breath and composure, Simonopio pulled on Martín's sleeve to insist they go back in to finish the job. They also managed to recruit Leocadio for the task. Between the three of them, they brought the heavy box out into the daylight after eight years of being left forgotten in total darkness. Reluctantly, Leocadio and Martín recalled the day when they themselves had very carefully stored it in the shed on the instruction of the lady of the house.

They broke out in goose bumps.

To Simonopio, on the other hand, the box seemed very beautiful. He thought that, if nobody needed it, perhaps they would allow him to store some things in it—provided the dolls were not in there. If they were, he would have to find them another prison.

That was the first test of his courage: to open it and then evict its possible inhabitants. When, with resolve, he tried to lift the lid, Martín stopped him.

"Don't. It's for a dead body. If we open it, it might want us to fill it."

Martín said nothing more on the subject to the boy: in a way, he associated the kid's arrival in the world with that box, and he did not think it would be a good anecdote to relay. He covered the box and then asked Leocadio to help him hide it again in the depths of another storehouse, *where no one'll see it, compadre, just in case.*

Simonopio knew about death. He saw it often in his stories about what would happen and in some that had already happened. But he had never seen a dead person's box. He did not want it. And Martín was right not to want it, either: that box was for neither one of them.

He spent the rest of the day cleaning. That night, once he was tired but settled in, with his bed made and in position, his godmother Beatriz arrived to inspect the results of his hard work.

"You're going to need a wardrobe and a chair, at least. And you need a window as soon as possible, Simonopio. What a dreadful smell! Are you sure you don't want to sleep in the house, at least until we finish the window and bathroom?"

He appreciated the offer but refused. His mind was set on that night being the first he would spend in his new sleeping quarters, though his godmother was right: with the door closed, the unpleasant smell of the years of airlessness had returned.

With the ventilation from the open door during the day and with the smell of the soaps and oils he had used, he had thought he had driven the stink away. But night had fallen, and he did not think it would be a good idea to sleep with the door ajar: it was his first time sleeping alone, even if Reja was still outside. He was afraid. Not knowing the words of Nana Pola's blessing, he had to invent his own, but he was unsure whether it would prove to be as effective as the one that had protected him every night until then. He did not know whether his words would persuade witches, assorted animals, monsters, or dolls to go elsewhere.

Or whether the words would protect him from the coyote.

After he closed the door very carefully, the bad smells invaded his nose again. He thought it was possible that, after so many years living in one place, they were reluctant to move, to be lost in the open air until their essence was gone. Now, in self-defense, they were clinging to the porous plaster on the walls and the old timber beams of the roof, and if Simonopio did not resolve it soon, it would not be long before they found his sheets, pillow, and mattress to be the ideal vessels in which to prolong their existence in the space where they had been born.

Exhausted, lying on the bed that still smelled clean—but unable to sleep because, in the dark, one's nose sharpens and something that smells bad begins to smell worse—Simonopio concentrated on breaking up the invasive stench. Before long, he was able to make out the individual smells. One by one, he tamed them with his nose in order to ignore them, until he came to the last one—one that, until then, all the other smells in concert had prevented him from detecting: the sweet scent of the enormous honeycomb his bees had built between the roof beams.

Now he felt comforted, because this was the smell that belonged to him. The one that he carried on his skin. The bees were glad of his presence and welcomed him, because he belonged there, too, with them, just like the crystalized honey formations.

For the time being, he escaped the fear he had been filled with. When he closed his eyes and opened not just his nose but also his ears, when he heard the vibration his bees gave off through the ceiling that covered and protected him, he reckoned he had made the right decision to take shelter there.

With his bees for company, he escaped the lingering memory of Espiricueta, the coyote in his story. Of Espiricueta with his stick, with his unfounded grudge, his threats, his dying land. Simonopio knew he would have time to grow and build strength for what would happen between them, and sleeping here was a good start. The next day, he would renew his efforts to follow his bees to the end of their daily journey, because it was important—he knew—that he understood what they searched for and what they would find before turning around to return home before nightfall. He did not know when he would do it, but he challenged himself to go a little farther each day. Guided by his bees, he would reach the end of the road.

Little by little, he forgot his doubts about how effective his blessing had been, because what better blessing could there be than to be under the protection of his bees?

And so, sleeping and growing under a living roof that gradually changed its rhythm and breathing to match his—that was how Simonopio would conquer his fear.

# 28

## *A Journey of Thorns*

Simonopio began his travels the next day, after resting better than he had managed in months: he would go in search of the treasure that awaited his bees every day of spring.

He knew that he would not find it right away, that it would take him a while to reach it, and that it would require a great deal of effort, for the strength and daring needed for such a journey would not be gained from one day to the next or just by wanting it.

The nearby paths he had explored over time had grown easier, but now he would have to go much farther, discover new trails and places. Make new paths.

What's more, after three months without exploring the hills as he normally did, he paid dearly for the lost time.

For the bees' path was not the path of men: while Simonopio took tentative steps, they flew over the thickets and thorns, without caring that there was no open road. The hollows between the sierras were no problem whatsoever for them; the slopes did not tire them; and the canyons— always difficult to negotiate for a two-legged animal like Simonopio— were no obstacle. If it rained on the way, they shook off the water. If the cold caught them unawares before they returned, they knew that, at the end of the day, they would be back in the warmth of their honeycomb, full of energy from their spring honey. They were never afraid, and nothing deterred them from their goal. Only death would stop them, and they did not mind dying in the act of completing their daily mission.

They had to complete the journey in one day, so they had no time to wait for him.

Simonopio, restricted by his human state and his young age, had to find or make passable trails, which slowed his progress. He also tired; he tripped, and when he fell, he cut his knees or hands. The rain soaked his clothes. The cold, when it came, seeped into his bones. The intense heat of summer and thirst made him stumble. The thorns in the undergrowth caught him, and the stones did their utmost to twist his ankles.

The fear that struck him at the sudden realization that darkness was coming and he was far from home made him turn around more than once and return exhausted, defeated, giving Nana Reja explanations with his eyes. She opened her eyes for him, and with them she said: *Keep going.* Then she closed them again. She had said all she needed to say to him. And the next morning, she said goodbye again with nothing but the movement of her rocking chair.

Little by little, his excursions that spring, summer, and autumn made his feet nimble again; he grew faster, his sense of direction sharpened, and his self-confidence returned and increased. With his daily, constant exercise, he also strengthened his bond with the bees. In doing so—step by step, hour by hour, and day by day—he shook off the fear just like they shook off the raindrops. And he felt stronger.

He knew that he still had time and that time would work in his favor: if he did not manage to complete the journey that spring or summer, he would do so the next or the next. In the end, he would do it.

The bees had been patient with him. They had waited for years for him to be ready to complete the journey with them. At the end of the road, something important awaited him, something they had always tried to share with him, to make him understand.

Soon he would see it. Soon he would know.

# 29

*The Train Passes through Alta and So Does Simonopio*

My mama immediately regretted allowing Simonopio to have his own space, because he started vanishing into the hills for ever-longer periods, until one night he returned neither to his bath nor his dinner nor his bed.

Alarmed, my parents summoned the peons for a nocturnal search, which proved fruitless: they spent hours looking for him on the road to La Florida, hoping that Simonopio had reached the estate before night fell.

My papa returned that night frustrated and worried. There was no trace of Simonopio anywhere.

"No sign of him."

That night, my parents did not sleep. There was nothing they could do except continue their usual routine: wash, change, turn out the light.

"We'll find him tomorrow, you'll see," my papa said to my mama in a comforting tone.

My mama, with the pessimism that comes only when the night stretches out without end, pictured Simonopio at the bottom of a canyon, unable to move, his legs broken, frightened, and surrounded by bears and pumas. Each time she closed her eyes, she saw the boy they loved so much utterly forlorn, facing a night that would undoubtedly seem more eternal to him than it did to her. Eventually, she stopped pretending to rest and went to the kitchen to make coffee. She turned on every light in the house and opened the shutters and curtains: if Simonopio was lost, he would see the lights in the distance and find his way home.

My papa, who got up to keep her company with the excuse that he felt like some coffee—a complete lie, because nobody knew better than he how bad my mama's coffee was—knew that Simonopio was not lost. That Simonopio would never get lost. He was sure of it because Simonopio had always managed to reach him without any help or guidance: if my papa was in the maize fields, Simonopio would find him there; if he was in the sugarcane fields, the boy would find him there as well.

Before that wakeful night, my papa had told my mama he'd been missing Simonopio since the boy's decision to watch over Nana Reja. Years ago, before Francisco grew accustomed to seeing him appear here and there, emerging from the bushes to meet him, he would ask, *Simonopio, what're you doing here? How did you know where I was?* But he soon stopped asking his stupid questions, because Simonopio would never answer him and because the boy's unexpected visits became part of his working day—the most pleasant part, perhaps.

However, after Simonopio stopped visiting him, after he decided to stay close to the house and then, later, to go on his solo expeditions, his absence was always a surprise. My papa did not comprehend why Simonopio, after ending his period of reclusion, had not come to find him.

That night, he was sure the boy had not gone astray. My papa had searched—as much as the darkness allowed—for any indications of where Simonopio might've gone, hunting along the path that led to the maize fields near Espiricueta's, where my papa had spent most of that day. He was certain the boy would've had no difficulty finding him. Simonopio always found the way.

No. That night, my papa hadn't been searching for a beloved child: he had been searching for his lifeless body. The lights shining in the house were a waste of electricity, but he didn't have the heart to take the hope or the good intentions away from my mama. Days later, he admitted to her that, when the boy didn't appear, he was overcome with the certainty that the boy had died, because what would prevent Simonopio from coming home for dinner and to sleep in his shed?

My papa filled his belly with my mama's coffee so he was awake and alert at sunrise, when he had summoned every able-bodied person to continue the search. At the agreed-upon time, he went to his bedroom to splash cold water on his face.

My mama had fallen asleep in the parlor, because not even for the sake of putting on a brave face had she been able to continue drinking the poor imitation of coffee she had prepared. I think it would have been better had she spent the night with her sewing, though I wasn't there to suggest it to her. Instead, she spent it either worrying about Simonopio or being surprised at my father, who served himself cup after cup without once grimacing in disgust.

My papa opened the front door without waking her, and the first thing he saw in the semidarkness was Simonopio waiting for him on the porch.

Do you have children? No? When you do, you'll understand what motivates any parent of a child who decides to go missing or disappear on an adventure to say, *When I find him, I'm going to throttle him,* or *When he comes down from that tree, I'm going to kill him.* I never understood it when I was the recipient of such affection, though I heard it a lot from the lips of my usually calm mother.

You must be a parent to understand that from great love there also comes a great violent impulse. You must have feared for a child's safety in order to comprehend and forgive the violence that hides or bubbles behind the anguish of anyone who, after giving up a son for dead, finds him playing at a neighbor's house or with his buttocks full of thorns from falling on a nopal. Or in this case, returning from an adventure on his own two feet, having suffered no apparent harm.

If you were a parent, you'd understand why my father's first impulse was to go up to Simonopio, take him by the arms, shake him, and keep shaking him until the boy fell to pieces—while screaming at him until he was deaf. But after two or three rough movements, my papa's shaking turned into a hug. A huge hug.

That was how my mama found them. She immediately felt the same impulse, which she must have contained because the job had already been done and because, after drinking so much coffee, she had to run off to the bathroom to empty her bladder.

As I was saying, my mama regretted allowing her godson to move to the shed. I suppose my papa did too. For as much as they tried, they could not understand why Simonopio would give up his role as a constant companion to my papa and go off without telling anyone, sometimes for up to three nights in a row. That same day when my papa gave him such a huge hug, Simonopio escaped again to wander unknown paths. They noticed that there was no blanket on his bed. Nana Reja, in her eternal place outside the shed—now his sleeping quarters—didn't open her eyes even to blink. She didn't seem anxious, which my parents took to be a sign that the boy knew what he was doing.

Yet they could not help continuing to worry about him. On one occasion, my mama said to him, "We're going to Monterrey on the twelve o'clock train tomorrow to visit the girls."

By dawn the next day, Simonopio had already left his shed.

My mama would always invite him along to stop him from straying when she was in Monterrey and my papa was on his ranches, but Simonopio refused and made his refusal known by disappearing. Before another trip to Monterrey, she said, "Come on, Simonopio, come with me. There's a circus with elephants, clowns, lions . . . I'll take you."

It was the only time Simonopio accepted the invitation. The temptation had been impossible to resist. But in the end, he had to return earlier than planned, because he couldn't abide being and sleeping in a strange place, far from the hills and his bees. I can imagine my sisters didn't help: Carmen because, with her romance, she had no mind to think of anything or anyone else, and Consuelo . . . because she was Consuelo, and perhaps because by then she, too, was in love. She never looked at Simonopio with kindness, let alone said anything friendly to him or devoted any time to a boy who was unsettled by all the new things in the city.

Simonopio waited for two days in Monterrey so that he could go to the circus. He endured those days only for the joy he imagined he'd feel when he saw real lions, he would tell me years later. But on the day when he went to the circus, people looked at him as if he were part of the show, like an interlude between the bearded lady and the man with six fingers on one hand.

*What are you looking at?* I can imagine my mama snapping at them, protecting her little guest and taking him to his seat in the front row.

First the elephant came out.

While the audience applauded, my mama noticed that Simonopio was gradually losing his vitality and excitement at being there, at seeing an animal that—he had assumed—would be monumental.

And it was indeed the largest animal that Simonopio had ever seen, but as big as it was, as Simonopio told me later, in truth what had a profound impact on him was that the elephant was dying, that it barely moved. That its color was not what it was supposed to be and that it was showing more ribs than one would expect. The elephant was dying from sadness and imprisonment. And the worst thing was that nobody seemed to notice. They kept making it raise one leg and then the other. They made it complete a lap of the ring with a woman fooling around on its bony back. And then balance on its hind legs while its trunk caught and threw a ball to its trainer.

Next up was the lion, with its tamer carrying a whip and a torch that he used to make the beast jump through hoops of fire. The tamer managed to get the lion to leap from bench to bench and roar now and then, but it was all a pretense, because in the big cat's eyes there wasn't the faintest trace of his fierceness. He lived, he moved, he roared a little, and—awkwardly—he did whatever the tamer requested with his whip, but he was dead inside.

That was when Simonopio's eyes welled up.

Then the clowns came out like a herd, because although the circus had only one elephant and one lion, it had more than a dozen clowns of all sizes, from a tall one to a dwarf.

Have you heard of coulrophobia, an excessive and irrational fear of clowns?

Simonopio proved to be instantly coulrophobic. Seeing those painted beings, with their strange physiognomies, parading in the ring near him and doing what they were paid to do, which was simply to behave like clowns, Simonopio burst into tears.

Not a whimper or a weep—no, a violent explosion.

I should explain that my poor mama had never seen Simonopio shed a single tear, so you can imagine the fright his coulrophobia gave her, especially since she didn't know that such a condition even existed. And if we now know that a word exists to describe someone who's scared of clowns, I think there should also be one for the clown who enjoys his victim's suffering. That day, it was as if all those clowns had a special radar for detecting easy prey for their torture, especially when it was a rich kid who'd paid a full peso to see them from up close.

Whenever she retold the anecdote, my mama would say that they went straight for him, and that she hadn't known what to do: whether to console Simonopio, apologize to the other people in her section for the racket, or beat the clowns with her parasol to get them away from the boy. She opted for the parasol, and to leave the place immediately with a sobbing Simonopio who, terrified and inconsolable, wouldn't stop crying for the rest of the night and until the next day, when my mama said to him, "All right, Simonopio, stop crying now: if we leave right away, we'll make the train to Linares."

On the way back, when they were passing through Alta—and without being aware of it—my mama lost the thread of the monologue with which she was trying to console Simonopio, and fell silent.

She knew, of course, that nothing remained of my grandfather who was executed by firing squad. If anything of him did remain in the world, she had no desire to find it. Furthermore, she had no desire for any remnants of him to linger in the place where he was shot. Why would he want to be there, when there were places he had enjoyed much more, like his haciendas or the library in his house?

Yet each time the train that took her to Monterrey passed through Alta, she couldn't help but peer through the window, fearing she would see an army lying in wait on the horizon, ready to attack the train as it had so many times before. Years later, she admitted to me that she also did it because of a strange fascination: to see if there were any signs of her father, to feel some kind of shudder produced by the force of the hatred and terror that must have gathered in the trees and the land itself, as silent witnesses to the violence and unwilling recipients of the spilled blood.

She never saw anything out of place, and she felt nothing but relief. On the several journeys she had already made, nobody had stopped them.

My papa had explained to her that, tactically speaking, the Alta hill was the perfect place for ambushes, which was why it had been used by various sides to inflict as much damage as possible on the enemy. Though it was the scene of many clashes, my mama never found any evidence of violence there, and the trees seemed as dry or as green—depending on the season—as any others: their leaves hadn't changed shape, and their hidden roots hadn't mutated in any way from being irrigated with blood and bodily fluids.

She would always look through the window there, she knew, and she would never lose the now-gentler grief that she felt at her father's absence.

Simonopio took her hand softly, distracting her from her contemplation and melancholy.

When they were back on Linares soil, it was as if the visit to Monterrey had never happened. Simonopio returned to his new routine as an explorer. Regardless of how much they told him not to go, that something might happen to him, Simonopio continued to disappear into the hills without warning.

My papa continued to hope that the boy would turn up to visit, but the days went by, and Simonopio never appeared in the fields. Seeing that my mama's plan to take Simonopio to Monterrey had backfired, my papa thought he would invite the boy on one of his trips to Tamaulipas—if what Simonopio wanted was fresh air and adventure, there was plenty of that on the cattle ranches.

Although the invitation excited him, Simonopio turned this one down as well. My parents' mistake was to think that Simonopio went wandering with no fixed destination in mind. Eventually, they would learn where he went and what he was searching for, but that wouldn't happen until many months later.

They had tried to have Martín go with him on his outings, thinking Simonopio would like the idea, but every time he tried to follow the boy, Martín returned frustrated.

"There we both were, then suddenly, when I turned around, the kid was gone."

After that, it was my father who offered to go with him, though he was very busy with his efforts to save the land. But Simonopio just looked at him fixedly, and my papa understood: *I don't want you to.* My mama told me that they even tried, unsuccessfully again, to get Nana Reja to talk him out of going alone; his nana squeezed her eyes shut. She never wanted to be involved in the matter, which my parents, at a loss, took as a sign that it was best they left Simonopio in peace to his expeditions.

With nothing else he could do, my papa gave Simonopio a light, easily packable sleeping bag, as well as a penknife that his grandfather had given him as a child. He also gave him a canteen and a flint with which to light fires to ward off the cold, darkness, and wild animals. If the boy was intent on spending so many nights out in the open, the least they could do was make sure he was well equipped.

"And no more walking off with the blankets from your bed, eh?"

Not even with time and effort did they manage to completely stop worrying. On one occasion, they saw him add a machete to his camping equipment, but now they said nothing. They didn't even discuss it between themselves. Each of them would just say, *Look after yourself,* and send as many blessings as they could think of with him.

The next time my mama returned to Monterrey by train and it went through Alta, she peered out the window as always. She didn't see the ghost of her father or any army lying in ambush. The trees were the same, and so was the land. The only thing different in the scene was that, in the distance, standing on a rock, she saw Simonopio waving goodbye with his arm in a wide arc that almost touched the clouds.

The same thing would happen every time she passed through there, in both directions.

How did Simonopio manage to travel so far on foot? How did Simonopio know when she was going to be a passenger on the train if sometimes she didn't even know in advance herself? My mama never found out. This was Simonopio. There was no explanation.

After the first time she saw him standing on the rock through the window of the moving train, my mama never searched for her papa or the armies again. Peering out through the window of the moving train, she looked only for him, and when she invariably found him there, her fear and nostalgia were banished.

# 30

*Where Does the Devil Go When He's Lost?*

"Where does the devil go when no one can find him?"

The boy's existence bothered Anselmo Espiricueta. It bothered him that the boy enjoyed the good life as a spoiled child of the señor and the señora. He had been born and arrived just a couple months after Anselmo's own daughter, and nobody gave her anything: neither regular meals nor a warm bed. She had nothing but her little girl's face. Nothing. And the boy, with his face kissed by the devil, had everything, from clothes to free time.

The boy did not want for anything.

If the kid decided he wanted his own room, they simply gave it to him. If the kid got lost, they searched for him, without understanding that the devil never gets lost. That the devil hides. That he plans, he waits, and then he ambushes. He takes you by surprise.

Anselmo Espiricueta did not understand the boss.

"He may have read books, gone to school, but what good's all that if he don't ask himself what the filthy kid does when he disappears?"

And he spent almost all his time nowhere to be seen.

Anselmo had his suspicions: he believed the boy hung around him all day and then followed him home at nightfall. He thought himself so smart and sneaky, that devil in a child's body, but sometimes Anselmo could hear his slow or hurried footsteps, depending on what his own footspeed was. Then the footsteps, which followed him persistently, would stop when he stopped. And Espiricueta would yell, *Come out, demon!* but the demon never came out to face him; he just resumed his stealthy footsteps when Anselmo set off again. The demon then followed him to his house and waited for him to drift off so that he could interrupt his sleep every night and ruin his peace. He never let himself be seen, like the demon he was, but Anselmo could hear him in every rustling branch, in every shake of the shutters, and in every groan that came from his two remaining children as they slept. Anselmo knew that, if he lowered his guard, if he did not bless his house every night, the devil in a child's body would come to steal his final breath from him, as he had already done with his wife and children.

Anselmo Espiricueta always felt the Morales's adopted child close, day and night, because as everyone knows, the devil does not sleep. Therefore, he always kept a furtive eye out for him when he left his house every morning, when he was clearing the fields, when he was taking up his rhythm to cut the sugarcane.

And he had felt his malignant presence on the night of the search that Morales organized.

When he received the order, Anselmo celebrated: if the demon was lost, he could stay lost, as far as Anselmo was concerned. He had no interest in finding him. He would not spend a single minute of his night searching, he decided. But then he thought again: the farther the boy strayed from his own home, the more likely he was to come to Anselmo's, and the easier it would be to catch him by surprise. This was his chance to do away with the kid.

As he arrived at the gathering point, he noticed that everyone was frightened to go out into the wild on such a dark night. They were also saying, *What's the point? The animals on the sierra must've gobbled him up by now.*

Espiricueta was also afraid to head into the hills in the dark, but his desire to find the boy, preferably alone, was greater than his fear. Because the boy lived—he was certain of it. Not even the animals would dare raise a claw to him, much less eat him. If they had not done it on the night when he was abandoned under a bridge as a newborn, that night when the devil had marked him with his kiss, they would not do it now.

Defying his fear, Anselmo went and called the demon by his name. "Where are you, Simonopio? Come out!"

But the wretched child did not want to come out.

Anselmo knew. He knew the boy had heard him, that the boy had been close, because he got goose bumps on every inch of his skin. But this demon was wise: he knew how to hide, like he always did.

Because he knew that, if he had found him, Anselmo Espiricueta would have killed him.

# 31

## *Only the Living Understand*

Francisco had just signed the final check he planned to send in the morning. His hand had trembled as he did it, though he would have liked to pretend it was from holding his horse's reins more firmly than usual—on his return from inspecting the cattle on his Tamaulipas ranch, he had been caught in a violent storm, so he'd had to control the skittish animal.

He had signed the check while sending a silent but heartfelt apology to the heavens, which was where he hoped his papa was enjoying eternity alongside the rest of Francisco's known ancestors—or the ones he did not know yet and would meet when he was summoned from up above as reward for being a man who lived by the law of God. But at that moment, as he poured sand on the moist ink with which he had traced the official seal of his name, he suspected his father was frowning on him or perhaps even wanting to send him in the opposite, fiery direction.

*Of my four children, you're the only one that survived, and you can't even do right by your father!* Francisco imagined him yelling from his cloud.

Thus, the booming storm of thunder and lightning. On several occasions during his journey on horseback, he had felt his hair stand on end because of a flash of electricity that had missed its target by a very short distance.

But Francisco did not stop: the world was for the living, and sometimes the living had to make decisions based on new information. Information of which the dead, like his father, knew nothing, because they had had the good fortune to move on before it emerged. Yellow fever had taken his father, but Francisco was still alive; not even the flu had defeated him. He did not want to be guilty of arrogance, but neither could he continue to live life always making decisions based on the views of someone who now lived on the other side.

The world changed, and one had to adapt.

In life, his grandfather and his young father survived the secessionist attempt—or an attempt, at least, to submit to the emperor Maximilian—of the then governor of Nuevo León, Santiago Vidaurri. This had led to the federal government punishing the state. The family land had been divided when the state lines were moved: the haciendas where they grew sugarcane and other crops remained in Nuevo León, while the cattle ranches became part of Tamaulipas. Like many other prominent landowners, they'd signed a document declaring themselves loyal to the fatherland, pledging not to support any new attempt at betrayal.

And yet, the rebellion that cost Vidaurri his life proved to be nothing more than an inconvenience to Francisco's father and others. After they made their pledge, nobody threatened to take their lands from them in a legal and systematic way. Had circumstances been different, Francisco was sure that his grandfather or father would also have made use of the family savings, spending whatever they had to in order to save the land.

But he agreed with one thing: he must not use the funds at his disposal—after the sacrifice of several generations—to buy himself luxuries he had not earned himself with his daily work. He was determined not to touch a single peso in the bank to cover the cost of

Carmen's wedding, for instance. It would have to be done according to his means and the times: an austere and intimate event. Likewise, with great discipline, Beatriz continued to sew her own clothes and those of the girls, while other ladies bought them ready-made or had them sewn by a seamstress. Equally, nobody would see the Morales family driving around in new cars, as others did.

To Francisco's mind, it was not that he had become a spendthrift in recent times. True, he had dipped into the gold in the bank to buy the house in Monterrey and all the new land, but that did not mean he had adopted a philosophy of "Spend Now, Worry Later." For he certainly worried now. And if, by acquiring these new properties, he bought himself a little peace of mind, that in itself was a reason to feel satisfied. It was worth the expense.

He was the first Morales to live under the threat of being stripped of his wealth, but he would not be the first to lose a single acre of the family estate. At least, he would not do so without putting up a fight.

With this in mind, he had just signed the check for the new tractor he had been coveting for years. On an impulse, he had also just ordered four wooden hives for Simonopio's bees. And he would take the rare step of buying everything using the family coffers. With money the fertile land of generations of Moraleses had been incapable of yielding in recent times. And he would buy it all in the United States—where else?

All the latest country wares were advertised in the *Farmers' Almanac*, including the most recent discovery: a maize seed created in Oklahoma to withstand droughts and intense heat. With these innovative seeds, Francisco could plant on tracts of land that had never been used for want of an adequate irrigation system. And water.

In the same edition, John Deere was also advertising a motorized tractor even more powerful than the original machine, which for years Francisco had been merely caressing in a photograph that he had cut out. With the new tractor, he could work more land in half the time it took him with a mule-driven plow.

With the investment he had decided to make, he would render his land more productive. And never before had putting the land to work been more necessary than now.

Francisco Morales did not like land being left idle. It was another practice inherited from his father and grandfather, he supposed: if you can't sow it, water it, fertilize it, and harvest it, you may as well sell it.

If it were that easy, he would already have sold a large tract. But during the economic depression and with the uncertainty of the war, the land reform, and the new law on unused land, who would buy it?

Now any unsowed land was eligible to be seized by the government and passed on to a resident of Linares, who would work it for a year and hand over a percentage of the yield to its legitimate owner, a payment determined in advance through a system of sharecropping.

Francisco had been practicing sharecropping for many years without needing a law to dictate it to him. He owned plots of land that were in the hands of trusted, hardworking men. Married men, with someone for whom they wanted to better themselves. Reliable men he chose, who nobody imposed upon him.

He did not mind knowing that someone else was occupying his land in such a way, and had seen the real benefit of forming partnerships: he provided the land, which would otherwise be left untended; he also contributed the seeds, water, and even the peon's house, in exchange for 50 percent of the crop. Fifty percent that neither he nor the peon would otherwise have.

However, he would never, without a fight, allow just any stranger—someone seeking to abuse the system and appropriate another man's land—to show up and, with a simple request, be allocated the land for no reason other than wanting it.

As part of his strategy to protect his land, some time ago Francisco had made the decision to distribute it in his own time and manner: he registered some of the family's land in the names of trusted friends with no agricultural property of their own. Honorable men who would act as owners of the small pieces of land in the eyes of the law, even if it was a mere formality. What's more, as soon as Carmen and Antonio were married, Francisco would ask his son-in-law to act as the symbolic holder of another tract. By verbal agreement, responsibility for the property and the rights to its use would continue to fall to Francisco and his family. With this covert but entirely legal measure, the risk of his land being snatched at the whim of the government was diluted, and he remained one step ahead of the authorities and those who coveted his property.

All the same, his satisfaction had not lasted long.

Now, with the new law on unused land, it did not matter how small a property was: if it was uncultivated, it could be seized from them for some stranger—with no knowledge or real connection with the land— to occupy it and tread all over it. The way Francisco saw things, the law was nothing more than thinly veiled expropriation. While it was true that, under the provision, the recipient's tenancy of the uncultivated land would last only a year, once the recipient was in possession of it, who would force him to leave? And if he did leave, would it be returned to the legitimate owner?

In Francisco's mind, the law was nothing more than a precursor to what was to come with the Agrarian Reform.

Francisco did not like being at the government's mercy. The new mayor, Isaac Medina, was a self-professed agrarian who, wanting to enforce the law, had formed a cooperative to oversee private property in Linares. The three members of the committee had named themselves as the judges of something everyone in Linares knew they were biased about. Francisco feared that their criteria for snatching a hacienda from its owner were based not on facts, but on whims and on the benefit to themselves or their friends. He did not think he was crazy to fear that, by decree of those arbitrary judges, anyone could be stripped of their best land without reason—on the pretext of the new law, but with the true motive of greed. They supervised the land, but who supervised them? The mayor who had appointed them?

No. Francisco did not want the fate of the land he had inherited from his parents and that he planned to leave to his daughters' families to be at the mercy of these people.

With the measures the government was taking, Francisco feared violence could escalate among the peons as they sought to take possession of land, or among the landowners as they sought to protect or reclaim their property. In Linares, the tension was beginning to be felt: each inspection by the cooperative was taken as a threat by the owners of the sugarcane haciendas. On the fringes, agrarians circled like vultures, with no permission other than what they granted to themselves or agreed to as a group. No longer content to settle for mere promises or rich men's scraps, the agrarians turned from scavenging birds to birds of prey. The attacks had begun, and several landowners were now dead. After the violent and illegal invasion of the San Rafael estate, landowners had been forced to form—and fund—a rural force to protect their interests.

Francisco considered himself fortunate to have retained his lifelong employees and to be able to lease the land to them without reservation. The newest peon had arrived ten years ago, and Francisco had not hesitated to offer him the same as the rest, because while he did not know him, he judged that the large family he had with him was the best letter of introduction Espiricueta could have: in Francisco's view, anyone with such a responsibility would never give up or neglect the excellent opportunity being offered to him. He would be loyal. Francisco still did not think he'd been mistaken. Espiricueta would never be a very capable farmer, and—perhaps even more so now, since the death of almost his entire family—he still struggled to get along with the others, but he quietly did what was asked of him and turned up to work without fail.

Francisco had resigned himself to it. Sometimes that was the most one could expect from somebody.

He cared little that Espiricueta remained unable to yield good harvests on his designated plot or to pay the agreed rent. Francisco listened to his complaints and excuses patiently: the land was bad, the water insufficient, the quality of the seed poor. He would take a deep breath and remember that it was better to have the land occupied by a trusted incompetent than by a greedy stranger.

Under different circumstances, he would have asked Espiricueta to vacate his plot by now. But Francisco still had unused land in Tamaulipas and in Linares and the surrounding area, whether because he had left it fallow out of necessity or because the violence had prevented him from investing in irrigation or in the new tractor. There was other land he had left idle because he had bought it when he was newly married, thinking of the many children he would have with Beatriz. The many children had not arrived, and instead the war had, at which time he lost the urge to begin something new on those properties. Carmen would soon be married, and Consuelo was soon to be engaged in Monterrey, too, he expected. Why leave two daughters who might never settle in Linares with the burden of tending to so much land?

With the new agrarian cooperative and its dubious judges overseeing it, the last thing Francisco needed was another plot unoccupied, so he resigned himself to Anselmo Espiricueta staying put.

Between the war, the deaths from the influenza, and the new opportunities for factory work in Monterrey, campesino labor was in short supply, especially men he could trust. During the three months he had spent in exile due to the influenza, people from the nearby rural communities had settled in Linares to escape the violence—whether from bandits or the army itself—abandoning their properties in a state of complete misery. All that was known about them was that they were desperate. Francisco would have felt the same if someone had appropriated his land or forced him to abandon it. Francisco might offer work to some of them eventually, but he did not want to give these people the chance to simply settle on his property. He knew that, in time and under the protection of the land reform, they would try to keep it.

The subject had been occupying his mind in recent times, until he found a solution that seemed perfect: among the letters he would send the next day, one would be delivered to Linares with a proposal for the Chang brothers, the Chinese men who bought vegetables to sell in the town's market: *Would you like to grow your own vegetables on my land?* He was certain the Changs would accept, for Francisco had been observing them for a long time. They were hardworking husbands and fathers, to all appearances honorable and honest, with a good nose for business. Francisco hoped the Changs would also see it as an opportunity, and he thought they would understand the advantages it offered, for as foreigners, they would have no chance of becoming beneficiaries of the reform.

Vegetable cultivation did not require large expanses of arable land or major investment. It would have to be done, even if his father cursed him even more for leasing land to Chinamen. Francisco reflected on the irony of the fact that he was being forced to break up his property of his own accord so that the government would not do it for him.

Sometimes, when he lay awake at night, it occurred to him that the government's attempt to make the countryside more productive, unstitching it into so many threads, would end up killing it like a plague. That the future was in cities like Monterrey, which had found a new calling, divorced from agricultural activity.

He could not imagine how the country would survive if it allowed the rural areas to die, for in spite of all the changes—the emergence of iron cities like Monterrey, all the technological advances, all the marvels of the modern world—if there was one thing that never changed, it was that people, whether of a city or a village, needed to eat every day.

Consequently, someone must continue to produce food. If only the government and the moochers would stop interfering . . .

He left the sealed envelopes on his desk. He was tired. He went to change into his nightwear, but the storm was raging on. He doubted he could sleep with all the noise, but he would try.

Recently, he had received a letter signed by the owner of Milmo Bank himself, alarmed at the unusual withdrawal from his account, fearful— Francisco suspected—that the Moraleses were transferring their funds to another bank. Despite that letter, despite Beatriz's increasingly minor objections, some friends' incomprehension, and above all, the thunder his father was sending him from up above that night, Francisco did not regret using their savings to invest in land, in a house in the city, and— now that he'd plucked up his courage—in the tractor and in extending the irrigation system.

Ironically, all the land he had acquired in Monterrey was unused— uncultivated—and nobody in the government cared.

It was time to turn his attention back to the estates and to buy the region's first tractor. If the government wanted agricultural productivity, he would give it to them. In the morning he would travel to Laredo. Irrespective of the letter from Patricio Milmo and despite the thunder and lightning persisting in the sky, it was time to slim the bank account down a little more, though he would make sure the investment in the tractor paid for itself. He would move it between his properties to use fewer hands on the crops and to produce more. And he would lease it to other haciendas at idle times, to cover the high cost of the kerosene and gasoline it required.

He heard a final clap of thunder.

"I know. You mind your own business, Papa; leave me to mine."

And with that, in the sudden silence of the night, he fell asleep.

# 32

## *An Old Look in His New Look*

Years later, my mama would always laugh when she recalled how my papa used the tractor for the first time, with the instruction manual in his hand and the clear intention, in due time, to train the most capable of his campesinos and turn over responsibility for the vehicle. However, he grew so fond of that steel monster that it took him months to let go of the wheel, arguing that it was a complicated and expensive machine, so it was unlikely that anyone other than him would be able to control it properly, without mishandling it. She understood that he wanted to make sure he could train someone well, but insisted there was no need for him to wash every last bolt himself, to grease the machine, or to cover it up like a baby every night.

"You have plenty to do aside from spending your time stroking a plow. Besides, your horse is missing you—he's growing fat from the lack of exercise," she said to him.

In the end, reluctantly—but remembering, as his wife had told him, that his destiny was not to spend his life following a mechanized plow around the fields—he declared that one of the peons would at last be given the honor of driving the tractor.

His original plan had been to plow all the fields, even the ones that had to be left fallow, to give the appearance he would make use of them.

He knew that the strategy would only work for one sowing season, but that was better than nothing. As it turned out, by the time the tractor finally arrived in Linares, his plans—and options—had changed.

After placing the order, and to keep him busy while he waited, my papa went ahead with his alternative investment plan in Monterrey, pretending that the regular work on the hacienda and the plans for Carmen's wedding kept him satisfied. He also tried to ignore his concerns about his godson, but that was a difficult task.

That past winter, my papa had thought he'd managed to stop Simonopio wandering so much by inviting him several times to spend a couple days on the ranches in Tamaulipas. There, my papa would see signs of the old Simonopio—his constant companion, the happy, fun-loving boy whom he had not seen for a full year. But when they returned to Linares, Simonopio would disappear again. Sometimes he came to find my papa, but only to join him on the way back from supervising the work. He would go off for hours, but not days. And though my papa did not understand the reason for his godson's melancholy, he felt satisfied and relieved that the boy had given up his constant solitary and dangerous vagrancy.

My mama told me that Simonopio's transformation—after he moved to his new sleeping quarters with his bees to begin his new life as a wandering knight—had been a shock, because while he had never been a silly child, there was always a sparkle in his eyes that only a child can have, whether it be of innocence or of blind faith in everything and everyone. My mama swore that, while it was to be expected that any child would lose this sparkle little by little in the inevitable transition to adulthood, Simonopio lost it suddenly, like a light going out, without giving them the opportunity to gradually get used to the new person who emerged in the blink of an eye.

Truth is, if I'd been the one who announced to them one day— in silence or with my absence, as Simonopio did, or with a rambling speech, as I would've done—that I was going off into the wild and there was nothing they could do to dissuade me, my parents would have taken a belt to me and said, *You little rascal, don't even try it.* With that, I would have quickly given up any plan to devote myself to wandering the hills, because I was always a relatively normal boy—although if she could, my mama, may she rest in peace, would say to you, *Normal? I had to battle with him all my life!* And like any normal boy, I hatched lots of plans for my life, plans for marvelous adventures, ideas that would change the world and eradicate injustice forever, all of which I gave up and forgot at the first sign of hunger, at the next invitation to play at a friend's house, or on receiving a stern look from my mama or papa.

But from that year on, Simonopio, who had never really been a normal boy, was even less so.

My mama believed that sleeping under the vapors and fluids of his bees changed his character, so she felt obliged to insist to my papa— because it was impossible to persuade Reja—that he in turn must insist to Simonopio that he move back into the house. My papa listened to her but didn't do as she asked, because he knew she was talking for talking's sake, as a mother does when she doesn't want to accept that her children have grown up and she feels obliged to continue fussing over them and organizing their lives. To decide for them. But her godson, this child with the body of a nine-year-old boy, had an old look in his new look, a look that suggested an unshakable wisdom and determination, like they had never seen in anyone.

So they respected his transformation. If he accepted the invitations to Tamaulipas, all the better. If not, they would try to insist, but then let him be. If he wanted to continue living under his bees' roof, they would let him, because though my papa had extolled the virtues of the system, he had been unable to persuade Simonopio to use the wooden beehives that would soon be arriving from the United States. The boy had accepted the gift when he told him about it, grateful for the gesture, but my father understood right then that the boxes would do little except gather dust. What must my papa have thought? That just by having the wooden hives nearby, the bees would have the urge to leave the one that had been their home for a decade?

No. For the bees to move, Simonopio would have had to ask them to do so, and he would never do that voluntarily.

Anyway, like I was saying: my parents had a peaceful winter that year, with no invasions and fewer worries about their godson, who kept relatively close. They rested a little. But if they thought Simonopio had gotten over his eagerness to explore the hill paths once and for all, they were wrong: once again, with the bees' first spring flight in 1920, Simonopio disappeared.

# 33

*Back on the Trail*

For a few weeks he had been feeling it in his bones, in his muscles, and in his nose: it was the end of winter. His bees announced it to him a day in advance with their frenetic, excited drone: *Tomorrow, tomorrow, tomorrow.*

Tomorrow they would go out again, like they did every spring. Tomorrow, winter would end. Tomorrow their life cycle and Simonopio's travels would recommence.

It had not been as solitary a winter as the previous one. Since it had not been so cold, the bees ventured out more just to keep Simonopio company, with no work to do, in no hurry, as if they forgot for a few months that their community's lives depended on their daily expeditions in spring. They flew without pressure, they stopped at will, and they returned whenever they wanted. They knew that the work had been done. They also knew that the work would soon be calling them back and that they would gladly heed the call. But in the interval between autumn and the following spring, the sole focus of the bees—aside from helping to keep the honeycomb warm for the next generation with their bodies—was Simonopio.

That winter, Simonopio was not idle either.

He knew that time had not lessened the danger Espiricueta posed, and that it would be a grave mistake to dismiss or ignore him. Simonopio's previous year's travels had not served to put such thoughts out of his mind; the purpose of the wandering was not to forget the fear the man had instilled in him. On the contrary: he fed the fear and allowed it to grow. He would not allow himself to become complacent, as easy as his days were, without the weight of that fear, without the weight of the responsibility he had taken on as the only one who saw Espiricueta for what he was: the coyote.

A coyote that, very deliberately, Simonopio had not seen again since the day he set foot on his land for the first and last time.

He was sorry to hurt his godfather with his constant absence, just as he was still sorry the family had been so alarmed on that first night he had improvised a camp away from the hacienda in the spring of the previous year and they had assembled a search party to look for him as night fell.

That night, Simonopio had camped close by. He had wanted to test his mettle spending the night alone but not very far away—he wanted to know that he could go home at any moment if his courage failed him. He expected to be afraid, but fear was not what kept him awake hours later. He missed his bed, for he had never slept anywhere other than a bed. The stones found their way under his blanket, making him miss his comfortable bed even more. Then he heard urgent voices. He specifically heard the desperation in his godfather's voice, telling the rescuers to spread out in one direction or another, calling his name.

He would have replied immediately were it not for the fact that Espiricueta was among the group of men, silent. Simonopio did not want to see him. Nor confront him. Nor did he want the man's hard eyes fixed on him. Which was why he had hidden in the bushes, dragging his improvised camp with him and erasing any trace of it, remaining silent. From there, he saw them pass by and go off into the distance. He watched Espiricueta come back and stop just a few steps away, yelling his name, urging him to come out. Simonopio closed his eyes, knowing that a look has the power to attract. A short while passed, which to Simonopio seemed endless. Espiricueta remained motionless, listening. Simonopio did not dare so much as breathe. At last the coyote, like the others, heeded the order to call off the search in order to resume it the next day.

Simonopio did not move from his hiding place for the rest of the night. Before they began searching for him again at first light, Simonopio returned home of his own accord. He would have liked to have cried the same tears that his godfather held in when he saw him, but Simonopio held back. He stopped at putting his arms around the man, though he could not reach all the way, remaining there until he felt peace return to Francisco Morales's body.

Simonopio would have liked to explain his intentions to his godfather, but he knew that, even if he could have enunciated the words correctly, he still would not comprehend him. There was no way to explain to them why it was so important for him, and for everyone, that he reach the end of his journey with his bees. He was sorry for every step he took away from his bemused godparents, who thought they were hiding their concern for him while they left him free to do whatever he needed to do. But not even that stopped him. He had come and gone on his expeditions many times, and he knew that, when spring arrived, he would do it again.

Not even in winter, with his exploring on hold, could he give himself the luxury of resting and therefore losing what he had gained. He was adamant that, when spring arrived, his feet would still remember every crack and every stone on the trail, and also that the trail would remember him: that it would accept his footsteps as it had learned to do through his efforts. He had also allowed himself some days off. Days to visit the ranches with Francisco Morales. Days to go out into the hills, making sure he returned in time to welcome his godfather on the road at the end of the day. He also traveled a long distance for his godmother, to that place that made her so sad, where the land still bemoaned the conflict.

But he would return to sleep under his bees, which he had rarely allowed himself to do during the hot months.

With his shed's new window open and with a great deal of patience, the bad smell had been banished during the hot days of summer. By the time winter arrived, when he had no option but to keep the window shut, only the scent of the honeycomb persisted, imbuing Simonopio with the comforting feeling of being enveloped and protected by the bees' unbreakable community. There, he slept in peace and slept deeply. And there his body had grown. He knew it because his pants told him so—they seemed to shrink of their own accord—as did the sore toes in his worn boots. Each time his godmother came to his shed to bring him new shoes or measure him to make new pants, she would say to him, *Ay, Simonopio! Carry on like this, and you'll be taller than me in a month.*

He liked growing. He liked other people noticing it. But what he wanted most was for the coyote to know it.

With the onset of another spring, he took to the trail again. His taller, stronger body traveled farther in less time. Reaching the place where he saw his godmother on her way to and from Monterrey was no longer a major effort, and he stopped there only to see her pass in the train and so that she would see him. If it was not a day when she was traveling, he would go on by without looking back, unwilling to make a promise; it was not up to him to heal that land. Not when he still had to complete his own mission.

But he would be back.

Little by little he made progress, encouraged by his bees: *That's it, keep going, not far now,* they would say to him. Inevitably he spent the night alone—the bees did not know how to survive out in the elements at night, so if they wanted to wake the following dawn, they had to return to their hive at nightfall. Whenever he slept far away, Simonopio chose his campsite very carefully. He lit his fire with the flint his godfather had given him, not because he was cold, but to warn other animals that the place was taken. For dinner he ate a mixture of soft oats and honey. He drank water from his canteen and then spread out his sleeping bag and climbed in it, imagining it was a cocoon that sealed in the smell of his skin—the smell of bees. With a hand callused from his constant use of the machete as he cut his way through the bushes, he stroked the smooth handle of the old penknife—the other gift from his godfather—as if it were a talisman. And then he fell asleep, revisiting or reinventing the stories he kept in his memory, especially the ones that reminded him he was the lion. The fierce lion of his imagination, not the lion that was dead inside that he had seen on his sad visit to the circus in Monterrey.

The next day he woke, usually after a peaceful night, feeling determined and ready to continue his exploring. The unusually hot spring breeze turned into welcome summer storms.

One particular summer's day, it was not his body being sated with rest that woke him. He was woken by an indeterminate yet irresistible smell, a smell that traveled in the warm morning wind, perhaps helped by the bees' wings. Then he knew: this was what called to them to make their daily journey. This was their treasure, and he was close to seeing it and touching it for the first time.

Contrary to his habit as an experienced camper, he left his equipment where it was, except for the machete. He would need that. He was anxious to reach the end of his long journey.

And he arrived, concentrating on swinging his sharp blade like a pendulum, hypnotized by the rhythm, cutting his way through the thickest bushes without being able to see past the thorny branch in front of him, and the next, and then the next, and then the next, until suddenly there were no more: just his bees' treasure. And his bees were there, waiting for him.

*You're here. You're here,* they said to him, buzzing around him. *Look. Touch. Smell. Here. Take it. Take it. Quickly.*

And Simonopio obeyed.

# 34

*The Flight of the Flowers*

The Villaseca Fair was coming to an end, and Francisco was grateful for the cool weather they had enjoyed throughout the last week of the festivities. After the Saturday dance at the Linares Social Club, they took advantage of the occasion to arrange Carmen and Antonio's interview with the Church for the next day.

They held a lunch for the fiancé's family and for the witnesses who'd come especially from Monterrey for the formality, which had taken place earlier that day with no setbacks or unpleasant surprises. The new Father Pedro, who had arrived recently from Saltillo to replace the old—and deceased—Father Pedro, was more than satisfied with the private interview with the couple and their character witnesses, declaring that there was no impediment to the marriage taking place that winter. This being the case, Francisco invited him to join them for lunch, and he gladly accepted. He was a newcomer in Linares, but he had soon sensed that little or nothing could be achieved there without the consent or support of the families of noble descent or "first society," as they called it, so any opportunity to get to know people better—and especially these people—he would take.

He was also bored of eating the tasteless food that Doña Inés prepared for him. That day, he would eat Doña Matilde's dishes at the Morales Cortés house.

On their requisite visits to Monterrey during Carmen's months of courtship, Francisco and Beatriz had forged a good friendship with their daughter's future in-laws. Now, at two tables in the shade of the great pecan tree beside the house, they enjoyed the perfect weather while they ate and then conversed, drinking coffee and sampling the candied pumpkin and little balls of pecan cajeta that Sinforosa had made for the occasion.

The conversation flowed pleasantly, and nobody seemed in a hurry to bring the afternoon to an end.

At the second table, the youngsters laughed in the way only young people can laugh: with ease, without the weight of worry marring the sound of a good guffaw. Francisco looked at them with envy, with an urge to sit at their table to remember, even if just for a moment, what it was like to be so free. And to forget, for another moment, that despite the perfection of the day—the delicious food, the cold beer, the whiskey on ice, the perfect weather, the good company—he was once again in real and imminent danger of losing a large part of his land.

He was doing his utmost to be a good host. He participated in the conversation and laughed at the right times. He proposed a sincere toast to the bride and groom-to-be. He thanked Antonio's parents for coming. He praised Beatriz's efforts with the food and his mother-in-law's with the dessert, and he even listened patiently to the new Father Pedro's petition, seeking his support for expanding the boys' and girls' charity schools.

"That way, fewer children have to go to the rural ones, Sr. Morales, because what the government teaches them there is to forget God and His commandments," the priest said to him, knowing the Morales Cortés family paid for all their workers' children to attend the Church's charity schools.

"Yes, Father, we'll see . . ."

Francisco Morales was a great believer in education. In all truth, he would have liked to have made a commitment then and there, given the clergyman's good intentions, but he could not: he did not know whether he would have time to devote to a new project in the near future. He did not know whether he would have money. He did not know whether he would have land.

That day, sitting in the shade of the great pecan tree beside his house, Francisco Morales did not know anything.

Beatriz looked at him from time to time, when the conversation allowed it, and from her eyes, a question reached her husband: *What's the matter?* From his eyes, the answer reached Beatriz's: *Don't worry, everything's fine.* But then Francisco's eyes involuntarily traveled back to the noisy table of young people, looking at them longingly.

On that day, the soon-to-be-weds were the center of attention; the only ones distracted were Consuelo and Miguel, Antonio's younger brother, since they only had eyes for each other, enjoying the early days of their courtship. He envied them that too. He remembered those young looks of love he had shared with Beatriz. They had not stopped—the love was still there—but they saved almost all of them for the best times, because life, the routine, got in the way, and war offered little respite or time for niceties.

He now tried to call to Beatriz's eyes with the force of his own, but she did not pick up on it, since she was discussing arrangements for the coming wedding with Antonio's mother.

From the corner of his eye, Francisco was surprised to catch sight of Simonopio approaching. They had not seen him for several days. Hundreds of bees swirled around him. He was ragged, covered in scratches and scrapes, and muddy, and his hair was stiff with dirt, but his stride was purposeful, and his smile so big, so bright, it lit up his eyes.

From Francisco's eyes, a message reached Simonopio's: *You're here, you're back.* And from Simonopio's eyes, a reply reached his godfather's: *I'm back.*

When the ladies from Monterrey saw and recognized the cloud that accompanied the child, one by one they let out a scream and hurried away from the threat, fanning themselves wildly as if they were the victims of an aerial attack. The visitors knew about the Morales Cortéses' godson, but no one had warned them of his quirks. When they saw Beatriz and Francisco approach the boy, who was enveloped in a veil of bees, they were shocked.

"Watch out!" some yelled from behind them.

Beatriz turned to offer some sort of explanation, but Francisco ignored them. While they often saw Simonopio with bees buzzing around him or crawling on his face or arms, it was unusual to see him surrounded by so many. That day, it seemed to be all of them. It was as if the entire swarm had gone out to welcome him or had joined him in his unusual homecoming. As if it was a special occasion. Such a number would intimidate anyone, but Francisco knew Simonopio's bees and they knew him. They tolerated him. They would not harm him and they would allow him to approach as they always did, so he did not hesitate to walk toward the boy. In the distance, he could hear Consuelo's complaining and her embarrassed apologies to her Romeo and the other young guests for the unexpected presence of the adopted child.

"Ay! Just look at him! What a disgrace!"

But Francisco left Beatriz to explain the situation and control their youngest daughter's flapping.

He did not know whether it was his proximity or some silent message from Simonopio that made them decide to stop escorting the boy, but suddenly, as if of a single mind, the bees ended their welcome parade and flew off in perfect unison.

Just one remained, perched on Simonopio's neck.

"Do you want to come meet everyone?"

Francisco was not surprised when Simonopio shook his head. In fact, he was amazed to see the boy there at all, not just because he had been absent for several days, but because Simonopio had never liked being present when strangers visited. Yet here he was, and the smile remained on his face.

"You're all right," said Francisco.

It was not a question.

Simonopio nodded as he removed everything he was carrying from his knapsack.

"What do you have there?"

Simonopio took out his sleeping bag, placed it on the ground, and unrolled the tight bundle. He took out something wrapped in a rag and handed it to his godfather.

"Shall I open it?"

Simonopio nodded again, fixing his eyes intensely on Francisco's. Whatever it was, the contents of the package were very important to his godson. Holding his breath, Francisco carefully undid the knot in the rag, remembering the day when he saw Simonopio for the first time, when he opened two similar, albeit larger, bundles, to find the boy and his beehive full of bees. So he thought that, in this case, he had better proceed with caution.

And when he had completely unwrapped the package Simonopio had presented to him, letting out the air held in his lungs, he uncovered its contents with relief: two hollowed-out orange halves, so old they had become shells of hard leather. Simonopio had bound them together with the rag to make a spherical container.

Francisco felt as if he were about to open an oyster shell to discover a pearl.

As he separated the halves, their contents fell to the ground in a fine drizzle of white. Francisco followed it with his gaze and then fixed his eyes on it, making no effort to pick up what he had dropped.

An exquisite aroma assaulted his senses.

"Flowers for the bride-to-be!" said Sra. Domínguez, who, now that the bees had gone, was curious to see what the boy had in his knapsack.

"You brought flowers for Carmen, Simonopio? Blossoms?" Beatriz, simultaneously touched and surprised, approached to see the little white flowers that did not grow in the surrounding area. "Where did you find these?"

Then, Francisco, who still had not raised his eyes from where the gentle breeze now lifted an orange-tree flower—a blossom—into the air, said, "Late bloomers. They're not for the bride. These flowers are for me."

And then he picked them up one by one, taking care not to mishandle the petals.

They all looked at him with surprise when, after securing the package just as it had been when Simonopio handed it to him, he went into the house without another word, followed close behind by the child of the bees.

# 35

## *The Blossoms' Destiny*

Francisco assumed Beatriz would take care of the guests, who were surely confused that their host had deserted them. He valued good manners highly and was aware that leaving had been in the poorest of taste.

But Simonopio had brought him the flowers, and until that day, Francisco had never received a better gift.

In his study, sitting at his desk, he carefully opened his godson's offering again. He was sorry to see that several flowers were bruised from falling on the ground and, of course, from the time they had been dead. They were beginning to decompose, and Francisco did nothing to prevent it. *Every living thing dies, even these flowers,* he thought to himself. Putting them in water would only delay the inevitable.

It did not matter.

Simonopio had torn them from their life on the tree for a reason, and Francisco, seeing them, understood it perfectly: they had fulfilled their destiny. He looked at Simonopio, who stood waiting patiently for the cogs in his head to shake off the dust and cobwebs they had gradually been covered with over the years of war, uncertainty, habit, and old traditions.

"You walked to Montemorelos, Simonopio. Over the hills?" He did not need an answer, because he knew it was true.

Mr. Joseph Robertson had planted those trees at the end of the last century, he told the boy. He had come to build the railway and had stayed there with his foreign ideas. One day, he went to California, and he returned with several freight cars full of orange trees that would take root in Montemorelos, without caring that they called him a crazy and extravagant gringo for not wanting to plant sugarcane, maize, or wheat, as men had done there for as long as anyone could remember.

"And that's what they all carried on doing. What we all carried on doing, too: planting near enough the same thing in near enough the same way it has always been done. And look where we are now: about to lose everything. But him . . . well, he's old now, but the trees he planted perhaps thirty years ago are still there, and they'll still be there when he dies."

The tree that had blossomed with the flowers Simonopio gave him had kept the earth in use for some thirty years. And in all that time, its owner had not needed to clear the land each harvest to start the next crop again, or needed to rotate the crop, because trees stayed, and once they began to bear fruit, they did not stop. What's more, Francisco had tried those oranges: they were extraordinary.

He decided at that moment that he would grow his own orchard. He would find a market for the oranges when his trees began to produce them, he told himself without hesitation, because after thirty years of proven success in Montemorelos, any concerns that the land was no good for oranges were gone.

Putting the ideas that were beginning to run through his mind into practice would be neither easy nor cheap, but he was convinced the answer to his problems lay in those little white flowers.

"Simonopio, I'm going to California tomorrow. Do you want to come with me?"

# 36

## *Everything Changes*

The movement of the train was lulling her to sleep. She would not fall asleep, because doing so in public would be in very poor taste. She told herself that she would just rest her eyes a little, close them for a while. Beatriz Morales did not know why she was so exhausted. Perhaps it was because, as a grandmother, all the traveling to Monterrey was all the more tiring.

Her two daughters were married now, and Beatriz was glad she was no longer obliged to go chaperone them during their courtships. She knew she would always go to Monterrey, that she would do it to see her grandchildren, but the feeling she had when she boarded the train to travel to see her beloved daughters—tense and aware that she was abandoning her post in the home—was not the same as when she returned to Linares, to the place where she belonged.

Sometimes the years went by in a blink: her daughters had grown up and gone to live their own lives. And now everything had changed in Linares.

Nothing had prevented Carmen's wedding, and then Consuelo's, from going ahead. It was a shame the young men's mother had died before seeing them marry, but that was impossible to remedy. Accordingly, both weddings were very discreet and austere occasions, conducted with great dignity and elegant simplicity. She was sure the guests who came from Monterrey had returned with a very good impression of Linares, particularly since both weddings had taken place around the time of local festivities: Carmen's on the day of the Virgin of Guadalupe, in 1921, after that additional year of mourning for Antonio's mother, and Consuelo's some months later, during the Villaseca Fair of 1922.

It seemed a long time ago now that she had thought that the celebrations would never return to Linares and that it was her responsibility to keep them alive so her daughters would know the traditions that had enriched family life for generations.

Now the traditional festivities had returned, but her daughters had their lives somewhere else. They would visit from time to time to enjoy them, of course, and they might bring their children as well, but the events would not carry the same significance for them because they had not experienced them as unmarried girls. For them, it would just be an anecdote with which to remember their hometown or their mother, who invested so much time, still, in making sure every detail of the festivities was organized to perfection. They would remember the compulsory period of mourning as a small town's idle pursuit, with the same formalities and dress that the people of Linares had always observed throughout Lent, waiting anxiously for the day of the Holy Saturday dance, when high society finally stopped wearing black and put on its best spring-colored clothes and dancing shoes.

At times, like now, Beatriz was overcome with nostalgia for the daughters that they had been and that they could have been had the story been different. But they seemed happy in Monterrey, with their husbands and with the children already born or soon to arrive: Carmen had just announced she was expecting her second, too soon after the birth of her son, and Consuelo was already pregnant with her first.

What Consuelo would be like as a mother remained a mystery, for Beatriz had never seen in her so much as a glimmer of maternal instinct or the tenderness only a woman feels for a baby, even someone else's. Even with a child on the way and full access to her nephew, she was still interested only in the same old things: her friends, her books, and yes, her husband. Beatriz hoped that would change when she had her own child. Carmen, on the other hand, had proved to be a very patient mother. Her first child, a boy that kept her and his nanas busy, was just over two months old and so restless and colicky, he barely slept—and never for long stretches.

When she visited, Beatriz witnessed the trouble he caused his caregivers and was glad she had left that phase behind her. Where had her energy gone? Lately, she felt so tired that, when Carmen came to visit or when Beatriz went to Monterrey, she would request to be left with him only after dinner when, bathed and tired from his unsettled day, he would let himself be held in his grandmother's arms until the two of them succumbed to sleep in the rocking chair.

She no longer went to the house in Monterrey as often as she had in the last few years. Her married daughters no longer needed supervision. Her responsibility for them, while not ended—because it never would be—had changed. Her life was in Linares, near Francisco, who was now so busy with his new orange orchards and the ranches that it was impossible for him to make the trip to Monterrey, as he used to do from time to time.

No. She did not want to travel so often to Monterrey, even for the grandchildren. They would have to come to Linares.

She could not complain; it was not as if going to Monterrey was hell. The house there was very nice; it was comfortable, though it was not the same as La Amistad, where her bed, her kitchen, her views comforted her. The ties of friendship from her youth had been strengthened by renewed contact with her friends in the larger city, and her new friendships were good and numerous, but they were not the same as her lifelong friendships in Linares. While she enjoyed the activities of the

Monterrey Social Club, she did not want to be involved in them. She owed her loyalty to the Linares club, which remained without premises.

Oddly, while she was in Linares, she missed and worried about her daughters, and when she was with them in Monterrey, she felt the same or more so about the people from her life in Linares. It was as if she lived only half a life: incomplete in both places. Because Beatriz felt bad every time she said goodbye to her daughters but felt worse when she went away from Francisco.

Her mother said the same thing on the occasions she agreed to accompany her to Monterrey, but even more so when, reluctantly, she saw her off at Linares Station: *Dear girl, your place is with your husband.* As much as it infuriated Beatriz when her mother said it, she had to admit that she agreed, because after the experience of the three months in exile, she knew that life stopped for nothing, not even for the needs of a woman abandoning everything, albeit temporarily, to be with her daughters and to get to know her grandchildren. Each time she boarded the train that would take her away from Linares and from Francisco, she was beset with the unpleasant feeling that, in her absence, their relationship would change and she would be left outside, like an intruder in her own home, a voyeur who can only look in through a crack in a closed window. She was afraid that, far away from each other, she would change and he would change in opposite directions, so that they would never find one another again. She was afraid that one day they would look at each other and not recognize each other's voices, intentions, looks, or the warmth of their bodies in the bed.

So Beatriz went to Monterrey as little as possible. Less and less often. She knew she could not help her husband with his work, which lately had kept him increasingly occupied. But she thought the least she could do for him was to wait for him and be there to receive him at night, to join him for dinner, to sleep with him very close so she could share her warmth with him and make him forget his doubts and worries, which were more than he admitted.

The changes they were facing now were not easy for Francisco, though he himself chose to make them from one moment to the next. On the day when Carmen and Antonio announced their marriage to the Church and Simonopio showed up with his strange offering, Beatriz had remained with the guests, waiting with all of them for Francisco to finish what he had gone to do in the house and promptly return. But the minutes went by and neither he nor Simonopio came out, so Beatriz began to worry. And, worse, she had run out of excuses to justify her husband's unusual—and rude—behavior.

When she went in to look for him, she found him in the study writing various messages for Martín to take to the post office so they could be sent by telegram.

"What're you doing, Francisco? We have guests!"

"I know, but they won't leave and I'm in a hurry."

"A hurry to do what?"

"A hurry to beat the land reform."

The response left Beatriz no less perplexed: How was it possible that some simple flowers had given him the inspiration he needed or helped him defeat federal law? Right then, there was no way to extract more information from him, because Francisco turned his attention straight back to writing his messages and did not consider his wife's presence again. She left puffing with anger and confusion.

Of course, when she got outside, she hid her feelings and offered excuses with renewed verve.

"Francisco sends you his apologies. He received news of an emergency on one of his haciendas but says to make yourselves at home."

With such a kind farewell from the host, the celebration continued without interruption. The person who seemed most reluctant to leave was the new Father Pedro, who kept asking Beatriz what time she expected her husband to return.

"I don't know, Father. With that man, sometimes it's best not to ask," she answered, allowing her resentment to show.

The hours seemed eternal, but finally the lunch, which became an afternoon snack and then an improvised dinner—when the group moved to the formal parlor and then to the dining room, hungry again, to enjoy the reheated leftovers—had come to an end. They would meet again the next day, since they were all invited out to La Florida for a day in the country.

"I don't know whether Francisco will be able to come with us. Sometimes it's what happens in this business."

She was right to offer an apology in advance: that night, Francisco informed her that he would leave for Laredo the next day, where he would spend a few days making arrangements for his journey to California, which he would then embark upon by train from San Antonio, Texas.

"What're you going there for?"

"I'm going to buy some orange trees."

Her husband's newfound dynamism, with its untimely decisions and impromptu actions, taking measures that all but contradicted everything he had been before—measured, conservative, forever confined to the patriarchal laws—sometimes gave Beatriz the desire to let the old her come out, the Beatriz who feared change and would not hesitate to object vociferously to the new Francisco.

But the new Beatriz controlled herself and listened. She agreed and later admitted that he might be right, as he had been about buying the house and the land in Monterrey, or about the extravagant purchase of the tractor, which ultimately proved a wise decision.

Now, this Beatriz had to listen to her husband's plans without showing any doubt. She had to try to ask specific, intelligent questions and draw on all her willpower to stop herself from saying what she really wanted to say: *And what will we live on until your orange trees bear fruit?*

What Francisco explained to her would change their lives. He would buy orange trees in various phases, for it was a considerable investment—another one. Then he would clear all the sugarcane plantations. At Beatriz's exclamation, he went on: "Remember that we have to plant all new sugarcane this year. But it's over; I won't plant it again. The orange trees will last decades. You'll see."

Yes, the sugarcane was renewed every three years. This year the cycle came to an end on their plantations, and the Morales family would no longer be sugarcane producers.

The news formed a knot in Beatriz's stomach, but she shared a little of it with the part of the heart that compresses with sadness. She had spent her whole life surrounded by sugarcane because her family—first her father and now her brothers—also cultivated it on their land. She had grown up surrounded by the green reeds that seemed to cover any land given over to them. She had been lulled to sleep at night by the wind whistling through thousands of plants and had woken, on blustery mornings, to the spectacle of the sugarcane rolling like waves on an enraged green sea or, when the breeze was too weak to ruffle them, standing still as a calm lake. What would it be like to sleep without their soothing sound? What would it be like to look out through the window and see the landscape of her memories mutilated forever?

What's more, Francisco would not stop at that: he told her he would plant orange trees on the unused land that very year. Or he would try, at least.

"You're going to have to buy hundreds."

"We're going to have to buy thousands, and that's just this year. Little by little I'll buy more, until we've filled all our land."

"And the maize plantations?"

He would not remove them until the first orange trees began to bear fruit. He would not commit the folly of leaving himself completely without income.

"Soon or later they'll go, too, Beatriz. The landscape of our estates is going to change little by little, even if it takes me ten years."

And while much of the land remained as it was before, the landscape around her had changed, and the old Beatriz, the one who feared any kind of change, sometimes got goose bumps in protest. But the new one, the extremely modern one who now wore dresses above the ankle—less fabric and less expense, after all—supported her husband unconditionally. She tried to see the good side to the change: at least the scent would be wonderful from time to time, when there were flowers. *If* there were.

When, a month after Carmen and Antonio had their prenuptial interview with the Church, Francisco and Simonopio returned with two railway cars loaded with root-balled sapling orange trees, several neighbors tried to dissuade him.

"It's madness. You don't even know whether they'll produce. And you're going to get rid of all your sugarcane and then your maize? What would your father say, Francisco?"

"That the world is for the living. That's what he'd say. And if orange trees produce fruit in Montemorelos, there's no reason why they won't here. You'll see."

Beatriz suspected that, in reality, Francisco feared that his father was spinning in his grave at the decision, but he had not let that stop him. And she conceded that he was right: one should not cling to old habits that no longer work in a changing world, even if it felt as if their estates had been hit by another revolution, a bloodless one. Even if she struggled to fall asleep at night without the sound of the sugarcane lulling her.

There was no going back now, and the orange trees quickly took root in the Linares soil, as Francisco had predicted. So, while they did not flower in the first year, let alone bear fruit—that could take up to three years—by the next year many people, including Beatriz's brothers, followed suit, now converts to Francisco's reasoning. When Francisco sent for more trees of various orange varieties that would bear fruit at different times of the year, others did the same.

There were some who struggled to change, whether because of a lack of funds to invest or because they refused to grow fruit trees—their fields were not ladies' gardens, they said. But in the end, even the most reluctant were persuaded, thanks to a recent exception included in the Agrarian Reform published in the Constitution: any land planted with fruit trees was exempt from expropriation.

Why fruit trees and not sugarcane? The published amendment offered no explanation, but the reason became clear before long: Secretary of the Interior General Plutarco Elías Calles—who would later become president—had just bought the Soledad de la Mota hacienda in the vicinity of the nearby village of General Terán, which he would thereafter devote entirely to growing oranges.

Francisco did not stop to remark or complain about the audacity of a politician enacting a tailor-made law for himself at his convenience. It brought him satisfaction to be one step ahead of any government plan to take his land from him, and if everyone in Linares and in the region saved themselves from being stripped of their property thanks to that law, then all the better.

Without neglecting the cattle ranches, and lamenting that the land in Tamaulipas was not as well suited to fruit, he had devoted himself body and soul to learning—from the books he bought in California—everything there was to know about orange cultivation. After ordering every last trace of sugarcane removed, he himself measured the distance between each hole they would have to dig to receive the orange trees, and then he supervised his men planting each tree. At night he returned home tired and went straight to the bathroom to wash off the earth stuck to his body by sweat, only to carry on working after dinner, studying the method for grafting the sweet orange trees that he would soon grow from seeds. He did not want to keep buying them from another producer.

For the first time in an age, Beatriz saw Francisco motivated. He had good days, when he seemed confident he was on the right path to save his family's property. She would have liked every day to be like that, but no: it was not in his nature to be so arrogant and triumphalist as to believe he had found the solution to all his problems in something as simple as changing direction. Francisco was a realist. And he had days when he was overcome with anxiety: the agrarians were still circling, and due to the cost of his scheme, he had not been able to finish covering all his estates. He knew it would still take him years.

One night, tucked up in bed, he said to her, "I feel like I'm in a race that I appear to be winning, for the time being. But it's a long, very expensive race, and I can feel them hot on my heels. And I'm tired."

"If you get too tired, tell me. I'll help you."

And there, lying in bed, Beatriz rested Francisco's head on her shoulder and stroked the hair on his temple like a child, until he relaxed and fell asleep.

Now *she* was tired, on her way back to Linares, and the rhythmic rocking of the train stroking its tracks had finally defeated her: for the first time since she began her railway journeys between Linares and Monterrey, Beatriz fell asleep. She was unaware of the ticket collector going past and allowing her to sleep, since he recognized her as a regular passenger. Nor did she notice when they stopped in Montemorelos, where passengers alighted and boarded. And in her deep sleep she did not realize they were passing through Alta: she did not look out, as she always did; or notice Simonopio's absence; or feel the slight but persistent movement in her belly.

When they reached Linares, the ticket collector took the liberty of waking her.

"We've arrived, Señora."

Dazed, drowsy, but most of all surprised and ashamed she had fallen asleep in public, Beatriz managed to open her eyes to find that, sure enough, they were at Linares Station. She picked up her purse. A porter helped her with her luggage—and all the better, she thought gratefully, because if it had been up to her, she would have left it where it was. She did not have the energy to carry anything. She wanted to be home, in her bed, so she could sleep again.

She was beginning to worry. At first, she had suspected that her chronic tiredness was due to the normal physical circumstances of her age and that the loss of interest in various activities to which she had devoted so much of her time in the past was something normal in a grandmother. But her friends were around the same age—some a little older, some a little younger—and none of them seemed so low in spirits.

She felt a knot in her stomach. One of her grandmothers had died young from pernicious anemia, which had first manifested in a general weakening of the body and mind. She hoped she had not inherited the illness, but she feared she was already exhibiting its early symptoms. She would make an appointment to see the doctor the next day. She would hate to cause more pain or anxiety for Francisco, but she could not willfully continue to ignore her discomfort. If it was bad news, she decided that she would confront it without wasting any more time.

As she left the station, she was surprised to find Simonopio waiting for her with a wide smile on his face. He had just turned twelve, but observing him closely, Beatriz thought he had grown even more in the last week.

"What have you been eating, young man? You're growing like a weed."

Simonopio walked up to her. Yes, at twelve years of age he was already taller than she was. Beatriz felt proud, though she also felt older than ever. It seemed like yesterday that Simonopio had arrived as a newborn, wrapped in a shawl and a cloak of bees.

And just look at him now: almost a man.

To her surprise, Simonopio had accepted Francisco's invitation to travel to California. Beatriz had watched them depart with apprehension, with the sudden worry that Simonopio would not manage such a long journey. But he returned a month later looking much like he did before, as if, in his month of absence, in the constant company of his godfather, he had reversed the transformation that he had undergone in his phase as a wanderer of the wilds. Still, from time to time, that mature look—so out of place and that saddened Beatriz so much when she saw it in his eyes—made an appearance. It was as if, for a moment, a prisoner that Simonopio kept inside him managed to escape, subjecting him to a harsh transformation that lasted until the boy—the one he still needed to be—imposed himself again and sent the invader back behind his eyes.

Francisco had sent her telegrams and letters to keep her informed of any news, uncertain how long it would be before he returned. From the messages, she learned that Simonopio was enjoying all the new things he discovered on their travels and that not even the foreign language was an impediment to him, since he made himself understood without speaking. A little jealous because he had not had such a good time with her in Monterrey, Beatriz learned that he did not complain or cry once. He went everywhere with Francisco and toured the orchards of young trees, row by row, to choose on behalf of his bees and mark the ones that would make the long journey back to Linares with some red ribbon that they gave him for the purpose.

On the first day, the people who worked at the orchard were surprised that the older man was so deferential to the boy.

"Are you going to let the boy choose for you?"

"If you knew him, you'd know why."

Francisco had started out on that journey, that idea, under no illusions that the trees would belong to whoever paid for them—as one would expect in any transaction. And yes, obviously he would pay for them, he would plant them on his land, and he would benefit from them. But as the days went by, witnessing Simonopio's excitement as they embarked on this new adventure that would take them north and to the other side of the continent, another idea presented itself, one that did not seem unfavorable to him but which he would share with no one except his wife: the orange trees would belong to Simonopio and his bees. There was nobody better than the boy to know which ones they would like, which would survive the journey, which would best adapt to his land to produce more flowers for them and more fruit for him.

With this in mind, he allowed Simonopio to choose and to overlook a few trees that seemed leafy and strong before stopping to mark one that, to Francisco, at first glance, seemed weak and bare. Simonopio knew what he was doing. Francisco, trusting him, let him be, without caring what the gringos—or the braceros—said. They had never seen anyone like his godson, who, from the first day visiting the orchards, attracted the Californian bees as if they had been lifelong friends. It was not long before he earned the nickname Bee Charmer.

Francisco suspected that a glance had been enough for the bees to understand that Simonopio was a kindred spirit, if not an equal, so he was not surprised when hundreds of bees abandoned their daily routine to approach his godson, perch on him, and cover his body to welcome him. The owner of the orchards almost had a heart attack, frightened by the sudden, unexpected, unprovoked assault. Francisco tried to reassure him, but the owner gave the order to wash the boy and his winged lining down with a high-pressure hose.

"Wait. Look."

To everyone's astonishment, all Simonopio had to do was raise his arms, and the bees all flew off as one, leaving the boy happy and unharmed.

And Simonopio was never alone again. From then on, every day, when he arrived early in the morning to continue the careful task of choosing the trees the Moraleses would live with for the rest of their lives, the bees came out without fail to meet him—albeit never with the grand gesture of the first day. Francisco supposed that, by the end of the day, like everyone who toiled on the orchard, the bees also had a quota of work to complete, a quota they could not neglect even to spend the day with their visitor, so they switched between their duties and their attentiveness to their guest.

Was it they, using the symbiosis they shared with the orange trees, who told Simonopio which ones were the best? Or was it simply Simonopio who sensed it? As soon as he began to wonder, Francisco stopped himself: there was little point in puzzling over it or trying to find reasons, because Simonopio was not equipped to explain them to him, nor Francisco to comprehend.

The important thing was that he believed Simonopio would choose well, and time proved him right. Of all the trees that made the long journey southeast, only two died on the way, and no more died after they were transplanted into the black Mexican soil. Now they all flourished, even if the fruit remained no more than a promise.

At the railway station two years after the trip to California, that December of 1922, all the first- and second-class passengers with luggage, and the third-class ones with knapsacks and crates, turned in surprise to see the strange-looking boy who had come to welcome the señora home. Beatriz thought that Simonopio, smiling, was approaching to embrace her, but she was wrong: he came just close enough to rest two hands on her belly.

She looked him in the eyes, and his smile widened.

# 37

*Slaves to Time*

We're nearly there.

It's been an incredibly long time since I was last in these parts, but I don't think the journey ever felt shorter. At my age, one realizes that time is a cruel and fickle master, for the more you want it, the faster it appears to vanish, and vice versa: the more you want to escape it, the more stagnant it becomes. We are its slaves—or its puppets, if you prefer—and it moves or paralyzes us at its whim. Today, for instance, I would like to reach the end of this story, so I wish I could have more time—that time would slow down. You, on other hand, might want this old man you've just met to be quiet so that you can put on your music or think about something else, so perhaps your journey is taking forever.

But let me tell you what I know, what I've concluded: it doesn't matter whether time passes slowly or quickly. What you can be sure of is that, in the end, all you want is to have more. More of those lazy afternoons when nothing happens, despite your best efforts to the contrary. More of those annoying arms that picked you up to stop you doing something crazy. More tellings-off from the mother who you thought was a nag. More glimpses, even, of your father hurrying somewhere, always busy. More soft embraces from the wife who loved you all your life, and more trusting looks from your children's young eyes.

Now, I'm sure my mama also wanted more time for many things, but at that moment, it would have been helpful had time done her the favor of giving her the space she needed to digest the news she received that day. A short delay so that, in her own time, she could find a way, and the right moment, to inform her husband, daughters, and the wider world that, fearing she was dying, she had discovered more life in her than she had expected.

My poor mama. Just imagine. She would be a mother again, when she had finally made peace with the half-infertile life that had befallen her. When she had come to terms with having only two daughters who, now adults, and both of them mothers, had made her a grandmother.

Life and time had decided otherwise.

My papa, the first to be told as the other person involved in the matter, was delighted with the news. It would be a boy, he foretold. My sisters were not so pleased: while Carmen had stopped at saying, *Ay, Mama!* Consuelo, less discreet and more inquisitive, asked how, why, and when. To which my mama, losing all her patience—which she had mustered, very intentionally, for that moment—replied, *Look, Consuelo. If at two months' pregnant you haven't figured out the how and why, I'm not about to explain it to you. And why do you care when?*

According to my sisters, that was the extent of her explanations.

# 38

## *He Who Must Arrive, Arrives*

Simonopio did not wish to go far from the house that spring. The first orange-blossom buds had appeared a few days earlier almost out of nowhere, and now, as if all the trees had agreed to a race, an eagerness to begin their cycle had quickly spread among them, and they put out shoots in abundance.

From the outset, he knew he would need to be patient with such young trees: the previous year, the bees—and he with them, now and then—had still had to travel a long way to the flowers they knew before in order to add honey to their hive. Now the buds in their orchard were not yet sharing their treasure of nectar, but the bees' patience was unlimited: like Simonopio, they went nowhere; they waited. They had waited for years for the trees, and at last the trees had arrived. They had waited patiently for them to flower, and now the trees were nearly there. They knew that at any moment, the first flower would open, generous, and from there a chain reaction would be unleashed that would fill the entire orchard with aroma, gold dust, and liquid gold.

When that first flower opened, it would mark the end of the bees' and Simonopio's long journeys forever. And for Simonopio, it would also be the signal for something else.

It was time to stay close. It was time to carry on waiting for the baby that would arrive, and that was where Simonopio's patience had reached its limit. He observed the buds more closely than the bees did. He knew that, when the first petal opened to the light, he would not stay to celebrate the profusion. No. He would rush off, because he knew that, with the first flower, it would be time to begin the vigil for the imminent arrival of the child that would come into their lives.

So he waited anxiously. He patrolled the orchard. He stroked a bud from time to time, taking care not to harm it, but hoping to persuade it: *Open, life's waiting for you. Open, so life arrives.*

And Francisco Morales, who with the first bud on the orange trees had begun to believe all his hopes would be fulfilled, observed his godson. As prepared as Francisco was to stroke the trees one by one as well, and as much as he fixed his eyes on them wishing they would open, he knew nothing would help: the flowers would open in their own time.

"Simonopio, go play. There's nothing to do here."

But the boy did not go, and neither did he.

They walked. They moseyed around. They inspected the irrigation and made sure that all the trees' roots were well covered in soft earth, that they grew straight, that there were no infestations. They kept themselves artificially busy during their long wait, inspecting things they had inspected many times, without finding any defects or problems. Until finally, when they reached the end of a row and turned around to start along the next one, they saw it: the first blossom of La Amistad's orchard. Simonopio did not give Francisco time to smell the flower. He took him abruptly by the sleeve and broke into a run, urging him to follow.

Confused, Francisco hesitated for an instant, but only for an instant. If Simonopio wanted him to follow, he would. There would be a reason. And he ran at the speed that his godson set along the shortcuts the boy took through the maze of trees in his orchard, without thinking or seeing where they were going. Without understanding why Simonopio had made him run to the house in such a hurry.

# 39

## *A Strange and Confused World*

I was born in April, though they expected me in June. I wasn't born prematurely—I was born on the day when I was meant to be born—which means that, when my mama discovered she was pregnant, I was three months older than calculated: she had conceived before the date of my sister Consuelo's wedding.

I wasn't the one who worked it out. It was Consuelo herself, who would always remind me: when I was a little boy, to confuse me; when I was a young man, to torment me; and then, when I was an adult, as a friendly joke—when she finally forgave us, forgave me for being born and my parents for making me. We managed, when she was old—albeit only in years—to start enjoying our relationship.

You should know we never spoke about it, but my own very personal theory is that a brother arriving late in life tormented her for a number of reasons.

My arrival, had it been early in their lives, would have taken my sisters completely by surprise. *Look what the stork brought us today,* the poor innocents would've been told, expected or even ordered to ask no more questions. The next day, they would've gone to school and announced to their friends that the stork had visited them to bring them a little boy. There would've been commiserations and rejoicing, some of their friends wishing the stork would visit their houses as well, but no more questions.

However, when I was born, when my sisters were married adults, there was no longer any mystery to it. They were not stupid. To their dismay, it became abundantly clear to them how their parents—grandparents now—passed the time in their absence. And not only that, but they also had to answer their friends' stupid questions and brazen comments when those friends learned, secondhand, that the marital activities of their parents had borne fruit.

As if that were not enough to justify the resentment she felt toward me, imagine my sister's reaction when my mama informed her—incorrectly—that they were due to give birth at the same time, so my mama could not be with her in her confinement, in labor, or in the weeks that followed.

My mama didn't live to see us make up, because Consuelo knew how to enjoy and prolong a good grudge. I think one day she decided to forgive me. Just like that. Better late than never, I suppose. By then, she was about to become a grandmother, and I imagine the time came for her to realize that even grandparents have hearts and that, if they're lucky, as she was, they still enjoy the marital activities for which she resented and criticized our parents for decades.

I never understood, even after we made peace, how it was that she was able to have such a good relationship with her husband and children. Did I tell you that, of all the men in Monterrey, she fell in love with Miguel, the younger brother of Antonio, my other brother-in-law? That's right: sisters and brothers.

The fruits of this double marriage kept me confused throughout my early years, because only the young parents—and perhaps the grandparents, but only by concentrating hard—could say with absolute certainty whose son or daughter was whose. Not only did they have the same surname, which rather complicated matters at school, but with their genetic mélange, Carmen's seven children and Consuelo's six were all born with the same coloring, nose, and even mouth. They were all from the same mold. There was not one pair of twins among them, but to me, that was how they appeared: twin cousins.

In the not-too-distant future, they would release me among that jumble of cousins—my nieces and nephews, who lived in adjoining houses—and I'd be completely overwhelmed. Not least because, as I was younger than some of them and the same age as others, people in Monterrey thought that I was just one of the crowd and that one of my sisters must be my mama. And I, who had never lived with them as sisters, admit that I came to think of them as my mamas in Monterrey—though I liked Carmen more than Consuelo in the role—and that my real mama was only my mama in Linares, where my sisters were my sisters.

I know it's illogical, but remember, I was a little boy, and small children sometimes need more clarification than we adults think it necessary to give.

One time, for instance, when I was something like four years old—an impressionable age—I heard my aunt Rosario say to my mother, *Ay, Beatriz, Francisco's going to drop dead tonight when he goes to bed.*

That prediction gave me a terrible fright.

The previous month, a seasonal laborer had in fact dropped dead as he worked in my father's orchard. Just like that. One moment he was stretching out his arm to inspect the ripeness of the fruit on a tree, and the next he was openmouthed and open eyed on the ground. Not even a blink: he dropped down dead. Simonopio had invited me to go with him that day to see the orange trees thick with fruit almost ready to pick, but what I remember most is the dead man, for we were quite near, so I saw him. What's more, for many days it was the main topic of conversation among the adults: he dropped down dead.

And that was the frame of reference my four-year-old self had when I heard my aunt foretelling that my papa would drop dead when he went to bed. How was I supposed to know there could be more than one meaning to the expression "drop dead"?

That day, my papa was supervising what I think must've been one of the first big orange harvests. I knew that meant he wouldn't be home until nightfall, so there was no way to warn him of his imminent death; Simonopio wasn't there to help me, having gone off on his own as he so often did. I knew I couldn't go from orchard to orchard searching for my papa by myself, because at that age, any distance seemed enormous to me, any road endless, and every turn I took would have seemed the same as the one before. Venturing out on my own would have only gotten me lost, without achieving anything. I knew that all I could do was wait.

I think that day was one of the longest of my life.

I was silent the whole time, barely moving from the spot I had chosen to look out for my papa arriving. I needed to warn him not to go to bed, to speak to the doctor, to hug me, to go confess. I didn't know what one did in such cases, when almost the precise hour of death had already been foretold. But I had faith in my papa: he would know what to do, if not to save his body, then at least his soul.

Why didn't I go to my mama so she could ease my worry? I suppose I believed she was somewhat complicit with my aunt. When my aunt made her deadly announcement, Mama had laughed and then changed the subject, which seemed like a blatant betrayal or at least proof that she didn't care at all about my father's fate.

When he finally arrived, exhausted, I had fallen asleep in his bed. In the end, sleep had defeated me in my vigil at the front door, but before I closed my eyes, I found the discipline I needed to move and go to the place where I would at least stop him from going straight to sleep. I was afraid he would carry me to my bed without me realizing, because once I was asleep, I was usually impossible to wake. But that night—it's what fear and anguish do—my papa woke me as he pressed his hand against my forehead, as parents always do to check whether their child has a fever, so unusual was it for me to go to sleep in his bed.

I lost my tongue and lost all my body's moisture through my eyes. Four years building my vocabulary, and at the crucial moment, nothing would come other than tears and sobs. When the words finally began to emerge, truncated and faltering, it was some time before my papa understood what was wrong with me. "I'm not dead, I'm here," he assured me. But in my faltering voice I told him, "But when you go to bed you'll die!"

I can only imagine the maze of words my papa must have picked through in order to understand me. Finally, between him and my mama, they managed it, and then they explained the misunderstanding to me. I forgave her, of course, but I would never look kindly on my aunt again: she fell out of favor with me forever, not because of the misunderstanding, which I admit was all mine, but because every time we saw each other, even years later, she would never miss the opportunity to tell "the anecdote."

I should explain that I see the funny side now. But at the time, I didn't understand, and certainly didn't like being laughed at because of it, not least because it wasn't the first or the last time something like that happened to me.

We'll talk about that later, if we have time. Slow down—you're going too fast.

Let's go back a little. Big as a foal and crying my lungs out, I was born prematurely only in terms of my mama's plans. She welcomed me with a mixture of fright and surprise that Tuesday in April 1923.

When it was no longer possible to deny that she had gone into labor, she thought that such a premature baby was unlikely to survive, and in the few months since discovering she had a lodger in her belly, she had gotten attached to the idea of me. Well, to the idea that she had formed of me.

Later, when instead of a scrawny weakling—which even the doctor had feared would be born only in order to die—she was presented with a heavyweight, she did not have time even to feel relieved. For when she saw me, when they placed me in her arms, it struck her that she hadn't finished sewing or crocheting my little cardigans, and that those she had finished wouldn't fit me, since she had made them with her delicate daughters in mind. She also remembered that the crib still required a fresh coat of paint and the mattress still needed to be beaten to rid it of dust that had gathered since Simonopio had used it. That even the Moses basket was still in the storehouse, and the diapers and other paraphernalia needed in the early life of a baby hadn't been put in the chest of drawers.

"I was going to start next week!"

My mama had taken some time to digest the news that she was expecting another member of the family. Then she'd decided it was best to wait until closer to the due date to prepare, because she didn't want to invest too much, especially when it came to hopes and dreams, in a pregnancy that might not be successful due to her age.

"Don't worry," my papa told her after the birth. "He won't be naked: Simonopio's gotten out all the clothes he wore as a newborn. I'm sure they'll fit. Lupita's already washing them."

"Used clothes?"

My papa, who had run home with Simonopio without anyone summoning him, took care of everything while my mama concentrated on giving birth. Remember that, in those days, childbirth was exclusively a women's affair—and it always will be, even if it's shared now—and men never went in to witness it, though the long wait was hard for them as well. So Simonopio killed two birds with one stone: first he kept my papa busy and therefore calm, giving him tasks. And in keeping him occupied in this way, he also managed to solve all the problems the new mother would think of by the time her ordeal was over.

He must've foreseen something.

253

"We've already gotten the Moses basket out, and they're cleaning it. Pola's putting the diapers where they belong and cleaning the room. There's time to do the crib, don't worry."

"We haven't painted the baby's room!"

That might have been the first time my father stood firm about my upbringing.

"We men don't care about those things, Beatriz."

And how right he was. I never cared whether my room was painted white, spotted, or dirty. Nor did I care when they told the story of how I was born unequipped, that I had to wear clothes and even use sheets that were not mine.

I never cared, because it had all been Simonopio's, and in that confused world I'd arrived in, the one thing I knew with complete clarity from the beginning, because he always told me firmly, was that he was my brother.

# 40

## *The Day the Mule Takes the Reins*

The señora had just given birth, and Anselmo Espiricueta did not understand why everyone was so happy: with a son in the world, Francisco Morales would be determined to produce more, to safeguard the land he had—by any means—and to keep it all.

More for him, less for everyone else.

The boss said nothing and shared none of his plans. He just gave orders: help the Chinamen with their vegetables, plant maize, harvest the maize, cut the sugarcane, pull it all up, and now dig holes and plant trees. Anselmo could do nothing if the boss spoiled the land by covering it in trees that would mean he could no longer grow good crops—food crops. So he kept quiet.

But Anselmo was neither blind nor deaf. Even though—to feign a lack of interest—he resisted asking questions, people around him talked. Some were critical of the reform, yes, but others praised the nerve of those who believed they had the right to have their own land, by whatever means necessary, fair or foul. The bosses had organized themselves and formed the Guardia Rural to try to ward off the agrarians, but before long, some—those who coveted land—were saying the law and its guns would do the talking.

One night when he left his house, sleepless and tormented by the incessant call of the many voices of the devil traveling on the wind, Anselmo found a group of men camped near his home. Their fire gave them away. After a moment of tension when they thought the rural force had discovered them, they allowed him to join them in the warmth of their fire. Perhaps they recognized the same zeal in his eyes that he had recognized in theirs, and they invited him to share their food, their drink, and their friendship.

They never camped in the same place twice: afraid the owners would discover them, and still without the strength to defend themselves, they moved stealthily around the remote parts of the haciendas, most of which were now converted into orchards. They had also found caves in the sierras, which they presumed Agapito Treviño had used in his glory days as a raider when he was fleeing the law, before he was executed by firing squad. Anselmo did not know who this Treviño was, nor was he interested in seeing the caves, but he visited his landless friends whenever they were nearby.

With them he found the camaraderie he had never felt with anyone in the region. With them he could talk about the family he had lost forever, or sit there for hours without saying anything and listen to their songs or hear them talk about the land they would have, the land they needed for their many children.

"I only got one," he told them on the first day, forgetting he also had the girl.

"Then make some more, compadre."

They made it sound so simple.

The image of Lupita, the washerwoman, making children for him went through his mind and lingered there. He had not seen her for a long time. He had always liked her. She did not visit the fields, and nobody asked Espiricueta to do jobs at the main house anymore. But he remembered her well, with her basket of wet clothes at her hip, walking toward the washing line and then hanging up the laundry without being aware that, each time she raised her arms to peg up a garment, her skirt lifted, revealing her slender ankles, and her blouse pressed against her generous breasts.

He would find her soon, he decided. He would make a whole new family with her, and he would have his own land, which would be as fertile as his new wife.

There was a lot to do before that could happen. Which was why Anselmo paid close attention to everything going on around him, for Francisco Morales was plotting something. A new son, and a new crop that was gradually displacing the old one, was no coincidence, though he did not yet understand exactly what it meant. They said to him, *Dig the hole for the tree,* and he would do it, without even looking up, but he did it singing—under his voice and through his teeth—the only refrain he remembered from a song he had learned in the warmth of a fire and that had never left his consciousness or his dreams.

> *Now the golden eagle has flown*
> *and the finch is chased away.*
> *At last the day must come*
> *when the mule takes the reins . . .*

There were times when, while he was supervising, Francisco Morales asked him, "What're you mumbling about?"

But Anselmo, interrupting his song, merely replied, "Nothing, Boss."

Like the law, for now, and like the guns, for now, Anselmo Espiricueta remained silent. For now.

# 41

*New Stories to Tell*

After so much patient waiting and such a long road traveled, life was at last what it should be: the flowers had arrived, and soon the fruit would follow. Now the boy Simonopio had been expecting for years had arrived, the one he had saved before the boy even existed, for had the Moraleses died of influenza, the possibility of him would have died with them. However, he had to find yet more patience within himself, because they would not let him hold the baby yet.

*He's very little. It's women's work.* Or *We don't want him to get used to being held,* they would tell him. They did allow him, at least, to sit at the side of his crib when the boy slept. They trusted him enough to leave them alone together. He watched over the boy, observing him while he slept in his crib, dressed in the clothes that had been impregnated with the smell, with the aroma, of honey by the infant body of their previous owner, his tireless protector: Simonopio.

He did not give the baby honey, as they had given him since his first few hours of life. But every day, when the little boy cried with his mouth open, Simonopio took the opportunity to delicately place a little royal jelly under his tongue. He knew that the baby liked it and that it strengthened him, because he noticed the ever-more-energetic movement of his arms and legs when he was content, his calm and deep breathing when he rested, and his prodigious lung capacity when he cried. Whenever he was in his crib, Simonopio did not take his eyes off Francisco Junior, because he did not want to miss a single moment.

That was how he memorized the child's features, from the gentle dip in the crown of his head to the soft cowlick of fine hair, like the fur on a tender peach, that formed between the barely perceptible eyebrows and that Simonopio insisted on stroking against the grain, in an experiment designed to ascertain whether the order of that perfect circle could be disturbed with the gentle, tender force of his rather callused finger—the finding of which was no: it was what it was and would remain like it was. He also learned which song soothed the baby when he woke up crying and which words made him open his eyes and pay attention—come out of his stupor and sleepiness—though everyone thought that a newborn never paid attention or took an interest in the world around it.

This was how, in that tiny face, Simonopio saw the boy he would become, the roads they would travel together, and the new stories they would create between them.

Simonopio drew on all his patience while, through the crib's newly painted bars, he observed the movements of little Francisco Junior, who did not stay still even while he slept. The temptation was very strong: he wanted to hold him in his arms. He *had* to hold him, he knew. The problem was that he was the only one who understood that, the only one who knew that this boy would be his responsibility.

The day would come, and he would wait patiently. For the time being, when they were alone, he spoke almost into his ear about the world, about the wild flowers, about the bees that buzzed at the window, insisting they should be let in to visit the newcomer.

He would wait until later to tell him the stories about the coyote. He did not want the baby to be afraid. He would keep them for when the boy was a little older and could understand that Simonopio would take care of that and of everything.

# 42

## *The First Drop*

I believe it was when the first of my children was born that my mama confessed to me that, for a longer period than was desirable, she had thought I was not entirely normal. That is to say, though I'd been born in one piece and with everything where it should've been, she was in some doubt about my mental capabilities.

I honestly was not offended. I suppose what happens to anyone is that, when they have a baby, the first thing they do is worry: count the fingers, inspect the ears, the belly button, the breathing. One asks oneself: Is it normal? Or in other words, as filled with joy as one is at the occasion, one is also filled, to one's surprise, with anxiety and uncertainty. My mama, seeing me in this state when my first child was born, saw fit to confess her own doubts in days gone by, to comfort me.

"Ah, Son, there's nothing to worry about. For the first three years of your life, I thought you were half-backward, and look at you now."

It had not until then crossed my mind that my baby might have some cognitive defect. I was worried only about a physical defect, like a sixth finger on one hand or something like that, so all my mama's comment did was put ideas into my already confused head. But it wasn't there, or then, that I asked her to explain this business of my alleged mental incapacity. I would do that later, when I was certain and had the peace of mind of knowing that my son's body had nothing missing and nothing that wasn't meant to be there, and that he reacted in the way the doctor had told me that any normal newborn should.

My mama was also told by Dr. Cantú that her son was normal. That despite her having a premature baby late in life, he was not backward. That while it was precocious and inconvenient—for his caregivers—that a ten-month-old boy should run all over the place, it was common for a child his age to neither perceive nor understand dangers or warnings, and that, consequently, he would constantly encounter problems and live with bumps on his forehead. Later on, when some ability to communicate was expected of me at the age of two or three, the doctor assured her that it was not unexpected that I did not talk because, as everyone knows, boys take longer to learn.

"But, Doctor, it's not that he doesn't want to speak—the boy's a chatterbox—it's just that nobody understands a word he says!"

In fact, my mama used to say that they couldn't shut me up. That I was so argumentative and so verbose that my papa swore that I'd be a lawyer when I grew up—which she doubted, because if she and the nanas couldn't understand anything I said, a judge certainly wouldn't.

What was happening was that I spoke my fraternal language, which no one but Simonopio and I knew. Simonopio had been silent for so long that everyone had forgotten that he wasn't mute. And he wasn't. He never was: all those years before I was born, he had kept himself company with his stories and his songs, telling them and singing them to himself in the privacy of the hills. They were the same stories and the same songs that had been sung and told to him in Spanish, but from his incomplete mouth, they came out in his own way, a way I learned at the same time as my maternal language, from the crib.

Because he was never silent with me.

Why did my fraternal language carry more weight than my maternal one at the beginning? I don't know, but I suspect it might've been because what Simonopio said to me, in my ear and in private, was always more exciting than what my mama or my nanas said to me. It's always more appealing to hear about big adventures than it is to be constantly reminded that it's time to take a bath, to go to sleep, to brush your teeth, or to wash your ears: stupid things for an active boy like I was.

All of this is pure speculation on my part. I don't remember deciding one day that I'd speak "Simonopio" and not Spanish. What I do remember is that I couldn't comprehend why no one knew what I was trying to say, even though I understood everything they said to me.

I was just a little kid, you see.

When I reached the age of three and beyond, still refusing to utter a single word that wasn't what my mama called "chatter," even my papa began to worry. It wasn't until someone found me deep in conversation with Simonopio that they realized or remembered that he had tried to speak when he was younger but had simply not been understood, and that now, under his influence, I was imitating his defect.

My mama admitted to me, once I was a father, that they had asked Simonopio to keep away from me until I learned to speak properly. And he had tried to comply, but I wouldn't let him. I followed him everywhere and demanded his attention. This I do remember: the empty feeling in the days—or was it months or hours?—when I believed, without comprehending, that Simonopio was mad at me, because he wasn't waiting for me when I got up in the mornings like he always did, and didn't pick me up right away when I approached expectantly with my arms outstretched.

As I said before, since I was very restless even as a baby, and wouldn't let anyone finish their chores, I was passed from person to person until I ended up with Simonopio, who was by then waiting impatiently to rock me to sleep—and later on, when I was a little older, to carry me out into the country while he sang his stories.

He was the interesting part of my life.

With him, I learned to climb trees and to distinguish animal and insect tracks; to throw stones into streams while I dangled my feet into the cool water from the bank; to cling to his back like a monkey while we crossed a stream on foot or swam across a river; to hide, without making any noise or moving, under a bush or behind a rock, the moment he told me to do so; to watch very carefully where I placed my feet on the hill paths near the house so as not to make noise or trip; to avoid the poison ivy, though I didn't always succeed; to aim the slingshot that he made for me, though I didn't yet have the strength to pull back the rubber band; to not use this on birds or rabbits, though I asked him what, in that case, it was for; to help transport some bees on my body without frightening them off with waving hands; to enjoy their honey and royal jelly even if sometimes it was for medicinal purposes, while we spent an afternoon at Nana Reja's feet. With him, I learned to appreciate the music of the *tambora* bands, hidden from the eyes that made him feel so uncomfortable, sitting motionless in a corner of the third-class marquee at the Villaseca Fair, or—more carefully and stealthily because, according to Simonopio, in the second- or first-class marquees, the looks were darker—to listen to the marvelous Marilú Treviño sing "La enredadera," which was his favorite, or "La tísica," which became mine the first time I heard it, seduced by the image it evoked in me of the girl dying of consumption while a dog howled under her bed.

He taught me to keep quiet while he told me his stories, without asking anything or demanding to know the ending before it was time, because, *Francisco, the ending only comes when it's meant to come and not before, so sit quietly, or I'll never be able to take you to listen to Soledad Betancourt's stories when she comes to Villaseca.* With this threat, I obeyed immediately. He also taught me to fall asleep while we looked up at the stars above the roof of his shed, when they allowed me, on warm days, to stay outside with him at nightfall; to tell the morning greeting of a bird apart from its call to a mate or its danger warning sent up into the air; to follow the bees with my eyes and to know whether they had just left or were now returning; to discern which tree would bear fruit first; to know, just by looking, whether the oranges were ready to be tasted, and to never pick them green to use wastefully as projectiles.

From one moment to the next, I lost all of this. We both lost it: Simonopio was left with his arms empty, and I at the mercy of the regimented activities they imposed on me at home. Perhaps he was prepared to make the sacrifice, convinced that it was for my own good, but, ignorant of the situation, which I would never at any rate have agreed to or cooperated in, I didn't allow Simonopio to vanish from my life easily.

One day, when I was supposed to be napping, I went to look for him and found him under the pecan tree that marked the boundary between the grounds of the house and its gardens, in the company, as ever, of some bees perched lazily upon him. I remember throwing myself onto him with no warning or care, in an attempt, perhaps, to become just another bee that he transported on his body.

His eyes opened immediately, showing no surprise.

"Let's go to the orchard," I said.

"We can't. You have to stay here."

"Why?"

"Because you need to learn to speak properly, like everyone else."

I went back into the house intrigued. Was that it? Speak properly?

My mama assured me that a miracle happened that day, for after waking from what she assumed had been a peaceful nap, I emerged from my bedroom cured, and surprised everyone.

"Mama, I want to go to the orchard with Simonopio to look for my papa."

In this complete and clearly enunciated sentence, I said the words *mama* and *papa* in the language that they understood for the first time.

Of course, that afternoon when I learned to distinguish between Spanish and "Simonopio," we went to look for my papa without impediment, without Simonopio returning to the silence that my mama had imposed on him, and therefore without depriving me of everything he taught me in his own language.

Then I became his translator. Although almost everything Simonopio said was just for me—in the moment, things that you had to be there to understand—some things were useful to others.

"Papa, Simonopio says the bees say it's going to rain tomorrow."

It didn't matter that the sky was completely clear. Simonopio was adamant that the drought of several months would come to an end and that we had to believe him, because it was true: the next day it would rain. I don't know whether my papa received the prediction with surprise, skepticism, or complete acceptance, because as soon as I translated the message, I ran off thinking about what the rain would be like.

That was the first rain in my living memory. That's the nice thing about that age: experiencing every event as if it were the first time. By the age of three, I must've already witnessed rainy months before, though at that age, the months are endless and the brain doesn't retain the memory of something as fleeting as rain, which my mama might have forbidden me from going out to play in.

I can just imagine her now: *The boy mustn't get wet or he'll get sick.* It's curious how we sometimes forget something as simple and as immediate as an appointment with the dentist or a birthday, yet never forget something as ephemeral as feeling a drop of cold rain bouncing and rolling on our faces for the first time.

In all my years, it has not rained again without me remembering that day and the pressure and silence in the atmosphere before the rain. The fat drops of water soaking my eyelashes and hair in an instant. The aroma of the countryside wet not from irrigation but from rain, which isn't the same. Going from the intense heat of the inside of the house to the immediate cool of wet clothes. Seeing—and hearing—the water finding the best way to come together, first running in brooks and streams, then reaching a tributary of the river. Ignoring my mama's warnings of *Francisco, don't get wet or you'll get sick and ruin your shoes and clothes.* The tremendous feeling of having something to be excited about: Simonopio had promised he would take me to the place where, with the earth moist at last, the toads that had spent months submerged to protect their delicate skin would come out.

Hours later, I returned soaked and covered in mud. They wouldn't let me in the house in that state, so Lupita undressed me and washed me in the laundry. I don't know where the clothes I wore on that adventure ended up, but my mama had been right: my shoes were beyond repair and no good even as a gift for the workers' children. I remember that, as she lectured me—*Spoiled child. Why won't you listen? You'll get sick and then you'll see, and look at your ruined shoes, what will you wear tomorrow?*—she made a point of sighing, so loudly it was more like a snort, before throwing the shoes in the trash.

My mama knew exactly how to add drama to her admonishments. Even now, I still don't know which sound rings most loudly in my ears: that fatalistic sigh or the emphatic clang of my shoes meeting their end at the bottom of the metal trash can.

Contrary to my mama's prediction, that night I didn't fall ill, but I did drop down exhausted. I slept deeply, happy with my memories and also lulled by a sound, because on my bedside table, in a box, the toad I'd adopted croaked for me—contentedly, I wanted to believe. A toad that, at the moment of emergence, had seemed confused by his sudden freedom in the boundless world.

Turn here. Slowly, we're almost there now.

# 43

*Unrequited Desire*

More than seventeen years wanting it. And the land would not come to him.

More than four years searching for her, looking at her, waiting for her, but the woman still did not so much as say hello or send a smile in his direction. He looked at her, and after doing it so often, he had noticed how she looked elsewhere, always elsewhere. Never toward him. For years, he had suspected that a lot of it had to do with the influence exerted on her by that parasitic demon she had helped raise from the day he arrived.

But Espiricueta knew that, with Simonopio, all he had to do was intercept him at the right moment so that he could erase him from his life. He was trying: he searched for him, he listened, he planned. He would find out where the demon went with the boss or the child that was always entrusted to him now, and he hurried out to find him. The problem was that he never did. By the time he arrived, the demon had gone. When Espiricueta waited for him on a road, between two points, he never appeared.

It was as if, sensing Espiricueta nearby, the boy created another path out of nothing.

The devil was the devil, but a woman was just a woman. What could the problem there be? What obstacle? What resistance? But there was. He felt it. Espiricueta had never been a womanizer, but he knew from experience that, with women, making eye contact was enough. Not with this one—she didn't even turn around to see him. What was it? What did she see when she turned away, when she refused to look at him?

The angle at which Anselmo had positioned himself that night enabled him to see precisely where she was looking. She stared as if trying to shoot an arrow, as if she could send a message to her love interest with the force of her gaze: *I'm here, come get me.* But it was an unrequited love, Espiricueta noted with satisfaction, because the elusive man ignored her and looked purposely elsewhere, always elsewhere—in whatever direction, provided she was not there, provided their eyes did not meet.

The woman did not seem to grasp it. She did not seem to want to give up.

Anselmo Espiricueta had been patient with this ungrateful woman, with her devotion to the boy and his tricks, but he did not forgive her devotion—even if it was only in a simple look with her big eyes—to any other man. The devil was the devil, but a man was just that: a man. And if she was looking for one, then he, Anselmo, would be adequate, just as the efforts to which he had already devoted too much time must be adequate for her. He waited for her on the road when she returned from town on her day off. He followed her when she walked through the dark on the nights when the señor and señora allowed her to go to Villaseca to dance in the pavilion to the music of the tambora. He also paid for a ticket so that he could go see her, even if from a distance, while she waited for someone to ask her to dance.

She was asked to dance less and less, and never by the man she most wanted to press her body against to the rhythm of a song, however much she tried to send him a message of love with her gaze.

The years were slipping away from Espiricueta, but they were for her, too, and fast. If he did not hurry, she would no longer be of any use to him. He wanted land and wanted a wife to fill it with children. He was growing tired of waiting for them to give him the land and for the woman to start seeing him as a man and not as a shadow she came across once in a while.

So that night, he had been bold enough, for the first time, to ask her to dance, even though he did not know the steps of the schottische that she liked so much.

With effort, she had looked around when she heard his voice to see him standing there, in front of her. But she did not look him in the eyes, or register his slightly imploring tone, or seem to care about the humiliation to which she subjected him when she replied that she did not want to dance, before quickly looking back at the object of her attention.

With that uncaring little roll of her eyes, she had made him feel insignificant. She had managed to remind him that he had nothing: no land, no wife, and no possibility of obtaining either by fair means.

Some of his friends, the more docile ones, all of them laden with children, had already obtained their plots: with so much pressure to give up their good land, the owners had yielded, but not the decent fields; instead they handed over some in Hualahuises, with less water and of lower quality.

Now those friends had their poor land. They had made do with whatever they were given.

But Anselmo Espiricueta would not be content with any old hand-out. He kept it to himself, but he was reaching the end of his patience waiting for his land, which was gradually, steadily being taken over by orange trees and flowers. It was a war against time that he seemed to be losing. Anselmo knew what the land he trod every day was worth. It was his; he worked it and deserved it. Just as he deserved the woman, for desiring her so much and for so long, for too long.

That day, his patience with the woman reached its end, and as was now his habit, he followed Lupita along the dark tracks to La Amistad.

# 44

## *They Happen in the Depths of Sleep*

Simonopio woke with a start. It was not dawn yet, but a terrible feeling of falling endlessly had shaken him from the depths of sleep, which was where he most feared going each night. He knew that bad things happened when one—when he—allowed himself to fall so far asleep. Bad things that he could not then see in the instant of the first warning, when his eyes suddenly opened, with no gradual process of waking.

His heart gave a sudden leap, seized with fear. Francisco Junior? No. He breathed deeply, relieved. Francisco had gone to stay at his cousins' house. He was safe. Simonopio knew it. Perhaps that was why he had relaxed that night, feeling unburdened of his ever-present worry for the boy.

Then what had it been? What had woken him?

He was no longer a child. He was sixteen but remained as afraid of falling into the void as he had been as a youngster huddling near his nana's warmth. He no longer had anyone to seek refuge with, for he could not allow himself. Little by little, training himself on the nights he spent out in the elements faraway, as he searched for his bees' treasure, he had acquired the ability to stop himself falling, to avoid passing a certain point while he slept.

And he almost always managed it.

Some years ago, he had decided that his fear of falling into deep sleep was not unfounded, for it came from the certainty that something would happen when he was absent from his conscious mind, with his mind's eye asleep and disabled, vulnerable, and therefore abandoning the world around him, the world that he cared about, to its fate. He had always sensed, from a very young age, that nothing stops when the lights go out, when the eyes are closed, and one sleeps deeply. Nothing stops: what must happen will happen, without the slightest consideration and without warning. Without waiting for the first light of the morning, without a witness, without a guardian, because the guardian abandoned it all, seized by sleep.

However disciplined, however determined, Simonopio sometimes failed and slept, traveling to the place where everything was forgotten, even his senses. Sometimes—most of the time—nothing happened, and Simonopio would wake up grateful that he did not need to feel guilt or remorse for his carelessness. Most nights nothing happened. But there were other times.

Much like this new day, still wavering between the darkness of night and the first light.

Simonopio hated knowing that he did not know everything. In these circumstances especially, he hated the fact that, after the shock of being brusquely woken from deep sleep, his mind did not connect with the world's energy as easily as it normally would.

His only certainty: something had happened. But what?

He climbed out of bed in the dark. He wet his face with the cold water from the washbowl. He dressed without needing to see. Then he took an oil lamp. He lit it. He knew that he had to go out and he knew where to go: toward the place where everything started, along Reja's road. Of that much he was certain.

But he did not know what he would find there.

# 45

## Revenge Is Not a Woman's Business

Lupita's funeral was in the past, but the pain was not. And Beatriz wondered whether her family would ever return to normal after the tragedy.

She doubted it.

Her daughters, with their husbands escorting them, made the trip to be present at the funeral of the young woman whom they had loved in life without realizing it. Now, all too late, they were grateful for every favor that Lupita, who had been only a few years older than they were, had always done for them gladly. Lupita had never said no to them, and there was never a day when they woke up and she was not already doing her chores, which she did not hesitate to interrupt to say good morning and ask them, *Do you need anything, girls?*

Now they wondered and regretted how many times they must have passed her by without returning the greeting, thinking only about their own things, and how many times they must have received her favors without so much as thanking her.

Now they felt devastated, understanding—for the first time, perhaps, and firsthand—the true meaning of death: that there is no going back and that anything that was not said in time would never be said.

Carmen and Consuelo did not arrive in time for the wake, which had necessarily been very brief due to the state of the body, but they were there in time for the memorial service and to witness the burial: the simple pinewood coffin slowly lowered to the bottom of the deep grave, the stomachs of more than one of them clenching when the clumsy novice gravediggers lost control of the ropes that held it up at each end, so that the feet descended more quickly one moment and, to compensate, the head did so the next.

It was a terrible occasion on which even the new Father Pedro struggled to find his voice and composure as he administered the blessings.

No other words were heard, but neither was there silence: the weeping established itself as an accompanying murmur, as if, once the cadence and tone had been set, no one dared break the harmony of their macabre chorus.

That day, there were a few dry eyes around the grave. Francisco did not cry. Beatriz did not cry. Nor did Simonopio. He had not stayed to say his final goodbyes, telling them neither where he would go nor when he would return.

Later, sitting on the armchair in her sewing room, Beatriz Morales heard her daughters' wails, but she was tired of listening to them now. They felt obliged to remain with her and tend to her in their mourning, and she understood that, at their young age, they would want to vent their pain and horror with this unstoppable verbosity. But Beatriz wanted silence; she wanted dry eyes, so dry they burned. She wanted revenge and wanted, most of all, to be the main witness when it was wreaked.

Impossible, she knew. Revenge was not a woman's business, she knew, and she repeated it to persuade herself. As a woman, she would keep out of the whole business, out of harm's way, and she would accept it, because she was a woman. She would not get her hands dirty, though her soul already felt stained, despite being a woman's.

She had already made her confession to the new Father Pedro. She had done it at home, in a moment of respite she had taken from the wake, where she had to maintain her composure standing to one side of the closed coffin they had placed on the dining table. First and foremost, she had to feign calm, resignation, and absolute faith, while the desire to kill ate away at her.

She had confessed in the half-light of her sewing room, sitting beside the priest, without the protection and anonymity of the confessional.

"Do not look at me, Father, please."

She did not want anyone to see her in that moment of weakness. However, she had thought confessing would help her purge her body of the violent adrenaline, never before experienced, which sickened and frightened her, for it revealed elemental facets of herself that came from a part of her spirit and her mind that had escaped any attempt to train it to be a lady and the example of Christian virtue that she was supposed to be. But it had not worked.

"Remember, Sra. Morales, that Jesus Christ requires us to forgive even our enemies. As penitence, say ten Lord's Prayers every day. Yes, for them. Forgive them in this way."

"Yes, Father. Yes, Father."

Before returning to the wake, Beatriz took another few minutes when the priest went away. She needed to recover a little before going out into the lamentation that had overtaken her house. The confession had not helped: she would not say one—let alone ten—Lord's Prayers for the murderer or murderers, because she would not forgive their savage act. That was the truth. She admitted it. If she followed the priest's instruction, pretending that she was praying for Lupita's murderers, the first person to see her hypocrisy would be Christ Himself, and Beatriz Morales did not want to stoop so low as to try to deceive Him.

It would take her years to move on from this newly discovered impulse for revenge, and while she stopped short of praying for evil to happen, she would pray for herself. She would make her Singer her confessor. She would pray. She would pray while she sewed. She would sew confessing. She would confess sewing. She would pray and confess to the rhythm of her feet on her Singer's pedal and the brush of her hands against the material.

She would confess her wrongdoing: she would pray asking for forgiveness for the promise she had broken.

Lupita had arrived seventeen years ago by way of her aunt, a former employee who, on the cusp of a war that would destroy men in one way and women in another, was looking for a safe place for her niece, no longer such a young girl at the age of twelve.

"We'll take care of her here, Socorro. Don't worry."

*We'll take care of her here. Don't worry. We'll take care of her. Here, me, us, Francisco, the nanas.* But one night: no one. No one took care of her that night. And she went. She went violently. They tortured her in life. They tore out her hopes along with her eyes. They sucked the laughter from her mouth. They squeezed her until her very soul escaped through her pores. They ripped her from life.

Someone did.

They did not know who. It could have been anyone in those hills, where a willingness to kill over something or nothing still prevailed. In those hills that were still infested with a plague of bandoleros who, with no trade or principles, roamed surreptitiously and without permission across land that, though they did not want—or it was not convenient for them—to accept it, was privately owned.

That Tuesday morning, they had woken up as normal, with no hint that anyone was hurrying anywhere, in trouble, or absent. Francisco, as ever, set off to perform his duties almost with the first light of the day. Beatriz, as ever, had taken longer, enjoying the unusual silence of the morning: for the first time, Francisco Junior had gone to spend the night at the Cortés cousins' house. Otherwise, the house would already have been filled with his noisy energy. She had given him permission to go on the condition that he be obedient for Aunt Concha.

"And no sliding down the banister, eh. You saw what happened last time."

By copying his cousins—or were his cousins copying him?—he'd ended up with a wound on his forehead that had to be stitched, while she held him down and he cried out and cursed at the same time. Later they had been forced to apologize to the doctor and his nurse, as well as to Beatriz's sister-in-law, who was pregnant with her fourth.

"Don't worry. It was bad luck. My sons are always doing the same thing."

And Concha never lost her patience or her cool. Beatriz pictured her then, surrounded by children running rings around her, yelling like revolutionaries. *Better her than me.* She sighed.

She left the bedroom and headed to the kitchen, surprised at the absence of the usual sounds of the morning routine in the house. She found Nana Pola there talking to Mati.

"What is it?"

"Have you sent Lupita on some errand?"

No. Beatriz had not seen her since she gave her permission the previous evening to go to a cousin's *quinceañera* celebration in Villaseca.

"Mati says she wasn't here when she woke up this morning."

"They must've snatched her, Señora." Mati, who shared a room with Lupita, had not waited up for her. "I always hear her when she gets back, because she makes more noise than a train. But today I opened my eyes, it was daytime, and there was no Lupita."

The clothes she had left on her bed, in her rush to get to the party, were still there: Lupita had not returned in the night.

"Send Martín to see if she's with her cousin or friends. Perhaps she stayed there to sleep."

Martín returned without Lupita, but with the news that she had said goodbye before eleven o'clock, and not even at her cousin's insistence had she stayed longer to dance: she was very tired and wanted to sleep. Martín had seen her there, too, from afar, but when he looked for her at midnight to head back to La Amistad, she was no longer there. He had not seen her on the way home. No one else saw her.

"Martín, go tell Sr. Francisco."

The search began in the Villaseca area, going door-to-door along the most common route between the house where the dance had been and the house where they were anxiously waiting.

"They've taken her," Mati said and repeated without understanding why they told her to be quiet every time she did so, given that, with each hour that passed, it seemed like the best possible fate for the poor missing girl. What she had started saying as a prediction had gradually become a wish: better that she had been snatched, taken as a live-in lover, and impregnated, than something worse.

By midday Simonopio had arrived, in a state. Earth from the hills covered his face, except where his tears, dry by then, had made paths of clean skin. Beatriz knew: Lupita was no longer missing.

Simonopio did not want to stay to rest or drink sweet chocolate for the shock. He just turned around and headed in the direction of the coach house. By the time Francisco arrived, looking for him, Simonopio had the cart ready. Nobody questioned him.

Martín refused to go with the rest of the men to recover the body. He did not want to see her like that, he said. Then Beatriz remembered Francisco's warning years before to his worker, after finding him flirting with Lupita: "Watch it, Martín. Not with the women of the house, understood?"

They had not had a problem of this kind with him since, but now Beatriz wondered what would have been had they allowed him to court her. Perhaps Lupita would not have gone out alone that night. Perhaps she would already have her own family. Perhaps right now she would be making her children lunch. But there was no sense in Beatriz allowing her mind to continue down such recriminatory paths.

It would never happen now.

Martín, on the other hand, had remained sitting in the kitchen, motionless, staring blankly, drinking—at Pola's insistence—the hot chocolate originally meant for Simonopio. Nana Pola was trying her best to console him, but he did nothing to help her as she cried silently, without trying to hide it.

Beatriz left before her mouth and eyes could pour out her feelings—it would offer no comfort and serve only to darken the atmosphere in the kitchen even more.

She went to look for Nana Reja. Perhaps with her it would be acceptable to sit and say nothing. When she arrived, she saw that the nana had left her rocking chair, which now rocked by itself, as if missing the weight and shape of its habitual occupant. Beatriz, alarmed, went to look for her in the semidarkness of her bedroom: she found her lying in bed, her eyes closed as always, and not making a sound, as she never did. Beatriz did not know how, but it was clear to her that Reja knew what had happened. Her silence and motionlessness, the way she barely seemed to breathe, away from the air and light that she enjoyed from her rocking chair, were her way to express her grief: alone, as ever, but away from the hills that called to her. And in turning her back on them, she punished herself; she repented.

Too much pain for such a slight body.

"We'll find whoever did this, Nana Reja."

Beatriz made a promise without thinking. Later she regretted it: what right did she have to make promises of such magnitude, if she had not fulfilled such a simple one made years before?

The nana did not react to her words or her intentions. Maybe she did not hear, Beatriz thought with relief.

Mati was in her own bedroom, crying noisily. Though she was much older, she had shared her space with Lupita since the girl had arrived. Beatriz decided not to go in. What for? For now, she did not have any words of comfort. She was grateful, then, that Francisco Junior was not at home that day. Who would have looked after him? Who would have explained it to him? She did not feel up to it. They would do it when everything was over. In two or three days, when her voice regained its strength and steadiness.

Today she felt neither strong nor steady.

Practical as ever, though she had to try hard to remember that trait of hers, Beatriz made a mental list of what they would need that day. With everyone busy recovering the body or struggling with their grief, Beatriz decided to carry out all the tasks herself.

"I'll be back soon."

After informing them, she went out on foot in search of the doctor, whom she found easily at the clinic. There was no rush. It was not a health emergency, but in any case, Dr. Cantú promised her he would come right away.

Finding the new Father Pedro did not prove so easy: the cathedral and all the churches had been closed by order of the government. Now the priest lived and conducted services illegally, dividing his time between various houses, including the Morales Cortéses', rotating his residence to avoid being an imposition or putting anyone at risk. Beatriz could not remember which family he was staying with at that moment, and while she did not want to speak to anyone, there was another visit she had to make: she knocked on her brother's door, though she did not want to go in.

"You'd best tell Sra. Concha to come, yes?"

"She's sleeping."

"Tell her to come."

She informed Concha succinctly, with no details, no drama, of Lupita's death. Concha did know where the priest was.

"I'll go find him. Please, keep Francisco Junior for a few days, until everything's over."

Then Beatriz went to look for the clergyman, who also gave his word that he would be there to receive and anoint the body. She thanked him, because it was no small thing: at that time, being a priest was a dangerous business, especially if the soldiers caught him administering a sacrament.

From there she went to order a coffin, whatever she could find: whatever was available that very day. She did not go to report the death to the Guardia Rural. She would leave that to Francisco.

When she returned home, she was surprised to find that, although the doctor and priest were already there, the men had not yet returned with the body. Later, she learned that they had stopped to clean it up a little by the side of a pool of water, so that, as far as possible, they would spare the women the horror of the appalling task.

Their well-meaning efforts proved futile: when a body had been subjected to so much violence, nothing could be done to clean it.

When the doctor arrived, he asked them to spread a blanket out on the kitchen table and lay the damp, half-naked body on top so he could examine it.

"Sra. Morales, if you do not want to be here, I can find someone else to help me."

"I'll stay. And Pola will too."

Lupita had been found at the edge of La Amistad, on the road to La Petaca, under the little bridge where Nana Reja had found the newborn Simonopio covered in bees. They had thrown her there, perhaps hoping the body would never be found, devoured by every insect or animal that took a fancy to it.

Simonopio had found her, and she had returned home. Now, how could they not stay by the side of this girl who had clearly suffered so much in the last moments of her life?

Her dancing clothes had been shredded. Her hair, which Lupita usually wore in a braid, was untied, tangled, and full of leaves and clods of earth. Her face, beaten and scratched, was beginning to show signs of rigor mortis, so there was no way to deceive oneself by pretending that the girl was sleeping peacefully. What's more, her eyelids, closed and bruised, no longer protected the absent eyes. Her neck was imprinted with marks from the murderous hands that had wrung it mercilessly.

When they removed her clothes, they saw the bite marks on her upper body.

"Animals?"

"No. Human."

"They did all of this while she was alive?"

"I don't know, Sra. Morales. I don't know."

"Well, when they killed her, she was alive," Nana Pola cut in, sobbing.

"Go, Nana. Yes, you'd better. Don't worry. Go rest."

But she stayed, though for the rest of the examination, no one spoke.

In the end, after washing it, the usual shine had been restored to Lupita's hair, clean and carefully brushed, as if its owner were still alive. But it was a brief illusion: the body was growing ever stiffer, and if they did not shroud her very soon, they would have to wait for it to pass.

"Fix her hair how she liked it, Pola. I'll go fetch a sheet."

Beatriz opened the cupboard where they kept the whites and took out a sheet made from the finest linen, the sheet that Lupita would have spread out on her mistress's bed early that morning, had it been a Tuesday like any other.

Now it would serve another purpose.

When she returned to the kitchen, Simonopio was there. Seeing her come in, with an urgent look, he handed her a bloody handkerchief. Beatriz braced herself: when she unwrapped it, she was horrified to discover Lupita's dead eyes.

Her first impulse had been to complain about the offering, saying, *You give your godfather a handkerchief full of flowers and give me one full of horrors?* But she reconsidered: it was Simonopio, and there was no morbidity or cruelty in him. Whatever he did, he always did it thinking that it was the right thing to do, and in this case, it was: a body must not be buried incomplete.

Beatriz put the eyes inside the folds of the white linen shroud, near the girl's hands.

"Thank you, Simonopio."

That was how Lupita went to the grave and how she would reach God: complete.

That night, Francisco and Beatriz took turns keeping vigil beside the coffin. Francisco went to sleep first. They offered pan dulce and hot chocolate to everyone else who wanted to stay. Beatriz knelt beside Socorro, looking at nothing except the succession of beads, saying nothing except Rosaries and litanies for Lupita. Beatriz was grateful that, with everyone concentrating on the Rosary's palliative rhythm, she did not have to face the aunt.

When Francisco returned—if not fully rested, at least ready to continue the wake into the early morning—Beatriz withdrew to her bedroom. It was her turn to rest, and with luck, her body would. But her soul would not, for it was as heavy as lead.

When she reached her bedroom and saw the unmade bed, she remembered that it had remained like that all day. Beatriz undressed but did not bother to put on nightclothes. She did not care. Nor did she change the sheets, even though Tuesday had gone by without anyone thinking to do it. She remembered the sheet in which she had wrapped Lupita's naked body, and shuddered. Tomorrow, she thought, tomorrow she would do it. Tomorrow she would do everything: *Tomorrow I'll change the sheets, I'll see my daughters, I'll look Socorro in the eyes, I'll bury Lupita. Today, I'll do no more.*

She lay in the dark, without falling asleep or reconciling herself to the new absence. Or the new reality. Before she finally closed her eyes, the mild, light smell of lavender that remained in the used sheets reached her nose. It was the smell of Lupita.

She cried. She gave herself permission there and then.

"But not tomorrow."

# 46

## *In Good Time*

Simonopio did not go far on the day of Lupita's burial. It was blossom season, and it was among the little flowers that he would find some peace. He walked from orchard to orchard, losing track of time. He walked tirelessly between the rows of trees, back and forth in the company of his swarm, which refused to leave him even though the day, the sun, and the flowers called to them to fly freely to enjoy the fruit of their labor. As the sun went down, they left him, because they would not face the darkness even to be with Simonopio.

Tomorrow would be better, they had said to him as they parted company. Tomorrow, calm would return. Tomorrow the flowers would still be there for them, for everyone.

Simonopio understood. Tomorrow, or the next day, he would let go of the memory of Lupita's dead body. Of the feel of her dead eyes in his hand. Of the time he'd spent lying beside her: her body cold—lifeless and cold—and his body alive and warm—warm but limp—given over to crying, with no strength or will to share the terrible news. He knew he had to do it, and he would, as soon as he found the strength, because he knew that his work would not end there: he understood that, after raising the alarm and handing over the body, he would have to go in search of Lupita's lost eyes.

Still lying like this sometime later, but calm at last, he sensed the peace of the place: Lupita had not died under this bridge—his bridge. Had that been the case, Simonopio would have sensed it, of that he was certain. Lupita died where her eyes lay abandoned. They had taken her here after she was dead—to hide her or as a message, he did not know. There were no longer any strange smells. He found nothing in the past or in the future that would enlighten him with the answer to the question that everyone would ask for years to come: Who killed Lupita?

He had seen the question in Francisco Morales's eyes. His godfather even ventured to ask, *Did you see anything, Simonopio? Or do you know anything?* But he shook his head. It was true: he did not know anything.

And although she had not asked the question, he had seen it in Beatriz's eyes, as well. He also noticed something else in both of them, something that seethed uncontrollably, transforming them: the thunder, the lightning, the deluge, the storm. He saw that they would search for the murderer and that, if they found him, they would struggle to hand him over to the authorities, to hand him over alive.

They would search for him for years, but he would evade them easily. They would never find him. Then Simonopio understood that no one would discover who Lupita's attacker had been and that no one would find justice for the murdered girl. No one but he.

When? Where? How would he recognize him? He did not know, but it would happen. In good time.

# 47

## Today, a Dead Desire

They were burying the dead girl today at the boss's house, but no one had sent him an invitation. There was no work today. Everyone was there, and only he was here. And today the land was his alone, and he did not have to be so quiet.

> *Now the golden eagle has flown*
> *and the finch is chased away.*
> *At last the day must come*
> *when the mule takes the reins . . .*
> *Oh, come it will*
> *the mule will take the reins . . .*
> *Oh, come it will, oh, it will come*
> *when the mule takes the reins*
> *when the mule will take . . .*
> *the mule will take . . .*
> *take the reins.*

# 48

## *He Who Lives by the Sword—or the Gun*

Francisco Morales was confused. If he had prepared for any eventuality, if he had sent his daughters to Monterrey to protect them from the danger and drama of the countryside, then why was he so surprised and shaken by what he had feared would have already happened on his land, to his people? Had he thought himself immune, deep down? Had he, in his arrogance, come to believe that certain situations always happened to others and not to his own people?

Lupita had matured from a noisy child who did not know how to do anything into a woman who had mastered her work, yet remained loud, chatty, and chirpy. Lupita had successfully learned to read with the same enthusiasm with which she attempted to learn to sew with the machine, though without managing the latter.

*You lack patience,* Beatriz had told her, also with little patience.

*Ay, Señora, if I can't draw a straight line on a piece of paper, how am I going to draw one with thread on a flowery material?*

In fact, Lupita had had a great deal of patience. She demonstrated it when she looked after Francisco Junior, a task that was far from easy, since only Simonopio knew how to keep him constantly entertained.

Now her death had been a blow for everyone. Because there were deaths and there were deaths. It had not been a stray bullet that killed her. Or influenza, or malaria, or yellow fever. She had not even been the victim of a revolutionary seeking a woman's company, of the kind that made off with a girl to bring him warmth and children. No, Lupita had fallen into the hands of a being beyond Francisco's comprehension, one that killed for the sake of killing. And worse: killed a woman.

He thought of the times in the past when, regretful, missing them, and faced with the evidence that nothing bad had happened, he had wanted to go to his daughters at the nuns' school in Monterrey to bring them home once and for all. Now he knew that nothing happened until it happened. Now he was facing the fact that he had let down his guard. He admitted that, with the armed conflict—the official one—abating, he had stopped worrying about the well-being of his people and focused on the well-being of his land and assets. Not even the government's war against the Church's faithful had moved him to act.

"All the real men are in Jalisco, it would seem!" his aunt Rosario had said to him at his refusal—and the refusal of every man in the region— to join the new armed movement in defense of the Catholic Church.

He did his bit: he offered shelter to the new Father Pedro. He donated money so that the Catholic schools could continue their lessons and so that the holy sacraments could still be administered, albeit in secret. But there was a big difference between that and joining the pitched battle.

His fight—yesterday, today, and forever—was for his land. His struggle, until now, had involved only books, laws, and trees, but Lupita's death tore him from his sense of security, from the false comfort he had taken from the feeling that he was winning the war over his land through ingenuity.

As long as there were those that coveted their fellow man's land, there would be no peace. There would be no security.

He knew who had killed the girl. He did not know his face, because it could have been anyone, but he knew his intentions and motivations. He knew his whereabouts. It might be this one or that one. It might be all of them. But he knew who Lupita's murderer mixed with, and now he was riding to join his men, whom he had arranged to meet near the scene of the crime to get rid of the agrarians once and for all.

Francisco had been content to contribute with a sizable sum of money to help maintain the Guardia Rural, the force that the land owners created. They patrolled, but it was a vast expanse of land, and however hard they tried, they could not be everywhere all the time. In the hills on his property, Francisco or his men often found remnants of cold fires, gnawed bones, hard pieces of discarded tortilla, a forgotten spoon, or even, on one occasion, a harmonica.

The agrarians moved from hill to hill every night or two to evade the rurales, and settled down to eat and sing their socialist songs under the stars as they plotted to rob those who slept placidly, like sheep, feeling secure.

Even after seeing the evidence of their incursions, Francisco had not been alarmed. He had always thought, *Well, they were just passing through, they've left without causing trouble, and they won't mess with me.* However, since Lupita's murder, he had not slept peacefully, because he knew that they were prowling around, surrounding them. And he would not sleep peacefully again until he could look his wife in the eyes and say, *It's over.*

The previous night he had made a decision: the agrarians would not pass through his land again. They would not spend one more night on his property. And they would not dare use his land as a pillow or mattress or for shade or sustenance.

On his land there would no longer be a single sip of water with which the agrarians could continue to wet their resentment.

When he reached the agreed-upon place, all his workers were already there. He dismounted and passed out the weapons and ammunition that he had bought illegally from the local army barracks. He could have acquired them on his next trip to Laredo, but he had not wanted to wait: he needed to arm his men better. The 7 mm Mausers were much more accurate over a much greater distance than the old .30-30 Winchester carbines that they already knew, even without being expert marksmen.

"You'll need to practice. I'll give you the rounds. With the gunshots that will be heard on our land from now on, we'll scare off the agrarians. We're all going to protect our women and our land, because if we don't do it, who will? So practice, and keep practicing, and if you see any invaders, shoot to kill."

"Yes, Boss."

Francisco Morales had never seen Anselmo Espiricueta respond with such enthusiasm.

# 49

## *The Aunt That Nobody Invites*

When I lived here, all of Linares's streets were numbered. Now look: Morelos, Allende, Hidalgo. Calle Madero and Calle Zapata run parallel, and two blocks down, they both meet Venustiano Carranza.

Just as the two men's paths crossed in life, they are now destined to come together on the streets of Linares forever.

I don't know whether, in the land of the dead, our revolutionary heroes are happy with the arrangement—whether being there has enabled them to settle their quarrels and grudges—but I can assure you that many of my relatives must be turning in their graves at the idea. I know that my aunt Refugio, in particular, must be grateful she isn't alive to have to leave her house on Calle 2, under the old nomenclature, and see it called Calle Zapata. And for my grandmother, Sinforosa, it would have been worse: her street was renamed Venustiano Carranza, who she always blamed for making her a widow.

Turn here.

That one, on your left, was my grandmother's house, which later went to my uncle Emilio, one of my mama's brothers, when my grandmother was widowed. Now, like everything in Mexican city centers, which have been invaded by stores, it's very down-at-the-heels, but at the time it was one of the largest and most attractive houses. I spent a lot of time there with the Cortés cousins, getting up to mischief. My mama always told me to behave or I wouldn't be invited again, which I didn't understand, because all I did there was copy my cousins.

I liked living in my house in the country, but waking up in down-town Linares also had its charm, because the sounds of the cathedral's bells, the milkman's whistle, and the knife grinder's flute were all so close. Then the evangelists would knock on the door to do their evan-gelizing, to which whoever answered would respond, in irritated silence, by slamming the door on them. Lady acquaintances, friends, or aunts arrived constantly, saying that they were passing by and stopped to say hello. The challenge for us, then, was to slip away without being seen.

And then there were the neighbors: on one side, Sra. Meléndez who—my cousins swore—practiced sorcery like the witches of La Petaca, giving the evil eye to anyone who crossed her path. "Never let her look at you, Francisco, or your balls will fall off."

You would've thought that, with that threat and the imminent danger that one could sense in the neighborhood, going to my cousins' house would lose its appeal. But no: it was very exciting to sit for hours on the sidewalk, playing marbles, waiting for the first sign that the witch Meléndez would come out of her house. We avoided her seeing us at all costs but took any opportunity to spy on her. And we would follow her, because everything seemed suspicious to us: if she went into the church, it was to perform a spell. If she was buying fabric, it was to make herself some new witch's clothes. If she was going to the drugstore, it was to obtain herbs for some potion. She moved with difficulty, as if one side of her body required the reluctant cooperation of the other. According to my cousins, the most conclusive proof of her devotion to the forces of evil was that the left side of her face, the side of the body where the heart is, belonged to another person.

"Look how, if one eye blinks, the other one doesn't, and when one side of the mouth speaks, the other side stays still. See? Two people in one."

Poor Sra. Meléndez. My cousins cared little that their mama visited their neighbor from time to time or that they went to the same church, frequented the same drugstore, and bought fabric at the same shop: one was a witch and the other was simply their mama.

That was the neighbor who was a witch, on one side. On the other, the Cortés house adjoined the Southern Star Masonic Lodge, which my cousin, with his endless ambition to be king, called on us to invade and conquer in a surprise attack. The first person had to scale the walls and then—waiting for it to be deserted, naturally—reach the heart of the enemy fortifications: the room with the round table and the swords. The first to arrive would not be made king; that would always be my eldest cousin, and there was no way to take his crown from him. Arriving first just gave us the right to choose the sword we wanted and to sit to the right of the throne, which according to my cousin, the king, was the greatest honor. As one of the youngest, I never got there first, and I barely had the strength to lift my sword, but my eldest cousin, who became the king as soon as we were through that doorway, made all of us knights: boys and girls.

I can imagine the freemasons' bewilderment when they arrived at their secret lodge and found that Member A's sword was now where Member B's should've been, or that one was missing because we'd left it under the table. They must've felt like the three bears after Goldilocks broke in. It did not take the freemasons long to deduce who their furtive visitors were and to complain to my uncle Emilio, who of course forbade his children from returning and threatened them with a beating.

While I had a great deal of fun at my cousins' house, I also spent some of my most boring times there, because when the time came for me to go to school, the Catholic ones had closed by legal order, so we children of good families went to clandestine schools set up in houses. By pure coincidence, due to my age and because I was a boy, mine was based at the Cortés cousins' house.

I think that's why it took me a long time to settle into studying. I was always confused by the fact that I wasn't allowed to do the same things as before when I went to school there—I was used to visiting a house where it was perfectly acceptable for me to mount the banister and slide down it, yelling; to bump down the stairs on my backside; to run in and out as I wished so that I could hear the various vendors going by; to attack the kitchen when I had a twinge in my belly; to go to the bathroom without having to ask permission from anyone; or to go into my cousins' room to fetch a toy. As a cousin, I could do anything; as a pupil, I had to learn to stay seated, without speaking, eating, or even going to the bathroom, until the teacher told us it was time to answer, eat, or go to the bathroom.

Becoming obedient was no easy task. I took any opportunity to escape, and knowing every suitable nook and cranny, I did not find it hard to go from hiding place to hiding place until I reached the front door and escaped into the freedom of the street to set off for my home on La Amistad. Of course, my intention was never to reach my house, because I knew what would happen: they'd send me straight back—forcing me, what's more, to apologize. No: my plan when I fled school was to lose myself among the orange trees. What would I do there all day? I didn't know. What would I eat? I didn't know. By that time, I had overcome my fondness for eating beetles. With luck there would be ripe oranges on the trees. Otherwise I would go hungry.

And how would I return home afterward? My plan wasn't a very elaborate one, and I hadn't thought that far.

I never found out what would have happened at the end of the school day when my mama sent Simonopio to collect me. I didn't even get to the stage where I felt hungry. I never had the chance, because my adventures as an escapee never lasted more than two hours. However much I tried to hide, Simonopio always knew somehow, without being told, that I wasn't where he had left me early that morning, and if he didn't find me on my way back, he would navigate through the orchard's trees like a bee searching for the only flower until he reached the tree that I'd climbed in order to hide.

Invariably, he took me straight back to school, without allowing himself to be persuaded by my complaints about how boring it was to be kept in all day with the teacher's endless blah-blah-blah. With a single disapproving look, he made me be quiet and go obediently with him. I didn't like him looking at me like that, displeased, or talking to me with the tone that the adults in my life used. He wasn't an adult: he was Simonopio.

"Never go out alone. It's very dangerous. Something could happen to you."

"What?"

"Something."

"Like what?"

"Like running into the coyote."

By then I knew what fear was, and the figure of the coyote was the root of it, so going out the front door, alone, at six years of age, was an act of courage in which each step took effort.

If I was so afraid, why did I never listen? Why did I run away from school again and again?

Now I think I kept reoffending because I knew Simonopio would drop everything to come find me. I think that's what I wanted. School bored me, I admit, but I easily could've found some other mischief to get up to right there, something that would keep me busy without needing to leave the building. But by then I belonged to the outdoors, and Simonopio had made me just another bee in his swarm. The clumsiest, yes; the most annoying, sure; but my days didn't feel complete if I didn't spend them with him, buzzing in the open air, playing the games that he and I played.

At school, my disappearance was always detected. The first time, they wasted a lot of time searching for me in every hiding place they could think of, but once they realized it was a breakout, they immediately sent a message to my mama, repeating the same thing each time thereafter: *Your son has disappeared.*

My mama told me much later that, the first time she received the note, she felt her heart stop from the fright, though by the time she had run to confront the negligent teacher and ask for more information, Simonopio had already returned me to my place. On subsequent occasions, she would take the news of my absence more calmly—after learning that what the school lost through neglect, Simonopio would find without fail.

I don't remember the spanking that first time I disappeared, which she gave me while she repeated everything that Simonopio had already said. No doubt it hurt, but I never learned anything by dint of a spanking, which was why, when one of my cousins asked to be included in my next escape, we didn't stop to pass the time in an orange tree. Emboldened, me by his company and he by mine, we went all the way to the tracks, hoping to watch the train go by. But since it was taking a long time, we decided to press our ears against the iron to hear it coming. Step by step, without realizing it, we went and made ourselves comfortable where the track bridged a ford. Maybe it was because of our age: bored of waiting, we forgot our lookout duties, and by the time we realized the train was approaching, it was almost on top of us. Not knowing where to run to save ourselves from the steamroller charging toward us like an enraged bull, we held hands, and emboldened once again, me by his company and him by mine, we leaped. It was not a great height, but we would have earned ourselves a fracture or two had we not landed on the padded softness of a nopal patch. When Simonopio found us—the first and only time he didn't return me to school—we were pricklier than the nopal, which we had left half-ruined, half-bald. Though in pain, we had no choice but to walk to my house.

The spanking my mama gave me that time—on impulse, without even waiting to extract the prickles from my backside—I will never forget. My only consolation was that, in the hours she spent trying to remove them one by one, she cried with me.

My duty-bound, long-suffering, and prickly schooling—it would be years before my skin was as smooth as before—was not yet a reality when I spent three glorious days at the Cortés cousins' house after Lupita's death. I must have been around four then, so as you'd expect, no one involved me in the tragedy. I simply learned, to my delight, that my stay—a simple invitation to sleep over that was originally to last one night—would be extended to a vacation of three days, though even that seemed very short to me.

By the time I returned home, everything had passed: there were no flowers, relatives wearing black, or traces of wax that trickled from the candles that must have been lit. The house had restored its order, but it had not returned to normal. When I asked after Lupita, Nana Pola ran to get my mama so she could give me whatever explanation she considered appropriate.

"Lupita won't be here anymore."

"Why?"

"Because her papa sent for her. He asked her to go home because they missed her a great deal."

Since mama was saying it, I had no reason to be suspicious. I didn't like Lupita not being there but understood that her family would want to see her, so I had that idea in my head for years. However, when I returned from my three-day vacation at my cousins' house, it was impossible not to notice that the atmosphere and routine had changed, and not just because of the woman's absence: Simonopio was gone too. I searched for him in his shed, but his body and his warmth were not there. I went to see if he was with Nana Reja, but she rocked and didn't respond to anything. I waited for him to arrive that night in the company of my papa, but my father returned alone and not in a talking mood. I searched for him all the way to the entrance to the orchard, which was as far as I dared go unaccompanied at that time, but there was no trace of him there either. I asked Martín, and he didn't reply. When I asked Nana Pola, her eyes filled with tears, and she ran off in search of Mama. I was afraid that, like Lupita, he had also been sent for by previously unknown family, but my mama quickly responded that he had only gone on holiday: *Just like you,* she said to me, *but he'll be home soon, you'll see.*

That night and the following nights, I fell asleep thinking about him, believing that if I thought as hard as I saw many people pray, he would hear me: as if nothing but my intense desire to see him could summon him from a distance. *Come, Simonopio.*

Several days passed without news.

With no Simonopio or Lupita to play with me, I would search for my mama so that she would read to me like she sometimes did, but she shut herself away, sewing endlessly—anyone would've thought she had taken it upon herself to supply uniforms to an army. When I woke up, she was already pedaling her machine, and when it was my bedtime, there she still was. And in the midst of all that, she didn't have so much as a scolding for me, not a complaint, or a story, or a caress. Not even a good morning or a goodnight.

Nana Pola and Mati were no help: sometimes I found them with tears in their eyes, but when I asked them why they were crying, they always answered that they'd just been chopping onions.

For years, I was afraid of onions.

There was something odd about my papa too. He was always busy: even when he was in the house, at the end of his day, it was as if he kept himself outside of his body, as if he'd left part of himself out among the orange trees. Everything he did around the house, he seemed to do mechanically. Now I know—I understand—that he had a great deal on his mind. But at the time I couldn't comprehend why my papa, who I didn't see much in the day, wouldn't pay me the attention I was used to receiving from him: we might not have seen each other much, but in the little time we had, we saw each other a lot.

In those days after Lupita's death, the only time he seemed to come out of his self-absorption was when other citrus growers came to discuss things with him behind a closed door. But even if I was silent and listened closely through the wooden panels, I couldn't understand what they were talking about with any clarity.

Before then, I'd just been interested in being able to play at whatever I wanted; now, after being away for three days, the little universe of my home had changed, and I wanted to know why. All of a sudden, I could not even gain access to my papa or mama in order to demand an explanation. I might've swallowed the story about Lupita having to go to her family, but sometimes, what children don't understand, they feel, and something monumental had happened in my absence.

With too much time to spare, bored, worried, I paid more attention to what was happening around me, to what the grown-ups were saying without realizing I was there, and there was one name that kept coming up: Agrarian Reform.

It was nothing new, but before that day I had not paid much attention when they mentioned it. I thought it was some woman they were referring to, like a gossipy, loud aunt nobody wants to invite to family gatherings.

*What could she have done?* I'd used to wonder when I heard her mentioned with disdain. Something bad, I was sure, and off I went to play without a care in the world.

At that disconcerting time at the age of four, when I listened closely, the penny finally dropped. I finally understood that the sin of this reform, *the Reform*, was that it sought to destroy everything that we were and all the work that my papa had done. I understood that it sought to take everything from us, from our way of life to our lives themselves, perhaps.

And for the first time in my life, I was afraid.

# 50

## *Nothing. Just Crickets*

Simonopio had found a certain amount of peace and distraction wandering among the endless rows of fruit trees, enveloped in the daily song of his bees, immersed in the stories that he had committed to memory, but in doing so, he completely lost the notion of time and his connection with life away from the hills.

He had left without considering Reja, without telling her, but what for, if she knew already? Simonopio needed to get away from the world to rest, like she did just by closing her eyes. For him, it was not so simple, because when he closed his, he continued to see life. So he kept them open, always open, to fill them with so many images that they did not have time to show him anything that was not right in front of him.

He had thought he was winning the battle.

Then, one night when the crickets chirped like any other night, an annoying, unintelligible, indecipherable whisper reached his inner ear. It had attempted to gain entry before, but until then, Simonopio had managed to repel it in much the same way one would wave away a buzzing fly. That night, he also tried to ignore it, for in the repetitive rhythm that those nocturnal insects laid down, he found another source of purification—one that he was reluctant to let go. However, the sound had persisted: it demanded to be heard, to stop being just an annoying noise, forcing Simonopio to allow it to take shape and become a whisper. It demanded the part of his attention that had taken a well-deserved rest, reluctant to come out of the scattered state in which it felt so comfortable. That part wanted to linger here, immersed in the sound of the crickets that talked for talking's sake, that chirped in their madness, spellbound by their own voices, making the same sound again and again without changing their rhythm, without changing their meaningless message, communicating nothing. Nothing. Nothing.

Simonopio wanted to remain in that soothing balm of nothing, but the whisper would not let him. It kept coming. It was like déjà vu: familiar and unfamiliar at the same time. Little by little, without him wanting or anticipating it, it began to take on meaning. Through repetition and insistence, it found its way into his ear, until Simonopio once more understood the language that he had needed to forget temporarily in order to rest the ether of his mind, the conundrum of his heart, the liquid of his bones, the seed of his eyes, the heart of his ear, the filter of his nose, the parchment of his skin.

Then he recognized the voice. He listened. He understood: *Come, come, come, come,* the whisper yelled, as repetitively and rhythmically as a cricket, but not without meaning. That *come-come-come-come* was an urgent call to him, one he should never have ignored for so long, let alone with so much intent.

It was the boy's word that called to him: *Come-come-come-come.* So he shook off his lethargy and left the indifferent concert of the crickets to return to the path he was meant to follow, concentrating on what would be his only companion on his return trip: *Come-come-come-come.*

Before long, he had matched his pace to the urgent rhythm of the call, and soon he was forced to trot and then to run at an ever-greater speed so that he would not lose it. But halfway home, in the darkness, the whisper suddenly stopped. It had gone to sleep. That silence tore at him, and the void that the absence of the call left now became a cacophony that thundered in his ears and would not let him breathe deeply or walk with certainty.

When, before sunrise, he reached La Amistad, he went straight to the house but found that they had locked the door. They had never done so before, but he supposed that in the new world without Lupita, they must have reconsidered and corrected their oversight. He was silent as he entered like a thief through the window in Beatriz's sewing room: the latch was designed only to hold against strong wind or on days when winter made itself felt, and not as an obstacle to someone breaking in, so Simonopio opened it easily. Treading softly, he was silent as he crossed the house until, reaching the corridor where the bedrooms were, Simonopio forgot about the loose floor tile, which, with its clunk, alerted Francisco Morales to the intrusion.

"Who's there?"

The hair disheveled by his pillow and the striped pajamas contrasted with the ferocity in his eyes and the cocked revolver Francisco held as he came out of his bedroom.

"Simonopio?"

"Uh-huh," he said, relieved as he saw his godfather lower the weapon when he recognized him in the darkness.

"What're you doing up at this hour?"

Simonopio had no way to answer the question, because it would have required many more words than a simple *uh-huh*. How could he reply that he had needed time for himself? He could not say, *I'm back and I won't leave again, I'll never leave him alone again.* Even if he could have uttered those words, Francisco Morales Senior would not have understood the message, so he just said *uh-huh* again, pointing toward Francisco Junior's room.

"He's sleeping, and you know what he's like—"

"Uh-huh," he answered again.

"Well, it's up to you. Good night."

As he turned to go into the boy's room, Simonopio's foot touched the noisy tile again. He spun around to apologize, but Francisco had already closed his bedroom door. Simonopio would have been very sorry had he woken his godmother with his carelessness. He knew that the last few days had been hard for her and doubted that she managed to sleep easily. He was not worried about Francisco Junior, who was still asleep, insensible. He wanted to shake him awake to tell him, *I've arrived, you called and I came, I'm late because I got lost for a few days,* but from experience, he knew that nothing and no one would be able to make the boy open his eyes until he was ready to do so. Francisco Junior slept deeply, and every night he surrendered to his dreams, unsuspecting, unafraid of falling to the depths to which Simonopio no longer dared go.

Simonopio sat on the rocking chair where four years earlier he had positioned himself to gaze at the newborn in his crib. This boy no longer slept in his baby bed: before he was two, they had been forced to move him to a lower one, because he insisted on trying to escape from the crib by climbing the bars and throwing himself at God's mercy, sometimes falling on his backside, sometimes on his knees, and less frequently—*Thanks to God and his guardian angel,* his mother said after a loud sigh—on his head.

The bars did not represent safety for him like they had for Simonopio as a small child: they were captivity.

The light of the new day began to filter into the room until it filled the space. During the process, which started slowly and ended in an instant, Simonopio barely blinked, concentrating, trying, in the slow and gradual luminosity in which the boy's face was bathed, to see the baby he had been and the man he would become, all at the same time. He had no difficulty making out the baby in those bones, assisted perhaps by his memories, but the face of the man eluded him: he saw promise there, but no certainty.

He decided that it was time to teach him more. Francisco Junior was no longer a baby, but if he was going to become a man, he had a lot to learn, and Simonopio was determined to teach him. In silence, he promised that he would never leave him alone again. No sooner had he made the promise than the boy slowly opened his eyes, as if he had heard it.

"You're here?"

Francisco Junior fought to emerge from his dreams, and seeing Simonopio there—sitting in the morning's soft light, the sun's rays that fell on him intensified by the dust that was normally invisible—he did not know, for the moment, whether Simonopio was real or just the product of wishful thinking.

"Yes. I won't go away without you again."

He did not have to say anything else. Francisco Junior believed him.

# 51

## *There Are Monsters*

At six years of age, I was old enough to go to school. Not that I wanted to, but I had no choice.

The person entrusted to take me there was Simonopio, who walked while I rode my horse: an old, slow, squat pony that I'd insisted on calling Thunderbolt. I'm sure that Simonopio would've preferred to keep carrying me on his back, like when I was younger and he carried me everywhere like that, but my papa wouldn't allow it anymore.

"You'll start sagging, Simonopio, and he'll end up with his legs dragging, without learning what they're for. Let him walk."

And so, I walked everywhere, except school, because before long it became clear that I didn't have the slightest interest in arriving on time. As part of my stalling strategy, I would stop to look at every worm or stone that crossed my path, to untie my shoelaces so that Simonopio had to tie them again several times, to sit urgently in the shade of a tree to rest my exhausted body and feet.

In order to avoid more conflict and to get me there as fast as a thunderbolt, they allowed me to ride Thunderbolt.

Simonopio spent the walk to school trying to educate me in subjects that were important in a child's personal development. While I was already learning to read and do my first mathematical calculations at the clandestine school, Simonopio tried to teach me to listen and to see the world like he did. I never managed to understand the murmur of the bees or to perceive smells like they did, or to see what was around the bend on the road or concentrate on trying to "see" my mama in my absence, or sense whether the coyote was lying in wait for me out of sight, hidden. Having never seen him—because as soon as Simonopio sensed him close, he made us hide, motionless, or change our route—I would say to him fearfully: *Let's go see him so I can recognize him.*

He never agreed.

"The less you see him, the less he sees you."

Simonopio's lessons did not stop there: he tried to make me see with my eyes closed and to remember what would happen the next day, but since I could barely remember what I'd had for breakfast that very morning, I was hardly going to remember something that hadn't yet happened. Then he asked me to see the day I was born, to remember the first contact with my skin, the first sounds in my ear, the first images that had poured into my eyes. However much I tried, I could succeed only in deciphering what was right in front of me: *A horse passed through here a short while ago,* I guessed. I never fooled him: anyone would deduce it when the horse in question had made use of the road to purge its intestine of its aromatic load.

I knew it was a source of frustration for poor Simonopio, and to please him—to be like him—I would make the effort to concentrate. But I was not yet seven, and given that I was a very active boy, I found it particularly difficult to stay still for a long time, especially when I was itchy from the mosquitoes that had eaten me alive in the night because I'd slept with the window open; when sitting down was painful because of the nopal thorns in my backside; when my stomach complained about the chorizo and egg I'd had for breakfast; when I knew I was about to face punishment for not doing my homework; when I knew I would have a miserable day doing letters and numbers, longing to go off with Simonopio to enjoy his day, which would be full of adventure, smells, and sensations; when it seemed more important to me that he should tell me another version of the story of the lion and the coyote; and when I didn't understand what all the things he wanted to teach me were for.

I arrived at school frustrated to see it appear in front of my eyes so quickly, when I would have preferred to just pass on by. That was why I thought Thunderbolt must be a thoroughbred racing horse, like the ones that competed at the Villaseca Fair.

Now I admit that Thunderbolt was nothing to boast of, though I felt important with my speedy mode of transport, even if it always got me to my destination more quickly than I would've liked. Arriving in the company of Simonopio also fed my arrogance and conceit, because the majority of the other pupils, who lived in the town, arrived on foot with their nana or mama, who never failed to look amazed when they saw us. For months, I thought it was because of my and my companion's bearing, and I always made sure I was sitting up straight when I arrived, elegant, as I imagined a knight on horseback must ride.

Simonopio would help me dismount, then he would climb onto Thunderbolt and rush off, almost without saying goodbye. Accustomed since he was a boy to the disdainful stares of the people in the town, he never fooled himself into thinking that a rickety old horse and a boy with curly, close-cropped, fair hair were enough to ward off the blatant looks, devoid of kindness, that sought to decipher the incomprehensible map of his face.

I was surprised when an indiscreet and careless boy asked if I was scared to be in the company of a young man with the face of a monster. I obeyed my impulse, and as soon as he finished speaking, I socked him. While I might not have left him with the face of a monster, at least I gave him a swollen eye. As punishment, I was sent to stand in the corner for the rest of the day, examining the texture of the wall, without even being able to turn around to watch the school day unfold.

That day I was more bored than ever, but I felt proud: I had defended my brother. But there was nothing I could do to defend myself against authority. When, still offended, I told the teacher that it was because the boy had said that Simonopio had the face of a monster, he replied that one should not hit someone simply for telling the truth.

The truth? Simonopio had the face of a monster? I'd never seen it that way. In Linares there were monsters, sure, but he wasn't one of them. For me, Simonopio's face was Simonopio's face, the one my eyes had seen since they first opened. Yes, it was different from mine, my parents', and my sisters', I knew, but his features were as familiar and as dear to me as theirs were. I didn't see the defect or any reason to be shocked. I saw only my brother, and I loved him.

There and then, I made up my mind to punch anyone who dared speak ill of him again. Simonopio was worth a day of punishment, or two, or ten.

That was my first fight, but not my last. The school kept complaining, and my poor mama didn't know what to say to stop me fighting. After a time, she tried to persuade Simonopio to let Martín take me to school, but he emphatically refused. He was responsible for taking me, and no one else. It wasn't that he wanted to provoke anyone or make me fight for him: *I don't care how they see me,* he said, *don't fight for me anymore.* But I was incapable of letting any offensive comment go. In the end, my mama went to my papa for support.

"Francisco: tell Francisco Junior to stop fighting."

"No. There're fights that are worth fighting."

Little by little the boys stopped making comments, at least in my presence. They all knew the consequences of mocking my companion, so they were better off keeping quiet. Anyone who wanted to be my friend soon learned that they would have to accept me with Simonopio by my side. With prolonged contact, the new friend did not take long to stop seeing his mouth and start seeing his eyes.

Simonopio resumed his silence when we had company, since no one understood him other than me. His wordlessness didn't matter, because being with him meant we could explore the orchard to find the row of orange trees with the most fruit strewn on the ground, rotting: perfect missiles for a pitched battle that ended when the bees, attracted from afar by the juice that ran down from our hair, arrived to take over our game, which always made me the winner, because I was the only one that didn't run away in terror at the sudden presence of the swarm.

Perhaps that was why I earned a reputation for being brave—or reckless, depending on whose point of view it was. Just as I had grown up used to Simonopio's unusual appearance, the same thing happened with the bees: I grew up with them, and I wasn't afraid of them. Or maybe the fact that I'd grown up with them meant they didn't harm me, because they knew me and accepted me, perhaps, to please Simonopio.

Nor was I afraid of the characters that I shared liberally with my good and not-so-good friends, telling stories I'd memorized: the Weeping Woman, the Egyptian mummies that roamed the streets of Linares at night—*Have you seen them?*—the witches of La Petaca, the doll, the vengeful ghost of Agapito Treviño, the vengeful ghost of the soldier abandoned to die in a cave, the vengeful ghost of my grandfather shot on Alta (heartfelt apologies to my grandfather). I should explain that all the ghosts had to be vengeful, or their power to terrify would be reduced. If the other kids wanted to hear about real monsters that roamed the area, I knew them all.

And friends or not, they listened eagerly: it must be that, even from the most tender age, we all possess a morbid streak that makes us enjoy feeling terror.

When she returned from a meeting with the social club ladies, my mama always said to me, *Stop telling silly stories, Francisco; all the mamas are complaining that their children are too scared to sleep.*

To be honest, I didn't care whether they slept or not: to each his own. I felt so protected that nothing stopped me from sleeping.

Nothing and no one troubled me in the depths of night—the time that children fear most—and in all likelihood, it was thanks to Simonopio, who took the time to teach me the words of the extremely effective blessing Nana Pola had taught him years before. Although, as someone who slept deeply, falling into deep sleep easily and with little in the way of a buildup, I never even finished a Lord's Prayer before dropping off—by the final *s* of "God bless," I was asleep.

Could those two words have been enough to protect me from night terrors? It seems so: they must have been sufficient to dissuade all the monstrous characters that tried to visit me in those vulnerable hours of the night.

Roaming mummies were no reason to lose or interrupt my sleep, which at any rate was so deep that, had the mysterious dolls—which Simonopio assured me lived on our property—walked or danced on top of me, I never would've known. If the Weeping Woman passed through asking after her children, she soon would've moved on, for I neither reacted nor replied. The ghosts, whether vengeful or not, never managed to move so much as a hair on my head, and in any case, they must've gone to frighten some other soul after using up all their energy without making me so much as open an eye.

The story I never shared with anyone was the one about the coyote, perhaps because its strange narrative evolved constantly. Perhaps because it felt like a private conversation between Simonopio and me: not even Soledad Betancourt, a professional storyteller who thought she knew every tale or legend, knew of its existence or of the danger of the coyote. Perhaps I didn't share it because I understood that the one about the coyote was different from the ones about the dolls, ghosts, and the rest of them. That the coyote wasn't a story, it was real. That it searched for Simonopio and me, for the lions that my brother assured me we were. That against that real monster, no blessing was possible: only precaution, nothing else. Or perhaps because, deep inside, it was the only monster—the only unknown one—that I really feared, day or night.

If even Simonopio feared it, then how could I not?

And on those nights when I couldn't shake it out of my mind, knowing that the constant repetition of *Lord bless, Lord bless, Lord bless* wouldn't do me any good, I changed my litany to *come-come-come-come*. And he never failed me. He arrived in the darkness, with no warning and without saying a word; he unrolled a mat on the floor beside my bed, and there he lay, in order, somehow, to make me match my breathing to his, to slow it down—slow it down until I was hypnotized. And with that human shield between my vulnerable body and any nocturnal threat from the coyote, I slept peacefully, deeply, without interruption.

I woke up happy to return to school again and spread terror among my willing peers.

When my mama asked me where I got so many strange stories from, I never admitted that Simonopio told them to me or that he had taken me to listen to Soledad Betancourt when she came to the Villaseca Fair or visited Linares of her own accord. There are things one knows instinctively, and in this case, my instinct screamed at me not to reveal my source. I didn't, because I suspected that it might spell the end of our outings to see a little bit of the world in the shows that came to Linares.

And I didn't want to take that pleasure away from Simonopio.

# 52

## *A True Wonder*

Simonopio was on his way back to La Amistad, riding across the town square on Francisco Junior's Thunderbolt, when he heard something he had never heard before. For someone used to hearing sounds, voices, and even thoughts using something other than his ears, it was surprising.

It was a wonder.

He stopped. He stopped right there amid everything and everyone, without caring that he was in the way and that people were giving him stranger-than-usual looks. He tried to locate the direction from which the metallic and unintelligible voice came—sometimes from the right and sometimes from the left, it seemed. It bounced off the drugstore wall, which sent it toward the square, where it faded a little among the trees and grew louder again as it left, before causing the same effect on the other side, echoing off the wall of Sr. Abraham's store, and then returning along the same route. Simonopio tried to follow the sound with his eyes, but he could not locate it because it moved more quickly than his vision, albeit without ruffling a single leaf on the trees that stood in its path.

The people around him were talking, walking, going about their business, and they did not seem especially surprised at the phenomenon.

Could it be that only he could hear it? That was very often the case, though now, at the age of nineteen, he generally knew how to distinguish between that which emanated from the world everyone inhabited and that which was exclusively his: the secrets that the world shared only with those prepared, like he was, to allow them in and to interpret them and commit them to memory.

This was new. He did not know how to interpret it. Amid the confusion, he couldn't understand the words reaching him from all directions. Quickly uttered words that interweaved and camouflaged themselves with a music of repetitive rhythms.

Then he saw the people begin stopping what they were doing and looking around also, trying to make out from what direction the racket was coming—it seemed to be approaching more and more from the right.

Attracted by the noise, the people of Linares came out of their homes and businesses. The ladies, who at that time of day usually spent an hour contemplating the Holy Sacrament in the church, had put their meditation on hold to rush out, their curiosity piqued by such a rare interruption. The teachers at the state-run schools—and those at the secret schools—could not contain their pupils, who in the excitement ran out onto the street to witness the phenomenon. Simonopio saw Francisco Junior in the crowd as well, but with a signal, he told him not to move from where he was.

Like Simonopio, everyone was wondering what the noise was, and it was not long before they found out. For at that moment, a pickup truck from which the sound seemed to spring forth turned the corner. Mounted on it, the tambora was playing at full volume.

And the voice? How was it possible that it was not being drowned out by the music that enveloped it? But it was not: over the music, the voice was growing clearer and more distinguishable with every turn of the truck's wheels.

Simonopio had always thought that Marilú Treviño's singing voice was almost miraculous, because while it was soft, it traveled with purity over the music of her instruments and other noises, without stopping until it reached each corner of the pavilion where she sang at the Villaseca Fair. Other less gifted artists were now using the new microphones, their voices taking on harsh, unpleasant metallic properties, albeit less so than this voice now was echoing around the square. Because then Simonopio noticed that was precisely what the man on the truck was yelling—not singing—into without respite: a portable, cone-shaped microphone pressed against his mouth, giving the announcer the strange appearance of someone trying to swallow something bigger than his head. He spoke so quickly and with such energy that Simonopio had to concentrate hard to make out a few of the words. Yet the people, who were multiplying and assembling to walk behind the slow-moving truck, seemed to understand him and celebrate his message. It was not until the vehicle passed in front of Simonopio that the words became clear to him. Over and over, the man was repeating:

"For just twenty centavos, come on Saturday at five o'clock to the old La Verdad Mill to hear Pedro Ronda, the True Wonder, sing underwater—with no equipment!"

The people applauded the announcement, no doubt excited for the event that would break the routine and also promised to be magnificent—wondrous.

Simonopio did not move from his saddle. He did not yell hurrah, cheer, or applaud. He did not even move to follow the party on the truck, like many other people were doing. Hearing the man clearly once was enough to unleash his imagination: How was such artistry, such skill, possible? Singing in public was in itself something that amazed him, which was why he never missed an opportunity to enjoy a show, whether at the Villaseca Fair or smaller events. But listening to someone sing underwater was unheard of, even for Simonopio, who sometimes observed the fish in the river when they approached to see him on the bank. However hard he tried, he could not hear or understand what they wished to communicate to him.

Who was this Pedro Ronda, the True Wonder, who would sing before all of Linares while submerged in the river in front of La Verdad Mill? What gift did this human have that even fish did not?

The truck and its racket drove off and turned down another street to continue announcing the party. The voice, which for a moment had been clear as it passed in front of him, turned back to metal and recovered its shrill meaninglessness. Once again it reverberated on the drugstore, faded among the trees, then bounced back off the Arab's store. The people who did not follow the truck went back to their work, emptying the square: the ladies returned to their contemplation, shopping, or housework; the men to their businesses; and the teachers to the more difficult task of shepherding their pupils back into their classrooms.

Simonopio decided to spur on Thunderbolt, who in the ruckus had made no attempt to move a single leg. He turned the horse around to follow the truck. When he reached it, he directed Thunderbolt toward the right side of the crowd. Then he spotted him: Francisco Junior had climbed onto that side of the vehicle and, as if he were part of the show, was waving at the people on the street, ready to remain with the caravan until the end.

Francisco Junior did not see Simonopio approach and get into position to heave him down and onto Thunderbolt's back, in front of him. Battling with a boy whose adventure had been interrupted and with a horse that was unaccustomed—and did not like—carrying the weight of two people, Simonopio turned around again to head to the Cortés house and return the child to school for the second time in less than fifteen minutes.

Francisco Junior kicked and waved his arms angrily. He seemed to think that he would miss all sorts of things if he did not go with the truck, but Simonopio also knew he took any opportunity to avoid being shut away for hours with his teacher.

"The show's not today; it's on Saturday. Today's a school day."

"It's ages till Saturday."

"It's just five days."

"That's ages. I can't wait five days."

"Yes, you can."

It seemed like a very long time to Simonopio too. But he would wait and so would Francisco Junior.

"Will you take me?"

"Yes."

"Do you swear?"

"I swear."

Simonopio figured he could quite easily raise the forty centavos it would cost the two of them. He would sell some jars of honey to the people on La Amistad. It was expensive, but it might be a once-in-a-life-time opportunity. Nothing in the world would have made Simonopio miss the chance to see Pedro Ronda, the True Wonder, who, with more talent than any fish, was going to sing underwater with no equipment.

# 53

*Alchemy*

Francisco Morales was in a bad mood. It was his normal state, of late, every time he dealt with Espiricueta, whether it was to agree to a date to inspect the land he had assigned the man more than nineteen years ago, to hand over the season's seeds or a new box of ammunition for his Mauser, or simply to ask amiably after his children. There was no getting through to the peon, who grew ever more uncommunicative and unsociable. He always put off the inspections that Francisco routinely conducted on all of his sharecroppers' land with the aim of finding ways to make it more productive. If Espiricueta answered a question, he always mumbled his response with his head down, without looking Francisco in the eyes like any upright man should address another upright man.

The years of protection had not been of any use to the southerner. The parcel Espiricueta occupied was the only remaining land on the Amistad estate that had not been planted with orange trees, because he refused to change. Francisco did not understand why, considering that, for some strange reason, the maize crops Espiricueta insisted on sowing did not thrive. Sometimes he suspected that the peon did not give his crops the care they needed, but whenever he decided to pay an unexpected visit, the son—what was his name? Francisco could never remember—was always plowing the land with his own sweat and brute force or irrigating it during their allocated irrigation time.

Even so, the Espiricuetas' harvest was never good. It was never even sufficient to cover the rent agreed upon in 1910. Now Francisco was reaching the limits of his patience. First out of pity and later because of the simple convenience of keeping his land occupied, he had overlooked this ineptitude and lack of productivity.

He could not put it off any longer.

He thought he had managed to frighten the agrarians away from his land, but they were not the only ones threatening the family property: there was also the agrarian bureaucracy, which never tired of sending official letters demanding to inspect the entirety of his properties, to check the deeds of ownership, and to confirm the legality of the transferals of land he had conducted years before to some trusted friends.

Francisco felt harassed. He seemed to spend more time doing paperwork and providing explanations now than he spent on the orchards and ranches. In Tamaulipas he had already had to give up a ranch, but in Linares he avoided expropriation through the deals he had struck, handing over more and more of the land in Hualahuises, which was the property that interested him the least.

He had defended his land in Linares by any means possible.

The orchards were gathering momentum: the orange trees had proved very productive, and there were ever-fewer setbacks from the army or bandits ambushing the shipments of fruit to various parts of the country and to Texas, where the market paid good prices.

With a great deal of pride but even greater relief, he had, in a relatively short space of time, been able to put back the large withdrawals that had depleted the bank account. However, that no longer mattered: two years before, in 1928, the Milmo Bank, which the Morales family had entrusted with their money for generations, had suddenly gone bankrupt, without warning or mercy. One day he received a letter informing him in very formal terms that everything he had believed he had—decades of savings, his inheritance—had vanished. His mind was still trying to solve the financial riddle, the alchemy, that had turned more than a hundred thousand gold pesos into nothing more than a piece of stationary full of apologies as empty as his bank account.

"We're going to have to start again. It's all gone, Beatriz."

"We have land and strength."

"You think so?"

"I know so."

"What're we going to do?"

"You, you're going to get up tomorrow morning like you do every day. Go to work on your land, like you do every day. And thank God that you were brave enough to use that money for useful things while you had it. And I, I'll wait for you here, doing my own things, as ever."

Beatriz was right: the Morales Cortés family's life had not changed because of the loss of a bank account that they did not depend on to live. Francisco had never stopped working for a single day out of the arrogance and vanity that comes with wealth. He had never lived like a rich man or envisaged himself living extravagantly in the future.

Thanks to the fact that they had used the money in the bank while they had had it, and more recently to the bonanza that the orchards had provided, they had even been able to cooperate with the other members of Linares Social Club to finally fund the long-awaited construction of the club's building, which was now making good progress. They also had the house in Monterrey and the land. They had the tractor that was so useful, though Francisco had to admit he was now admiring and stroking another cutting from the *Farmers' Almanac* advertising a much more modern and compact model—albeit with a heavy heart, for they were unable to purchase it in their current situation. Thanks to that gold, he had been bold enough to change their land's calling, and the investment had paid off twofold: with the success of the oranges as a crop and as protection from any major expropriation.

He mourned the loss of the gold, of course—how could he not? He even joined a group of creditors from Linares and Monterrey to file a suit against Milmo Bank, though he could not see how, by legal means, they would be compensated for the loss of their fortunes. They organized meetings, they ranted and raved, they cursed, they complained, and some even cried. It was all for nothing: Francisco suspected it was much easier to make a mountain of gold disappear than it was to make it reappear again from nowhere.

His fortune was gone, but his property was not, which was why, now more than ever, he felt not only the obligation but also the need to defend what he had left. Why he could no longer allow himself the magnanimity he had shown Espiricueta. Why he went to him to inform the man that, if he did not agree to plant orange trees on his allocated plot, he would have to leave.

The news did not go down well with the campesino.

"I been working my land nineteen years, but I wanna plant tobacco."

Francisco was surprised to hear so many words strung together coming from Espiricueta's mouth. And the business with the tobacco was news to him.

"Tobacco was planted here before the sugarcane, but it didn't work. And you've been failing to fulfill our agreement for more than nineteen years. This is as far as it goes: you do what you're told, or you leave. It won't cost you anything. I'll bring you the trees. You plant them and tend to them. Oranges sell, and it's the best way to stop them taking our land, Anselmo."

Silence.

"I'll see you here on Saturday. I'll help you get started."

# 54

*It's the Best Way to Stop Them Taking My Land*

"Yes, I'll see you here Saturday."

Instead of irrigating his maize, though it needed water, Anselmo Espiricueta went to practice with his Mauser.

# 55

## *Not All Saturdays Are the Same*

I remember those five days of waiting.

When I climbed onto the pickup truck, I did so imagining that I was running off with the circus and would learn, like Ronda, the True Wonder, the trick of singing underwater. It's not that I wanted to earn a living by singing under the surface; rather, I imagined that, if one was able to sing in such an unusual and adverse environment, first one would have to be able to breathe like a fish in water. And just think of all the big adventures that such a skill would bring me.

How many Saturdays had I lived through until then? It was April 1930, so I calculate that, up to that point, there must've been 363 Saturdays in my life so far. Not that I paid much attention before I started school, but from then on, every Saturday seemed glorious to me because I didn't have to go.

At almost seven years of age, I had experienced seven Holy Saturdays, which were the most eagerly awaited because the color and activity returned to Linares life after what seemed like never-ending monotony, traditionally beginning on the first day of Lent. Then there were certain Saturdays when the Villaseca Fair came to town, when the best quarter-mile horse races were held. Those seemed special to me. There were also the Saturdays in the summers that we spent with my cousins on one of the ranches, trying to remain submerged for as long as possible in the pools that formed on the river banks—hence my intense desire to learn Ronda's aquatic skill.

That Saturday in particular was, for me, the Saturday of all Saturdays: my seventh birthday coincided with the underwater spectacle, and the whole town was gathering at the event that, at times, I persuaded myself was being held in my honor. I imagined Ronda, from his place underwater and with the show in full swing, saying clearly through the bubbles, *May the guest of honor come forward!* And there I'd be in the front row.

Yes, the wait was long.

During those torturous schooldays leading up to the Saturday that was so eagerly awaited, so widely publicized, and so very much mine, no one—neither pupils nor teachers—spoke of anything else. *Impossible,* the adults said. *Impossible.* The innocents said, *But he said so! He said it through the megaphone and we all heard it!* As if saying it through a megaphone was a sort of guarantee. But one and all would attend the aquatic recital: the line had been cast, and we were all fish ready to bite.

Two days before, in the square, on the streets, everyone stopped to discuss the matter, asking one another, *Are you going?* Just like that—no need to specify what event or what day they were referring to. They all knew, and then they would say, *See you there? What time are you going?*

*Well, it starts at five.*

*But we could go earlier. Take some food.*

*We could spend the day in the country.*

*Let's take tortas and lemonade.*

*Let's meet at twelve, then.*

*To get a good spot.*

Getting a good spot would be crucial.

That Saturday, even the storekeeper Abraham closed up shop at four in the afternoon. All the field workers had asked for special permission from their bosses to work a half day. The barracks, which some years ago had appropriated the town's largest hospital building, left just two soldiers—two that were being disciplined—so that the rest could join the party. And no parent, even the most skeptical, had been able to deny their children the Saturday outing.

Except mine.

Every day of those five I had to wait, I embarked on a new campaign to persuade my mama and papa to go, without success. I believe they must've been the only ones to categorically refuse to pay the twenty centavos each to someone they declared was a con artist exploiting the gullible people of Linares. Not even my own attempts at extortion—all my friends were going, it was my birthday—forced them to yield.

I wasn't too worried, because I had Simonopio's promise: he would take me, and if my mama and papa wanted to miss out, that was their business.

As ever, whether fast or slow, time always passes, and grain of sand by grain of sand, every date arrives. And so the Saturday that all of Linares had been waiting for also arrived.

# 56

## *Sharing Sweat and Shade*

She had brought up her children with discipline, following the rule that one should not say yes to everything, but by the Saturday in question, Beatriz Cortés de Morales had tired of saying *No, no, no* and *Please, leave me in peace,* because her petitioner, in spite of—or because—his seven years of age, was indefatigable and relentlessly stubborn.

There were moments in the last five days—which had seemed like weeks to her—in which she had been about to give up and say, *Go on then, go see that Ronda, that wonder, that good-for-nothing.* But the family already had plans for Saturday, and they did not include wasting time and money on a refugee from some nearby village who, in the ten years he had spent living as a parasite in Linares, had done nothing but extract money from people of good faith using trickery.

The event on Saturday was just another ruse.

Beatriz did not know what people would find when they went to see the aquatic singer's show. To some extent, she understood why— needing some kind of distraction after the years of hardship they had lived through and the years still to come—even the most suspicious townspeople would give in to their curiosity.

The interest in Ronda was just a pretext for many people.

With the excuse that Ronda had given them, why not enjoy what promised to be a warm, lazy spring day by the riverside, sitting in the shade of the trees, surrounded by family, games, good food, and friendship? Beatriz suspected that some were looking forward with glee to what the evening would end in: some good jeering—which Beatriz knew would be well deserved—at the performance of the supposed underwater singing. For them, twenty centavos each was money well spent, because they would enjoy the day, spend time with their neighbors and friends in the open air, and then enjoy the mass mockery—which they might even instigate themselves—of someone who undoubtedly deserved it.

For twenty centavos each, they would have an anecdote to enjoy for years.

For one reason or another, it seemed that everyone—both the credulous and the cynical—would meet at La Verdad Mill. Even Francisco's workers had asked for a half day off, and while he refused Francisco Junior, as their boss, he had allowed them to go.

He tried to dissuade them, but if they wanted to spend twenty centavos on stupid things, it was their choice.

That Saturday morning, when they woke Francisco Junior, his father said to him, "I need you to come to work with me today."

And his mother added, "And when you get back, I'll be waiting with a birthday cake. What do you think?"

Finally, they had found a way to silence the boy's incessant begging to go to see Ronda.

Francisco would not achieve what he had originally set out to do that day, but even so, he wanted to continue with the plan, albeit on a smaller scale: he would take Francisco Junior to start planting the orange trees he had set aside for Espiricueta's land. Francisco did not believe it was too early to involve his son in matters of the land, to understand what would be his inheritance. And by the same token, it was time to strike up a closer relationship with his only son, a relationship he felt he had neglected, first because of the boy's young age and later because of the problems and distractions of being the head of a family in troubled times.

In the absence of any peons or Espiricueta—who Francisco assumed would make himself scarce that day, reluctant as he was to make the change Francisco had proposed, and who he assumed would be attracted, like everyone else, by the gathering at the river—the two of them would plant five or six trees by themselves. They would take a picnic, and then the father would give his son his birthday present: the old .22-caliber rifle that had belonged to his grandfather.

"Yes, Beatriz: he's old enough to use it. With me."

He would teach the boy to be cautious, to aim, and to fire, but also to care for the rifle and clean it in the way that it merited after use.

Francisco was certain that this special gift would compensate for not being able to join the crowds at the river, which would end only in disappointment. The rifle, on the other hand, would offer excellent opportunities for father and son to spend time together. It would provide a way to find common interests that would remain with his son for his whole life, as Francisco hoped the .22 itself would, so that in the future, his son could leave the precious object to his own sons.

Francisco's father had also given it to him at a young age. With rifle in hand, having learned to use it with skill, Francisco spent entire days and nights feeling himself grow as a man with his father by his side, practicing shooting, going with him to his ranches, warding off rattlesnakes, standing guard at night to watch over the cattle on its journey to be sold in Texas, hunting white-tailed deer, salting and drying their lean meat in the sun so it would last all season, drinking bitter coffee boiled without a filter in the pewter pot, and saying little, because his father was a man of few—though always precise—words.

He had learned to listen to and memorize every one of the words that his father very deliberately said to him, because there was always a lesson in them, even if they were said in jest and took Francisco a long time to understand. Like when his father advised him, with great wisdom—*Because it's worse for blonds, my boy*—to never go out in the sun without a hat on.

"And always walk on the shaded side of the street, so nobody tries to borrow money from you."

That was one of the lessons that took him the longest to understand: Why would someone ask to borrow money if he walked on the sunny side of the street, but not the shaded side?

Idiocy, he concluded, after maturing a little and becoming a little more sensitive to the pleasant sarcasm that sometimes appeared in his father's scarce words: when there's shade, only the idiots walk in the sun.

It was time to teach Francisco Junior to walk in the shade, to tell him about his grandparents, about what the family had earned through its own efforts and lost by the design of others. He would tell him about how painful death is, but also about the absolute pleasure of life. He would have to wait a while longer to tell him about the value of a good woman, though it was not too soon to tell him about the value of good company and the respect and care that, as the landowner he would be, he owed to all those for whom he was responsible.

He did not know where to begin and had admitted to Beatriz that he felt a little nervous—inadequate, perhaps. Not as wise as his father.

"With the first turn of the cart's wheel: that's where you'll start. And don't be in a hurry to teach him everything today."

It was true: it had taken his father years. He would take his time too.

While Francisco loaded the cart with the grafted saplings grown in his own nursery, as well as a pick, a spade, and the rifle wrapped in canvas, Beatriz organized everything else, eager to enjoy this one day of peace, because even Pola, Mati, and the new girl had asked permission to go to the river.

"Mati, make some egg tacos with potato and chorizo. Wrap them up well and then pack them in the basket. Fill up the bottles with lemonade so it lasts them all day. And you, Lup—"

It was almost three years after Lupita's death, but Beatriz could not get used to her absence or stop saying her name. *Lupita, Luu—, Lup—* was the first thing that came out of her mouth when she spoke to the new washerwoman.

Out of necessity they had hired another young woman, a girl from a good Linares family, but Beatriz could not get used to her or rid herself of the knot that had formed in her heart since Lupita's death. It must have been why she could not become fond of the new servant, even though she was a very hard worker, good natured, and patient with Francisco Junior.

She knew that it was not fair on poor Leonor, as she was called, who had arrived knowing that she was coming to replace a dead girl, not least when Nana Pola and Mati insisted on reminding her of it every day with some comment, some subtle, others not so subtle: *Ay, how we miss Lupita,* they would say, or *Lupita left the clothes so white.*

"And you, Leonor," Beatriz corrected herself, "look for a sweater for Francisco among the winter clothes, because he's going to need it. I hope it still fits him. Pola, take two blankets from the chest and put them in the cart."

Her husband and son would not be cold.

The weather, usually warm in spring, had taken them all by surprise. That Saturday of Francisco Junior's birthday, against all forecasts and logic, the day had begun wintry: windy, cloudy, and cold.

"Simonopio told me yesterday that it would be cold today and to wrap up warm."

"Then why didn't you tell me yesterday, child?"

Her son and godson had kept her in the dark, which was why she was there now, at the last minute, ordering Pola to look in chests she had not expected to open again until autumn. *Next year I'll keep them out until June,* Beatriz thought, feeling cold even inside the house, so she took the opportunity to pull out a woolen shawl for herself. Beatriz almost felt sorry for the aquatic singer, for whom it would be impossible to cancel the show, and for all those who would be cold on that disappointment of a day in the country, but something distracted her.

"Señora, I found a moth in the blanket chest."

*If it's not one thing, it's another: in a house, it's one emergency after another,* she thought.

"Come with me, Pola."

A plague of moths could ruin everything in a few weeks if not dealt with, and Beatriz, alarmed and like the good housewife that she was, was already dealing with the matter when the cart, pulled by a horse, slowly left the grounds. For this reason, she did not see that Francisco, magnanimous, had allowed his son, on his birthday, to hold the reins. Preoccupied with the invasion of insects, and by then a little dizzy from the camphor vapors, Beatriz did not go out to say goodbye.

# 57

## *To Each His Own Path*

Francisco Junior had gone out early to say that he could not go with Simonopio to see Ronda.

"Come with us, Simonopio. We're going to work."

Despite knowing it would be the first time that the boy explored the fields without him, Simonopio did not accept the invitation, because it was also the first time that father and son would spend time alone together away from the house. The boy would be safe with his father. With this in mind, it was not difficult to turn him down: Simonopio did not want to miss the show at the mill.

If it had been his godfather who had invited him, Simonopio would have accepted immediately, of course, because there was nothing he would not do for him, even if it meant missing a true wonder. But he would nonetheless have spent the whole day wanting to be somewhere else, wanting to be at the river, wanting to see Pedro Ronda sing underwater with no equipment.

Simonopio had waited anxiously for that day, looking forward, as well, to taking Francisco as he had promised, because he knew that it was an event that would only happen once. But he was glad to see the boy set off with his papa, taking the reins, excited to be going to work with him. Perhaps they would go to one of the orchards. They would make a fire when they rested, to keep the cold at bay. They would eat together in the shelter of a tree, wrapped in the blankets he had seen Nana Pola load onto the cart.

He was not breaking his promise to the boy by going to the river without him that day, he thought. Simonopio saw it in Francisco Junior's eyes: after five days thinking of nothing else, the spectacle of the man who would sing under the water was no longer so much as a memory for him, so privileged did he feel to be spending the day by his father's side.

One day Simonopio would go with them, but not that day: that day belonged to the two of them and to nobody else. While he made a fire for Nana Reja, to protect her from the uncommon cold, he saw them ride off on the cart and waved goodbye in silence. They both returned the gesture, happy to be setting off together. And Simonopio knew then that Francisco Junior would never forget that day. That it would mark him forever. In any case, Simonopio promised himself with conviction that he would remember every detail of the event at the river to tell the boy about it later.

He would go alone because, just as he had not accepted Francisco Junior's invitation, his bees would not accept his: it was spring, but it would be cold for the next four days, and they preferred to stay in their hive, waiting for the sun to come out again.

Taking the bees' paths that only he knew, in the opposite direction from the two Franciscos, Simonopio was the first to reach La Verdad Mill, with the exception of Ronda's eldest son, who, learning that people would arrive early to enjoy their day in the country, had installed himself there so that no one could pass without paying their twenty centavos, which Simonopio gladly handed over. To Ronda's treasurer's surprise, his first audience member walked a little ways into the freezing water before climbing onto a rock that jutted out in the river.

Simonopio did not care that he had gotten his legs wet in order to reach his rock, nor did he care about the cold: from there, he would enjoy a prime view of the show without needing to move or sit among the sea of people that would arrive. Had he been with Francisco, he would not have been able to reach the spot; sitting around soaked for hours would surely have made the boy sick.

He took out the jug of honey with its wax seal that he always carried in his knapsack and, tasting it, settled down to wait patiently.

# 58

## On the Longest Road

So many years have gone by and so much has happened that I must admit I don't recall what road we followed or how long it took to arrive where we had to go. What I do remember is that everything was new to me, so I can assure you that the wheels of our cart did not touch the road between La Amistad and La Florida, which was the only one I would've recognized because of the dying tree with its twisted branches—only one of which sprouted leaves—or the enormous rock that looked like an angry man trying to block the road and that, intimidated, I always imagined to be looking at me as we passed.

That day, the paths previously unknown to me led us to places where, from the cart, we could inspect the river's water level and the work the men were doing in the orchards we passed.

I think they saw us approach with some apprehension, fearing that the boss had thought better of allowing them a half day and would assign them new tasks. But my papa just passed by, giving his approval to whatever they were doing, without stopping for long.

The men must have been relieved to see the back of him, riding away.

At a certain point, we began to see people walking or riding in the opposite direction. Everyone was going to the river except us. I didn't care anymore. Monday would arrive, and my schoolmates would talk of nothing else, and they'd ask me why I hadn't gone. I didn't care. The mystery of Ronda's wonders disappeared from my mind, though new wonders had taken their place: driving the cart, feeling that I was helping my papa with his daily work, sitting shoulder to shoulder with him, listening to his observations and plans for the immediate or distant future.

We weren't getting anywhere, but I didn't care about that, either, because, while I tended to torture my parents whenever we went on the endless trek to Monterrey—asking *Are we nearly there yet?* until they were dizzy—that day I think I sensed that, in reality, what mattered was the journey and not the destination.

We stopped early for lunch. We no longer saw anyone heading to the river. It was as if we were the only inhabitants of the countryside, aside from the magpies, the rabbits, and the rest of the small animals we took by surprise on the way. I ate the egg tacos with potato and chorizo, resisting the temptation to complain that chorizo always upset my stomach, which my mama never remembered.

I don't know if it was the heaviness of the meat in my belly, the proximity of our destination, or the hours I'd spent away from Simonopio—the only person with whom I'd gone exploring—but I suddenly felt a knot in my stomach and a feeling of blindness. I felt safe with my papa, but I suddenly realized that, in all the hours we had spent together, he hadn't once predicted what would be around the next bend in the road or over a hill. Nor had he stopped to interpret who had been there before us or who would follow. And not even once had I seen him look beyond the horizon for the presence of the coyote.

"Do you know the coyote?"

"Who?"

"The coyote that looks for Simonopio and follows him, because he's a lion."

"A coyote that's a lion?"

"No. Simonopio's the lion. The coyote's the coyote that we never let see us."

"You're afraid of a coyote?"

I didn't know how to answer: I didn't want to admit that I was afraid of something, because if I did, I doubted that my papa would invite me to go out with him again. Suddenly, he seemed to understand me.

"It's a story I told Simonopio a long time ago. Just a story. When you're with me, you have nothing to be afraid of—I'm your papa."

He stopped the cart. We'd reached the place where we'd dig the holes for the trees.

"Anyway, look."

From among the blankets in the back of the cart, he took out the smallest rifle that I'd ever seen. A .22, he explained, passed from his grandfather to his father, and now from my papa to me, on my seventh birthday. It would be for me to use only when I went out with him, and very responsibly.

I liked the birthday gift, but I was more pleased with what it meant: today was the first outing together of many. I forgot all my apprehensions.

"Help me measure and dig the holes. Then we'll plant the trees. When we've finished, I'll teach you to load and fire it."

By the time we'd finished the holes, he was covered in sweat and I in earth from head to foot.

"Your mama's going to give us a scolding."

"She scolds you too?"

# 59

*And a New Road*

I don't remember what happened after that. Just that, three days later, I awoke in my bed, confused, and my mama was crying inconsolably, unable to answer my questions.

"What did I do? What happened?"

She just cried, unable to explain to me that life had sent us down a new road.

# 60

## *It Will Hurt*

Despite feeling bound to his memories, for his whole life, Francisco Morales Cortés has denied that he remembers what happened on his seventh birthday, that eagerly awaited Saturday, after he and his father had worked all day digging holes, back when they still called him Francisco Junior.

He has denied it so many times that he's persuaded himself it's true. *I don't remember,* he said to himself and his mother, to his grandmother, and to Dr. Cantú, who tended to him, but also all his life to his sisters; to the family; to his classmates at his old school and later the ones at his new school; to his fiancée, who would later be his wife and soulmate; to his daughter the psychologist: *I don't remember; I was concussed from the blow.*

All his life, his friends and family allowed him that single omission from his memory, first in consideration for the blow to the head and his young age, then out of simple compassion, and finally, once again, out of cautious respect for his old age.

His mother, who had her own interest in forgetting the details of that day, protected his amnesia while she was alive.

"Leave him in peace. If he says he can't remember, it's because he can't remember. Anyway, why would he want to remember?"

# 61

## *Yes. Why Would You Want to Remember, Francisco Junior?*

You were better off, over the course of your life, not reliving what happened, what you witnessed: a boy just turned seven that Saturday, on your birthday, such an eagerly awaited day. Some survival instinct helped you to send the harsh reality of those minutes, those hours, and the following days to a dark dungeon in the depths of your mind; to enable you to return to being a healthy, playful boy in no time, one who would become a successful, well-balanced, happy man.

You locked that reality away in a cage like a prisoner, but you didn't throw away the key, and today the day has come to let it out. It's time to end the story, to fill in the gaps.

All of them.

So, take a deep breath: let the memories of that day come out. Remember your own, but recognize and incorporate the memories of others, as well: the ones you'll allow to enter you only today, even if they're uncomfortable, even if they're painful, even if it seems as if they'll make your heart stop.

# 62

## A Consecration at the River

At the expected time, the people farthest from the mill began to call for silence, and like a wave, it gradually spread. A deeper silence than the one the new Father Pedro could command at the moment of consecration took hold: no one coughed, no one whispered, no one fanned themselves, and no one adjusted and readjusted the veil on their head or their tired hips on the seat. No one even had to tell chatty or naughty children to be quiet.

At the riverside, everyone understood the importance of complete silence.

It was as if even the birds understood. All that could be heard was the river's current, the creaking of the great wooden mill wheel propelled by the force of the water, and higher up, the water pouring from the top like a fountain.

The fact that the mill had fallen into disuse did not mean that its wheel, which had never been dismantled, no longer worked. While there was water in the river, it would do what it had been designed to do since it was installed there decades before, only now without the productive purpose of milling sugarcane: turn.

One day in the future, without being maintained, it would rot and collapse. Meanwhile, since it was abandoned, it provided entertainment to the town's children, who dared one another to hang from it as it rose, to see who could last the longest dangling there and to see who could manage to go all the way around. A dangerous activity that had already claimed the life of one child, who failed to surface from the water alive, having gotten stuck on a branch under the wheel.

That day, since it was cold and their parents were there, no one attempted the feat. That day the families ate on the riverbank; they drank, talked, laughed, played, and even snoozed, all to pass the time until the big show.

Which had arrived.

Simonopio—who had remained motionless for hours, missing the company and conversation of his bees and sad that Francisco Junior was not there, in spite of his prime spot on the great boulder in the river—readjusted his position expectantly. And then, covered with his robe, appeared Ronda, who until then had not allowed himself to be seen. Simonopio noticed that he did not seem very happy about having to remove the garment: as impressive as his underwater talents may have been, he was not immune to the cold. It may also have been that he was afraid of getting sick, but he had summoned the town to see his aquatic concert, and even people from Montemorelos had shown up. There was no going back now, no postponing the event: he had taken a tidy sum of money, and now he must deliver.

At last he took off his gown, handed it to his son the treasurer, and leaped from the bank into the water in front of the wheel.

# 63

## *Ronda's Singing*

Nobody recognized the first few notes of the corrido that traveled loudly from ear to ear, but it did not matter: Ronda was singing. They had seen him go underwater, and now the audience could hear his voice and listen to his song. In unison, everyone—including the disbeliever who had prepared in advance to pelt the failed subaquatic singer with rotten fruit and vegetables—let out a loud sigh of admiration. Ronda, the True Wonder, was singing under the water. They could all hear him, but even so, some bent forward as far as possible to hear better, while those a little farther back stood to try to see something.

The cries of *Sit down*, *Out of the way*, and *You're stopping us from hearing it* marred the incipient concert somewhat, though by then, those with the clearest view began to protest. Yes, it was true that Ronda, the self-proclaimed True Wonder, was singing underwater without any equipment, but he was not submerged; instead, he was behind the stream of water that fell with the constant movement of the wheel. There, standing on the firm riverbed, loudly and out of tune, he sang a song he had composed himself. Neither the singer nor the performance was a wonder of any sort, and so the complaining began, because singing under a mere sprinkle, without breathing equipment or a microphone, was an ability that every one of them possessed without the slightest need for skill or mastery, much like Ronda himself.

"What's happening?"

Those at the back were unable to see the silhouette of Ronda behind the stream of water, but those at the front gladly explained the situation to them, so that they could join in the spreading discontent. Even those who had gone there that day expecting a ruse felt offended and conned: even for a trick, Ronda's was very cheap, and not worth the twenty centavos he had taken from them.

Simonopio had not expected a trick. He had gone to see a wonder, which he thought had begun when Ronda dived in. He had felt his heart skip a beat from the excitement, but it resumed its normal pace when he saw the man emerge from the river behind the stream of water. The song that Ronda sang was not even very good: Who was interested in the sorrows of a man whose mule was dying? That was something that could happen to anyone, on any day of the week.

Still, he did not understand why the audience was complaining so much. Ronda had not even lied: he was singing underwater as promised. The people, themselves, had believed what they had wanted to believe. Simonopio immediately lost interest in Ronda and concentrated on the faces, voices, and furious rage of the crowd, though he did not feel tempted to join their vociferous and foulmouthed complaints. Rather than conned, he felt disappointed. Had he been able, he would have thrown himself into the water and left, but he did not want to push past all the people who were pressing ever closer to the river, demanding the return of their money from Ronda's son, the treasurer. Tired of the yelling and complaints, Simonopio remained motionless in his spot, trying to rid everything and everyone from his mind. But it was not easy.

He'd had enough: enough yelling and enough of the negative atmosphere that prevailed. He had been sitting on that freezing rock for too long already. He could no longer ignore the cold or his frustration. He had invested a lot of time over the last five days trying to imagine how someone could sing underwater, and to witness it, he had turned down the invitation from Francisco Junior, who had gladly and generously wanted to share his papa with him.

He decided that he would apologize to the boy, and while there were no wonders to tell him about, Simonopio knew Francisco would laugh when he heard how they'd started throwing leftover food at Ronda. He would also tell him how the waterfall the con man hid behind was so thick that no bread or tomato could pass through it— that the projectiles hit the stream of water only to drop into the river. He would tell him how it was not until it occurred to someone to throw an orange, hard, that Ronda began to receive the reward for his musical efforts, by force. He would tell him—and this he knew would make the boy laugh—that even certain ladies from the social club, tired, freezing, and bored after the long hours waiting out in the elements, had lost their composure and, in the swarm, had begun to talk and shout just like the rabble they would never allow into their exclusive club or the first-class pavilion at the Villaseca Fair. Still not daring to leave his spot, Simonopio recognized that positioning himself on that rock to see the show had not been the best idea. Now he felt trapped there until the people decided to leave, because swimming across the river to the far side would not be sensible: it would mean getting wetter and returning home on the longest route.

He decided to be patient. It would not be long before the people left, with or without their money, and then he could go back to La Amistad.

It was too late to join the two Franciscos, but the wait would be more pleasant if he could see them, so Simonopio decided to sense them. His body was trapped on that boulder, but he could allow his mind to fly, and so he did. He made himself forget the curses, his own disappointment and that of others, the complaints, flying oranges, failed singing, centavos, and pesos, and in doing so, he went to where his godfather and Francisco Junior were. His mind flew toward a day in harmony. He perceived some chorizo that upset a stomach and the sense of anticipation from aiming and firing a rifle. He arrived at some badly made holes in the ground and some unplanted trees. He felt breathless as he sensed the weight of some infertile and hostile land. He saw the hatred in some eyes that were watching them and sensed the determination behind the sight of a weapon about to be aimed at them.

Then he knew what it feels like when one's heart really stops. A beat, two. Then he knew what a heart feels when it misses a beat, two, then remembers that, to live, it must beat again, even if the first beat hurts as if the chest has been split open. He knew the true horror that one feels when, without needing to be asleep, one falls endlessly; when the world collapses. He knew how one feels when, without warning, an uncontrollable pain invades the body, so great that it cannot be contained, so great that, in order to go from that moment to the next, in order to survive, one must let it out or cease to exist.

Before diving into the river's icy water to swim to the bank and then penetrate the thickest part of the mass of people, without slowing down, without caring whom he knocked over, the strange boy of the Morales family—the one everyone who witnessed the events that day had thought was mute—let out the most powerful scream they had heard in their lives. The most desperate. The most painful. Stunned, all at once, they stopped complaining and yelling at Ronda.

From where had he appeared, and what had caused such a cry? None of those present who saw him run off in the direction of the hills—like he was possessed, some would say—were ever able to explain it. On the rock where he had spent almost the entire day there remained a pair of shoes that nobody retrieved.

# 64

## Leap of Faith

"She scolds you too?"

What questions the boy asked!

Of course Beatriz scolded him when warranted, and she put him in his place when he deserved it. But Francisco Morales would not have admitted that to his son, at least not that day, so he did what all fathers do instinctively: evade the question, avoid answering, change the subject.

"Come on, let's go plant the trees."

Father and son climbed onto the cart to bring the orange trees closer to the roadside. The trees were not heavy for an adult, but their weight and size meant that it was not easy for a seven-year-old boy to move one without damaging it. Francisco saw how his son imitated his movements and how he looked up, hoping for his approval, and he thought, *This is how we build a relationship; this is how I'll teach him to be what he must become: little by little, as Beatriz says—not all at once.*

He climbed off the cart and took all the trees down. Then he held his son's hand and helped him jump down onto the irregular surface of the road. Francisco Junior was not content to just drop down and plant his feet on the ground; instead he propelled himself upward to prolong the leap and, in doing so, make something simple into an exciting adventure. Francisco Senior wondered how long ago he had stopped doing the same thing: jumping higher than necessary without knowing how he would land or what consequences there would be. Picking up the first orange tree—a product of his orchard but, before that, the fruit of his imagination and daring—it occurred to him that having dared to change the agricultural calling and perhaps the history of an entire town was comparable to taking a great leap like his son had just done with complete faith.

Satisfied, happy with the result of years of hard work, he brought the first tree to the place where it would strike root forever.

And then he saw him in the distance, on the hill: accompanied by his son, Espiricueta had arrived. Late, but there he was.

# 65

## *The Return*

Stop, please. I need air. Pull over. I want to get out for a minute. Just a minute. To be honest, I never thought it'd be so tough coming home, and for me, my home always started on this road my ancestors made, now bordered with dying and dead trees.

They must've thought they'd be eternal, that they'd never age, that they'd never die. Now look at what's left of them.

# 66

### *See, Listen, Understand*

Francisco Morales, who until the age of seven they had called Francisco
Junior, climbs out of the taxi that collected him that morning from his
house, as quickly as his body allows, tangled as it is by age and disuse.

The young taxi driver looks at him with confusion and alarm.

He is afraid that someone of such an advanced age might decide to
die in the car—because, first off, at his young age, he has never seen a
dead person, and second off, he does not know and wonders how dirty
death would be if it arrives. He decides that it might be very dirty, so he
prefers that, if the old man is going to die, he should do it out of the car,
which does not even belong to the driver. He does not want to have to
explain to the owner or have his pay docked for the cost of cleaning, so
he responds immediately to the elderly gentleman's request to pull over.

Protecting the integrity of the vehicle is his priority, but what makes
him get out after his passenger is curiosity: he cannot leave things as
they are. He has to know the end of the story, even if he hears it with
the old man's final breath.

That morning, Francisco Morales had called the taxi company that,
whenever there was a need, was normally called by Hortensia, a woman
hired by his children when he was widowed, to act as housekeeper and
nurse. He did not feel that he needed a nurse, since he was still capable

of meeting his most basic physiological needs without help, but he would never object to having someone to take care of him.

He did not call Hortensia "Nana"—at his age it would have been ridiculous, but what difference was there between her and his nana Pola?

Just affection. A minor thing.

He'd made the call obeying a rare impulse for someone his age. That morning he had woken ready to follow the routine that had bound him to Hortensia for more than fifteen years. A routine of distant friendship: she in the kitchen and he in the comfortable La-Z-Boy, a gift from his children one Christmas, which he had gradually tamed and molded to the contours of his body. Now he spent all day in the permanent, soft embrace of his seat, getting up only when he began to feel the pressing and pinching of his elegant reclining rocking chair, which tired long before he did of the constant proximity.

Sometimes it seemed to him as if he were turning into a marble statue by Rodin, the one called *The Thinker* that he had seen once in Paris, sitting for eternity in the same position, because he could not be bothered even to recline the seat a little or use another feature of the La-Z-Boy, which was for elevating the legs.

In this way the hours passed of their own accord and without warning. They faded away. There, with the curtains closed and in the dark, between visits from a child, grandchild, or great-grandchild, he closed his eyes and ears, though the television was always on as a window into the world. What could he see or hear on that glowing cube, on that idiot box, that he did not already know? In his long life, he had seen it all, and he did not want to watch reruns of anything. Because sometimes it was as if everything were a repetition: the same mistakes, the same warning signs, and the same governments, even if the faces changed.

No surprises. Ever.

He closed his eyes and ears, and he locked himself away in the past to remember, because the only repetition he could tolerate was that of the memories with which he had filled his life.

But that day, he had lifted the receiver and called to request a taxi like an expert. He had filled his wallet with money, and without saying anything to Hortensia, who was as ever in the kitchen making one of her aromatic soups, he went out into the midday sun to wait for his ride, which promptly arrived. He did not sit in the back seat, as any paying passenger is expected to do; he sat in the front, to see everything with his eyes wide open.

"We're going to Linares."

He silenced the young driver's objections, assuring him that he had enough money to pay for the return trip as well as the gasoline. He had enough to cover the cost of the entire day, if necessary.

Sitting in the front, seeing the road unimpeded, he started to tell the story that he wanted to tell, the story that none of his children or grandchildren, prisoners of the hurried pace of modern life, had wanted to hear other than in bits and pieces, because they always interrupted.

*Is it true you threw yourself off a bridge once because a train was coming?* they must have asked him once or twice.

*Yes.*

*And what happened? How did you survive?*

*A nopal patch saved us.*

*And what was it like?* his interviewers asked, before, as usual, immediately losing any real interest in the question and then losing the thread of the conversation, because their cell phone rang with a call or beeped with a notification that they had been tagged in that thing called Facebook, or with a message that included a kindergarten's photo of the day, in which a member of the new generation of the family appeared.

*Look. Do you want to see it?*

*I don't have my glasses, but thanks.*

That day, he decided to tell it from start to finish, even if the taxi driver was not interested in an old man's story. He had always remembered, but since life had been put on hold by his widowhood; by his old age; by the silence, the immobility, and the isolation, the details of his story had grown ever-more vivid, more colorful, more present. As always, he tried to contain them, control them, but his memories had surprised him that day, requesting freedom, air, light. *Let us out,* some asked him. Others took him by storm and said, *Let us in now.* It was as if, that day, they had all decided to assail him at once, to flood his senses—the five that convention acknowledges, and the others that he knew existed but that he had never been able to access, use, or even understand: the ones of which Simonopio had spoken to him when he was a boy and that he had never had the patience or time to study and develop.

Tired of resisting so much, Francisco had surrendered to the battering.

Now he had to let the memories that whirled around him in or out, or he would explode. Now he understood that they spoke to him, that they called to him, that something had been calling to him for many years, but he had resisted seeing or hearing, or it had been impossible for him to do so, surrounded by the busy everyday life of an enormous city.

That day it was imperative that he listen to the *come-come-come-come* that called to him and that he relive the story in which he never, even when he was young, thought he was the protagonist. Now, at last, he managed to fill and understand the hidden gaps in the story he had thought he knew in full.

He climbed out of the car because he needed air, even though he had the window open.

But going out does not improve his condition, because Francisco Morales still needs air, as he will continue to need it until he reaches his destination. As he will continue to need it until he finishes telling the story like he has never done before: with the new spherical vision that Simonopio had tried with such enthusiasm to teach him and that he has only just started embracing. The vision that is now enabling him to understand and to feel tenderness for a new, experienced, and older mother of an irrepressible child. That helps him sympathize with Carmen and even with Consuelo, and understand the crosses that his father had to bear—understand them in his belly and in his cells and no longer just as a simple, if bitter, anecdote. To understand, if not forgive, the envy and resentment that drive one to kill, and also to decipher and finally embrace Simonopio's world as his own.

# 67

*But Simonopio's Image Invades Your Mind,*

Francisco, and it's not the one with the gentle eyes and generous smile that you like remembering so much: the image of the young man surrounded by bees and sun, who took you to school, happy, pulling on Thunderbolt's reins for too short a time. The mental portrait you see now is not the one you took with you when you went and the one that has accompanied you all these years since you left. No, the image you see today behind your eyelids, the image of him in your mind's eye, is one that you've never seen before. The face you see on him today, so many years later, is one of absolute suffering, unfiltered, with no pretenses or condescension.

And you suddenly feel the greatest pain of your life invading you, a pain that must be let out or you will die. You comprehend that the pain belongs to someone else, but it is your responsibility. You know that it comes from the past, though it has reached you only these many years later. Now you know that the pain is called Simonopio. You think about it for a moment with the little good sense that you have left, because you feel your windpipe seal, and the thin trickle of air that reaches your lungs barely oxygenates your blood and is only just enough to make a lucid decision. With no energy in your old body to vent the pain from your body with a great scream to rival the one that Simonopio let out on that Saturday, your birthday, your only option is to continue telling the story.

You turn to the taxi driver, who you now know is called Nico, even though at no point during the journey have you asked him his name, nor has he offered it.

"That's better. Shall we carry on?"

Yes, Francisco. Get into the cab. Reach your destination. Carry on, Francisco. The memories and the pains, all of them—yours, other people's—from start to finish, they require you. Today they will not let up: you must go to them. It hurts and it will hurt more, but you're on the right path.

# 68

## *Following the Bee Trail*

Simonopio had to go cross-country. Using the map of the hills he had made in his mind during his endless walking in pursuit of the bees—the map he also traced on the land, through the vegetation, with the weight of his body—he chose the fastest route and ran at full speed.

He could not feel his heart beating. He could not control his breathing or see beyond the next hill. He knew it was beating, that he breathed, and that the world existed beyond his field of vision, but only because he was still alive, moving, and with a destination in mind. If it was cold, he no longer felt it. He didn't care anymore. If he trod barefoot on stones, branches, or thorns, driven by compulsion, he could only take a firm, quick step and follow it with another, and another, and another, and as many as were necessary to take him to where everything was calling to him, to where he had known he would be called all his life.

With each step he sent out his own urgent and repetitive signal: *It's today, come today.* Deafened by anguish, he did not know whether he was receiving a reply.

Indifferent to the scratches, he stopped for nothing. He did not reduce his speed even to carefully make his way through the thorny plants, which had grown back since his last visit. He did not stop, as he normally would, to admire the view that suddenly opened up of the tallest hills from an angle that could be appreciated walking on only that route. When an unsuspecting rabbit crossed his path, he did not stop to let it pass freely. For the first time in his life, he ran thoughtlessly, indifferent to whether he caused alarm or damage in the hills, and not even an encounter with the bear that roamed that area would have stopped or diverted him.

He had a long way to go and very little time: the day of the clash between the lion and the coyote had arrived, and he was going to meet his adversary.

He did not know whether he would arrive in time.

# 69

## . . . Dies by the Sword—or the Bullet

He could not help it: seeing Espiricueta in the distance, standing on the hill, darkened Francisco's good mood.

True: it was what they had agreed—though he had thought it canceled—and working with the campesino had been his original intention when he had brought Francisco Junior with him that day. But now that they had spent all this time alone, he did not want to share the day with anyone else. They had begun a task together, and he wanted them to finish it together. He knew that, had they had help from the beginning, had Espiricueta arrived on time, the same task would have taken a few minutes, while he—a clumsy digger—and a small boy who returned more earth to the hole than he managed to extract would have taken around two hours.

Now that he had the first tree at the edge of its hole, he decided he would ask Espiricueta to come back the next day, when they would start to plant the new orchard in earnest. For today, Francisco and his son would plant these trees alone, and Francisco Junior would always remember that, as a boy, he had started an orchard with his father.

He and Francisco Junior still had work to do that day, but it did not matter. He had enjoyed himself with his son, being inefficient and sweating together in spite of the cold, and the boy seemed to have enjoyed himself too. That night they would arrive home hungry and with blisters on their hands, but satisfied at a job well done and at their achievements that day, which were far more important than the five trees they would plant.

After that long day of work, they would drop down dead, he predicted.

He waved his hand, expecting the gesture to be returned. Instead, he saw Espiricueta raise his hand—not to return his greeting, but to accommodate his Mauser and take aim using the sight, nice and slowly, without rushing, no doubt holding his breath, like any expert marksman would do when he wants to hit a target.

It took Francisco Morales Senior only an instant to realize that Anselmo Espiricueta was not aiming at anyone behind him, and to understand with horror that the campesino would fire the weapon Francisco had given him using the bullets he had also provided, insisting the man practice to improve his marksmanship. And in that instant, he concluded that the target was him, and with him, his son.

Just an instant.

He turned, with the intention of protecting Francisco Junior with his body, and the shot rang out, echoing between the hills of the land that still belonged to him.

# 70

*. . . Lives by the Sword—or the Bullet*

Anselmo Espiricueta went to meet the boss as they had agreed. He arrived early with his son, almost at dawn, which was the usual time to start work. But the boss had not arrived and—after several hours sitting there, cold and hungry, resting against the trunk of a tree at the top of a hill—Espiricueta, at his son's insistence, had been about to give up and go home, resenting the boss's lack of consideration.

A peon's time, he concluded, is not worth the same as the boss's, who, breaking his word, had not showed up at the agreed-upon time. Then he felt disappointed: he had waited anxiously for this day—not for the excitement of changing the crop or out of curiosity, like everyone else who went to the party at the river that day, but because it was the day when he would begin the life that he had been planning for so many years.

Espiricueta had interpreted their meeting that day as a threat, but it would be the last time that anyone dared threaten him: he, in turn, had responded with a serious promise that he intended to fulfill. And it had nothing to do with orange trees.

With this in mind, Anselmo remained on that rise, not knowing when he would have another such opportunity to defend his land from the man who wanted to snatch it from him with incomprehensible changes, with changes that, like everything, were good only for him and his family. Anselmo's belly was beginning to complain by the time he saw them arrive in the afternoon, carrying trees and spades. He stopped his son in his immediate impulse to go to their boss's aid.

"No, my boy. Not today."

He forgot his hunger. He forgot the cold.

And so, out of sight of his boss, who had not stopped to wait for his obedient peon's arrival, father and son watched the other father and son struggle to dig five badly made holes. And seeing them—clumsy, tall, white, and elegant campesinos—confirmed what he had always known: the fields belonged to those who worked them, those who knew how to do things, how to plant, and not to those who supervise everything from on top of a horse without dirtying their hands.

"This land's mine."

He had waited for years and would not wait another day to remove the trespassers from his land. All the patience and all the waiting that he had in his body and spirit, all the silence he was capable of, he had expended a long time ago.

And if he had spoken into that woman's ear to end his silence, spoken to her close up, as close as possible, mostly about her wrongdoings—*You didn't look at me when I looked at you, and now you won't look at anyone else*—while their sweaty bodies fought hand-to-hand, eye to eye and chest to chest, one to live and the other to kill; and if in the end he had felt pleasure on his skin in depriving her of her life with fingernails and teeth, and pleasure in his ears in hearing her breathe for the last time, now he had no problem doing the same, but from afar, armed with his Mauser, with which he had practiced and practiced and caressed like a lover, for want of a woman.

That day, he wanted his voice and his will to be heard in gunfire, to rumble like thunder.

The boss, with his boy, had managed to bring the first tree into position. But Anselmo Espiricueta would not allow a single one of those trees on his land. He stood, to be seen. The boss, with his usual arrogance, waved at him; and with the arrogance that Espiricueta revealed for the first time, he aimed his rifle.

Contrary to what Francisco Morales thought in that tiny instant, at a distance of just over three hundred paces, Espiricueta was not in the habit of taking a deep breath and holding it before firing. As he aimed at his boss's head, Anselmo Espiricueta did what he had been doing for years when he practiced.

He sang.

> *Now the golden eagle has flown*
> *and the finch is chased away.*
> *At last the day must come*
> *when the mule takes the reins . . .*

And he fired.

# 71

## *So Close and Yet So Far*

Simonopio was close when he heard the bang. Close, but too far, too late, and now the air that he breathed had changed: now it smelled of burned gunpowder and of death, and the absolute silence in the hills, after the gunshot, thundered in his ears and punctured his heart.

# 72

*Irrigating the Land*

Francisco did not feel the impact of the bullet.

All he felt, without understanding what was happening, was his body losing its strength, flying forward, and falling face down on his son.

Suspended for a moment between voluntary verticality and permanent horizontality, between lucidity and confusion, Francisco had the time to think that, when he reached the end of the fall—why was he falling, if it had been so long since he last fell to the ground?—he would tell Francisco Junior that it was time to go home, because he felt tired and they would not finish planting the trees that day, *but tomorrow we'll come back, we'll finish, we'll irrigate them and watch them grow, you'll see, the trees grow fast, they bear fruit fast, but you have to protect them from infestations, from the cold, from the dry season, from the Reform. You'll see. When you're older, you'll see: these trees that we're planting today will bear a lot of fruit, and you'll bring your sons here to get covered in earth, so their mama scolds them, which is what mamas do: they lecture you because they love you, because if they didn't do it, who would put us right, Son?*

Then he remembered that they had not finished planting the trees: *Don't worry, but let's hope someone remembers to irrigate them, because I'm tired and I might not come tomorrow. I might stay in bed, so that Beatriz spoils me with caresses and pampering. Now as soon as we can, we'll head back in the cart, because she's waiting for us with hot chocolate and a cake for you, and sure, to scold us, too, for the earth that you're covered in: sometimes mothers do that, but don't worry, Son, it's your birthday, and today I'm going to ban any nagging.*

No. As soon as he could, he thought—now facedown on the ground, feeling the effects of the blow to his left temple against a stone, and trying without much success to spit out the earth that had entered his mouth—that the moment he regained his breath a little, he would tell Francisco that it was best he went home without him.

*And tell your mama I'll come later, as soon as I can. Tell her to wait for me to have dinner, because she has a cake for you. It's your birthday today. I wanted to show you everything today, but she stopped me. She said to me, "Bit by bit, Francisco." And she was right: bit by bit. But I'm tired now. Look at me lying here. You go, but stay in the shade. Let me rest in my shade. Run so you reach the cake before the candles go out—they don't last long. You'd better blow them out, blow hard, because I can't now. I'll stay to water the trees, soon as I can, because if you don't irrigate them as soon as they're planted, the roots don't take. The roots are important, Francisco. Water the roots. Come on, Francisco, we're a long way from home. Run now, or the candles will go out. I'll watch you go, Francisco. Go on. Where are you? Have you gone?*

Then he heard it: a little sigh that seemed to come from the earth beneath him, a little groan. He understood—remembered—with apprehension that he had fallen on top of Francisco Junior. Worried, he thought that Francisco Junior would not want to come back to work with such a clumsy papa who fell and crushed him under his weight. He had to move to let him go, to let him breathe, and as soon as he could, he would roll over to allow him out from the prison under his body. As soon as he could.

*Now Beatriz will be mad at me for sure.*

*Are you all right? I'll get up right now, Son, wait,* he tried in vain to say; no sound came from his mouth.

The blow had dazed him, he thought, and he tried to remember the last time he had fallen, but it would not come to mind. When he was a child, no doubt, and no doubt he would have gotten straight up, brushed off his knees, and carried on with the game—playing hide-and-seek, which had always been his favorite. And how he had liked hiding among the close rows of sugarcane, paying no attention when they told him, *Boy, you'll get bitten by a snake,* but none had ever bitten him: he had gotten lost only once in the depths of that maze, going around and around without finding a way out, seeing nothing but the matte green of the sugarcane in front of him and the blue sky above as his only, useless, guide. Finally, with great relief, in one of the spirals that his feet took him on—though his head had now surrendered to his being completely and eternally alone—he came out into a clearing. But only he had noticed his absence, only he had felt lost, and the eternity he had spent lost in the undergrowth of the sugarcane field might have been just ten minutes in the known world: the other children continued playing without interruption. He did not cry with relief when he reached freedom; he contained the urge. But he had to take only a single deep breath to resume the game of hide-and-seek, and it was only a few more minutes before he forgot the terror he had just felt.

Now he needed more than a moment to regain his breath and his bearings; he was no longer the agile, quick-to-recover child he had been before. Now a fall felled him like a great tree that, once felled, does not stand up again. *Perhaps this means I'm getting old,* he thought fearfully.

Now he felt a pressing need to stand and shake off his fear. Urgently. Urgently because . . . Why urgently? He had to stand up because he had fallen, but why had he fallen? Something had pushed him. *Where's Francisco Junior?* Out of the corner of his eye, he saw the tree they had been about to plant, hoping to see Francisco Junior come out from behind it with a leap and a scream to surprise him, but then he thought that a tree with such a young trunk would be no use as a hiding place, even for such a small boy. And there was not a single sound. Only the wind blowing through the distant bushes and then softly, but icily, across his face. And he did not like that silence, for he had never known it to exist when Francisco Junior was in the vicinity.

He tried to call to him, to scold him: *No more hiding, Francisco. It's not the time for hide-and-seek. Come out now—you're scaring me.* The words formed in his mind but not on his tongue or in his breath, because he barely had the strength to breathe, and only without filling his lungs to full capacity. Then he heard it again: a weak sigh coming from underneath him; and he remembered again that, when he fell, he had fallen on top of his son, and that now Francisco would be asphyxiated under the weight of his father's body. Under the weight of his father's clumsy decisions.

Then all the confusion that had seized him suddenly went away, though with his mind clearing, there came no relief or solution to his predicament. With his mind clearing, there came only terror.

He tried to move but could not. He tried to feel his son underneath him but perceived only the icy wind caressing his forehead, the cold earth under his face, and the hardness of the stone that he had hit with the side of his head.

Then he remembered Espiricueta in the distance and a greeting of lead.

A greeting that had hit him in the back, he concluded, because he noticed with desperation that his head was the only part of his body that seemed to work, and with great difficulty: all the feeling in the rest of his body had gone. In front of his eyes he saw a hand. He identified it as his own from the scar on the knuckles and the long, crooked fingers that he had inherited from his father—*Yes, that's my hand.* He recognized it, but it no longer recognized him: the hand, which had always been so fastidious, refused to obey his order to clean the earth off, to quickly get out of the way of the stream of blood that was running toward it. That reached it. That wetted it.

That hand was the only part of his body that he could see, and it seemed as if it were the only part of him that remained, because without seeing the other hand, his arms, his torso, his hips, his legs, it was as if they did not exist.

Then he understood that his body had succumbed to death before him.

And his heart—that organ that one feels beating, if not in an insensible body then beating in the soul—his heart broke. But now he could not even surrender to the impulse to wail. He did not have the air for it. There was only moisture for the tears, which flowed freely and without shame and which, in his imagination, watered the orange tree and mixed with the blood that he knew he was giving to his land, draining him, even if he could not feel it.

He had always gladly given everything to his inherited land: family, mind, time, youth, sweat, study, and even secret tears. But he never imagined that it would also demand wailing and blood. That it would demand his son's life.

*Will this orange tree nourished with my blood and tears grow strong? Will our blood be noticeable in its fruit? I'll never know,* he concluded.

*This is death,* he told himself. *This is my death and my son's, which I cannot prevent, however much I want to.* Then he wanted to see his daughters one more time, but especially Beatriz, because he had always thought he would die looking into her eyes.

In the end that he had imagined, they would both be old, as they had promised each other, and by then, they would have had time to say everything to one another and to say it many times, without caring that they repeated it, without ever growing tired of it.

He had thought there would be time.

Now, too late, with no air in his body, he wished he could give her one—because he would have strength for only one—of those intense, loving looks that he had been saving up in order to use them in better times, for want of time, for want of energy, because he had been busy with his routine and because he had surrendered to his worries. If he had his wife in front of him just one more time, he would find a way to repeat in a single look all the tender words that he had said to her since they met. He would make sure that this last look would even create new words just for her.

Now it was too late, and while he wanted to find only words of love and parting, he could find nothing but words of pain, sorrow, and recrimination.

Would she accept them?

Because if Beatriz were there, stroking his aching temple, holding him, sharing her warmth with him, he would be able only to ask for her forgiveness and humbly accept any words of admonishment that came from her mouth, from her mind, from her heart, *because I deserve them all. I deserve every harsh word, if not for the earth that our playful son is covered in, then for my overconfidence and arrogance, for choosing to be blind, for not wanting to see what I had in plain sight for so long: the danger at home. I would ask forgiveness for opening the door to him. Forgive me for beckoning death, for waving at it when I should have run. Forgive me, Beatriz, for killing with my clumsiness the son that I gave you so late and who I'm now taking away from you so soon.*

He would have asked for her forgiveness, had he been able, for the earth that would cover their son forever. For that earth, he would. But it was too late for apologies and certainly too late to make amends, because then he heard him, softly, in a low voice, but growing in volume, growing closer: the chorus that he had never understood because he had never paid attention, because he had never wanted to, because it had never been important until that moment.

*Now the golden eagle has flown*
*and the finch is chased away.*
*At last the day must come*
*when the mule takes the reins . . .*

He heard Espiricueta's dragging feet a few steps away, and had he been able to speak, Francisco would have pleaded with him for the life of his son, who at that moment was surely fading, little by little, between the earth and the heavy body that killed him while it protected him. He could not see his child, but he wished he could at least feel him one last time, speak to him one last time in life, even just with his eyes, to say, *I tried. I tried and I failed. I failed you: I told you you'd be safe with me, to not be afraid, and I was wrong. But now you really must not be afraid, Son. We'll go together. Take my hand, squeeze it. We'll go together. Jump high. Jump. Nothing will make you fall now.*

Francisco Morales was no longer capable of doing anything except waiting. And knowing what was coming, in the silence imposed on him by a bullet, he sent up a fervent prayer—perhaps not conventional, but certainly from the bottom of his soul and with all the strength he had left: *Let it be quick, don't let him understand, don't let him suffer; better that I kill him, that my body suffocates him before the man hurts my adventurous son, my brave son, who is about to meet his executioner, because there's no return from this adventure; may his death be painless and may he know no fear; God, may his life end quickly; let it be quick . . .*

Close—too close—to his face, he saw some worn old boots that, without consideration, lifted the dust around him, preventing him from taking in the small amount of clean air that his body had the strength to inhale. He saw them stomp on the hand that was no longer his, and he was grateful that he could not feel anything. He closed his eyes, expecting to be kicked, but he opened them when, instead, in his ear he perceived the moist, warm breath of Espiricueta singing to him softly, almost with tenderness.

*. . . when the mule takes the reins . . .*

Had his body still belonged to him, he would have felt a shiver run through it. Instead, he felt the sword on his neck, ice cold.

But he would not feel the bullet that killed him.

# 73

## *Too Late*

From a distance, still running, without allowing himself to slow his pace or close his eyes for anything, Simonopio saw the coyote walk up to his godfather and give him a kiss, like Judas. Then he saw the second kiss: of lead, of death. He saw Espiricueta stand up, satisfied, to show his son the outcome of his violence on the despised, now lifeless, body, and goad it irreverently with the toe of his boot.

There lay the lion at the coyote's feet, killed by the hand of the coyote, like in many of the versions that Simonopio had constructed without wanting to, unable to avoid it, of the story his godfather told him when he was a boy. He had seen it since then but had not understood: he was not the only lion that the coyote bore a grudge against, that it hated; and on that day of confrontation he had feared so, he was not the fallen lion, no. He had been safe at the river—he reproached himself—distracted by a banal show for which he had reneged on the promise he had made to Francisco Junior one morning, years before, at the foot of his bed: *I won't leave you again.*

He had reneged on it to watch a show and had abandoned Francisco Morales and his son to their fate. The price that everyone would pay for his doing so would be very high. Life had changed because of his carelessness, if indeed life continued for anybody.

Where was Francisco Junior? Close. He could feel him. Simonopio could not see him in the distance, but he had to find him before the coyote. Had his godfather had time to get him to safety?

No.

The coyote's attack had not been from the front, with warning. He had attacked from behind, cunning and treacherous as he was, with the heat of two bullets that penetrated the body of the boss, the first target of the day. Reading or feeling his intentions, Simonopio understood that he would take care of the lion's son later, and would do it at close range, without rushing. Because the coyote is not afraid to face a cub that he can enjoy killing slowly, as he had killed Lupita, sinking his teeth into her, tearing off her flesh and ripping out her eyes, blocking her air, seeing—with surprise—the tears run down in spite of her empty eye sockets, and, growing weary of the screams, squeezing her until she was silenced forever, then standing and carrying, dragging her to the bridge over the river and dumping her there unceremoniously, abandoning the dead eyes where Lupita's body had abandoned life.

Simonopio did not stop at the realization, the hatred, or the temptation to seek revenge. He kept running, calling to Francisco Junior with one step and to his bees, which he felt were close, with the next. They had responded to his call, defying the cold despite the knowledge that many of them would die that day. Ready to sacrifice themselves.

*We're coming, we're coming,* they said to him as a swarm, in unison, and the sound began to echo between the hills until it became a storm, a hurricane in honor of the dead lion and in defense of the child in danger.

Simonopio thought the coyote would react, but Espiricueta seemed deaf to everything except the sweet sound that still resounded in his ears—one gunshot from a distance and a second at point-blank range—and, to a lesser extent, the voice in his head demanding that he find the child and kill him as well, to blow away every last obstacle to his claim on the land once and for all.

As he ran, Simonopio saw Espiricueta's face change: under the father's body, which he rolled over uncaringly, he had found the son, whom he lifted into the air, gripping him by the shirt and shaking him.

The boy's weak sobs reached Simonopio's ears. Still alive, but on the way to death.

This time Simonopio let out a roar: he was a lion throwing himself into the defense of his pride.

Simonopio had arrived too late to save one of them, but with help, he was in time to save the other.

Perhaps.

# 74

## *The Devil's Thunder*

Anselmo Espiricueta had not been in any hurry coming down from
the hill after firing the first shot. He had given himself time to pick up
his knapsack and the used, still-hot Mauser cartridge, which he put in
his pocket as a souvenir while enjoying the smell of burned gunpowder
that enveloped him.

It was not the perfect shot he had planned. He had wanted to hit
Francisco Morales in the forehead, to blow his brains out, to destroy
his eyes and his height, to wipe the arrogance from him forever, as
he had imagined in so many practice sessions. However, Morales had
not cooperated, and what Espiricueta had envisaged as firing on an
easy, static target had proved more complicated: guessing his worker's
intentions, he supposed, the boss had turned around to run. Instead
of hitting him in the forehead, he had struck him in the upper back. It
was not the same.

"But dead's dead," he boasted to his son.

He could not recall whether he had spoken to his son of his plans,
and he supposed not, because after Espiricueta fired, his son had seemed
surprised and a little frightened, though he would never question his
father's actions. When Espiricueta took the first step down the hill, his

son just followed him quietly. They left the horses tethered to the tree: they would not need them for their descent.

Satisfaction filled Espiricueta's lungs as he breathed deeply with each step. As ever, he sang the chorus of which he never tired. It had taken him nineteen years—aside from the rest of his previous life—but in the end, he had done it: with a single shot, he had changed his life forever.

*At last the day has come . . .*

He would no longer live his life stooping, servile. The day had come when the mule lifted its head and refused to recognize the boss, because he knew, like he had always known, that nobody tells a landowner what to do; that owners do not suffer hunger, hardship, or worries, which is why they grow tall and straight and look everyone squarely in the eyes.

And that was him now: the master of his land.

He breathed in the new air of his property, filling his lungs with land and freedom.

*. . . when the mule takes the reins . . .*

In his reverie, he walked without looking up. He walked without devoting a single thought to the Morales boy, for when the father fell dead, Espiricueta banished him from his mind. However, as he approached Morales's blood-soaked body, the boy's absence surprised him. He stopped a few paces away, annoyed.

Had he climbed onto the cart? It did not matter: Espiricueta would find him. The boy was dead even if he didn't know it yet.

He was also surprised to find that Morales's body was still alive. He was almost disappointed with himself, but then he realized he had not missed his target: he clearly saw the wound where the bullet had entered the back and the blood running under the body, which meant the projectile had passed through.

He was breathing but choking. He was alive but dying.

Not wanting to be a part of what was to come, Espiricueta's son kept his distance, preferring to rummage through the Moraleses' cart. Espiricueta did not care: like the land now, this moment belonged to him and no one else.

He approached and trod on the lifeless hand to prevent the wounded man from defending himself in any way, but Morales did not react: he did not groan with pain or try to pull his hand from under the boot that insulted him more than it hurt him. The only parts of Francisco Morales that seemed to still be alive were his eyes and mouth. The eyes, weeping, understood that their end was coming and realized who would be responsible for it. The mouth tried to form words, without success. Francisco Morales seemed to be trying to plead, though Espiricueta was no longer interested in what the boss wanted to say to his former-peon-turned-executioner. Espiricueta was more interested to see that the boss was now irredeemably prostrated at his feet, against his will. He observed with enthusiasm that all the arrogance and elegance had now left his body and face.

The day had come when the boss was silent and the peon spoke, and it gave Espiricueta pleasure to have him as a captive audience: Francisco Morales had no option but to listen to what he wanted to say to him.

He had already said it to him forcefully with a bullet. Now he would tell him with a whisper.

Espiricueta then decided that missing the target had been for the better: it had given him time to administer death up close, intimately— almost like Lupita's; he would see the precise moment in Morales's eyes when he realized he was dead, even if he still breathed.

He moved closer to the living dead man, crouched down, and bent over him, and as close as one does with a lover, he sang into his ear, as he had always wanted to do.

> *Now the golden eagle has flown*
> *and the finch is chased away.*
> *At last the day must come*
> *when the mule takes the reins . . .*

As he did so, as he repeated the words that had remained with him for too many years, repeating them like an obsession, like a prayer, he promised himself it would be the last time they came from his mouth.

It was time to change his tune.

Standing again, he aimed the barrel of the rifle at Morales's neck, and without hesitating or prolonging the moment, he fired, satisfied with the effectiveness of the weapon. The bullet ended its journey like a flash of lightning, but its thunder lingered in his ears like a constant reminder that there was no going back.

"Dead's dead."

Hearing his own voice, enveloped in the thunder that rolled on, enabled him to make out another quiet sound: a groan, almost as soft as a sigh. Then he noticed that under the father's body lay the son's, dying little by little, suffocated by Morales's dead weight. Espiricueta was glad that he did not have to waste time searching for him. Pleased to know that the boy had been trapped, that he was suffocating. Espiricueta could leave him there, remain with him until the little body no longer had the strength to breathe in, remain with him until he died, and then enjoy the irony of it, almost as if he had killed two birds with one bullet. But he reconsidered: Why wait, when he had already waited so long? Why not kill him and solve the problem once and for all?

With the toe of his boot and with great effort, he managed to roll the dead body, and he saw that, though it had lost part of the face where the bullet exited, the forehead remained intact, and the blue eyes, open, now looked up at the sky. For a moment, and with a shiver that traveled across his skin, he feared that the boss was still alive and turning his accusatory eyes toward him—but no.

"Dead's dead," he reassured himself.

Now he had the boy at his feet, just as he'd had the father: alive, but half-dead. Without the weight on top of him, the child began to move, to take in more air, determined to cling to life.

Espiricueta helped him, ignoring the signals his son was giving him in the distance. His yells of *Something's coming* meant nothing through the thunder that grew ever louder in Espiricueta's ears. Nor did he notice—and at any rate he would not have cared—that the Moraleses' horse was bolting, terrified, as if the weight of the cart behind it did not exist. There was nothing more important at that moment than finishing what he had begun: he gripped the boy by the shirt and lifted him, shaking him violently so that the thick mist that had taken possession of the boy's awareness quickly dispersed, so that he, too, would know who would kill him and how.

He took his knife from its sheath.

When the boy opened his eyes, he did not notice the blade that threatened them. He just stared at Espiricueta and, weakly, said something that Anselmo heard without understanding.

"Coyote."

Then, inevitably, Espiricueta heard a roar that exceeded the thunder in his ears, and he knew immediately that it was the cry of the devil, who was coming for him.

After so many years searching for him on the roads without finding him, without coming face-to-face, that day he knew the encounter would be inevitable, and fear seized Anselmo Espiricueta. He did not want to see him anymore, he did not want to confront him, but he understood he could no longer avoid it. He looked up and saw several things at the same time: his son speeding away, the devil in a boy's body now grown into a man, and behind him, above him, in front of him, as if he had opened the gates to hell itself, a living, furious, vengeful storm.

A winged storm that came to take him. The thunder in his ears.

# 75

## *Killing and Dying*

On the longest run of his life, the interminable sprint that seemed to take him nowhere, feeling his thirst and the effort of his roar tear at his throat, feeling his lungs compressed from traveling over the path that he had traveled only once before, Simonopio knew the precise moment when Espiricueta feared for his life, when he let go of the boy, who fell onto the soft ground among the mounds of earth that his father and he had made while they dug holes.

He noticed Francisco Junior was not moving, but he breathed.

He saw that Espiricueta was running, pursued by the violent cloud that, implacably, came closer to him with every second, and which sooner or later would take revenge. That the son, despite his head start, would not escape the bees, either, now that they had come out of their hive in response to Simonopio's urgent call.

For him, at great cost, they had defied the cold and their own instinct which, with good reason, had prohibited them from venturing to this land all these years.

They knew what they were there to do: they would kill that day, and most of them would die doing so.

Without turning around, Simonopio had first heard them behind him, but they soon caught up and then overtook him. He had never seen them fly so fast or with such intensity; they were of a single mind and a single idea: kill. Simonopio, who had always lived surrounded by them, felt afraid when he found himself in the eye of that storm, even knowing that their fury was not directed at him and that they knew their target. They would take revenge against the man who, by existing and treading on a territory, had banished them from there forever.

Simonopio saw them pass over the bodies of the two Franciscos without stopping, but he did not look beyond there. It did not matter if Espiricueta managed to climb the hill and tried to hide in the wilds. The bees would find him wherever he went, because now he was in their sights, and bees never forget: even if they failed that day, even if it took them years and several generations, Espiricueta and his son were dead men.

When Simonopio finally reached his godfather's body, he barely looked at him with sorrow: he was just an empty shell. There would be time later—a whole lifetime—to mourn him.

Right then, there was no time. He cared about only Francisco Junior now. Only life. It was cold, and night was falling.

"Francisco. Francisco. It's me. I'm here now," he said as he examined him, receiving no response.

On the side of his head, near one eye, was the cut that Espiricueta had managed to make with his knife before dropping the boy. On the back of his head was another wide and deep wound, perhaps from hitting a stone when he fell. He was bleeding from one of them, but not from the other anymore: the earth had absorbed almost all the blood his body had been prepared to give it. He also had at least one rib broken by the impact and the pressure of his father's weight.

Francisco Junior was breathing with difficulty due to the fracture, and Simonopio noticed that he himself was short of air. He would not be able to fill his lungs until they were away from there, from that toxic air, from the coyote's land. He was filled with uncertainty. What should he do? Moving Francisco would hurt him, but not moving him would kill him. He decided he had to take him away quickly, to safety, because until Simonopio was certain the coyote was dead, he remained a danger.

And it was growing colder. And darker.

And the coyote was at large.

But the horse had bolted.

It was impossible to take Francisco Junior to the house in the state he was in: cut, battered, unconscious, almost frozen.

"I'll carry you, Francisco. You sleep. I'll take you home tomorrow."

With Francisco in his arms like when he was a baby, mindful of his head and trying not to squeeze him too much, because of his ribs, Simonopio headed into the hills with the sole intention of trying to reach a place where it was easier to breathe, anywhere outside of the coyote's territory.

# 76

## The Worst of the Bad

At ten o'clock that Saturday night, with the moth plague under control, if not defeated, with dinner cold after several hours of waiting, and with the candles on the cake still unlit, Beatriz Cortés de Morales once again allowed panic to set in.

It had been hours since Pola, Mati, and Leonor, after witnessing Ronda's disappointing trick, returned to fill her in on the details: the con, the stream of water, the pelting with oranges, and finally, Simonopio's scream.

While she had not been surprised at how the performance ended, Beatriz was alarmed by Simonopio's unusual outburst. Hearing the news, a knot formed at the entrance to her stomach: something had happened to make Simonopio cry out in such a way, from nowhere, like never before, and she was afraid that the reaction had something to do with Francisco Junior. *But he was with his papa, so what could happen?* she thought, trying to stay positive.

By eight o'clock in the evening, she had sent Nana Pola to ask Martín and Leocadio whether they had seen their boss out there that day: *In the morning or around midday,* they replied when she found them on the way to town, where there was a dance that night.

They had seemed fine at that time. They were happy, Martín and Leocadio said.

However, when ten o'clock arrived and they had received no news, Beatriz sent Pola in one direction and Mati in the other. One to the dance to fetch the men, and the other to inform Emilio and Carlos Cortés: the two Franciscos were missing.

They all came quickly, which made her feel even more anxious: it meant that her fears were not unfounded. They promised that they would search for them, that they would find them. The two had surely taken shelter from the cold and would return early in the morning, they predicted hopefully before setting off.

Beatriz spent the night sitting at the dining table, where a birthday cake awaited an absent birthday boy. She didn't want anything, thanks. Coffee? No. Hot chocolate? No.

"Shall I sit with you, Beatriz?"

"No, Mama. Go to sleep."

"I can make you some tea—"

"I said no! Leave me in peace!"

And Sinforosa left her, disappointed and unsettled but without resentment, understanding and sharing her daughter's anguish. She went to stand guard herself in the solitude of her bedroom, seeking the refuge that the beads of her rosary offered.

From her place in the dining room, without moving, Beatriz watched the sunrise. Had it been possible, she would have stopped herself blinking so that she would not miss the moment when her husband and son appeared on the horizon. When it happened, she did not know what she would do: She would run to them, that much was certain, but what would be the first thing that came out of her mouth? A scolding or an expression of relief?

She would cry, she knew. That day she would cry.

At around seven she saw the cart appear over the near horizon, escorted by several riders. She ran, as she had predicted she would do.

But as she approached, she saw that it was not Francisco who drove the cart. It was Carlos, her brother.

She stopped dead because of the sudden lack of air in her lungs, but also to prolong her ignorance, even if for just another minute. And had she been a little less brave, had she been a little less aware of her dignity as the wife of the owner of those lands, she would have turned around and locked herself in her bedroom, blankly refusing to hear news of any kind.

Instead she stood there, motionless, with her knees trembling and her heart immobilized, waiting for the news to roll its way to her head-on. And so her ignorance lasted not even a minute longer: they had found the cart and its horse out in the fields, abandoned. They had found Francisco farther on, beside some holes in the ground, watched over by only a sapling orange tree. Murdered.

That much she understood.

The knot that had formed at the entrance to her stomach the day before seized the rest of Beatriz's body, from her brain to her limbs and even her eyes. Then it seized her ears, so that she could no longer hear, and her vocal cords, paralyzing them to prevent her from screaming.

There she stood in the middle of the road, without asking anything or moving, blocking the path of the funeral carriage and more bad news. But she understood that, now that they had arrived, there was no way to stop them, even if she remained standing there all day.

And yet she stood firm, waiting for them to arrive of their own accord, without her help.

"Beatriz . . ." Was it her younger brother who spoke to her? Carlos? When had he lost his distinctive playful manner? When had his face taken on this severity, this pallor? she wondered as he spoke. "Francisco Junior . . ." It was her brother, but she did not recognize him like this and did not want to know what he would tell her. "Can you hear me? Beatriz!"

But his elder sister, lost in the middle of her own road, did not find any words, nor did she seem to understand any. Then he took her by her arms to hold her up, or to hold himself up, to hold her or to be held by her, to console her or to be consoled, or simply to make her react. He did not know.

"Beatriz," he said, rubbing her arms until he saw a reaction in her eyes. Carlos managed to give her the news a second time: "Francisco is dead and Francisco Junior, he's missing."

He could no longer contain his sister other than by force when, out of the blue, at full voice, she began to scream Simonopio's name, again and again.

Perhaps she had not understood, Carlos thought, and in his desperation, he joined his sister in her yelling, but shouting for the only person he could think of.

"Mama!"

# 77

## Satin from Another Age

She had not wanted to see the body. She did not want to clean it or change the clothes. What she had done with great composure for her father and for Lupita, she refused to do for the man with whom she was of one flesh, according to the law of God.

*What clothes would you like us to put on him?* they asked her, but she did not answer.

Nor was it she who organized the wake or notified relatives and friends of her husband's death. She had not thought of her daughters, nor of paying for the telegram that would be sent to them, nor had she asked at what time they would arrive. When she was asked whether she minded them using the coffin they had kept, well protected and covered in a storeroom, she did not even question what a casket was doing in one of their storerooms: she would not remember, until she saw it closed on top of the dining table, that she had bought it herself unnecessarily on the day that Simonopio arrived. That she had had it stored in case it was needed one day.

As it was today.

If, after almost twenty years, the satin inside was yellowish and not white as it had originally been, she did not care. Francisco would not care, either, and she knew that, had he been able, he would have said that *men don't pay any attention to such things* and that there's *no point in spending money on a new one if we already have one that's perfectly adequate.* What would the aunts and ladies of the social club say about it? She did not care about that either. No one would see the inside, because the one thing she had firmly requested was that the coffin be kept closed at all times.

She did not want anyone to see him like this: dead, defeated, destroyed.

Her mother had changed her into mourning clothes after giving her a few hours to calm down and, on the doctor's recommendation, several cups of lime-blossom tea for the nerves.

"Hurry, Beatriz," Sinforosa said to her when she was doing nothing, "the people are arriving now."

They had taken her to sit beside her husband's casket to receive the guests, who offered her their condolences without caring that she did not want to hear them.

To one side of her, they had also pulled up a seat for Nana Reja, who left her rocking chair to make her slow journey to the dining-room-turned-mortuary. Nana Reja had known her boy Francisco since he was newly born. Now she would sit with him when he was newly dead. And Beatriz knew that the little old lady was not as insensible as she sometimes seemed. That she was suffering. As if Nana Reja struggled to pass air in and out, she gave a deep groan from her chest every time she inhaled, though it was audible only to Beatriz, only to the woman who shared her pain and who soon began to imitate her.

No one offered condolences to the wooden woman. Nana Reja sat, closed her eyes, and did not open them again during the entire process. The visitors walked past her as if she had nothing to do with the events.

Beatriz, on the other hand, did not want to close her eyes for a single instant, not even to get away from the tide of people coming toward her.

She had not had the strength to say or yell *no*, she did not want to see anyone or speak to anyone; she did not want anyone to speak to her or look at her; she wanted to be left in peace, because she felt dead, defeated, and destroyed herself. If they could find another coffin in a storeroom, they might as well put her in one too: she, the one with the murdered husband and the missing son, to whom she had not gone out to say goodbye for the last time for no reason other than to attack a plague of moths.

Sitting there without blinking, she was aware of Francisco's recent, violent, cruel, and permanent premature absence.

Permanent. From now onward. Forever.

She knew that sooner or later she would have to face it. The day would come when she would need to contemplate a life in complete solitude, filling the hours of the day in order to survive them, and surviving the empty nights.

She knew that her grief for Francisco would come out.

For now, that pain was almost stored away, waiting. She had controlled it out of necessity with the other pain, the more demanding one, more urgent. Because that day, she did not have time to think about her widowhood or to receive sympathy from anyone, for she wanted to ask them all: *What are you doing here keeping vigil over a dead man if there's a living child out there, lost in the cold?*

If she had been able to trust her body not to betray her, she would have gotten up immediately to wander the hills yelling Francisco Junior's name until she found him. But at that moment, her body could not remember how to speak, let alone walk or hold itself up without a chair with a back keeping her upright.

She was the mother of a missing boy, but she did not have the strength in her body or the courage in her soul to stand up and go in search of him, for fear of what she would find or what she would never find, destined to wander the sierras calling to her lost son for eternity, like the Weeping Woman of legend.

She allowed herself to be embraced a little and allowed the compassionate words to float around her, but she did not let any of them in, because at that moment there was nothing that could distract her from the fear and uncertainty, from the void she felt at the core of her existence.

She had been the daughter and then the orphan of her father, to which she had grown accustomed. She had been a wife and was now a widow, to which one day she might resign herself. She had been a mother and . . . What does one call a mother who has lost a child?

Amputee? That was how she felt.

Now she was an amputated mother.

How does one resign oneself to that? When?

People approached her; they spoke to her; they offered her advice for which she did not ask. They offered her food or drink, but that day she could only look out through the window to the horizon, concentrating, waiting, longing for the miraculous appearance of her missing boy. And there was no room in her head for anything other than the silent cries that resounded inside it ceaselessly: *Where are you, Francisco? Are you cold, Francisco? Are you alone? Are you afraid? Are you hurting anywhere? Are you alive? Francisco!*

While dressing her, her mother had assured her that her brothers would continue the search, which the Guardia Rural had also joined, and which they would continue until the child was found.

"Simonopio must be looking for him as well, and if Francisco Junior's alive, he'll find him, like he always does, you'll see."

"And what if he's dead?" Beatriz said, refusing to look at her.

"If he's dead, he'll also find him."

Would he already know? Would Simonopio know that his godfather was dead and that Francisco Junior was missing? If Simonopio lived, he would know. If Simonopio knew, then he would find him. But Simonopio had not returned since the day before, either—not since they saw him run off from the river in a sudden and inexplicable manner.

Simonopio was missing, too, like Francisco Junior. They were not dead. Just missing.

*Francisco.*

*I can't feel you. Are you cold, Francisco? Where're you hurt, Francisco? Are you alone? Are you afraid? Don't be afraid of the dark—what else can it do to us? What else? Simonopio's coming for you. Can you hear him? Simonopio: Can you see him? Where are you? Are you hiding? I can't hear you. Have you gone? I can't feel you, alive or dead. Not alive, or dead. And I didn't go out to say goodbye. Where are you? Alive? Where are you both, Simonopio? Are you alive? Dead? No, no, no. No, Francisco. Francisco, are you alone? Are you alive? Are you cold, Francisco? I expect you've lost your sweater by now, Francisco, or gotten holes in it, child. And the blankets? I gave you blankets. I think I did. I gave you two. Or was it three? They were blue. The good ones. But I didn't go out. I didn't say goodbye. I didn't say goodbye to you both. I had to save the other blankets. It was very important. It doesn't matter. It doesn't matter if you lost them. Come. Come home, now. Come to me. Alive or dead, come home. I don't care about the blankets. Don't be afraid now. Nobody will scold you. Are you hurting anywhere? I don't have the strength. I don't have the strength to come find you. I don't have the strength to lose you. Are you alive? Francisco, Francisco, I can't feel you and I didn't say goodbye. I can't feel you because I didn't say goodbye. I didn't say goodbye. Why didn't I say goodbye? How stupid I was, Francisco. Are you hurting anywhere? Something hurts inside. Something broke inside me and if it doesn't heal today, it will heal tomorrow . . . No. No. It won't heal if you're not here. It won't heal if you don't come back. It will never heal. Come back or it will never heal. Where are you alive, Francisco? Tell me. Where are you dead? Why didn't I go out? Are you cold where you are, Francisco? I am, and there's no blanket that will make me warm. Bring him now, Simonopio, bring Francisco, and you come as well. If I'd gone out, I would've stopped you, Francisco. I would've known.*

*Somehow, I would've known. I would've stopped you. It hurts. I'm hurting. Perhaps you're not, anymore. Not if you're dead. And if I'm hurting, I'm hurting because I'm still here, waiting for you. Alone. The waiting hurts. The doubt hurts. Francisco, Francisco, Fr . . . Are you alone? I am. Are you afraid? Me too, Francisco. Me too. Me too. Very much. Afraid of knowing and of not knowing.*

Dead or alive, if Simonopio was alive, he would find him—because, dead or alive, she wanted him back: to welcome him or to say goodbye to him. Even if she went after her Franciscos, with that final goodbye.

Before nightfall, in the company of their husbands, Carmen and Consuelo arrived from Monterrey to take charge of the preparations. They had imagined that on arriving they would collapse with grief into their mother's arms and that she would console them like she always had. But seeing the state she was in, they understood, alarmed, that they did not have time to break down, that they had to take responsibility, because at that moment their mother was not capable of anything, not even offering comfort.

The family were all present, they said, so they announced the Requiem Mass and burial of Francisco Morales the next day.

They struggled to coax Beatriz away from her husband's coffin, beside which she had stationed herself to keep vigil not over the deceased but over her missing son.

# 78

*Honey on the Wound*

Francisco Junior was lost.

Many hours had gone by, but the body was still unconscious in his arms, and Simonopio had been afraid for the same number of hours.

"Where are you, Francisco? Come back."

Simonopio sang all the songs he knew to him over and over again. He told him all the stories, except the one about the lion and the coyote, because not even he wanted to remember either of them.

Sometimes the soul must be allowed to rest, kept away from the things that hurt it.

"Is that what you're doing, Francisco? Resting?"

He had walked with Francisco in his arms to this place with clean air away from Espiricueta's land, to what was more like a crack in a rock than a cave. It was not the ideal place to spend the night, but it offered some protection against the cold wind. In any case, he could not have gone on any longer: the run from the river had exhausted him, and carrying Francisco was no longer as easy as it had been when he was a baby.

So he had headed to this place he knew from some other occasion. He sat down, resting against the base of a rock, without letting go of Francisco, refusing to return him to the cold earth where he had spent so long under his father's body. He was sorry that he had not brought his overnight bag, thinking that he would only be out for a few hours, though he was grateful that he never went out without the old pocket-knife his godfather had given him. From the small inventory he had in his sack, he took out his jar of honey and dabbed some on Francisco's wounds, to protect them. His arms would have to be enough to shelter the boy from the cold.

But he did not sleep, for fear of falling into the depths, like Francisco.

When the boy woke—Simonopio decided during the first night—they would go to fetch the cart in order to return home. But Francisco Junior would not wake up. The new day arrived and went, but the boy remained lost in unconsciousness. Simonopio knew that, by then, his godmother would be in a state of anguish because of her dead husband and missing child, and he would have liked to alleviate her suffering in some way, but it was impossible. He also knew that a group of men was searching for them, but they were far away and heading in different directions, and there was no way for Simonopio to go find them: on no account would he leave the boy alone or move him more than necessary.

"I won't leave you," he repeated between stories, between songs.

He had broken his promise once. He would never do it again.

Francisco would be all right. The boy would wake up, Simonopio told himself, though he was uncertain whether he was predicting it or merely hoping.

But Francisco was not waking up, despite Simonopio's attempts to bring him back to the world with his voice.

Little by little, drip by drip, he gave him all the honey that he had taken with him to the river. With a corner of the blanket, Simonopio persevered in collecting the water that seeped and filtered through the rock, so that, drop by drop, he could also keep the boy's tongue and body moist. Now the honey was all gone, and soon he would have to decide whether to get up and walk, to set off home in spite of the boy's delicate condition and the danger of the coyote.

Because while Simonopio knew that a search party was scouring the hills, he did not know whether the coyote was among them, as he had been on that occasion years before, when they had given Simonopio up for lost. He could not know, because his bees remained in an unfamiliar silence from which they transmitted no news to him of any kind. Simonopio did not know with certainty whether they had managed to hunt down the murderer. He did not know whether they had survived the night to continue the hunt the next day.

Almost forty-eight hours had passed when, finally, he sensed that a search party was close. He decided it was time to come out of hiding. With his pocketknife in his hand as a precaution and Francisco Junior in his arms, trying not to mishandle or move him more than necessary, Simonopio went out to meet them.

He saw with relief that it was Uncle Emilio Cortés, accompanied only by Gabino and Leocadio; although Simonopio preferred Martín, both men could be trusted. He trusted his uncle especially, and he knew that Uncle Emilio had not stopped searching even to rest or eat. Even so, Simonopio flatly refused to hand the boy over to him, because he was still the one who had to carry him, in spite of the many hours he had spent doing so, in spite of being exhausted, in spite of his cramping arms.

He and no one else would take him to his mother.

# 79

## *Alive or Dead*

Francisco Morales's burial was at noon that Monday, just after Mass, which the new Father Pedro had gone to great pains to make moving and personal, speaking of Francisco Morales with genuine respect, admiration, and affection.

His daughters broke down in tears in anticipation of the pain of missing the father whom, with so many preparations and legal formalities to take care of, they not yet had the chance to miss. Sinforosa, the deceased's mother-in-law, saturated one of the handkerchiefs she had brought with tears. The other handkerchief, which she had given to Beatriz, was still unused, for only one pair of dry eyes remained in the church: those of the widow, who was incapable of paying any attention to what was happening around her.

Years later, once she had built up the strength to talk about the episode with Carmen and Consuelo, Beatriz continued to be unrepentant of her rude—albeit temporary—catatonic state, because it had protected her from suffering the same pain she had suffered during the funeral process for her father, when she had remained sane, despite the loss. If, in the days of her husband's wake and burial, some well-intentioned visitors had told her that what had happened was a test from God, she did not listen. If other insensitive and senseless people spoke to her of the two angels, summoned by God, that heaven had gained, she did not take it personally. If the new Father Pedro had approached her, declaring that her recovery hinged upon her capacity for forgiveness and upon prayer for her dead husband, her missing son, and the enemy, she pretended that she was made of wood, like Nana Reja.

All of a sudden, all that remained of the whole process was the three masses that would be offered for the salvation of Francisco Morales's soul, since he had died without being anointed. Beatriz would go: her mother, showing a strength that had appeared to have faded when she was widowed, would not allow her to do otherwise, just as she would not allow her to refuse to eat, wash, and sleep, even if all Beatriz wanted to do was look out of the window and be the first to see her son return.

Alive or dead.

The day would come when she would thank her mother for her stubbornness, but not yet.

She would go to the three masses, because custom and her mother made her do it, but she would pray for the return of her son: the prayers for Francisco could begin afterward. He would understand. There was no rush.

"Beatriz. Look at me, Beatriz." With effort, she did as her mother asked. "Leocadio came for the cart."

"What . . . ?" It seemed impossible. She would have seen something from her window.

"I don't know. Pola told me. He quickly came and went without saying anything, but not that way," she said, indicating the road Beatriz could see from her window. "Out the back, down Reja's road. Do you want to wait there?"

For years they had called that path Reja's road, because it was where she always faced, even if she did not look at it; it was where she had gone in search of a crying baby, and also from where she had returned, baby in arms, on the same cart for which they would wait that day together, one on her rocking chair and the other in a straight-backed chair. One with her eyes closed and the other with her eyes wide open.

Both looking for their boys.

*Alive or dead? Alive or dead? Alive or dead?* they both asked silently to the rhythm of the nana's rocking chair.

When the answer was finally about to come after almost two days of asking, Beatriz Cortés, widow of Morales, was tempted to return to her window to look the other way. She had thought that she would prefer to know. To find her son even if he was dead. Then it occurred to her that the worst thing might be to learn that her son had died with his father; that it would be worse to receive his battered, lifeless, decomposed little body, which she could not refuse her attentions—even if they were mortuary—because for what remained of her life, she would never forgive herself such neglect.

She did not move from her place, but she closed her eyes like Nana Reja. It was impossible, however, to close her ears: she could hear the cart's wheels and the horses' hooves on stones and earth growing closer and closer. Closing her eyes was useless and it made it worse: what her eyes did not see, her mind imagined. So she opened them, so she stood, so she walked out to meet the cart, so she saw that neither Francisco nor Simonopio were riding on its front bench, so she concluded; she contained her breath, her body, and her tears, and she said, "He's come home dead like his papa."

# 80

## *An Empty Roof*

If Simonopio had gone to his shed to rest and not off into the hills, it was not just to keep his promise to not leave Francisco again; it was also because, while he had not felt them before, suddenly the wounds on his feet began to hurt, a lot, and putting on shoes and walking off seemed like a very bad idea. Then he remembered that he had lost the only shoes he had, that in the rush, he had left them almost as an offering for the river to devour. He also remained in his shed because he needed the comfort of what remained of the beehive under his roof, of the queen bee and of the bees that, because of their young age, had not gone out when he had called them.

They also needed him: they were all in mourning. They had all lost too much.

Under the great, almost-vacant structure they had built over nineteen years between the roof beams, Simonopio allowed himself to sleep, to put the vigil on hold. He also gave himself permission to rest the wounds on his body and heart.

After cleaning himself up, eating, and drinking, because he had not done so since he'd found Francisco Junior, Simonopio slept for two days straight. Sometimes he opened his eyes a little to find Nana Reja sitting at the foot of his bed, or rocking beside him, but his eyes closed again of their own accord. Perhaps it was that Simonopio did not have the strength to open them for long enough to explain to the little old lady, with a look, everything that would change their lives, all the grief that life would bring. Or perhaps it was that his eyes still refused to be the messengers of the news.

At other times he had sensed that his godmother had come to see him; that she offered food or fresh water; that she touched his brow; that she stroked his cheek; that she cleaned the cuts on his hands, face, and feet and applied ointment; but he had not been able to escape his stupor to ask after Francisco, to respond to anything, or to thank her for her kindness.

He was aware of the words she said to him during the time she was in his shed, tending to him: Francisco had improved, he was regaining consciousness at intervals, he spoke a little, he was asking after him.

"The doctor says you did well not to move him much, because of the blow to the head and the broken rib."

Remembering how Espiricueta had shaken him and thinking about the pain it must have inflicted on the boy—aggravated later by each step that Simonopio had taken with him in his arms—almost made him come out of his slumber, but he did not allow himself to do so: he reminded himself that Francisco was now safe. Francisco was receiving the attention he needed, and now Simonopio also had to rest in order to be ready for the decisions that would soon have to be made.

Simonopio would wake up only when he sensed that Francisco had completely regained consciousness. That was the time frame he gave himself and that he would obey. With this decision made, Simonopio forced himself to remain insensible to everything, from the unease he felt at the almost-empty and silent roof under which he slept to Nana Reja's rhythmic rocking and the never-changing parting words of Beatriz: "Thank you, Simonopio. Thank you. Forgive me, please."

He had understood the reaction of his godmother who, seeing him arrive with her boy in his arms, without knowing whether Francisco was dead or alive after two days of continuous anguish, had received him with a slap.

He understood: it had been that or to fall to pieces, and true to her essence, Beatriz Cortés de Morales had opted to be strong. Once she recovered her young son, the spark had returned to her eyes, the storm that broke out when Lupita died and that had slowly faded over time.

Her fury was not directed at him. Her fury was for the coyote.

There was nothing for which to be grateful. Nothing to thank him for. And nothing to forgive.

# 81

*Your Mama Never Forgave Herself That Slap,*

and until the day of her death, as sane as she always remained, she continued to berate herself for the violent error.

It's true. My mama continued to sew on her Singer until the end, in her eagerness to remember the good things, forget the bad things, and have the strength to face life's surprises, good and bad. By the way, she never wanted the electric sewing machine that I gave her—*It doesn't sew the same, it doesn't sound right, I can't make my hands comfortable,* she would say, always finding some defect in it—so she would die with stronger legs than a marathon runner from so much pedaling to the rhythm that brought her peace and that she lost only when, in her absorption, the memory of the welcome she had given Simonopio that day popped into her head. Her rat-a-tat, rat-a-tat became a disordered rat-a . . . tat that ended in tangled thread and straying material. Then she would stop without finishing the project and wander for a while around the house as if lost, feeling desolate, going over the events of my seventh birthday and wishing she had behaved differently with Simonopio, with my papa, and with me.

But that had been her reaction, and it could not be undone, despite the regrets and wishes that stayed with her for the rest of her life: if only she had hugged him, if only she had told him that she had also thought of him, that she had also feared for him.

In her defense, I should explain that she did just that with Simonopio as soon as she had the chance, which was what mattered, though it never seemed enough to her. What was given, was given, and that slap was certainly given by my mama who, for the rest of her life, with unwavering certainty, with stabbing remorse, would say that it was the first—and last—time she had hit anybody.

She never wanted to listen to my objections: the spankings, my spankings, did not count as hitting as far as she was concerned.

"Anyway, you deserved them. Simonopio did not," she replied whenever I tried to contradict her.

# 82

## *Unanswered Questions*

Her brother Emilio was so proud to be the one who found Simonopio and Francisco that Beatriz did not have the heart to tell him that it was Simonopio who found him.

Beatriz appreciated the great effort to which all the men went, searching for her son without rest. Though she did not know the details, she knew that Simonopio had saved him. How could one understand or explain what Simonopio did? Explain his sudden and inexplicable escape from the river? She had always suspected it, but for Beatriz, this was the first irrefutable and direct evidence of her godson's special ability, his very particular gift that she had always treated discreetly and discussed with no one except her husband.

She felt a nip in her heart: her husband was not there anymore.

Nobody asked where Simonopio and Francisco had been or what they had done while they were missing. All Emilio and the men knew with certainty was what Simonopio had been prepared to share. While they waited for the cart to transport Francisco safely, Emilio asked Simonopio if he had seen anything, and he nodded.

Emilio and the men had already had their suspicions, but they were glad to have a witness, even if he was a mute.

"We found Espiricueta's and his son's horses on the hill, up above . . . above the place. Was it them?"

Simonopio nodded firmly.

"What happened?"

Simonopio refused to answer that question, and no one, not even his godmother, Beatriz, would learn the details from him.

Simonopio knew there was no way to recount them, for even if he had been able, even if he could have made himself understood, he would never have verbally reproduced the cruel images that would remain in his memory forever. It would mean causing everyone more pain, which he refused to do. In any case, how could he communicate the humiliation, the anguish, the terror, the horror, the pain, the cruelty, the coldness, and the loss that he had witnessed? It was not possible. He could not, and he did not want to do it. Overwhelmed by the memory, instead of answering, Simonopio had burst into tears, until, without realizing it, he moistened Francisco Junior's face with his drops of grief.

With rough slaps on the back, not knowing the right thing to say, Emilio tried to console the youngster, who seemed not to know that men must not cry, at least not in front of other men. But Simonopio did not stop sobbing until the cart that transported them was approaching the house.

Even without knowing the details, what everyone at first suspected became an irrefutable fact: Simonopio had witnessed Francisco Morales's murder, and the culprit was Anselmo Espiricueta. They also mentioned the son, but Beatriz doubted that he would have pulled the trigger. However, she did not doubt for a second that his father was guilty.

They had both vanished, and their disappearance was a mystery that caused alarm.

The Guardia Rural were searching for them, though Espiricueta had not returned home and nobody had seen them since before that Saturday. They had left no trace. They abandoned the horses, and they did not leave by train. Everyone reached the same conclusion: the pair were still roaming the hills, evading justice, perhaps living in caves; so they thought it wise to offer a sizable reward to anyone who informed on them. They also decided that guards would be posted around the Morales Cortés house, in case the pair decided to attack again.

Beatriz knew that they did not have many funds available, since the bank had embezzled their money, but she would not skimp. She would figure out later how to pay rewards and salaries, even if she needed to borrow against the next season's harvest. And she would see what she would do, what Beatriz—the civilized Beatriz—would demand when they were caught. She would see what she would say—or what she would scream—face-to-face with her husband's murderer. She also had a primitive Beatriz inside, one she would never allow to come to the surface: the vengeful woman, the one she normally kept well under control, for if she let her out, primitive Beatriz would not be satisfied without at least gouging out the murderer's eyes and tearing his skin to shreds.

Impossible. Impossible, even if they found him. She was a woman, and revenge was still not a woman's business.

For the moment, there was one thing she could do to begin to satisfy her urge to hurt the murderer back.

"Go to the Espiricueta house with the tractor and tear it down."

Leocadio and Martín looked at her, clearly distressed.

"With the girl inside?"

"What girl?"

"The daughter. Margarita. They left her there."

Then she remembered the girl who had been excited to receive the clothes and ragdoll Beatriz had sewn for her, that day when Beatriz tried to offer her condolences to the family; the day when the man tried to attack Simonopio, still a child; the day when she returned home having decided to ask her husband to get rid of the campesino.

She had left it unresolved—she could not remember why—and had done nothing to drive the murderer away from her family when she still had time. She had been negligent. She had ignored her instinct and the evidence, and they had paid a very high price for her carelessness, changing their lives forever with a painful absence.

It was her fault.

She wished she could say *sorry* to her husband, but it was too late. It was too late for everything now.

"No. Pull the house down, but let the girl gather her things and come out, of course. She can leave if she wants. Give her money so that she can take the train. If she wants to stay, take her to the nuns or find work for her in a house. I don't want to see her or know anything more about her."

She did not receive anyone during those days.

Her oldest friends arrived to keep her company, to distract her, to congratulate her on finding her son, but she had no time or desire to be distracted.

Her reclaimed son was still unwell. When Francisco Junior was back to his usual self, when they no longer had to answer the same questions every time he woke because he could not retain the information, when he stopped saying sorry for some mischief for which he imagined he was responsible, when she stopped crying every time she looked into his confused eyes, then she would consider whether she could recover something of the Beatriz she had been. There would be time to see what kind of life she would build.

That woman changed once again by violence no longer had a husband, and for now, she did not want friends or distractions either. Now she was a woman in charge of everything by herself: from the weekly wages and the moths that had returned, to the planning for the future.

Her Singer was calling to her, constantly, with its siren's song: *Come and forget about everything; lull the pain to sleep with the rat-a-tat, rat-a-tat.* Beatriz did not allow herself that promised rest. It was not the time.

There would be time later. There would be time in the future, though it was impossible to think ahead.

Now it was time to tend to what was in front of her and to feign the strength of days gone by, to at least give her mother a well-deserved rest, because since that April Saturday, Sinforosa had filled every gap Beatriz had allowed her to fill during the days when her daughter was lost in anguish. Beatriz was now grateful to her for everything that, at the time, she had complained about and resented. She was grateful that her mother had never allowed her to fall, that she had prevented her from crumbling completely. And Beatriz was also grateful to her for delaying the three masses for Francisco until a better date, without Beatriz asking her to do so.

Her mother had returned to her copper pot, stirring the goat milk and brown sugar while she prayed, tireless in her search for comfort with her Rosaries. For whom did she pray? For her murdered son-in-law's soul? Possibly. For her grandson's health? Certainly. For her daughter with the weight of the world on her shoulders? Hopefully.

Beatriz, on the other hand, spent hours beside her injured son's bed, looking at him, watching over him as he slept, waiting for him to wake a little more clearheaded. When her daughters sat with her, she did not answer their questions about what she would do now. She did not know yet. For the first time in her life, Beatriz Cortés de Morales did not know what to do with the rest of her life. And what was worse: with her son's life.

She was afraid.

To escape their questions, their pressuring her, she left Carmen and Consuelo taking care of Francisco Junior while she went to tend to Simonopio for a while—he needed her, too, even if Nana Reja never left his side, even if Nana Pola took on the role as well.

Or perhaps it was she who needed him.

Maybe she needed to see forgiveness in his eyes, because she could pretend that the anguish had made her crazy and that it was madness that had dealt the young man a slap and not her, but Beatriz Cortés did not like fooling herself and did not like denying responsibility for her actions. Madness or not, Simonopio did not deserve to be treated in such a way, and now she would devote herself completely to making him understand as much and to earning his forgiveness.

When Francisco and Simonopio regained their health, perhaps she would have time to think about the future.

Before very long, she would have to prepare herself and find the right words for the answer she would offer the moment her son regained his senses and lucidity, and began to ask about his father.

She hoped that, by then, it would be necessary to give him the bad news only once. That his mind would have cleared enough for him to understand and to retain the information. That he would suffer it only once, because the one thing that was certain was that he would suffer and it would hurt, just as she was beginning to allow herself to feel the pain and the loneliness.

"Mama, hurry. Francisco Junior's awake, and he's asking for papa and for his .22."

She did not feel ready to answer the question yet, but would she ever? Was there a better way to tell your son that his papa is dead, that he was killed? No. There were no alternative answers; there was just one, because death is final.

"I'm coming. And, Carmen: your brother's called Francisco. Just Francisco."

The only Francisco they had left.

# 83

## *Your Father Died, but All You Thought About*

was the .22.

No, no, no. Maybe it was taken that way, maybe my mama and my sisters took it that way, but no.

One of the last things I remembered from that Saturday was the moment when my papa gave me the rifle. I couldn't remember, I didn't care, whether it was of fine wood in a light or dark tone.

I never touched it, like I never touched the promise that, in giving me the rifle, my father made me.

And hence my problem, because it was not the rifle that I really wanted when I asked after it. It was my papa who I was looking for, because he had told me that the weapon was to use only when I went out with him.

The gift of the .22 meant that we would spend a lot of time together, and I believe that, in my mind—confused by the head trauma and by my age—I thought that, if the rifle appeared, my papa would appear, too, to invite me to go with him again.

In asking for the .22, I was remembering my papa.

But the rifle never appeared.

# 84

*No. Espiricueta's Son Took It.*

We always suspected it.
   Now I know.

# 85

## *If Your Mother Had Known*

what happened to them, maybe she would've made a different decision. But a month after the tragedy, she still had not ventured out of the house or allowed you out, in spite of the fact that you had almost fully recovered, that you had energy and wanted to play and even had an appetite to return to school.

The guards remained outside the house. As far as she was concerned—as far as everyone was concerned—the murderer was at large. He roamed and threatened. They feared. So not even in Simonopio's company did they let you out. Beatriz Cortés didn't want to take her eyes off you, the miracle that you now were, her only Francisco, because the new scar on your face reminded her of what she had lost and how close she had come to losing everything.

# 86

## *The Future's Somewhere Else*

Beatriz Cortés de Morales knew she was sick with something that not even Dr. Cantú would dare diagnose. Physically, there was nothing wrong with her, but something that resembled a cancer called *poor widow* had been eating away at her, and she sensed that, the more the cancer grew, the more her essence would disappear.

How tempted she was to give up and surrender to it forever.

Poor widow. Forever, like her own mother. Growing old, poor widow. Alone, poor widow, because the man who was supposed to be with her through the years, until life ended, had made a promise that he only half fulfilled: *I'll never grow old, and I won't let you either.*

How tempted she was by the friends that visited her every day and lavished her with pity, with *poor you*s, offering to fix everything for her, even doing the shopping, though they would not manage to buy what she liked. What relief that they all allowed her to cloister herself without questioning it, thinking that it was in order to mourn her husband. For the same reason, nobody expected anything of her anymore, neither her attendance at the meetings of the social club ladies nor her presence to supervise the construction work. They did not even expect her to contribute with her good taste when it came to buying or designing the furniture and fittings for the new building.

How enticed she had felt at her brothers' offer to manage her land, workers, and crops—*You mustn't worry about anything, Beatriz*—allowing, as they would be prepared to do for the rest of their lives, the newly discovered indecision of their elder sister.

For the moment, her—previously—unusual hesitation manifested itself in matters of the land, which had been her husband's concern before:

*Shall we plant more or leave it for another year?*

*I don't know, whatever you say.*

*Shall we sell all the grafted trees?*

*What do you think?*

She knew that, if she gave into it, the hesitation would also appear in other areas of life:

*Shall we move him to a different school? Will he celebrate his First Communion this year or next year? Who will be his godfather? Will he go away to study? What color shall I wear? Can I go to Monterrey?*

Rat-a-tat, rat-a-tat . . . How pleasant it would be to lose herself for hours, bewitched by the hypnotic rhythm of her Singer, forgetting her fear, rat-a-tat, rat-a-tat, her uncertainty, rat-a-tat, how inadequate she felt, how alone, forgetting her son's questions, his demands to see Lázaro the Resurrected, her eternal debt to her godson, the elderly mother who resented her abandonment, and the recovered son, who now resented the constant attention he received. Rat-a-tat, rat-a-tat, rat-a-tat, rat-a-tat.

What a great temptation she felt to escape from the cruelty of the empty nights, the darkness, the loneliness, the cold bed, the sheets that gradually lost the aroma of the beloved body that had been wrapped in them for so many years.

But time does not stop. Despite the painful absence beside her, the sun came up and set each day, though as a veteran of loss, this fact no longer surprised her so much. The empty hours of the night do not pass unnoticed, because in their unrelenting cruelty, they do not allow one to rest; they force one to think, and they demand a great deal. Because it is at night that fear is most frightening, yes, but it is also when sorrow becomes deeper and one regrets what one did or did not do more.

It is in the deepest darkness that one sees things most clearly. Just as the memories tempted her to give up everything for their desert of blackness, they did not allow Beatriz Cortés even the slightest myopia. What she saw in that clear, if unintentional, retrospective forced her to shake off any temptation. It forced her to decide to heal herself of the darkness with which she was filled, but not with unnecessary medications: with willpower.

A month had passed—*A whole month, already?*—since Francisco's death. If she did not do it for herself, she would do it because she owed it to him: she would get back on her feet, she would reunite with the strong woman that he had left at home when he died, charged with the care of their son and all their affairs.

She was still afraid to leave the house. That was the truth. Because that Saturday in April, Espiricueta did not just take her husband from her. He also took her peace. Thinking about sending Francisco to school once he was back to full health filled her with terror. She feared that Espiricueta would take him by surprise, like the wolf in the stories. The same fear made her prohibit dear Nana Pola from going to fetch the daily bread alone, as she normally did. Now Martín always had to accompany her, which neither of them was happy about.

But she would not cede a single part of her life or free will to anyone anymore. She decided as much on the night when she found peace in a sweet song that was not being sung to her. She would make her decisions freely, and with free will, she would banish the fear. She remembered the promise that she had once made to no one but herself: not even in her old age would she allow herself to become anyone's shadow. She would never be set adrift, at the mercy of other people's decisions. She would never allow herself to stagnate.

It was the same night when, with regret, she remembered stopping her husband from proposing a radical change, back when changes terrified her, when she clung to traditions as if they defined her family. They should go to Monterrey, Francisco had begun to suggest on those nights when he allowed himself to lose heart, but she had never allowed him to continue talking; she had never allowed him to set out the idea in full. She had always refused to let him continue chewing over his crazy plan, but encouraged him to carry on with the same thing, doing the same thing, in the same place, and with the same people.

Leave the ancestral home? Leave the friends with whom they had shared their lives for generations? Leave the promises that life had made them?

She had flatly refused.

And what had happened to those promises? What right did she have to think they were guaranteed? The permanent absence of her husband had given her no choice but to admit it out loud, so that she would never forget it again:

"Life offers no guarantees. To anyone. It waits for nobody. It has no consideration for anyone."

How arrogant she had been to have felt that, just by existing, she deserved the best in life, that she was worthy of being at the top. How arrogant for not realizing that, believing herself strong—a pillar in her husband's life—in reality, she had been paralyzed by her fear of change, which was why she had prevented him from carving out a different destiny for himself, for them, for everyone.

Her arrogance had taken away the possibility of Francisco living until old age. It had prevented him from fulfilling the promise he had made when she sat on his lap, years ago, on an afternoon when they laughed together.

Clinging to the past had cost him his life.

It was a price that Beatriz refused to allow her son to pay as well.

How many times did she have to learn the same lesson? How many times did she have to forget and relearn that life veers in all directions? That there is no limit to the amount of times a person can be knocked down, because life doesn't believe that third time's the charm?

She needed no more lessons. The third time had taught her the lesson she would never forget. Even if it took the rest of her life, she would recover from this third lesson, because she felt that it was her duty. But a fourth would kill her.

Then it struck her that the future was no longer connected to the past. And her mind was made up.

"The future's somewhere else," she said into the air, in the dark, wrapped in sheets that no longer smelled of her husband.

# 87

## *Had My Mama Known Everything,*

maybe she wouldn't have decided to move us to Monterrey, I don't know.

Or perhaps she would've done it anyway.

Because the house's familiar nocturnal sounds hounded her, rather than comforted her, and even the clunk of the loose floor tile, which had been so useful before, now irritated her. The idea of roaming the long halls reminded her of her constant and permanent loneliness. The smell the house gave off stopped her sleeping at night, and the absence of the buzzing of bees woke her in the morning.

Had she allowed time to pass, would she have gotten used to it? Would she have found peace again between those beloved walls?

We can never know what would've been, only what was.

We had a good life in Monterrey. We didn't have savings, but we had the house there, and we had the land we would sell little by little, if necessary. My mama put her brothers in charge of selling all the family property in Linares—which, in the meantime, would continue to produce. The crops would be sold under their close supervision. The sharecropped land was left to the workers so that they could finish paying for it with fixed installments—a symbolic amount—for the next five years, when the land would be wholly theirs at last.

The ranches in Tamaulipas were the first to be sold, at a cut price but just in time: the buyer who had taken advantage of the opportunity to pay a ridiculous price to the widow of his neighboring ranchero had most of his property seized shortly afterward by decree of Lázaro Cárdenas and in accordance with the law.

My papa had died, but the Agrarian Reform was alive and kicking.

We never returned to Linares, even to visit. My grandmother decided to come with us, always supporting and staying with her daughter without hankering after her old life, even if the new people, the new rhythms, and the new places overwhelmed her. There, she finally took off the mourning clothes she had worn since my grandfather's death. She saw her grandchildren and great-grandchildren every day, and that compensated for how unsettled she felt living in a city. What she never understood and never approved of was my mama making the crazy decision to enroll me in a new school: a secular—senseless, my grandmother would say—institution called the American School Foundation of Monterrey.

"It's all gringos and atheists and *aleluyas*."

"I don't think so, Mama. I don't care: he won't have soldiers greeting him every day when he goes in and out, making sure the children don't say a single Lord's Prayer."

The federal government's war against the Church raged on, even if shots were no longer being fired. When I received my First Communion that year, it was as if I was betraying the fatherland: at night, in secret, in some family's home, the ceremony administered by a priest who, in the street, in view of everyone, pretended not to be one.

The Catholic schools continued to exist behind closed doors.

But you didn't have to hide to go to my school. There was no need to pretend you hadn't learned what you learned there. The diploma I'd receive would be recognized by the government. We were exempt from singing the socialist national anthem, a requirement Cárdenas soon imposed on other schools. And very importantly, there were boys and girls together in the classrooms, and I always liked girls a lot—even if, as a kid, what I enjoyed doing was terrorizing them with my stories imported from Linares, with the legends I told them at recess, when we sat in a little circle in the shade and, enjoying their suffering, they begged me, *Tell us more.*

For the first time in my life, I was happy going to school.

I shared my tales of mummies and ghosts there, the other children's stories about cattle rustlers paling beside them. There the legend of the doll was kept alive, recycled over and over and surviving until my own children were pupils at the same school, in a more modern building.

There, when I was a little older, I became obsessed with H. G. Wells's *The Time Machine*. Because I could never forget what I lost that Saturday. And once I'd become a science fiction fanatic, I began to believe and dream that a time machine would be the solution to everything. I would travel back in time, to that birthday Saturday. Somehow, I would save my papa and wipe away the sadness that sometimes caught my mama by surprise; the nostalgia for her old life that assailed my grandmother; the feelings of guilt with which I was filled, without knowing why, about my father's death; and the feeling of abandonment that I never overcame. Of course, I soon learned that it was not possible: that there is no way to go back in time to fix the past.

But there you go.

In the corridors of that school, I met the girl who would be my wife, though when we shared the building, I barely looked at her because she was so young, and she didn't like me because of my absentmindedness.

It was also there that I prepared myself to study for a degree in the United States, though my mama objected to my first choice of university.

"You're not going to Texas A&M. Study whatever you want, except agriculture."

How right she was. In Monterrey there was no place for land or tractors, only for iron of another kind.

# 88

*You Built a Good Life . . .*

Sure, but I never managed to shake off the bittersweet memory of
Simonopio, because all the good memories were tainted with his abandonment of me.

# 89

## We've Arrived; Turn Here

"But what happened with Simonopio?" Nico the taxi driver asks eagerly while he follows my directions.

This is his first intervention since we left Monterrey.

I realize now that he had been silent not from boredom, as I had thought at the beginning, nor from a desire to be elsewhere or to turn on his radio, but so that he would not interrupt my flow or the story that I began to tell us this morning, after we closed his taxi's doors and set off. And I know that, had we met before, had we had more time, this young man—who has been told very few stories or tales in his life—could have become my friend.

But there's no time. There's no choice: we've arrived, and the *could haves* don't exist. Nico has nothing to worry about; I'm not trying to delay my story anymore. All the versions of this story, which besieged me for years inside the walls of oblivion that I put up, took me by storm today. They're other people's versions, they're mine, and together they're a sphere: I see the whole, and I can no longer ignore it or leave it unfinished.

I feel compelled to reach the end.

# 90

## *Sweet Ignorance*

When Beatriz decided she never wanted to walk the halls of her beloved house or the streets of Linares again, nor continue to receive sympathetic looks, when she decided to take up her husband's idea to invent a new life in Monterrey, she did so with the intention of including everyone.

Her son, of course, had no choice: he would go wherever she said they would go.

He was lucky to be of an age that had enabled him to recover more quickly than she, Beatriz thought. While she still vividly remembered her unconscious, injured son, he no longer recalled on what side the fracture had been, and on the back of his head, his hair had already covered the wound that had required twelve stitches. When he looked in the mirror in the morning, he did not even notice the scar on his temple, still red to one side of his eye, and that still made her shudder: to him, it was as if he had had it all his life.

She was also surprised that he spoke of his absent father with enthusiasm, sometimes in the past tense, but sometimes in the present. He seemed to forget, or to not understand, that death is permanent. It was as if he did not understand that his father had not gone, like on many other occasions, on a temporary visit to one of the ranches. Sometimes, at night—because at night, as she well knew from personal experience, there is no hiding, distractions, or pretending that something that will be remembered for a lifetime has been forgotten—he spoke unintelligibly and whimpered in his sleep.

I had never done that before.

When Beatriz—when my mama—came to check on me, alarmed by the screams that came from my sleeping consciousness, Simonopio was always there, trying to erase the bad memories forever with gentle but firm strokes on my forehead, between my eyebrows, just like he had seen my mama do when I was a baby. He sang to me in a low voice, without interrupting his song when his godmother came into the room.

My mama did not understand his words, though she recognized the notes. Before long she grew accustomed to that language exclusive to Simonopio and me, and before long she thought it beautiful, because Simonopio had a melodious voice. It was a voice that enveloped you, soothed you, and took you away not only from an orphaned boy's dreams but also from the fears and doubts of a widowed mother. Of his godmother.

It was a comforting voice.

Although I never woke during those nocturnal serenades, today I can see my mama sitting on the old rocking chair, without interrupting, without intervening, but without going away. She did not want to miss a single minute of the strange coexistence of her son and the godson that life had given them. Because one night, between one sweet-sounding song and another, she understood that, while life offers no guarantees, sometimes it does offer gifts; and understanding that, accepting it even without being fully aware of it, the bitterness, the grief, and the deep wound of Beatriz Cortés, now the widow of Morales, began to heal, and her determined streak began to reemerge.

If she had fallen into a dramatic downward spiral from the moment of her husband's death and my disappearance, that was the moment when the descent ended. It would be the point from which the new

Beatriz would rise up, the one born from sheer willpower and the one that would last for as long as there was life in her body. The arrogant Beatriz she had been when she was young; the new fearful one; and the other, even newer, more battered one learned to live together in peace until they completely merged. It would take years, and the climb would be slow, but everything starts somewhere, and for her, it had begun listening to Simonopio's songs.

Determined, she called everyone to the dining room one morning: Grandmother Sinforosa, Pola, Mati, Leonor, and Simonopio. At that meeting she didn't explain to them—and she never did—all her reasons. She just said: "This land's not for a widowed woman with a small child, so we're leaving."

They did not all accept the invitation: Leonor didn't. Nor did Mati. One wanted to marry, and the other wanted to be a grandmother to the grandchild that had arrived. Pola said neither yes or no, but no one was in any doubt.

Discussing it with her daughter in private afterward, my grand-mother, Sinforosa, understood that the reasons for moving went beyond a simple inability to manage the land alone, but she did not say any-thing. She agreed that it was more sensible—safer—for my mama and me to leave Linares, even if it meant breaking ties and losing traditions. And when her daughter asked her if she wanted to stay behind and live with one of her brothers, Sinforosa didn't think twice.

"I'll come with you."

My grandmother, Sinforosa, wouldn't have liked being a burden or being burdened, as she knew would be the case if she stayed to live with the daughters-in-law.

"Anyway, it's you that needs me, Beatriz."

Simonopio had left the dining room in silence, as ever, but with a look of resignation that my mama wanted to interpret as acceptance.

"We'll take Nana Reja, of course, and Simonopio."

She knew that, of them all, Simonopio would struggle the most with the change, so she was prepared to find him something to do in Monterrey, to which Simonopio had refused to return since the visit to the circus. They would find something he liked, she was sure. In Monterrey there were also hills and even mountains. Enormous mountains. Simonopio might like to come and go, to explore it all.

Perhaps.

The decision that had been so hard to make soon became the center of Beatriz's attention and even her enthusiasm. Because once she accepted the idea, she also decided to make the change immediately: to the displeasure of many, they wouldn't wait until the end of the school year or for me to receive my First Communion there, or for her friends' daughters' debuts, much less the parties at the new Linares Social Club premises.

Why, if she wouldn't even go?

No. As soon as she finished organizing everything, she would leave and take me away from there, far from the dangers to our lives and land. Far from the temptations and dependencies.

Many tried to dissuade her, including my uncles—her brothers—who repeated their offer to manage all her affairs.

"Help me sell everything and manage everything until it's sold. Nothing more."

"Think about Francisco's future."

"That's all I am thinking of, but the land is the past."

They accepted the task but warned her that it would take time, not least because many properties were in the name of friends of her husband's, and her brothers would have to persuade them to pretend that it was they who were selling them. Beatriz was not surprised that all of them, without exception, agreed to return what belonged to her as a widow. My papa had always chosen his friends well: none of them went back on their word, recognizing that the land they were safeguarding on his behalf from the agrarianism belonged to Francisco Morales's widow. They would gladly help her to sell it.

Little by little my mama tied up the loose ends, keeping herself busy, gaining some respite from the emptiness of the night, when she sought refuge in the comfort that the songs of her Singer and of Simonopio brought her, even if one was mechanical and the others were not sung for her.

And while my life and my days were filled with Simonopio, with his stories and his songs, to my mama, Simonopio's life now seemed empty and sad.

It wasn't resentment, she was certain: he had hugged her after one of her constant requests for forgiveness for the slap, and Beatriz was relieved at his show of affection.

It wasn't that. Then what was it?

It was the mourning that affected him: since he had come out of his shed, barefoot, two days after returning, the look in his eyes had never been the same. In the first few days, Beatriz had concentrated on his physical well-being. But, distracted by her concern for her son's recovery and adaptation to life without his father, she had overlooked the emotional state of her godson, who had lost a father more than a godfather.

And it was also desolation: weeks passed, and she did not notice that what woke her earlier than usual was the absence of noise: the absence of the buzzing with which, through her window, the proliferation of bees that had installed themselves in the shed's roof nineteen years earlier had lulled her to sleep, their hum making it so easy to cling to sleep for the last hour—or the last minutes—before facing the day.

They had arrived with Simonopio, and they had stayed ever since.

However, now the silence of simple birdsong woke her in the mornings. Inexplicably, Simonopio's face was now free of bees—when even in winter, provided it was not too cold, there had always been some perched there, and in spring or summer they had followed him like a flower. Now, in midspring, Beatriz could see his green eyes and long eyelashes without their extensions of moving wings. She could see his mouth just as God had given it to him, without it being covered in bees, as if they wanted to hide it or feed off his smile. She saw that his skin was not blemished by a single mole, when before it had always seemed like he had several, even if they changed position with every glance.

She didn't know for certain, having been distracted for weeks and lost in her new widow's grief, but she suspected that the bees had left Simonopio completely alone since the day of Francisco's death.

Why had they abandoned him? Why had the creatures that had helped him live deserted him?

Seeing Simonopio spend the day talking, singing, and telling stories to the one audience member who offered his full attention and participation, my mama thought that she could ask him what was wrong and receive a reply from his little interpreter. She decided she would do so a short while later, and went away without approaching him. She would ask him tomorrow, but tomorrow became the day after tomorrow, and then a week or two.

And she didn't ask.

Had she been brave enough to ask, what would have prevented her from pressing him to tell her what had happened that Saturday? Nothing would have stopped her, even knowing that it would be painful for everyone. She knew that questions hurt him, and the last thing she wanted to do was cause him pain. But she was even more afraid of hating—and never forgetting—the answer. She also feared what I, as the interpreter, would be forced to narrate, to know, and to remember.

And there were things that it was better not to know.

We would leave in order to forget the bad things: the absences and the abandonments. We would go to remember just the good things. And in our ignorance, we would heal.

# 91

*Song from the Past*

As ever—whether it passes slowly or quickly—time definitely passes, and from grain of sand to grain of sand, every date arrives.

And so, sure enough, the Saturday of our departure also arrived.

Everything that needed to be packed had been packed. Everything that needed to be given away had found its new owner, including my papa's clothes, because, living in heaven—as they'd told me he was—he would no longer need them. We also gave away my Thunderbolt, who would've been very unhappy in Monterrey, because on those city streets he would've had nowhere to run. He would be happier in my cousins' orchard, where they had promised to take good care of him.

My mama took her old furniture to replace the pieces in Monterrey, which were of inferior quality and of much less sentimental value. She took a chest of winter clothes and another one of summer clothes. She took her Singer and all her fabric and threads. She packed the few family photographs we had. They were few, perhaps, because it was a very expensive service back then, but it might also have been because they had thought there would be time to take more. From the kitchen they took my grandmother's copper pot and her big wooden spoons. Nothing else.

They packed very little for me: some clothes and a few toys. I didn't have much, and in the little chest that they assigned to me, there was still some space: space enough for my .22 rifle, the only reminder of my papa that was mine, very much mine. But it was a space that was impossible to fill, so, leaving it empty, we closed the chest.

We said goodbye to all of La Amistad's workers, and there were some tears. Most of all I would miss Leonor and Mati, who until then I had thought of as part of the Morales Cortés family, such that it was inconceivable to me that they wouldn't want to come with us. Nana Pola, on the other hand, cried with sadness because she was leaving, because she would leave behind everything she knew, but I suppose it would've hurt more had we left her, and that drove her to follow us.

She would live with us for the rest of her life. She would know my children and, entirely by touch, my grandchildren, because, *Francisco,* she would say to me when she was old, *these eyes of mine can't see anymore.*

She had worn them out seeing me grow up.

Two years after we moved, when I was nine years old, the nostalgic adventurer that Nana Pola was, she discovered that, among the performances in the pavilions of Monterrey, Marilú Treviño and Soledad Betancourt would appear on the same day.

"Want to come with me, Francisco?"

I gladly accepted. I had grown up with their stories and their songs, with their voices in my ears, and it had been a long time since I had seen them last in Linares.

My mama gave us money, and we went on the bus. When we arrived, we bought tickets valid for the whole show, though Nana Pola warned me that we would have to return home by eight.

"Why?"

"Because it's when the good-for-nothings come out."

Those good-for-nothings sounded interesting to me, but I'd learned not to insist when it was obvious the battle was lost before it had begun. Nana Pola had declared, with an authority that seemed to emanate from the Ten Commandments, that we wouldn't see the good-for-nothings, and that was that. Intelligent boy that I was, I recognized that all I would achieve by being foolish was Nana Pola saying to me, *Well, in that case, we'll just go now, without seeing anything.*

Thinking that the time would go too quickly, but resigned to the limit imposed, I followed her to our seats on a bench.

First Marilú Treviño would appear in the marquee, and then, after the jugglers and the magician, Soledad. I only managed to see Marilú. We even had to leave before she finished her evening repertoire, compelled by the people around us.

"Señora, take that screaming boy away—we can't hear a thing."

Compelled or not, I was relieved to go, to escape the notes of those songs, the depth and lightness of that familiar, gifted voice. I refused to explain or to wait for Soledad Betancourt to take her turn.

"I want to go home now, Nana."

Now I realize how disappointed my nana Pola must've felt to miss the rest of the show and how much she must've regretted not inviting the neighbors' nana, the only friend she had made so far in Monterrey.

"The jugglers are next, Francisco. Then there's the magician," she persisted, trying to persuade me, with those vaudeville acts, to stop crying.

But I, who hadn't even cried when I woke from my concussion with a broken rib, did not want to stop. And not only that, but the more she asked me not to cry, the more I clung to my sobbing and even enjoyed it. I was convinced that I had every right to throw my tantrum. I, who when I woke from my coma, still concussed, confused by my state and by the abruptness of my papa's departure to heaven—an innocent who didn't understand that to go to heaven, one first had to die—barely reacted, barely cried when my mama told me.

"Francisco, your papa's gone to heaven, and he'll watch over you from there."

"Why?"

I realized it was a question that was hard to answer.

"Because God called him."

"But he didn't say goodbye to me, and I lost the .22 he gave me."

"He did say goodbye. You don't remember because of the bump, but he did say goodbye, because he loves you very much. And don't worry about the rifle anymore."

And that was that. The explanation had been given, and I devoted myself to getting better so I could go back to being the restless boy I was before.

Hence my nana's confusion: Why was I crying, then? What had made me cry? I didn't answer any of her questions or any that my mama asked me when we arrived home. I went to bed and didn't come out for dinner.

Do you know what? Two years before, on the Saturday when we moved, I had gotten up with more energy than ever, ready to live near my sisters and nieces and nephews, excited to find a good school in Monterrey, but even more excited to go there with Simonopio for the first time.

For days I had been talking to him about what we would do in Monterrey: we'd go to the Monterrey Pool to swim, for starters. It was summer, so it would be tolerable to dip our bodies in that water that came from the Santa Lucía Spring and that they dammed for the delight of the city's inhabitants before letting it continue its natural course toward the Santa Catarina River. It was very close to our house, so we could walk there whenever we wanted. We would take my nieces and nephews, who were afraid of going in because they imagined that, because of the spring, a great underground viper would appear from the water to devour them. For years I had been assuring them that Simonopio would protect us from a thousand and one vipers, no matter how big they were, and this was my chance to prove it.

"You'll take care of us, won't you, Simonopio?"

I never waited for an answer, because, believing that I knew it, I considered it said—and I was also in too much of a rush to continue planning our new life to stop and wait. And it was from talking so much that I didn't notice that Simonopio wasn't contributing so much as a *yes* or a *no* to the conversation.

That it was a monologue and not a dialogue.

Then the Saturday morning of our departure arrived. We had to get in the car that would take us to the railway station. And Simonopio didn't show up. And my mama said to me, *Come on, Francisco.* And I said to her, *No, not without Simonopio.* And Simonopio was nowhere to be seen. And neither was Nana Reja. And the rocking chair had disappeared with them. And in Simonopio's shed, there was nothing left of him or his bees. And even the little mountain of crystallized honey that had formed in one corner over the years had disappeared.

Then I realized. And then I accepted it: Simonopio had gone and taken everything. Everything, except me.

I went back to the car, and we left that place forever. I would've liked to have told you that I left calmly and obediently, that I didn't say anything during the entire journey, because boys are brave and they don't cry. The truth, because I'm too old to hide things now, is that Martín had to run after me. I didn't get very far down Reja's road, because I was blinded by tears and short of breath due to the continuous scream that could not manage to transmute into the two words that whirled around in my head.

Forgive me: it's not true that I returned to the car. To say that would imply that I did so voluntarily, but no. Martín took me back there. He carried me all the way in spite of my flailing legs. I think I would've bitten him like a wild animal had I not continued with my screaming. He put me—kicking—in the car and then the train.

My mama tried to calm me down. But anything she said was futile; I wasn't listening. I couldn't and I didn't want to. I didn't want comforting or explanations, because there were none. I think I was still looking around me, then, in the hope that Simonopio would arrive at the last minute. I think that, despite all the evidence, deep down I still believed it was impossible that Simonopio had abandoned me. When the train started up without him, I clutched my chest. When the train's wheels began to turn, all hope died.

And with the strength of my chest, and perhaps also my stomach, I contained my sobbing. And the contained sobbing turned into nausea. I vomited all the way. I vomited so much and for so many days that my poor mama thought I'd die. And I did, too, but boys don't cry, and how proud I felt that I would sooner have a brush with death than allow myself to live crying over him, missing him, remembering him, talking about him.

It was a trick; saved-up tears come out sooner or later, and mine came in an explosive crying fit that evening at the performances, as I listened to Marilú Treviño sing the same repertoire as ever, the one I'd liked to hear so much in her voice and in Simonopio's: the songs I'd only ever listened to in my brother's company. The first notes of the music transported me to giant-height on Simonopio's shoulders, to warm days swimming in the river, to the toads that croaked at nightfall, to the summertime cicadas, to the orange-tree mazes, to the footsteps of a bee on my face, and to its sound when it flew off. It transported me to his peculiar and beloved smile and to his stories, to the mysterious lessons to which I always enjoyed listening, though I never understood, then to the space in my chest, to the lost rifle, to my papa's involuntary absence and the premeditated absence of the person I always thought loved me like a brother.

So, from a distance, in his total absence, I punished Simonopio with my silence: my mouth would not utter his name again for years, and slowly but surely, my mind stopped thinking about him, because I made it.

I began to talk about him again, with a nostalgia that out-weighed any bitterness I had harbored, when I had my first—and only—girlfriend, during that period of newfound love when one wants to know everything and share everything, without limit.

She asked me about my life in Linares, and I told her, at first trying to create an edited version of events. I spoke to her about my cousins, about their house-turned-school, about Thunderbolt, about the orange wars, the river, the nopal thorns, but none of these anecdotes seemed interesting. They all fell short. I soon realized there was no way to address those themes, to tell the stories well, to inject emotion, if I refused to acknowledge Simonopio's existence.

Thanks to him, I had anecdotes to tell, and that was the reality that I understood during that exercise in narration. Without Simonopio as a protagonist in the story of my life, there were only loose threads. To talk about Linares was to talk about Simonopio. I accepted, with resignation, that talking about myself, openly and honestly, necessarily meant talking about Simonopio. And it was in talking about him, remembering him, that I realized I'd never forgotten him; that I'd never stopped missing him, though I could never forgive him.

My mama found us talking about her godson one day. She hadn't heard me mention him for years and hadn't spoken to me about him, either, sensing that it was a painful subject. She even came to think that her son had forgotten her godson over the years. She was surprised and glad that this wasn't the case.

Memories are a curious thing: while I always felt fortunate to have a few photographs of my father, they ended up contaminating my memories of him, because I looked at them so much, they gradually replaced the flesh-and-blood man whose body had a smell, whose voice had a timbre, whose hair would ruffle, and whose smile, when he unleashed it, was more contagious than the flu.

In those old photographs, people were almost always captured at a forty-five-degree angle: looking into the distance and never at the camera; always serious; and for some reason, mostly in their formal clothes, in black, with every hair in place.

I kept memories of my papa, sure, but from looking at those cold, impersonal photographs printed on paper, before long I erased his smell from my nose, his voice from my ears, his warmth from my skin, and his face in motion. The wrinkles that formed at the corner of his eyes when he smiled or exerted himself, like when he dug five holes with me for five trees, faded from my mind. I remembered the holes, I remembered the trees, but my papa was always rigid, at a forty-five-degree angle, like the image recorded on paper.

Forgetting him in this way was very painful, especially during my teenage years, when I felt most guilty for my failure to remember his essence, when I tried to dream up a time machine like H. G. Wells's—if not to save him, then at least to retrieve him.

We didn't have a single photograph of Simonopio, though. And like I said, for a long time I refused to think about him. Nonetheless, when I opened myself up to doing so, out of love for my girlfriend or whatever it was, Simonopio remained intact in my memory: his smell, his voice, his warmth, his laughter, his eyes, his gestures when he spoke to me, his songs, his stories, his lessons, his words in that other language I learned from the cradle, his hand when I held it, his back when he carried me, his resignation when he found me wandering, his serene company when I was unsettled.

Life got in the way; routine interrupted me; the years caught up with me. And while I no longer had so much time to spend talking about him, or such an eager listener, I never lost Simonopio. And while, at first, the memory of him was more bitter than sweet, as I became an old man, the bitterness gradually faded.

It took me a long time, but I believe that, with age, I managed to understand Simonopio's motives for leaving me: What would've become of him living in Monterrey? In Monterrey he would have slowly died of sadness, of weariness, of loneliness, of incomprehension.

In Monterrey he would've died before he died, like that circus lion he had seen as a boy.

# 92

## *A Heap of Masonry*

I was born inside this heap of ashlar masonry, plaster, and paint a long time ago—it doesn't matter how long.

In that time, the stones retained the order the original builder had given them, and one on top of the other and side by side, they formed the home of several generations. Look at them now, just strewn everywhere. When they demolished the house, they did so without consideration for what they might have been destroying with it: anecdotes and smells, memories and echoes.

My essence.

This town became a city and was reinvented, and without giving up agriculture—preserving the oranges that the men of my papa's time grew there to save the land from strangers' hands—it was also filled with industry. And so it was transformed, it grew. It became a city, and eventually there was no longer space for the last orchard still within the urban area: La Amistad. The orchard that my papa created from some blossoms that reached him after a long journey.

I suppose the new owner will build a residential or commercial development here. It's no longer a place for a house built large out of necessity, but also simple, without luxuries or grand adornments. A house without historical value for anyone other than me, the last of the original owners.

I came today believing that I wanted to see it one final time to contemplate the last traces of my childhood, to touch the bricks that protected me when I was a boy, to try to capture, even if just once more, the aromas that had wrapped me up warm and that still define me to this day. I thought I would find it the same, unalterable, and that when I saw it, sitting in its shade, it would be easy to remember everything and everyone. That it would be less painful.

I was wrong. Though this was always the destination—and still is—I did not need to come here to remember. And the memories are as painful here as they were in my house in Monterrey or on the journey today.

They're painful because they had to be. And I came because I had to.

Contrary to what I had believed, what I came searching for isn't here, strewn among these ashlar stones. It was never here, because it was always in me, disappearing from this place, from these ruins ever since the day when I left with my mama for Monterrey. Because my papa was right that time when he took up a feather duster as a weapon: houses die when they're not fed with their owners' energy. And this house, recognizing no other owners after us, began its slow return to the land on the day we closed my chest, a process that continued when the last bee left its hive, when Nana Reja and her rocking chair turned away, and even more when Simonopio's presence could no longer be felt.

Without realizing, in that chest in which my belongings traveled and that I always believed to be half-empty, I had packed all my memories. All of them. Intact.

The living house where I was born—the house that has been utterly dead since they knocked it down—gave me everything that defined it when I left. Its stones are strewn about without rhyme or reason, but the machine that finished it off could not destroy its echoes or the clunk of the floor tile or its smells or its nocturnal creaks. Because I took them all with me, just as today I brought with me the smell of the soup that Hortensia prepared before I left my home.

Just like when I was a boy, on my return, as an old man, I brought with me my memories of Simonopio. Complete. Intact.

# 93

## *The Future without Him*

Since long before my mama's first public announcement that our future was to be in Monterrey, Simonopio knew that was how it was and how it would be.

There was a future in Monterrey, but it didn't include him or Nana Reja, however many times we invited them to share it with us. He knew that, if they agreed to come with us, they would both be slowly suffocated to death in that city that had already tried to squeeze the life from him on his only short visit there. And he knew that, if he went, the story that he had worked so hard to weave would change irredeemably. He knew from the first moment that they would not follow what was left of the Morales Cortés family, and it was from that moment that his heart slowly began to break.

When my mama asked him to help her pack this or that, he did it quickly so he could be back by my side, keeping me company, as soon as possible. I continued to recover faster than my mama thought possible, but slower than was tolerable for me, for while my body healed, my mind was already jumping and spinning. It needed constant distraction to keep me still, and Simonopio provided it because he knew that, without him, I would get bored, I'd be restless, and what was worse: I'd start misbehaving. Simonopio would speak to me about anything except that Saturday of my birthday and the days that followed it, when he had thought me lost even when I was in his arms. I didn't ask about it, and Simonopio was grateful.

Thinking about that old day was painful, just as every minute of the new days was. Because Simonopio had known since he was little: one day the lion and the coyote would face each other. And the story that the wind, the trees, and the young bees were already telling of that day was one that Simonopio would've preferred never to hear, never to know, and most of all never to experience. Life would change, he had predicted since he was a little boy: his own, his enemy's, mine, his godmother's, everyone's, and nothing would ever feel normal again.

And he was right: it had changed for all of us.

His godmother seemed to want to go back to being whole again, but her husband's death and the days of anguish and not knowing anything of her son's whereabouts or well-being had made her crumble. The process of reconstructing herself would be very long, and Simonopio would not see it reach its conclusion, though he was glad to know that it had already begun: she feigned strength, as she would do for a long time, and by feigning it she would end up believing it, and by believing it, she would make it reality.

She would be all right, and with her, Grandmother Sinforosa, Nana Pola—who had of course agreed to come to Monterrey—and I would too. But he would not be there to witness it.

Simonopio would miss us all, but my absence in particular would leave him with just half a heart: the half that kept his body alive. I would take the other half with me to my new life; I would pack it in my chest; he would give it to me gladly so that it stayed with me forever, so that I could do something good with it, unburdened by the unbearable weight of the painful events.

Simonopio did not know when, but the day would come when I would be ready to remember. To return.

Still by my side, making the most of the time we had left in the last few days, Simonopio spoke to me about everything and nothing. Unable to go out walking in the fields, as he would've liked—prevented by my recovery and my mama's understandable prohibition—Simonopio kept me entertained by talking to me about what the bees knew and how they knew it, and he reminded me how important it was to listen. To listen to what life sometimes murmurs into your ear, heart, or gut.

"Listen carefully and pay attention, Francisco."

He told me the same stories as ever, and I listened as I always had: always as if it were the first time.

And just as he did every night to soothe me in the depths of my nightmares—which I wouldn't remember the next day—the night before the Saturday of our departure, Simonopio kept vigil over me during the dark hours of the night; making the most of every minute; stroking me between my eyebrows, where I'd had the swirl of fluff as a baby; talking and singing into my ear about the truth.

Impassive, peaceful now thanks to the hypnotic effect of his voice and his words, I slept deeply, and not even when Simonopio shook me gently that night to pull me from my unconsciousness did I perceive any of the words about him loving me like a brother. Not the first ones, not the middle ones, and not the last ones, the most painful ones, the parting words:

"Goodbye, Francisco. You're going because it's where you'll grow into a man, where your future is. I'm staying. If I go with you, I'm finished. If I leave them, they're finished; everything's finished. Do you understand? No. You won't understand for a long time, but when you do, will you come back for me? Will you come back to find me? Yes. Goodbye, Francisco. I'll be here waiting for you."

When he left that bedroom where he had spent so many nights watching over me, he found his godmother, my mama, waiting for him expectantly.

"Have you packed Nana Reja's rocking chair?"

She had been repeating it to him several times a day for weeks: *Don't forget the rocking chair,* or *We'll have to cover the rocking chair well so that it doesn't get damaged during the journey.* It was her indirect way of making it clear that the family wouldn't abandon the nana, and that, if the nana went, it was a given that Simonopio would too. It was the way in which she believed she made him feel the obligation, but which in reality communicated what she had already sensed from the beginning: that he did not include himself in our future.

That a goodbye was coming.

Simonopio shook his head. There was no point in pretending anymore.

"Ay," she sighed, like she did when I got up to mischief. The difference was that this sigh wasn't one of exasperation but of resignation. "Do you need anything?" Simonopio wouldn't need anything, so he turned down the offer. "What am I going to tell him? What're we going to do without you?" My mama didn't wait for a response, because the questions weren't for him. Still, she went on. "Will you take care of her?"

He nodded. Nana Reja was part of his life, and leaving her wasn't an option.

"Goodbye, Simonopio." With the hug she gave him and which he returned to her, they said everything to each other without words.

# 94

## *Goodbye, Francisco*

Dawn that Saturday took them by surprise on Reja's road, but not as far from the house as they would've liked. Nana Reja advanced slowly. It was not the lack of light that prevented her from moving more quickly, because she walked with her eyes closed anyway.

And they carried very little: a few clothes of hers in one knapsack, and a few of his in another.

The day before, the bees had not had to struggle so to move, because with no particular attachment to the place and the structure that had given them refuge for so long, but which was now too big for them, they had installed themselves temporarily in one of the wooden beehives that, years before, had been bought for them along with my papa's tractor.

The bees had arrived with and because of Simonopio. Now they would leave with and because of him.

Which was why, from the first light of the previous day, the few that remained had allowed Simonopio to take them to where everything began, to the place where fate had woven the stories of their lives together for the first time, under a bridge, to the place where they would build a new hive, another one that would grow as successfully as the last. The land and the orange trees still needed them.

Transporting Reja's rocking chair had posed more problems, but the nana refused to leave it behind, and Simonopio understood: it would've been as if, all of a sudden, someone decided to abandon a leg, just like that. So, the day before, without being seen, he had made a separate trip, carrying the chair up the hill to where they would continue to live, where it would await the arrival of its old companion.

On the day of their departure, their inadequate goodbyes weighing heavier on their shoulders than their knapsacks, they stopped when the first ray of light appeared: Reja pretending she needed a rest and Simonopio that his new shoes were uncomfortable.

Looking back, they knew they would see the house waking up for the last time, and neither of them resisted the temptation to do so.

It was from the top of the hill that Simonopio saw me searching for him in his shed. It was from there that he then saw me come out, my face distorted. And it was from there that he made out the words that my mouth could not form through my screams and tears: *Come-come-come-come, Simonopio, come-come-come-come.*

My unanswered call would torment him forever. How easy it would've been to go to me. To forget everything. To forget debts and commitments. To forget all the danger for a few more days by my side. He wanted to run after me, his resolve weakened. But he controlled himself: his destiny was the same as the destiny of the blossoms that had borne fruit on that land. If he left it, he would wither. My destiny was in the city. Our lives—our whole lives—depended on our separation.

*Goodbye, Francisco.*

Simonopio closed his eyes so he wouldn't see me leave. He turned around with my cries swirling in his ears, and he hoped that Nana Reja would turn as well, to continue the walk to a little bridge that crossed a stream where, years before, Nana, the bees, and Simonopio had begun their story.

# 95

## *I Always Thought*

that it was Simonopio who'd abandoned me.

It never occurred to me that it was me who abandoned him, leaving him only with the hope that I would return.

# 96

*It Took Me Longer Than He Thought It Would,*

but in the end, I returned.

In part—and with no remorse whatsoever—I'll blame my lateness on the fact that I became the man he saw in my future: a man who might not have gone through the same trials as his father, who might not have been forced to defend his land and son by shielding him from a bullet with his body, but one who always did everything possible to live his life with integrity, with courage—which has always come in useful in these parts—and to stick close to his family.

That man would not have been able to come when he was young, with the ties he had forged in his life, with the urban roots he had put down and watered and which depended on him so completely.

Time passed, and it has been years since anything or anyone depended on me, whether for sustenance or for character. Not even as an example or for company. It has been a long time since I became superfluous, unnecessary. For a long time, in complete and resigned solitude, all I've done is sit on a faded old La-Z-Boy, waiting for my life to end so that I am reunited with those who went before me.

Why didn't I escape before falling into that? Why didn't I listen? Why didn't I return?

I admit that I also owe my lateness to a factor that Simonopio did not count on and for which I now blame myself and nobody else: the same stubborn energy that, as a boy, drove me to insist and insist until I got what I wanted, I invested in the resentment that came from feeling abandoned.

For some reason, perhaps because I didn't remember how it had happened, it was easier for my child's mind to understand my papa's death, even if I always lamented it.

But Simonopio's abandonment, on top of my father's absence, was impossible to overcome. It made me believe, at the age of seven, that, contrary to what I had thought, Simonopio did not live for me or because of me. I know: at that age I was an egotist who thought the sun revolved around me. *I* and *me* must've been my favorite words at the time. It was a very tough blow, realizing that Simonopio made the deliberate decision to leave me, that he packed whatever was important to him—without forgetting anything—and neither said goodbye to me nor offered me an explanation.

I thought that meant Simonopio wasn't bound to me like I felt bound to him.

And for a long time, I banished him from my mind, just as he had banished me from his life.

Later I spoke of him again, and I began to remember him with more fondness as the years went by, though the bitter questions never stopped seeping into my memories: Why didn't he even say goodbye to me? Why pretend that he would come with us, when he didn't intend to do so? Why the deceit?

So much time lost on those senseless questions.

*Listen carefully and pay attention, Francisco,* Simonopio told me, but I didn't listen or pay attention.

Until now, when I've finally opened myself up to truly seeing and listening to everything, as he had tried to teach me, as he asked me to do with the last words he said to me. Now I know and I understand why he did it, the reason he hid it from me and deceived me: I was the only person in the world who, with my stubbornness—and my blackmailing, perhaps?—could have managed to dissuade my mama from moving. He knew that I would've refused to leave Linares had I learned in time that he wouldn't be coming with us.

And he couldn't see any possibilities for my future in Linares, as much as he tried to find them. I don't know exactly what he saw: perhaps just a life cut short by drowning under the mill wheel at the river or another bullet that hit its target. Perhaps my life would have ended because of another stunt with a train in my wild young country life. I don't know. All I know is that something there would have stolen my days and years from me. In Linares there would've been no falling in love, no studies, no children or worries. Nor would there have been the pain of losing my wife, hemorrhoids, or the digestive problems of recent years. I'm not the same man now, I know, and that's why Hortensia makes nothing but soup.

I very much enjoyed the whole of what now, looking back, I can see is my life: the many good things and the not-so-many bad things—old age included, because it wouldn't have happened had youth not also existed. I am what life has made me. I would've been nobody without Simonopio's sacrifice, and I'm grateful to him for it. Only now, but I am grateful.

He let me go, he saw me leave, and he let me break his heart when I turned around and climbed into the car to leave. I, me, I, me . . . I never learn. I'm stubborn: I keep doing the same thing. I'm an old man and I keep doing the same thing. I'm back here, and I keep on and keep on.

# 97

## But It Wasn't All about Me

With my departure, he was left alone, sharing Nana Reja's fate on this land, sharing the fate of the flowers and bees, waiting for my return. Owing a debt for my life and committed for life.

A question would plague my mother every day and night of her life: *What happened to the Espiricuetas?* When she was brave enough to say it out loud, to nobody, to God, I could never hear it without adding a silent question of my own: *What happened to my .22?* She replied, as I also replied: *God knows.* Those questions were impossible to answer at the time.

Until today.

On the day my father died from two bullet wounds, my .22 ended up with its new owner at the bottom of a ravine.

And there it still lies, slowly disintegrating out in the elements, returning to the land, which reclaims everything—from flesh to iron.

Although iron lasts longer than flesh.

It's what remains on the land as a souvenir of that Saturday when it was my birthday: Espiricueta's son was already dead before he had finished falling to the bottom of the ravine. The bees showed him no mercy, no matter how fast he ran, or how he tried to escape them, and in spite of the rounds he fired at them from the .22.

It was all in vain. All of them died, yes, but not from a bullet—they died killing him.

The son met his end without knowing his father's fate, and the father died without even thinking of his son, just minutes later. But he didn't fall like his son into a ravine, or make the same futile attempt to kill the bees with his Mauser, or even try to hide from them, perhaps sensing that it would be of no use.

They attacked him first from behind, like he did with my father. He died enveloped in them, terrified, curling up like a newborn with his body covered in wings and stings. He died knowing that the devil had sent them after him, that the demon had stung him to death. He died a long distance from his son, facedown, tasting the earth that he had coveted so much.

They did not take long—bees, father, son—to turn to dust. They did it for Simonopio, but the bees, in their swarm, died to save my life and to avenge my father and the land stained with the blood of its owner. The debt was mine, but Simonopio took it on.

And I never thought about them; I never noticed their absence or questioned Simonopio. I didn't even stop to notice his sadness and loneliness in the days before I left.

I never thanked him for the sacrifice.

Now I know that very few of the bees that answered Simonopio's call to save me returned to the hive. Those few arrived weak from the cold and from the heat of the fury that they didn't expend with their sting. Their queen and their young welcomed them home; they were received by a silence full of regret and echoes in the void. They were received by great uncertainty: *What will become of tomorrow? What will become of the flowers, the trees that produce them, the land that needs us? What will become of us, Simonopio?*

Simonopio took shelter under this pain every night until I left, but he needed only one night to know what he had to do for them.

Their numbers reduced, they needed care; they needed someone to complete their memory, to pass on the flying map to the new generations. Just as they had guided him, now they needed him to be their guide and teacher. They needed time, and they needed to rebuild their strength.

I always thought Simonopio was mine: my brother, my guide, my savior . . . but Simonopio belonged to them. Just as they belonged to him. Before he was mine, he was their brother, their son. Simonopio of the bees, the bees of Simonopio. That was how it was from the beginning. It was the first thing he knew in his life. They told him with their first whisper into his ear; in the early hours of his first day, when wrapped in their warm wings, they introduced him to life.

And they reminded him on the first night Simonopio spent under his cold, empty roof.

Simonopio would've slowly died in Monterrey, without doubt. But for me—just to protect me from the pain of his abandonment—he might have given himself over to that incomplete life and to death. He might've surrendered to the limitations of those of us who live deaf and blind with just five senses.

But he knew that the few bees that remained in the hive, the ones who saw him being born, the ones who protected him and guided him all his life, the ones who were his first family, they needed him now more than I did. He was theirs and they were his. Both, in turn, belonged to the land, the land they'd filled with orange trees after many patient years and many journeys in the hills. He could not break their pact. There was no way that one part of the triangle would survive without the other.

If he went away, he would die a useless death. Without him, they would die, and without them, the land and the trees for which they had fought so hard would too.

It was not all about me.

Even without infestations, even without frosts, Linares had a very poor orange harvest for the next few years. The owners, accustomed to abundance, counted the fruit one by one and counted them again, but however many times they did so, there was no mistake: there were spaces in the crates that they could not fill.

None of them missed the bees. None of them went to the trouble to count them.

Only Simonopio did.

# 98

## *And Here I Am*

Stubborn, foolish, egotistical as I am, I'm still talking to you, knowing that he has been waiting patiently for me all these years, that he's waiting for me on the other side of that hill, along Reja's road.

# 99

## *He Knows I've Arrived,*

but he's patient: he has waited so long that he doesn't mind waiting a little longer.

He has all the time in the world.

Nana Reja's rocking beside him, in that world that allowed them entry and welcomed them, under the bridge where they both spent their first hours and saw their first light. They're waiting in that world where there is no time, where they've kept a space for me.

I want to go, but I'm afraid. I'm afraid of them seeing me as I am now: an old man. I worry that Simonopio's waiting for me to climb orange trees again, to hunt toads, to crack nuts with our teeth, and to fill me, unashamedly, with the heirs of the same lice, fleas, or ticks that inhabited our bodies decades ago.

But I forgot how to be a child a long time ago.

*Listen carefully and pay attention, Francisco.*

Now I can hear him clearly, as if he were speaking into my ear, but I resist. He's calling me with his familiar voice, singing to me with his beloved voice, but I'm afraid. I'm afraid to look him in the face and admit to him that for years I denied him and that for decades I closed my ears and eyes, on purpose, to his calls. That the last fifteen years I have wasted doing nothing, and now that I can see, hear, and understand the things I could not before, I recognize that his call to me was there, ever present, constant, strong.

I'm afraid to look him in the face and read his disappointment in me there.

# 100

*But Now These Bees Are Flying around Us,*

and I understand what they want to tell me with their murmur: *Come-come-come-come, come quickly, come quickly, run.* And I know that he sent them to guide me to him.

Now I hear, too: it's a little child's sigh coming from inside me. I search inside myself, deep inside, and I find the boy that I was. He didn't disappear with the years, as I'd believed. He was waiting for me, and he spoke to me like Simonopio did: protected in the depths of my memories, silent sometimes, but patient, waiting to be invited out.

In him, in me, there's no place for rancor or resentment anymore, and he's excited, I'm excited, because the day has arrived at last.

He greets me like an old friend and reminds me that we were once brave and bold, that we didn't stop for anything. He asks me to set off as soon as possible; he's bored, he says, and the excitement that he feels to get back to our orange wars, to run free, to climb trees at will, to play hide-and-seek, to swim in the river, to hold Simonopio's safe hand, fills me and infects me.

And I allow it to do so.

The memories are no longer distant. They're no longer measured in years. They begin to be measured in pure excitement.

Now he holds my hand. I hold his. He asks me to follow the bees along Reja's road, because at the end of it, our brother is waiting for us. And I say to him, *Wait a minute. There's something I have to do first,* because though I'm starting to cast away the old man that I became day by day, I'm still tied to a most basic feeling of responsibility—to the last bond to my mama's teachings. I can't forget it so easily. I can't go, just like that, purely because of the enormous excitement of a reunion.

I look at you, Nico, and I know that you already know what I'm going to say:

"I'm not coming back with you."

You look at me in astonishment, but nothing will stop me now.

"Take all the money from my wallet but tell this story to my children. They only know pieces of it. It's time for them to know all of it. Tell them I loved them very much, that they were worth the years I spent without seeing my brother. Tell them to walk in the shade. To listen with their eyes, to see with their skin, and to feel with their ears, because life speaks to us all and we just need to know and wait to listen to it, see it, feel it."

I know all too well that these lessons come late, but I wasn't ready to teach them until today.

I'm filled with regret at all the time I wasted, in which I could've told them everything in person, when it counted: when they were small, when they looked at me with stars in their eyes. Now it's too late, and the message, delivered by a stranger, will have to be enough.

"A safe journey to you and to me. I'll leave you now, because the boy that I was, the one called Francisco Junior, is insisting and insisting. Right now, he's saying, *Come on, Francisco, let's go now, stop talking, I want to get out.*"

And all I can do is listen and pay attention.

Because this boy's always been very tenacious or very stubborn, depending on the situation and on who was saying it. Which is why I know that, before we reach our destination, he will have managed to get all the way out, to leave the old man behind once and for all, and to run like he hasn't run for so long. He wants to reach his destination quickly. The blossoms' destination, Simonopio's, his own, his, mine, before the sun sets. Because once there, with his little hand—now with no visible veins, no blemishes, no lines—he'll take his brother's young hand.

As he has waited for so long to do.

I turn around and take a hesitant step. Then another. I realize there's more strength in my body than there has been in years. I follow the bees, growing more and more agile and quick, with the old horizon behind me. We walk without looking back, because on this journey, all we care about is our destination.

# NOTES AND ACKNOWLEDGMENTS

This is a novel inspired by the true story of a town in the citrus-growing region of northern Mexico.

There's no greater freedom than writing a piece of fiction, even when inspired by historical events like mine is.

The key word here is *inspiration*, because it opens up endless possibilities and allows me—I allow myself—the prerogative to shape certain events, at my convenience, to develop the novel as I imagined it.

This is what they call artistic license. No department in any government issues it. You issue it to yourself as you please, hence the freedom.

Nonetheless, my research for this novel was very extensive. And while respecting the historical events and technical aspects—just as they were—was very important to me as I told the story of my fictional characters, I wasn't so concerned about respecting the exact dates. Many are as accurate as my research allowed: Ángeles's government, the dates of the wars, the Spanish influenza pandemic, the references to the Constitution of 1917 and the law on idle land, for instance. Others not so much: the exact date of Ángeles's visit to Linares, the law on fruit trees, the beginning of Linares's evolution toward citrus growing, certain events in the region's Agrarian Reform: in some cases, I put two and two together; in others I brought the dates forward a few years.

In this book I sought to be faithful not so much to the historical details as to my imagination.

This is why Simonopio exists in these pages. Why I suggest that all of what is now an important citrus-growing area exists because of a boy's journey and the vision of some bees. It's why I take the liberty, in *The Murmur of Bees*, of including a hard-fought canasta tournament, though it would be twenty years or so before some bored Uruguayans invented the card game. This is also why fictional characters, extracted from my imagination, coexist in the novel with characters that are in some or all the history books (I decided, for all the fictional ones— except Espiricueta—to use typical surnames from the novel's location, though this doesn't mean that the people really existed). And this was why, in another perfectly acceptable clause in the artistic license I awarded myself, I also included some characters that exist, or existed, but not in the context in which they appear in this novel. Like Soledad Betancourt, my own nana, who was the storyteller in my life, from cradle to bedside to rocking chair. I was lucky to have her. I also know that I am a lucky writer in many ways. I'm grateful.

To Wendolín Perla, my wonderful and intrepid editor at Penguin Random House Mexico who welcomed me, an unknown writer, when I came knocking on the door: thank you.

To Simon Bruni, for the day he picked up *El murmullo de las abejas* somewhere in Spain, "listened closely and paid attention," and decided to transform it into *The Murmur of Bees*. Thanks to your art, the murmur of bees sounds beautiful in English.

To AmazonCrossing and the possibilities it offers: a world of new stories, ideas, and sounds within reach.

I am grateful for the opportunity I had to interview some remarkable and much-loved people before their final departure, and for the energy, enthusiasm, and patience with which they answered my questions. They are gone, but they left their mark on me, in this story, and in the lives they touched during their time in this world.

# ABOUT THE AUTHOR

*Photo © 2014 Juan Rodrigo Llaguno*

Sofía Segovia was born in Monterrey, Mexico. She studied communications at Universidad de Monterrey, thinking mistakenly that she would be a journalist. But fiction is her first love. A creative writing teacher, she has also been a ghostwriter and communications director for local political campaigns and has written several plays for local theater. Her novels include *Noche de huracán* (*Night of the Hurricane*), *El murmullo de las abejas* (*The Murmur of Bees*)—which was called the literary discovery of the year by Penguin Random House and named Novel of the Year by iTunes—and *Huracán*. Sofía likes to travel the world, but she loves coming home to her husband, three children, two dogs, and cat. She writes her best surrounded and inspired by their joyous chaos.

Follow her on Facebook and Twitter or visit www.sofiasegovia.com for more information.

# ABOUT THE TRANSLATOR

*Photo © 2013 Thomas Frogbrooke*

Simon Bruni is a literary translator from Spanish, a language he acquired through "total immersion" living in Alicante, Valencia, and Santander. He studied Spanish and Linguistics at Queen Mary University of London and Literary Translation at the University of Exeter.

Simon's many published translations include novels, short stories, videogames, and nonfiction publications, and he is the winner of three John Dryden awards: in 2017 and 2015 for Paul Pen's short stories "Cinnamon" and "The Porcelain Boy," and in 2011 for Francisco Pérez Gandul's novel *Cell 211*. His translation of Paul Pen's novel *The Light of the Fireflies* has sold over a hundred thousand copies worldwide.

For more information, please visit www.simonbruni.com.